PRECIOUS THINGS

He discovers value beyond triumph and success

A Novel By
JB Gatling

Cover Photography by:
Library of Congress Control Number:
ISBN 978-0-9904534-3-7 (hardcover)
    978-0-9904534-4-4 (softcover)
    978-0-9904534-5-1 (ebook)

Dedication

The influence of ancestors

What is to give light must endure the burning.

---Eleanor Roosevelt

Contents

Part One:
Stones In the Crown

Chapter One:
Long Island, NY

KYLE LEANED BACK IMPATIENTLY in the moonlit darkness. He remained concealed behind the east-facing overhang of the boathouse next to the camp's creaking floating docks. In front of him the edge of the ink blue sea pulsed softly beneath the large fleet of neatly tied sailboats.

Sail Shape camp was otherwise quiet at one-thirty in the morning with summer insects tucked in and muzzled until dawn.

Having already removed a set of oars and three life jackets, Kyle waited for his friends.

Finally hearing faint footfalls from the trail that passed several feet beyond his location he whistled softly; Alan and Skip soon joined him.

"What took you guys so long," he said?

Before they could answer he grabbed the oars and tossed the life jackets at them. They fell in behind as he led the way down to the rowboat.

"Sorry Kyle" Alan's reply was barely audible.

"I was up and ready, but it was only twelve o'clock. I blew it trying to get some extra sleep."

When he stopped Kyle turned and looked at Skip who had yet to say a word.

"I'll bet Alan woke you up twice, Skip," he said to the yawning teenager.

3

"Yeah, I think he did."

"But I didn't forget the swag bag," he proudly announced as he slipped an old backpack from his shoulders.

They gingerly boarded and pushed off. Within fifteen minutes they entered the salt marsh area that opened to a lake; cabins dotted the gently slopping hill that rose beyond the far shoreline.

Kyle would never forget his chance discovery of the place three years earlier when he was exploring the coastal areas during his afternoon duty-off period. He couldn't have imagined before then that an entire camp, a camp full of fascinating girls, would be so close to *Sail Shape*. And who would have believed that he had spent time alone that afternoon with one of them, the intelligent and beautiful Brooke Saunders?

Both he and Brooke had agreed after their first time together that secret meet ups were the only viable approach. It made sense because once alerted, adults at both camps would have shut down the relationship that they'd developed and very likely would have taken much more drastic action.

They were the same age and while people would later say they were from entirely different sides of the track, they had a common passion. Meeting together in the wee hours was the only way to safely share it.

During that summer and each summer thereafter, Kyle made three or four secret trips over to see her.

Brooke would always recruit two or three younger girls from her camp to join in with them. They had to have special character traits that convinced her they were able to flourish within a multi-cultural experience and master the skills to fit in. Kyle did the same with boys from *Sail Shape*.

Most importantly they each stressed to their younger charges the necessity for strict secrecy, always reminding them of the danger and reprisal that everyone could face if secrecy was compromised.

As Kyle pulled strongly on the oars over the final yards, he remembered that this would be his last run over and that college next month would end their three-year relationship. All he could think about was how much he would miss Brooke.

"Kyle?"

Alan was speaking quietly from his facing seat at the stern.

"Tell me again why this thing has to be so secret?"

Kyle looked at him.

"There's a complicated answer and one that works at two in the morning."

"The last one is short and sweet—we keep this thing under wraps to protect the lives of everyone involved and we never take chances, period."

Aware of history, Kyle said it knowing that he wasn't exaggerating.

Alan seemed to accept the justification while Skip appeared to have fallen back off to sleep.

As they drifted silently into the dinghy dock Alan yanked Skip's arm; his head snapped up.

"Sometimes the ends justify the means," Kyle added quietly as an afterthought.

✳✳✳

Brooke Saunders would not see Kyle or anyone else at her camp during the early morning hours as had been so carefully planned. She was over one hundred miles away being watched by a pair of Pinkerton security guards. Her father had arranged for them to remain all night outside of her bedroom suite at his Park Avenue penthouse.

Her forced helicopter ride earlier that day over the entire length of Long Island had been traumatic. Yet now sitting helplessly alone in the dark and waiting, was far more stressful.

From what little she'd learned at camp before being interrogated and hustled away it was clear that the cover had been completely blown from the secret rendezvous by Shelley, her flawed recruit.

What irked Brooke more than anything was that she should have seen the entire disaster developing much earlier and put a stop to it. From the moment that Shelley had expressed more than casual interest in what Kyle physically looked like as well as in intimate details of his personal life she should have recognized that she made a bad pick.

Curiosity blossomed into obsession when Shelley ignored the established protocol and contacted Kyle independently with a racy email about her yearnings to be paired with only him during the pending get together. Brooke finally took strong action. After they quarreled and Shelley angrily accused her of trying to keep Kyle all to herself, Brooke removed her from the group.

What she hadn't been able to figure out was how much detail Shelley had revealed to camp authorities about the activities.

When the director and her senior staff summoned Brooke into the office the initial line of questioning was vague and borderline salacious. Yet they didn't tip their hand and expose how much they really knew. It was as if they were holding back because they were not sure about key facts. Brooke didn't care; she let them guess and told them nothing.

Nevertheless, Kyle's arrival at the camp docks in the still of the night would confirm what every leader assumed the secret activity to be—an enormous and dangerous breach of camp security.

The underlying assumption behind those beliefs was revealed moments before her father's security detail escorted her to the helipad. She overheard an old staff counselor gloat about having accurately predicted the entire disaster decades ago when the town ignored the objections of many residents who didn't want inner city ruffians in the camp neighborhood under any circumstance.

Brooke shuddered at the recollection and instinctively reached for her cell phone; but it had long before been taken away.

Kyle and his friends were on their own. She could only pray that his intelligence and instincts would allow him to evade whatever trap had been set.

***

Kyle signaled for them to follow him down the path through a large grove of oak trees. They kept very low after turning down a narrow connecting trail that circled around the lake with only waist high shrub cover. Within minutes they approached the cabins that revealed themselves behind an open field strewn with wildflowers. Kyle knelt and looked in that direction for several minutes. The cabin area appeared to be more shrouded in darkness than he remembered; perhaps a safety light had blown.

Otherwise, things seemed the same as always.

They crossed the fragrant field on hands and knees as the rustic collage of buildings loomed in front of them. Everything was quiet; the thought crossed his mind that maybe things were a little too quiet. He paused once again and observed for another several minutes before finally heading to the supply shed far off to the left. Skip and Alan stayed close.

As they silently approached the building Kyle was certain that he saw a momentary glint of light reflecting from beneath the window of a cabin thirty yards to the right. It was an unfamiliar marker.

Sensing something, he abruptly stopped and looked over at the other buildings once more. That's when he realized what had been bothering him; there were no signs of life anywhere. No clothing had been left out to dry; no boat shoes or other objects were arranged around the stairs; and none of the usual sounds of heavy slumber induced by a long activity-filled day were heard.

He swiveled around and quickly gestured for Alan and Skip to turn back. Confused by his signal, they froze.

Seconds later three large LED light panels hidden by the police fired up with blinding brightness. A deep amplified voice ordered them to place hands behind heads and lay face down on the ground.

Skip looked around furtively after the demand, trying in vain to wipe the glare from his eyes. Alan jerked his head at Kyle and silently moved his mouth. Then his hands shot straight up in the air as he peed his pants.

Skip had instinctively started to back away in the direction from which they'd come. The booming voice ordered him to halt. Instead, he panicked and bolted away from the light while ripping off his backpack.

Kyle always believed that he did that so he could run faster to the boat; police claimed he was reaching for a weapon.

Before he had retreated twenty feet deafening shots rang out.

By then Kyle had dropped onto his stomach. He stared up with his hands clasped behind his neck and heard the sizzling ordinance streaking overhead.

Each bullet struck true, jerking Skip's body into a lifeless pirouette before he collapsed.

Alan had stopped screaming by the time he was dragged to his feet and handcuffed but he continued to stare at Skip's crumpled body. The image of his best friend, lifeless and still, would remain with him throughout his life.

✳✳✳

As Brett Howard approached the parking area, he remembered his last visit to the same city hall complex three decades earlier. In the face of stiff resistance to the construction permit for his camp and to everyone's astonishment but his own he had won; *Sail Shape* was born.

That triumph seemed long ago.

After circling the large parking lot three times he found a single space in the last row of the auxiliary section. By then he was highly agitated.

Ten minutes later and still walking he wanted to know why in God's name were a dozen or more yellow school buses parked so much closer than he was; shouldn't they be out somewhere dropping off or picking up kids?

Finally spotting the green space in the distance that fronted his destination, he saw what appeared to be extensive lines of demonstrators, four or maybe six rows deep. They were organized in a wide rectangular pattern, almost sentry-like, at the base of the open staircase that ascended to second level entry doors. Some of them were holding signs.

Great, a picket line he groused out loud while seeing no way through the blockage; just what I need, city workers wanting more benefits and cash.

Yet he didn't hear chanting or shouting coming from the protestors.

As he moved closer, he saw that the throng consisted almost entirely of students, high school age and even younger. And they were moving but very slowly. Heads were down and hands were clasped in back as if they were collectively contemplating something profound. Stick-mounted signs were randomly spaced throughout. Written on them were the names of New York City public schools, the roughest ones.

He was about to circumvent the assemblage following the lead of others who were also blocked when the human tide slowed to a halt. Silently on each side of the dense rectangle a narrow corridor opened through which he alone was allowed to pass. He walked past dozens of bowed heads.

On the other side and without answers he climbed the stairs. Halfway up he finally saw it set off by itself on the very top step—a brown wooden casket draped in white. Skip's name and birth and death year were sewn into the material in large lavender letters. Glossy cutouts of sailboats were attached to every side.

The shrine's personal impact on Brett was immediate; it caused an overwhelming sense of loss, failure, and guilt. It made him easily remember Skip's face from among the hundreds of other campers that were registered for that same summer session. And he distinctly recalled the teenager's casual disjointed manner but also what a nice kid he was.

After entering the building, he looked back down at the students for several minutes. He recognized more than a few of his summer campers among them.

The vast collage of idealistic faces made him remember a similar group of young people from long ago on a college quad in California who were eager and hopeful and innocent as well. He had tried to help their cause, to lead them at that time, but he couldn't save them all.

Suddenly he understood the entire connection that was staring back at him. It was more than the obvious one that the students were there to raise awareness, empathy, and social action over Skip's death—a mission dramatized by the coffin. There was another crucial one–*Sail Shape* still mattered and that as its founder and leader, he still mattered.

Leaving the window, he continued down an empty corridor. Along the way his mind flashed back to the boisterous army of

Sail Shape believers that thirty years ago had packed the hearing room before he and his team arrived.

With no similar effort to turn out parents, friends, and supporters this time he didn't expect any allies today. The bottom line that everybody knew was that the camp would be found guilty of allowing young men to trespass onto private property. That transgression and not Skip's death had dominated the headlines since the police shooting.

He paused for a moment before the tall composite door. After checking his watch and fastening the middle button of his snug fitting suit jacket he stepped inside.

Besides the stenographer, chairman, and four council members elevated in the front, two-dozen spectators were seated around the spacious hearing room. They quietly signaled that they were on his side as he made eye contact.

"Mr. Howard, sit down."

Without looking up he recognized the irascible voice of Dan Quigley, the very same chairman despite the passage of thirty years.

He listened to Quigley's dry reading of a prepared statement, zoning out while appearing to pay attention. It was all political theater anyway he reasoned. His lawyer had assured him that the expected negative ruling today would start the appeal process and that *Sail Shape* had a decent chance at winning.

Hearing Quigley wrapping up he reached into his briefcase and removed the document that held his version of reality. All he had to do was stand up and submit it to the stenographer; nothing more was needed.

But he strongly felt that something more was very much necessary although he had kept that conviction close to the vest. He didn't believe that his well-meaning attorney could understand how deeply he had been offended back in the day by the gavel-wielding chairman's crassness and naked prejudice.

Because of that he was convinced that he needed something extra to counter Quigley's self-righteous attitude, the one he had arrogantly displayed when he had tried his best to prevent *Sail Shape* from ever being born.

As luck would have it, he happened to remember the newspaper coverage about the drug bust involving Quigley's fifteen-year-old grandson. It happened almost ten years ago. Despite being caught red-handed selling hallucinogenic drugs to classmates, the young man received no jail time and a suspended sentence. Later he went on to finish college and graduate school.

Brett made the connection between the grandson and *Sail Shape* because Quigley and his oldest son, the boy's father, had donated fifty thousand dollars back then to several traditional prevention-based treatment programs. They had tried to keep it anonymous, but he had been able to confirm through his contacts that it was their money.

That secret cash symbolized the hypocrisy that had dampened his efforts to expand *Sail Shape* over the years. The entrenched establishment at times opposed him vociferously, yet the minute there was trouble with young people in their own ranks they went about funneling dollars to a select group of safety net programs. But rarely were programs like his on the receiving end of those dollars.

Were race and class he asked and not for the first time the real reason that solutions like what he offered were resisted? On how many occasions had he proclaimed in public meetings that an ounce of prevention was worth a pound of cure; often it had fallen on hostile ears. As he'd gotten older, he had grown more conservative and at times he had buckled when facing stiff pushback from the opposition.

He'd been too damn constrained and too passive in his advocacy, he admitted.

In fact, after the bruising Chicago camp opening years ago, backing out when opposition from the other side hardened had become his modus operandi. His usual excuse for doing so was that he could more efficiently deploy his resources elsewhere.

But retreat had cost him at least four camps around the country over the years; they were facilities that never got constructed even though the needs in the communities he had planned to serve were most acute.

Quigley finally finished and was pointing at Brett with his index finger.

Ignoring the insult Brett stood up and left his prepared remarks on the chair. He was determined to change the dynamic.

He was going to talk about the power of prevention and the value of investing up front to keep kids on the right path. And he would list the many benefits that *Sail Shape* had brought to the table in Long Island and at all the camps across the country.

After admitting that a grave mistake had been made in the supervision of his Long Island campers, he would apologize and commit to strengthening procedures and personnel. He would also place the entire event within the context of the young people that both camps serve and remind the council that despite the deceit, as far as anyone knew no harm was intended or caused by the actions of any of the teenagers involved.

Then he was determined to expose Quigley's ancient animus and bias; first by pointing out that *Sail Shape* was the kind of program that would have prevented his grandson from pushing drugs within blocks of today's hearing. *Sail Shape*, he would add, was a prevention-based program deserving of support rather than scorn.

He would hear the gavel banging loudly after that and endure the drubbing from Quigley's irritating voice accusing him of being out of order.

But maybe his two-dozen supporters would vocally object to such treatment and let their loud disapproval be heard throughout the hearing room.

After order was restored, he was determined to confront Quigley—while shocking the four unwitting council members—about his secret and hefty financial gifts to programs in the area with very similar goals to *Sail Shape*.

What was it about those programs and their leadership that earned the chairman's respect and generous dollars he would ask and when would *Sail Shape* ever receive equal treatment rather than discrimination?

Chapter Two:
London

"JOSHUA, WE REALLY MUST DO SOMETHING big to mark this milestone. It can't just be our usual end of year celebration. This is number ten you know, an entire decade; that's a significant amount of time."

"We've also had our fifth high honors class matriculate out to university. Not just to Cambridge and Oxford as you are aware, but to several other top-rated schools."

He looked back at her with a neutral expression, not wanting to be enlisted into something for which he was not ready.

Mirra kept going.

"Look sweetheart, I accept that you like to keep a low profile, I respect that love; I really do."

"I know it's because the last thing that you want in your life is to emulate the overly famous Brett Howard, but remember, he is your dad."

She saw the momentary frown skirt across his face; she had gone too far.

"That's all today for my amateur psychoanalysis, I promise," she said before quickly trying a different approach.

"But remember, the celebration would be for all our kids, including their heroes, the graduates. What better way to inspire the younger ones to keep excelling than for them to rub shoulders with the pioneers?"

She kept advocating; her breathing was hardly affected by the brisk pace they were laying down on the jogging trail.

Occasionally her enthusiasm grated on his nerves; she could be relentless at times.

"And you know what else," she persisted, "I'm also sure that every one of the graduates would travel back for the event."

Mirra was certain because she had secretly polled them and gotten everyone's pledge.

They were running through the far northwestern turn in Hyde Park approaching Kensington Palace. Mirra's effortless strides were in sharp contrast to Joshua's military-like cadence. As always when they completed the turn the spirit of Princess Diana was omnipresent. Despite her long-ago death she continued to attract scores of floral bouquets and hundreds of gifts and artwork from adoring fans. Dozens of admirers were there again today, solemnly sitting on the well-tended lawn across from the palace grounds.

Passing the familiar scene so often over the years, they barely noticed the trove of items and humanity rimming the black gold tipped gates that walled off royalty.

There's was another typical civil dawn run, the kind of workout they loved within the shelter of the lush six-hundred-acre urban respite. A bonus for their conditioning was the occasional appearance of mounted riders from the dozens of equestrian trails that laced the park. Mirra enjoyed those moments even more than him and on occasion she would turn on her sprinter's speed to challenge one of the horses, holding her own for at least twenty-five meters.

"It's very important, I hear you and I completely agree," he said slightly out of breath.

"I really don't want to slight the kids either. Tell you what; we'll mark it with something special. But we need to figure out a way to do that so the press doesn't get hold of the thing and turn it into something it isn't supposed to be—a media circus revolving around our lives. "

Mirra frowned. She would never understand his reluctance to take the rightful credit that he deserved. After all, when he launched the student warehouse he did so entirely with his own money, and he continues to finance the vastly increased operations to this day. They were tutoring close to three thousand poor and disadvantaged students every year. Most made their way from very difficult situations to after school warehouse programs.

She remembered his mention of the word warehouse years ago when she first met him; she didn't get the connection at all between the name and what he was trying to achieve. But later when he was actively recruiting her to come on board in an executive role, he explained that he was determined to build a deep bench of talent, a warehouse of gifted and motivated kids.

"Well lover you know my feelings," she said.

"You take no credit for the success while you're spending a small fortune keeping the whole thing going. And there's no legacy there yet. If you dropped dead tomorrow, how would it all carry on without you?"

"If I dropped dead tomorrow, or even right now given this pace," he said grimacing, "you'd take over everything. You're pretty much my legacy, you know that."

It reminded him how isolated he'd become from his family and friends back in the states. Mirra really was the one who would carry on in his absence, not that he was planning to retire from the field anytime soon.

As they approached the last stretch of the run, he raised the arc of his arm and shoulder motion higher hoping to get more lift from each stride.

And he cut his talking short to focus on breathing.

Mirra looked at him again shaking her head. She remembered the first time she laid eyes on him. She was a newly minted graduate with a doctorate in education administration at the time. She had arrived in London from Jamaica years before to complete an arduous PhD program. Barely surviving on the last of her scholarship money she had nonetheless allocated some of it to attend a wealth-building seminar for recent graduates. Even without a job in the works she was optimistic that sound investment advice would pay ample dividends after she landed something; it had.

Joshua was one of three bankers that presented. Unlike the others he'd struck a chord in her as she listened. When he was winding up, he reminded them that there was more to life than the proboscis against the grindstone; he smiled when he said it. He finished on a more serious note by admitting that he wanted to live his own passion and live to uplift the passions of others. He hoped that each of them would do the same during their careers.

It was a memorable talk; she was impressed.

Later she learned that he had already sketched out the early outlines of the warehouse concept, but there was no brick and mortar yet and no students.

The best part of the whole thing, her falling in love with him, had happened weeks after she joined the fledgling warehouse team. It was an intense time; they worked shoulder-to-shoulder planning, buying real estate, outfitting the building, sourcing staff, and recruiting students.

"You look a bit winded my love," she said, poking him. "I would challenge you to the last half K back home, but you might very well take a pass on that, right sweetie?"

To answer he veered quickly left through the trees, pounding his way down a slopping shortcut trail with the hope of building a lead to hold her at bay.

Joshua lingered; he enjoyed a long hot steam shower in preparation for the upcoming stressful slog at his London equity-trading firm. It struck him that many of his fellow owners would simply retire to their private library that morning to run their operations remotely. All it took was a six-figure investment in the latest technology. But he was never tempted; he headed to his closet.

His group at the Fleet Street shop included forty high-octane stock traders; he had hand picked and hired each one. To him they were like family, and he remained the only owner to appear in the pits with his traders from time to time where fortunes were made or lost in lightening fast deals.

Most owners in his circle frowned upon his chummy practices with his employees. The London elite had always shunned rubbing shoulders with the up and coming.

But on more than one occasion his humor stoked by his morning run had broken the grinding pressure in the pit, allowing his team to stay loose and sharp and score big wins. He liked to think that part of the recipe that allowed them to outperform the larger blue blood outfits year after year was greater teamwork with his crew fueled by a sense of mutual respect and shared purpose.

Before showing up today though he had another matter to attend.

After grabbing his leather satchel, he closed the fifteen-foot mahogany doors behind him. The nearby idling Jaguar quietly eased in front of the broad whitewashed steps just as he reached the bottom.

"Good morning Mr. Howard," the driver said, keeping his eyes fixed on the rear-view mirror.

"I received your earlier text about the extra first stop, Mr. Howard."

The thought occurred to Joshua that it had been five years almost to the day since he was fortunate to hire Harold away from a soon-to-retire investment banker. And it had almost been that long since he had stopped urging Harold to call him by his first name.

"Good morning, Harold," he replied cheerfully as he settled into the plush rear seat.

"Yes, the syndicate offices on Bainbridge. I should be out again by nine, but I'll text you if it looks like an earlier end."

"Very well Sir."

Harold launched them into London traffic. After twenty minutes spent skirting through narrow urban city streets, they arrived at the motor route where he quickly muscled the stretch sedan into the far-left lane. They maneuvered around cars, buses, coaches, and motorbikes.

Although Joshua had lived in the London for a dozen years, he continued to experience the latent anxiety that they were clamoring ahead on the wrong side of the road.

He reached for the console telephone to relieve the tension.

"Hi darling, I suspect you're still in the shower washing that lovely hair of yours. I forgot to mention that I want to stop in on the ex pat dinner at Grosvengers this evening just to log some face time with U. S. bankers. Cocktails at nineteen thirty; will likely stay for no more than one hour. Please meet me there after that hour and plant a big kiss on my cheek as I make my excuses for an early departure. Love you love. Text me if you can't make it, please. And by the way, nice final sprint this morning on your part. I believed for a moment that I had you beat this time; what a foolish thought. Ciao."

His extra stop was of an entirely personal nature. A life-long passion, competitive sailing, was front and center. The stakes couldn't have been any higher and today's meeting was a critical planning tipping point because the America's Cup was being contested in San Francisco in two years.

He and his fellow investors had plunked down twenty million pounds plus a hefty bank note in pursuit of the prize and were keen to wrest the Cup away from the wealthy American defender. But the final choice of the challenge crew and the selection of racing captain had yet to be determined.

Given the size of his own seven-figure stake as well as his long racing experience Joshua was determined to convince the other investors that he should be the captain of the syndicate's challenge boat.

There would be opposition; he had anticipated it. Most would fall into one of two camps—investors that believed the syndicate should hire a full time pro or those that wanted a skipper who had competed at a high caliber during the previous Cup race.

Even though he'd never skippered in a race for the Auld Mug before Joshua was certain that he stacked up in experience against any full time pro because he'd been sailing and racing since childhood. Though still an amateur under racing hierarchy's strict classification scheme, he believed that he had the necessary skills to be successful.

Deep in thought he gazed out at London's drab class B commercial buildings. His mind harkened back to the first time his father pushed him out alone into that clear lake in Albany, NY. After the firm shove, Brett had patiently watched from the shore as he drifted away—Joshua was alone in his boat, a wide-eyed youngster in early panic mode. Then his father shouted at him to bring his boat back in using the sails just like they practiced.

Piece of cake he probably thought at the time after he snapped out of the momentary paralysis.

Worry about the approaching meeting intruded on his nostalgia.

He grew more convinced that notwithstanding the ultimate decision about a skipper a wildcard at the meeting might be discussion around the disposition of the crew and the ultimate quality of teamwork and leadership to yield a tangible advantage. He figured that he might have the edge there.

Months ago, the syndicate recruited the potential crew and backups. They hailed from all over the globe, each of them hungry to be a part of the winning boat to beat the Yanks. Good men all he believed, and he had raced with them on many occasions during the dozens of shakedown training regattas over the past several months. They had responded well to his helmsmanship; that could also weigh in his favor verses bringing in an outsider.

In the end he knew that he needed to see how it all flowed at the meeting, so he dampened down his adrenalin level, saving it for his ten-minute pitch in front of his peers.

✳✳✳

"You look lovely and sexy this evening, sweetheart."

He said that as he held Mirra's hand high up above her head within his own. His eyes were drawn to her tall athletic figure that braced a form fitting black pantsuit. Curly natural hair framed her nutmeg brown oval face and large expressive eyes.

Responding to his compliments, she twirled gracefully like a dancer. Posing, she struck a wide-legged model's position, hands on hip, shoulders back.

"My dear," she said, mirth in her voice, "you know that flattery like that is completely unnecessary if you want to get intimate with this package later."

She quickly flashed her engaging smile.

It was the same buoyant spirit that had often lifted him up during his times of loneliness in London. In fact, over the years they each had become a de facto emotional support to one another in lieu of distant and disengaged family.

"And by the way lover," she said, moving closer after glancing around.

"How did it go at the syndicate this morning? Will you be the racing captain?"

He answered her quietly because Cup preparations were guarded like a military secret not only in London, in all the cities around the world where challengers were prepping.

"It was a partial," he said.

"Most of the other private investors backed me at the meeting. But one big bank held out and pushed for a pro. I really think they have one in the wings, probably a nephew or son. I'll get to the bottom of it though. So, it's a stand-off for now."

He hugged her around her waist and drew her closer, gently squeezing the air from between them

"It'll come down to a couple of possibilities," he said.

"One, an on-the-water race off against the best skipper the bank can put up or two, I've got to kick in another million pounds or so to increase my investment percentage to where I can elbow them aside."

Mirra frowned for the briefest moment before smiling.

"Then I suspect that I know how that will unfold my love, you're going to race and kick the want-to-be skipper in the knickers. Am I right?"

"That's one more reason that I love you, Mirra. You can discern what's best for me; even sometimes before I've finally decided what course to take. And yes, I'm leaning in favor of doing some knickers kicking as you say quite soon out in the English Channel."

At home later that evening Joshua sent a text message to his favorite warehouse student, an east African orphan and computer savant named Jemal.

He authorized him to research the identity of the bank's skipper as well as to compile a backgrounder. But he admonished his young protégé to keep the research confidential and untraceable.

The last thing Joshua needed at this stage was the embarrassment that would attach to him from a blown snooping operation with his fingerprints all over it.

They stayed awake later than usual that evening enjoying each other's company within the secluded dimmet in the master suite. Gray staccato shadows played on the walls as rich fragrance of sage wafted from a jade incense holder.

He snuggled closer, pressing himself against her while feeling her bare back and smooth buttocks warm his chest and groin. His free hand rested lazily atop the mounded slope of her hip.

His lips brushed her ear ever so lightly when he whispered that her idea to host an anniversary party at the warehouse was a fabulous one and that they should plan the event as soon as possible. He followed with a kiss to her cheek.

She reached back for his face and brought it gently to rest in the cradle of her neck, holding it there with a light touch.

She replied softly that it would be a grand time, one that they would always cherish.

Feeling his urgency, she shifted to face him, meeting his embrace with her own.

Chapter Three:
Sarasota Training

So far training had gone well for BG and her sculling crewmates. It was a welcome break from the previous months of winter conditioning back on their frigid New England college campus.

That torture included weightlifting, endless running, aerobics, and long hours in simulated sculls tethered to medical clip-on leads that recorded more than they needed to know. They were all happy now to be back in Sarasota for two weeks of on-the-water preparation. All they had to do was row strong.

As a senior on the varsity heavy crew, it was BG's last year. From experience she understood that what they accomplished in Florida would make all the difference in the world during the spring season. But at this point the only long-range goal for her and her teammates was to avenge the heartbreaking loss to Princeton at last year's May championships.

After another drenching workout under the relentless Florida sun, she sat exhausted on the bench outside of her locker. She finally stored her cleats and gloves, tossed her dripping singlet at the laundry basket, and grabbed a towel from the stack on her way to the shower.

"Hey BG, some of us are going to BIGG's steakhouse tonight. You up for beef and beer?"

It was the loud masculine voice of her crewmate, Katie.

Katie was brazenly staring without averting her eyes.

BG wrapped herself in her towel.

The invitation wasn't unexpected, and she knew that deep down she wanted to accept, that she secretly wanted to be closer to the pack as she called them. It had always been harder for her to avoid them when the team trained away from campus. That's when she had no real excuse since there were no convenient outside commitments that she could claim as alternatives.

But she needed to get out of her room, and she wanted some companionship.

"Sure Katie, what time are you all heading over?"

"We're meeting in the dorm lobby at seven-thirty."

"Okay, I'll see you then."

As she stepped into the shower, she wondered whether she'd made the right decision; Katie could sometimes be annoyingly aggressive after drinking.

At seven that evening BG's cell phone sounded with her mother's distinctive chirp.

"Hello mother dearest."

"Hello baby girl. I hope this is a good time."

Lailani plunged ahead without waiting for an answer.

"There's been a…development at *Sail Shape* in Long Island. We didn't want you to find out on the news."

"Find out what?" Is everything okay?"

"No everything isn't, not by a long shot."

Lailani's voice lowered.

"We don't have a lot of the facts yet but one of the young men from the camp was shot and killed, by police."

"Oh my God mom; what happened?"

"It started at a nearby camp, a wealthy girls' camp. Three *Sail Shape* boys apparently left in the middle of the night. Somehow the police had been alerted beforehand."

"The girls' camp had already been evacuated when the boys arrived. The press claims that one of them reached for a gun before he was shot. It's just crazy, where would he get a gun?"

BG couldn't make sense out of what she was hearing.

"That just…doesn't add up, mom. I know exactly where that girls' camp is located. Some of my college classmates attended it at the same time I was enrolled in daddy's camp back in middle and high school; talk about one degree of separation, that was it. I'd often joke around with them about how close the camps were physically but how they were miles apart socioeconomically."

"What's missing mom in what you've told me so far though is why the boys would go there in the middle of the night in the first place. I mean there are close to one hundred girls in the west cabins at *Sail Shape*, and that was years ago when I was there; must be an even higher enrollment now. If the boys were hot on socializing, they could do it at *Sail Shape* after hours. We certainly used to in the old days."

BG hesitated, having accidentally revealed to her mother an ancient secret.

"Sorry mom, but it was only good clean fun back then, honest."

"Thanks for waiting all these years to tell me," Lailani said.

It made her wonder about what other secrets she'd missed during her daughter's childhood.

"Anyway baby girl, the truth is we really don't know the complete set of facts. But the newspapers are claiming that some manner of a sex ring was ongoing, something steamy, and that it had been going on for several years right under everyone's noses. You can't imagine the lurid headlines that are already appearing locally. And it's all about poor black kids taking advantage of innocent young girls."

"A sex ring," BG responded.

"I just can't believe that. Daddy always had a very strict selection process for each camper---maybe too strict if you ask me. The kind of wild unmotivated kids that would pull something crazy like that were weeded out early in the application process. You know that's true, mom."

"I don't know what I know any more except that what has been reported doesn't add up for me either. We just wanted you to hear about it from us first."

"How's dad taking all this?"

"You know your father; he's agitated in the extreme at the campers for jeopardizing everything he'd worked for out there. But at the same time, he's been in touch with the guardian of that boy who was killed as well as the parent and grandparent of the other two young men. He's offered all the support he can. Your sister's law firm is going to represent them."

"Keisha's firm? But won't they disqualify her?"

"Maybe, I don't really know the technicalities. But I do know that she's got the experience. Your father thinks that since she's not representing him or the camp there should be no issue. We'll just have to keep them all in prayer."

Without responding to her mother, BG shook her head and silently mocked her; everything's always kept in prayer. If she had a nickel for every time her own issues had been kept in prayer by her mother, she wouldn't need to maintain a 3.5 grade point average to keep her science scholarship. Instead, she could've paid most of her tuition with all those prayer nickels.

"Mom, thanks for calling and letting me know. I really hope everything turns out for the best. But none of it will bring back that young man."

She looked at her watch.

"I'm sorry to be short but I've got to head downstairs to meet the team."

"Okay baby girl. But before you go, have you talked to your brother recently? Joshua hasn't called me for weeks. And he's still not talking to your father. They haven't spoken in almost two years now."

Hearing that length of time surprised her.

"I'll let Joshua know about this. We still Skype and text. No worries, Joshua is doing well. He still enjoys London and Europe. And of course, he has someone special in his life; they've become close over the years."

BG could have kicked herself; she realized that once again she'd accidentally spilled the beans, this time about her big brother's love life. She'd have to text him and apologize.

Lailani hesitated after hearing it, waiting for more detail; but BG remained silent.

She tried to tease out more.

"A love interest. He's certainly kept that under wraps from me."

She paused again; BG stayed mum.

"Baby girl, you take care and good luck in the upcoming races."

"Thanks. Yeah, we take on the Huskies in the first round. It'll be a real test of our conditioning and teamwork after this camp. We'll be ready.

" Thanks for calling and letting me know about this, mom."

"I certainly wish I had better news to share; anyway baby girl, have a good time with the crew tonight."

***

After draining her fourth bottle, Katie leaned back and rested her head on BG's shoulder.

Momentarily surprised, BG glanced around while others at the table continued their own conversations, seemingly without noticing.

"I know that this makes you uncomfortable," Katie said quietly as she snuggled her head closer to BG's face, "but I'm enjoying it very much, please let me."

"And since I'm so cozy," she asked while looking up, "tell me, did you get your acceptance letter from med school this week? Are you really going to abandon me for wildfire-stricken California?"

"Katie," BG said sharply under her breath as she moved her shoulder from beneath the warm head of curly black hair, "please keep it together!"

Katie sat up; her frustration and beer breath directed at her friend.

"You know what my dearest crewmate, no one's fooled by your straight act. When are you coming out? All of us here had to make that decision at various times in our life. Me, I declared at thirteen, much to the shock and dismay of my father, the illustrious Wall Street banker. My mom always knew. Him, who knows? He's yet to come out himself by the way and he'll be sixty-five this September."

"And while I'm at it," she said clearly on a roll, "I've always wanted to ask you, what the hell does BG stand for anyway, Boy Girl?"

Katie laughed and burped.

"For you Katie, BG means Be Good. And thank you so much for the psychology lesson. But I thought you were a history major. You must have switched to a double."

She instantly regretted saying it because it came out with more sneer than she intended.

Katie turned to her again in frustration and spread her arms wide.

"I may not have a degree, but I know this, suppressing who you are is a huge health risk."

Katie lowered her voice after taking in her crewmate's stern glare.

"It leads to all kinds of internal conflicts," she said quietly as she once again leaned her head back against BG's muscular shoulder.

"And one day if you keep it up, you're going to blow a gasket. I really hope I'm there when that happens so I can help you pick up the pieces while nursing you gently to health. And besides you know, I have an insatiable appetite for chocolate; and I'm certain that you'd love my vanilla. Which would make the nursing part with you even more special. Did I ever mention that before?"

Katie turned and smiled devilishly.

BG couldn't help but shake her head and laugh along as well.

They heard loud tapping of silverware against glass and turned to the head of the long rectangular table. Sharon Steiner the bulked up assistant varsity strength coach stood looking at the team; it was time for a Steiner pep talk.

"Ladies, ladies and also gentlemen," Sharon said as she beamed broadly at the table full of women. Several enthusiastic grunts and high-pitched cheers responded to her.

"I just want to say how proud I am of each one of you. I haven't been away from the sport as an athlete long enough to forget what it's like in the trenches. Not long enough away to forget what each of you must endure on a day in and day out basis, including the grueling academic work. Thank you for that dedication."

She looked around the table for a moment and appeared to almost choke up as she said the next part.

"You all know that our first trial race is right around the corner. Whether we win or lose isn't important to me. What is important is what I know I can expect from each of you women on race day. I know you will take your mark. I know you will be off strong and smooth at the horn and that your stroke count and power output will match our hundreds of drills over these past months. And at the end of it all I know you'll each be winners because that's precisely who you are."

"Grind on ladies," she said holding high a glass of water!

Chapter Four:
Finding Mother

SISTER SARAH CATHERINE ISABELLA furtively peeked around corners. For good measure she double-checked all deep recesses and each study area at the far end of the chapel library because she wanted to be certain of being alone before placing her satchel down on the large, varnished table.

Because the other sisters had retired to the cloisters or to their rooms for prayer, the coast was clear again this time.

After smoothing her nun's habit around small hips, she sat down and removed her high bonnet hat, setting it well off to the side.

Before beginning she turned to the expansive picture window and watched the golden California sun slowly slip beneath the gray edge of the shimmering Pacific.

Getting to work she unpacked several color-coded folders, setting them out neatly in front of her.

After that she carefully removed worn content from each folder, arranging the familiar papers and documents in chronological order. She pressed hard against the many attached sticky notes to secure them as best she could, applying adhesive tape where needed. On some of them the pencil mark notes had long begun to fade and over time she'd carefully retraced the letters in ink.

Every piece of paper was a shred of possible evidence. Looking over it all she thought about the enormous amount of time that it had taken her to get this far.

Ten years ago, almost to the day, she finally rejected the vague and contradictory stories told to her by the nuns about her birth and childhood. She concluded that they were lies at worst or half-truths at best; they didn't add up.

Not one of the nuns had been willing or able to answer her most basic questions about who she was and where she'd came from. Nor would they respond to her burning desire to know who her parents really were. When she reached her teens her reaction to the pervasive obfuscation was a deep suspicion that important things were being hidden.

Something within her spirit had convinced her that her real parents had to be alive, somewhere. That's when she first set out on her journey to locate them. Perhaps it was only her unshakeable faith in her quest that made her believe she was closer to her goal now than she'd ever been.

Yet she realized that she was fighting an uphill battle. Everyone knew that orphans were liberally scattered throughout Catholic nunneries around the world. They were the sisters with no history. Most of them placidly accepted the grim truth that they would never know their heritage, would never meet the people who conceived them in love and for unknown reasons abandoned them to the church.

But Sarah was a perceptive and determined young woman who had always listened carefully to every story told to her and the other girls by the nuns. Each story had a common thread that ended with the same lesson, other than the church and Lord no one else loved them. She refused to believe in the uniformity of that narrative—there had to be exceptions.

The first early clue that she picked up on was in middle school. One of the nuns let slip that she was not a California girl or even a west coast girl. The old nun had taught her years earlier in grade school and had developed a liking for Sarah, almost as a grandmother. During one of their many chats before the sister passed away, she had chided Sarah for being too rambunctious and a true heir to that New York City verve.

But the other nuns had already played a fast one on her, concealing her age by saying that she was two years younger than she really was. That had thrown a wrench into her early efforts to nail down her date and place of birth. The official lie was entirely plausible when she was growing up given her naturally slight frame and girlish features.

The inconvenient arrival of her menstrual cycle, presumably two years early, had been another clue that maybe she was older; she had always felt that way. After that she started to systematically look for clues using whatever reference volumes she could find.

Her research accelerated when the sisters installed a networked state of the art computer system linked to the Internet and to all the order's convents and facilities. At first, she was overwhelmed by the dozens of genealogy sites that promised everything. Then she slowly began to access information and databases that had been difficult or impossible before.

But the photographs and reams of information had proven mostly useless for years until she discovered a small news story published recently in the Post.

She looked at the headline again.

Rich MBA Dame Kidnapper and 3 Chums flying the coop after 25 Years on ice in Bedford Hills/Attica Slammers

To Sarah's delight a grainy archived photo was included with the article; it was likely taken at the original trial. It was an image of the woman and the three other convicted felons. Only the woman's image had retained enough definition to still be recognizable because she had stared straight into the photographer's lens, almost like a deer framed in a spotlight.

Putting the facts in the article together with the fragments she had gathered about her own circumstances, Sarah believed that she was the woman's daughter.

She reached for the grainy photo and gently cradled it in the palms of her hands.

My mother's name is Melinda, Melinda Smith.

*** ***

Stewart squinted and peered across the dusty Attica prison yard. He spotted his partner. Predictably Chauncey had chosen a quiet spot to the right of the laundry building. He was sitting with his back against a dirty brown wall as he faced the heatless autumn sun.

As he casually approached Stewart looked around to gauge whether they would have privacy this time; they mostly would he concluded despite the ever-present heavily armed guards rimming the high perimeter platform. They were marking his progress across the open space, weapons and spyglasses trained at him.

"Twenty days Chauncey, twenty days until we leave this shithole behind us."

Chauncey looked up, shading his eyes as Stewart sat down.

"I really can't fathom how we made it, Stewart. My own mind isn't the same. I think I've lost it, so much of it anyway."

Hearing Chauncey's comment riled him; he slammed his palm down on the cold metal bench.

"The only two things we've both lost for sure my friend are a fortune and twenty-five years of our lives. We can't recapture the years, but we damn sure can recapture a chunk of that fortune."

"I don't know what you're talking about, as usual. But you know very well that my own parents disowned me before the verdict came down. I was zeroed out of the will, the property, the trusts, everything. I showed you that stuff; remember? All my riches turned to ashes; my old man lit the fire, damn him. I hope he's twisting in hell right now.

"I remember. And I told you to keep the originals. Did you?"

"Yeah, I still have it all."

"Good, we'll certainly need it when we get out. And by the way, the only thing faster than your fall from money was my plunge. Of course, I had far less than you to lose, but my folks wrote me out of everything the minute the charges against us were filed, well before the trial. They didn't want to take a chance that a civil suit might target their assets. I guess it's the same ritual that most of us sons of Abraham observe with death, we must be in the ground by sunset on that day or as close as possible thereafter. My inheritance, same thing, in the ground and buried at the first sign of trouble."

Stewart nonchalantly looked around again, making sure no binoculars or cameras were trained on their mouths before he continued.

"There is a way back Chauncey. I've been thinking about the execution of a plan for a long time. It's what I did while you read all those steamy fiction novels."

Before continuing he covered Chauncey's hand with his own for an instant before taking it back.

"I've also thought about us and what we've grown to mean to each other in this...place. Only our devotion to each other has made it bearable."

Chauncey was pleased as always to hear that, but he was also intrigued by what Stewart had mentioned earlier.

"A way back, what way back, "he said after sending a secret kiss?

"When we're released a few days from now we'll be starting at the bottom Stewart, is that what you mean? And yes, at least we'll be doing that together."

"No, not the way I see it, not at the bottom. Like I said, I've been studying the law surrounding the documents from your old man's estate; I've had the time, that's for sure. The law library here isn't perfect but it was good enough for my needs, our needs."

"You see," he said, "that Long Island deed of trust is our vehicle back into the game. And we're also going to exploit the split between your mother and your father when they were alive. As I read the press clippings from those days, I really think that your mother was the prime mover behind your disinheritance. It's easy to pin it all on him, but I think he had her help. It's just the scorched earth way that the whole thing went down; female emotions involved, my opinion."

Chauncey reclined back against the wall and considered the possibilities.

"Maybe so, but I tend to doubt it. It's true though that my mother had a distain for my lifestyle. My father on the other hand had always supported me and cut me slack. But soon after we were indicted, I was notified that I had been removed from every bank account, credit card and depository instrument. Just before the verdict came down there was more pain. The wills, real estate documents, and trusts were all redrafted as if I never existed."

Chauncey sat forward with his elbows on his thighs as he held his head in his hands. Suddenly Stewart's theory didn't seem that crazy after all.

"Perhaps he did want to keep the peace at home, so he very well may have been doing her bidding. And when I think about what happened to the Long Island property—gifted to some black charity for crying out loud, it's got my mother's diamond crusted fingers all over it. For that two-faced phony it would've been the perfect one two punch at my face—look good in your phony liberal charity circles and stab me in the back at the same time."

"But how can we prove any of it, and why would it matter; they're both dead and long gone?"

"Not to worry, I've got an angle. And I've also taken a lot of time over the past few years to learn trust law. I'll bet I could pass that portion of the bar exam right now with very little effort."

Stewart glanced around then looked down as he spoke, just in case.

"This is the deal—your father's estate lawyer, his old prep school buddy Chase Hadley, made a monumental error—or perhaps he was just sloppy—when he drafted the revocation document that took that Long Island property from you. He omitted a key word that was included in the original grant."

Chauncey smiled thinly but he was lost.

"Doesn't sound like a big deal, right? But it is, it gives us a solid argument that the omission was intentional and done as part of your father's plan to thwart your mother's vengeance."

"Chauncey my love, we'll use that mistake in our favor to reclaim that pricey chunk of real estate."

Chauncey was encouraged, even though he remained clueless about the technicalities. Stewart's passion made him feel optimistic.

"What about Cy, Stewart? He's been in here with us the whole time, even though he's drifted away in the past few years. We can't cut him out of this, can we?"

If it were solely within his control that's exactly what Stewart would do. But there was no way he could risk walling his plan off from everyone, especially from someone with Cy's smarts. As a reality check he had shared the detailed plan with him, asking that he calculate the odds of a successful recovery if they were to bring a lawsuit. Cy said the odds were 84.9 % in their favor. Cy—a true quant if ever there ever was one— was rarely wrong.

"Don't worry, he will get a cut."

To keep Chauncey emotionally on track he didn't mention that their other co-conspirator, Melinda Smith, might also need to be in on the scheme.

***

Reverend Mother Helen Regina Desedore' eased back into her stuffed leather chair and looked across her cluttered desktop at her favorite student. Sarah was bright, resourceful, and doggedly stubborn. Those qualities were why she'd been accepted into Cal Berkeley's medical school program, the first sister from the convent ever to be admitted.

Underneath her desk a white Shiatsu rescue dog curled its soft body around the Reverend Mother's feet while its human patiently contemplated the consequences of Sarah's recent request—permission to travel all the way to New York—on a mere hunch no less—to see a woman that may have abandoned her to the church a quarter century before.

Was the request beyond the pale, or was this God's will? The Reverend Mother sought the Lord's guidance as she discussed the matter.

"Sarah, you know don't you that many children who seek their biological parents are more often disappointed at the end of that search because they find nothing. If by grace they are successful they discover that there were good reasons they were given up for adoption, they were not wanted and they were not loved. I don't want you to be bitterly disappointed my child if

35

this woman happens to be your biological mother and yet denies it; or worse yet, she recognizes you as her own and denounces you. I would spare you both of those pains."

They had been speaking for thirty minutes and Sarah remained undeterred.

"Yes, Reverend Mother, I know those possibilities might be the likely outcome; or she may in fact not even be my biological mother at all and may pretend to be to gain something. I have prepared myself for these things. You see I have already forgiven my real mother. I cannot be hurt again. I only want to give her a hug and perhaps a kiss. I only want to tell her that I forgive her and love her."

It would deeply pain her to deny Sarah, but she could see no other path forward as she considered all sides of the problem.

What would the order do she had asked herself when a substantial number of orphans discovered that their parental origins were capable of being discovered simply by using the Internet network as Sarah had done? And how many might be emboldened to demand access to the hidden archives of the church itself to discover the truth about the thousands of unholy internal relationships that had produced children.

And to what end the Reverend Mother asked herself? To find the answer that was already known; that the children of those relationships were not wanted or loved? The more she considered it the more she was convinced that without strict discipline preventing such unbounded inquires the order would surely weaken and possibly collapse.

The Reverend Mother rousted the sleeping Shiatsu from around her feet and leaned forward.

"This journey that you request would be without precedent, Sarah. Do you truly feel that you are the only young woman who would wish to seek her parents to the ends of the earth? This is a natural deep human instinct in us my child. Yet how are we to prioritize these many natural desires to visit the past for some evidence of the truth? In what way should we determine that one request is legitimate, and another is folly? I cannot see an equitable method to mediate among the many issues that are sure to follow from your actions."

"And who would be there to comfort you Sarah when this woman, this felon, walks away from you without caring?"

Sarah's tears flowed over her hands that concealed her face.

***

Melinda Smith sat on the thin mattress that partially covered her steel bed. She folded a few more belongings into a scratched-up suitcase.

Expectantly, she listened for the hollow echo of footfalls from the warden and her attendants signaling their approach to her cell. It would mean that she would soon leave her place of incarceration, the tomb known as Bedford Hills. After so many years the reality that she would do so hadn't sunk in.

What would confront her on the outside?

The question filled her with dread.

She latched the valise and stood up, waiting,

She remembered that the warden had promised a free taxi ride into New York City. She reached into her pocket for the address of the rooming house. Other than the five hundred dollars that she'd saved from her prison job it was her only lifeline.

They walked for what felt like miles through dank stuffy tunnels and dim hallways. Melinda was sweating heavily, and her feet throbbed in her old stiff shoes that had not been worn since the first day they processed her into the facility.

She'd heard about but had never seen the exit area. Prisoners' folklore claimed that it was filled with clutching jealous spirits that tugged at one's soul to prevent departure. She didn't believe that.

Finally, she spotted the exit area in the distance —a vast concert-like chamber, empty and shrouded.

On the other side of the hall was a broad steel door beneath a green-lit exit sign.

The warden stopped and pointed.

Melinda moved on alone, the ricochet from her painful pumps grew louder in intensity. The sharp booming sounds became a jagged mental assault, an early migraine trigger she feared.

Halfway there she felt a cramping weakness in her legs and shoulders and joints, there was just too much walking. To ease the pain, she switched the valise to her other hand but that hardly helped. Shortness of breath grew more severe; she had to stop soon and kneel for a moment; she couldn't go on.

She felt the warden's eyes on her back.

Stopping for air she tried to still her rising panic; despite swaying she stayed on her feet. The cold fear that she would never be allowed to leave again pushed her slowly forward. Finally at the door she slumped her back against the barrier. Looking back across the vast hall all she could think to do was wave.

She turned around and forced all her weight into the stout door, pushing thighs, shoulders, back, and arms into it before it grudgingly yielded with a loud screech.

She stepped into blinding sunlight.

Shielding her eyes, she searched for the taxi within the immense fenced-in enclosure. There it was, or at least the form of an automobile, some one-hundred yards. An image of someone leaning against the passenger door emerged through the yellow glare; the image shifted and then raced to Melinda as she approached.

Melinda had an unexplained urgency to be nearer to the figure coming at her; she tried to pick up her pace, but her movements were slow motion.

Soon she could see a nun wearing a habit and a high bonnet.

At last, they both stopped and stared.

Melinda stared in awe at a slightly built young woman, one that looked almost exactly like she looked decades before.

***

Cy peeked across the chessboard at his hulking student who was covered with tattoos on every visible piece of skin. Lex was over six and a half feet tall and weighed four hundred pounds. He sat very still with heavily muscled shoulders hunched over the chessboard as he did every weekday at his 3:00 P.M. lesson.

This was a special time of the year.

The annual prison chess tournament was approaching, and all the players would compete for the grand prize as well as for lesser category prizes. The grand prize was 72 hours of one week away from mandatory prison work shifts, with pay. Lesser prizes meant less time away from the drudgery. For these high security inmates who'd been locked away for more than twenty years, winning was extremely significant.

Cy always had difficulty focusing on his chess master duties even during tournament week. The lack of focus was exacerbated by his twenty-one-year tenure in his current position. It was because he had been a chess Grandmaster on the outside before his incarceration. And it was also because the competence level of his students was so far below his talent that staying awake while teaching was his greatest chess problem. Nonetheless, he managed to remain mostly alert to impart a variety of minor insights.

He'd earned the lofty title of prison chess master after he was promoted from the game room ward where he was only allowed to teach checkers. The checkers class continued to have five times more inmates in attendance than he could count on with chess, but he didn't miss that infantile environment.

The fact that he would soon be released from Attica added another major distraction. He continually recalculated the long odds he faced outside of prison to reintegrate back into society. No matter how he varied his input assumptions he saw no more than an 18 percent probability of success for himself—unless of course Stewart's illegal scheme was successful, which pushed his chances to almost 50 percent.

He hadn't regretted hugely inflating Stewart's odds of success when Stewart had asked for an analysis of his scheme because he doubted that Stewart's knowledge of the true odds would have motivated him to set the plan in motion. Ergo Cy comfortably concluded in his mind that the ancillary benefit to him outweighed the antecedent prevarication that served as catalyst.

Cy's approach to students at this time of year had to be ecumenical as far as preparation for the tournament was concerned—everyone got equal coaching.

But Lex had brought such passion to his lessons that Cy was inclined to encourage him. Unfortunately, that fueled the false belief in Lex's small brain that he was one of Cy's best students and that he had been receiving extra prep.

Tournament rules paired inmates of like ability against one another from rank beginner to intermediate, but those distinctions were often imprecise. And as happened every year several entrants had sandbagged, hiding their true skill level to draw an easy opponent in the early rounds.

When tournament day finally arrived, Lex was paired against a superior sandbagger; the match ended after five moves. While no one dared openly make fun of Lex, the snickers behind his massive back were audible. Unfortunately, Cy had shared a big laugh over an unrelated issue with one of his students at the very moment Lex was checkmated.

Paranoia had always been a serious affliction at Attica. The result being that nearly all inmates believed they were victims of false accusations and vicious cabals. Unfortunately, Lex's particular form of paranoia was clinical and deep-seated.

After hearing Cy's laughter, he imagined that he had not only been cheated in his lessons, but that Cy had unfairly prepped his opponent.

How else could he have lost so quickly? The rage and confusion consumed him as he glared down at the chessboard.

After a few moments he stood up from the table with the white plastic king hidden in his meaty left hand. He walked over to Cy, approaching him from the front. When he was within arm's reach, he lunged forward, grabbing Cy's entire neck within the vise grip of his right hand.

He stabbed repeatedly and mercilessly, gouging the aorta until the spurting blood soaked them both. By the time ten prison guards were finally able to drag him away, it was over.

Flat on his back and barely consciousness Cy no longer felt searing pain. Outside his closed eyelids and almost beyond hearing he could sense a great flurry of activity. Yet he was leaving it all behind, drifting slowly from his body.

He thought about Stewart, Chauncey, and Melinda before the end.

Recalculating the likelihood of the three of them recovering millions of dollars without his help; he was certain that the new odds were well below 20 percent...

Chapter Five:
Lailani

LAILAANI WAS CONVINCED THAT THE KILLING at the girls' camp would mean enormous change to the life that she and Brett had shared. No matter how much she prayed about it that premonition never changed.

The stress from it all forced her to remain in her office at the end of another long day. She sat at her desk quietly as dusk settled over the city. Earlier she had turned off the lights as well as her computer, leaving a silent stillness.

She was thankful that Brett had remained laser focused on the needs of the camps while staying on the periphery of the many marches and protests that had erupted throughout the state and nationally in support of Skip and against police brutality. The last thing she wanted was for him to become the public face of those demonstrations, all of which had their own distinct agendas.

Her beliefs about it had hardened over the recent weeks. For Brett and the national organization, she believed that it had to always be about focus on the mission, about *Sail Shape*. It had to be about the job that he was destined to accomplish. Diluting that in her mind, no matter what the promised end game, meant compromise and failure.

It didn't mean that she wanted to shade the protestors.

She strongly supported their hopes and aspirations. They wanted justice in so many shooting cases that simply defied explanation. That they had added Skip's death to the growing list, she fully understood.

Nevertheless, the protests in support of *Sail Shape* had the potential to strip and compromise the energy and resources required to advance the mission of the camps.

How do you reconcile two conflicting points of view that both hold merit, she asked herself?

It all seemed to add up to a consuming fire right now; she was convinced that there was a force that was slowly drawing them into the maelstrom where they would lose control.

Worrying about it had made if difficult for her to sleep solidly of late.

Without thinking she messaged the small gold crucifix that hung from her neck.

Reaching across her desk she lifted a heavy glass picture frame with both hands. The quickly fading light from the window behind her was refracted within the cut glass. Its soft glow surrounded a photo of her and Brett from many years ago. They were reclining together in a beige beach chair, cuddled up in each other's arms. Behind them was the pink sand beach of Bermuda. They were so much in love then, she remembered.

She reminisced about that distant time, and it made her happy. Was it the last overseas vacation or was there one more after that? Being unable to remember made her sad. They had let so much stuff and so much activity build a wall between them.

She set the frame down.

She still loved him, didn't she? Not like before she admitted, not as intensely. She continued to feel that she wanted to be there with him, didn't she?

No, she responded firmly; not with the current version, the one he'd grown into over the years.

What happened to that long ago version she asked herself in an audible whisper?

Whatever became of the boy she loved when they were seven-year-old kids together, that best friend that she ran and played with around Albany streets? What happened to the original Brett Howard?

She knew the answer, both the good and the bad of it. He had been absorbed into the man she married many years later, the man with an all-consuming vision.

She wanted desperately to reconnect with that ancient version of him, the one that had plenty of time to listen to her as well as time to love her. But did he want that too? Had the thought even crossed his mind in the past ten years?

Maybe if she were three thousand miles away with a big check in her hand to support *Sail Shape* programs, she might see him and engage with him more often; at least until she handed over the check.

Turning serious again, she wondered if her failure to work shoulder to shoulder with him at the camps —rather than her having stayed focused on building her own business—was a cause of their estrangement. Would he have loved her more if she had been his loyal secretary, his Girl Friday keeping schedules and rustling the campers?

Sadly, she realized that her sarcasm wasn't too far off the mark considering their history. Didn't he always prioritize anything associated with *Sail Shape*? Wasn't there always accommodation made for fundraisers, patrons, and camps visits anywhere in the country but not for her or her accomplishments?

And had he ever shown one bit of genuine joy in what she had been able to accomplish with her business, she asked? Had he ever set foot inside this office, even once?

Her mind drifted deeper into sadness, a result of both the darkness and her melancholy. The dual assault made her remember her two greatest losses.

She shuddered at the unwelcome memory of her extended bedside vigil with her dying mother. Her mother's death had been the culmination of something that Lailani had long known was coming despite her young age at the time; she had smelled it for weeks, but her young mind hadn't recognized the nature of the scent.

That palpable sense of impending loss from so long ago felt so familiar to her now, so much like the downward trajectory of her marriage. Now as then she sensed an unwinding of energy, a type of entropy that would extinguish the future.

Is there an imminent death ahead for Brett and me; is that what this means?

No, not necessarily but then again quite possibly, she responded, the response came not from her religious faith but rather from her rational, secular mind.

Everything can't always be inevitable, pre-programmed and bible scripted she added. What law beyond ritual recitation made her relationship with Brett immutable? She admitted that her emerging beliefs and doubts were alien to her traditional religious teachings.

Yet were they not evidence of her emerging maturity, things that life experience had taught? It had also taken courage for her to embrace the view that there are often events with no rhyme or reason. And if the religious retort is that it's all part of His plan, doesn't that make everything part of the plan. Does it not follow from that orthodoxy that what we do is therefore meaningless since it's all pre-planned?

Better keep those heretical thoughts private she warned herself.

Yet wasn't what transpired around the second great tragedy in her life, the death of her sister, the clearest example that something was missing in the establishment point of view? She remembered her vague feelings about it back then and slowly over the years the recognition had taken hold.

Years ago, her older sister's death or the death of either one of them was the farthest thing from their minds. Nevertheless, they made a silly sisters' pact after Keisha, her sister's oldest, was born. They vowed that if anything ever happened to either of them, the survivor would raise the other's child as their own. At the time Lailani had no children but her sister had assured her that the pledge would attach when she had them.

A little over eight years later her sister was dead. The why of it was beyond the ability of the human mind to comprehend, she believed; the thought that maybe there was no why began to creep into her brain. Yet how many times had church leaders and comforters seemingly twisted the tragedy to fit it into a neatly laid out plan? She was skeptical back then and she refused to buy it, she remained so.

In her spirit she would always believe that her sister's life was redeemed through Keisha, as if her sister's influence from heaven had kept watch and vigil over her daughter. And what a fine woman she turned out to be. So, it's not all gloom and doom by any means she recognized as she tried to cheer herself up.

Perhaps her faith was evolving. Or was it starting to crumble.

Interrupting her thoughts, the desk phone rang loudly, sending a piercing red flare into the room's darkness.

Who could that be at this hour, she wondered before glancing down at the receiver's interoffice light?

Its's Remy, working late as usual.

Remy, best friend, confidant, and right-hand executive who'd helped keep the staffing organization they'd built together ship shape and mission focused.

Lailani picked up the phone.

Remy was excited, said she was heading down the hall to see her.

"Lai, I just got off the phone with Tony Calibri," she said after the door flew open and she swept inside.

"You remember him of course, right? He still owns Execustaff."

"Hey, why is it so dark in here," Remy asked as she flipped the light switch on?

"I was just sitting and thinking, that's all," Lailani replied.

"Of course, I remember Tony. He reached out to us several years ago. He wanted to talk about a merger or a buyout back then. Handsome guy as I remember him, right?"

"Exactly. Well, he's back. He just made quite a pitch to me on the phone. He wants you to fly to California as soon as you're able to sit down with him to talk face to face. Could be a match made in heaven, those were his exact words."

"Anyway Lai, I pulled up Execustaff's financials after the call. They've done quite well. And they have a big fat checkbook dedicated to expanding their business—three acquisitions in the past five years. What do you think girlfriend, are you up for a trip west?"

Lailani instinctively swiveled her chair around to gaze out at the array of orange splashed autumnal trees rescued from the surrounding darkness by the city's recently installed LED array. They dotted the small park in front of the building and formed sentinel-like bursts of color along the streets beyond.

Lailani realized that she should be flattered and extremely interested in Tony's call. He'd come calling twice now. LR staffing obviously presented an attractive opportunity for him. After all, she and Remy had started out as a tiny proprietorship twenty years ago, just the two of them putting together the pieces to jumpstart a small business.

Now they staffed over 700 independent contractors in five regional centers in New York. Revenues were solid and most importantly their reputation was stellar. Every year they topped the small company best-in-class rankings for providing the most motivated and prepared medical staffing support.

But she understood that accolades were never the end of her dream because as much as she enjoyed running her own business the broader strategic options and resources that a larger company could bring to the table had always interested her.

Lailani remembered that when Tony's offer first surfaced several years ago, she'd found the idea to be quite tempting. Brett on the other hand had been one hundred percent negative about it. Why he was against even considering the possibility of a combination had been a mystery to her. In the end she'd been dissuaded by his strongly held views. That had been a huge mistake on her part.

This time she was going to fully investigate the facts. She'd also pray about it more earnestly and be guided by those prayers.

She swiveled to face Remy who was watching her carefully.

"Remy, this does have great potential and I also feel your enthusiasm over it. Please ask Jacqui to set something up on my calendar with Tony in the next few weeks. I'd be more than happy to meet him in sunny California. That's especially true with early fall creeping in around here."

After that they laughed and joked together about the possibilities. They ended up calling the whole thing California beaming, the perfect phrase to capture their aspirations. They'd each heard so many things about that place but separating fact from fiction took a back seat to good fun over possible Rodeo Drive shopping sprees, Hollywood celebrity hunting, and brilliant Malibu sunsets.

"Your travel schedule is really starting to get busied up," Remy mentioned offhandedly.

"With the addition of the California trip you could be away from here more often than Brett over the next several weeks. How will he ever manage things at home without you," Remy asked in jest.

Lailani thought about that for a moment. Strangely, it didn't bother her at all—either the being away part or Brett's possible discomfort. She shrugged and frowned at Remy, signaling that she could care less.

Watching her friend's dismissive gestures made Remy quietly anxious. She'd never seen her blow Brett off like that before. She wondered whether Lai's sitting alone in the dark had anything to do with it.

***

Lailani decided to meet her former manager at the downtown Woolworth's lunch counter like they used to do years ago. At that time Jan was a conscientious and highly skilled contributor at LR Staffing. She was that strong hands-on RN that helped instill discipline and pride into the ranks of the temporary staffing team. When a prestigious hospital needed a competent RN staff manager for a short or long-term assignment, Jan was always Lailani's number one choice.

Lailani didn't hold it against Jan when she resigned with only two weeks' notice and accepted full time work at Slater Memorial. Loosing highly capable members of her team to aggressive employers looking to cherry pick the best was always a risk. But what Jan did after leaving Slater was a mystery. She'd completely dropped out of touch, and no one had heard from her in several years.

However, rumors had circulated in the past year that she had been working in private nursing for a very rich clientele downstate. No one who could confirm that. Lailani did learn one reliable fact, medical needs for Jan's mother brought her back to Albany every so often.

Then, out of the blue, Jan had called her to say that she needed to talk about an urgent matter that couldn't be shared over the telephone. She volunteered to fly up from Manhattan for the meeting.

She was seated at the lunch counter when Lailani arrived.

They hugged for a long time before sitting down on the old-fashioned rotating stools, facing each other like they used to do years ago. Clearly, they hadn't lost the chemistry between them, and they genuinely enjoyed seeing each other again.

"Jan, you look wonderful. Is it true you're doing private duty downstate now? That work must be a fountain of youth for you. You look great, girl,"Lailani said.

Her compliment was more than idle flattery because Jan looked like she had reversed the aging process entirely. She was trim and fit and there were no wrinkles or crow's feet around her eyes. Her face and neck as well as the skin on her hands were smooth and glowing. Lailani's trained eyes could discern that Jan had been under the knife; but a top-notch surgeon was involved.

Jan blushed.

"Oh, thank you so much Lai. Yes, I'm doing private duty in the big City. It places me in frequent contact with several specialists. They offer the fountain of youth, for a high price!"

They laughed.

"And look at you Lai, you look wonderful, and you haven't aged a bit since I last saw you, what eight, ten years ago? Your youngest girl should be about ready to graduate from college, right?"

"Yes, indeed she already has, Jan. Baby girl started medical school in August. But she's not close. California fever struck; she followed Brett's old footsteps to the Golden State."

"That's wonderful. You must be so proud. And how are Joshua and Keisha doing?"

"Well, he is far away over in London and he's quite successful there, in banking."

With that generality Lailani concealed her sadness over the enormous emotional and physical distance from her son.

"Keisha is right here in Albany though. She made partner a few years back at the Harpin firm downtown," Lailani said quickly.

"You must be so proud of all of them. Time flies, doesn't it," Jan said.

"Yes, it does. How's your mother Jan, did she ever stabilize from those painful liver problems she'd suffered from?"

"Thank you for asking, I think that's finally behind her. But Mom has slowed down quite a bit over the past year, just age. She remains optimistic that she can continue to live on her own. But soon, I'll have to have that dreaded talk about assisted living communities and what's best for all of us."

"And how's Brett," Lai, Jan asked before nervously answering her own question?

"Well, I know the Long Island shooting was difficult for both of you. But how is he holding up?"

"It's been extremely challenging to say the least. The negative publicity has put the entire national organization under a huge strain. And there's been a movement among some of the wealthy residents out near the camp to shut it down. One of the mayoral candidates has vowed to do just that if he's elected; and he's leading in the latest poles."

"Lai, that's why I wanted to speak with you privately, I've heard some things that are troubling."

Jan casually looked around after that. She waited until the nearby waitress finished re-wiping the already clean countertop.

"What is it Jan," Lailani asked in a lowered voice, "what could you possibly know about *Sail Shape*?"

"I only know what I've read in the paper the past few weeks, Lai. I mean those reports that some poor inner-city kids from *Sail Shape* were having a tryst with several wealthy girls at an adjacent camp, right? But regardless of the truth or falsity of that, why the police had to shoot that young man I'll never understand."

Lailani instinctively recoiled at Jan's characterizations. She was about to push back against them when Jan leaned in closer.

"But Lai, I also learned something a few weeks ago merely by chance that puts that whole investigation and the reporting around it into serious question. The more I thought about it the more I realized that you needed to hear it."

"Hear what, Jan?"

Lailani's heart was racing.

"As I mentioned I've been doing private duty in Manhattan. It's very private duty for the wealthy set. They don't go to hospitals you know—too much publicity. Abortions, cosmetic surgery, rib removals, you name it; they get it done discretely."

"Well, a few days before they shot that boy one of the real estate big shots on the East Side had arranged for his daughter to have an abortion at our clinic. She was sixteen and superbly indifferent about the procedure, showing none of the usual remorse that we see in those circumstances, even the fake kind."

Lailani reached into her purse for a leather-bound pad and started jotting down what Jan was saying.

"Anyway, I was approaching her recovery room when I heard her on her cellphone. To be polite I hesitated before entering. But she was speaking loudly as if she didn't care who heard the conversation. What she said didn't make sense to me at the time. After reading the articles about the shooting later I began to piece together what she was alluding to. And you know what, she was involved somehow with the girls at her camp that were planning to meet the *Sail Shape* boys."

Lailani looked up from her pad.

"So, she was camper, Jan?"

"Yes. She left camp days before the shooting on the pretense of an illness, but the real reason was the abortion. She talked about being angry at a girl named Brooke. Apparently, Brooke had removed her from an activity because she sent a message to one of the boys coming over for a visit. I think his name was Carl, or maybe it was Lyle, I don't remember, sorry."

"This young lady talked about how she would soon fix Brooke for good and blow the whole late-night charade to smithereens. There was intense jealousy between them, that's for sure."

Lailani looked wide-eyed at Jan.

"Jan, Brooke was the name of a young woman from the girl's camp, she was evacuated before the shooting occurred; her helicopter flight back to Manhattan made all the papers."

"I know Lai, I read that too, that's why I called. But none of what that girl talked about was in the papers."

Jan looked around again before continuing.

"There's more; the girl, Shelley was her name by the way, went on to talk about her abortion; that also seemed related somehow. She told whomever she was speaking with that she was beginning to show, that's why she had to have her procedure before parent's weekend. It may be that one of the boys from *Sail Shape* was involved with that. It all seems to be part of one big, related issue from what I heard."

"Oh, and I almost forgot, she said that she would give the girls' camp director a song and dance story about what was really happening."

That's it, that all I know, Lai. I hope it helps."

Jan sat back on the swivel stool and allowed her shoulders to slump. She was visibly relieved that she'd finally shared everything she could remember.

"Jan, the truth will always help, thank you so much. You're right; most of that information was ignored or omitted by the news outlets. I'm going to report what you shared to Keisha who's representing the boys. I'm certain she'll want to speak with you about this. Please work with her when she calls."

"I will Lai, I will."

Lailani was anxious to pass on what she'd just heard. She touched her friend's shoulder before standing up.

"Jan, we all still miss you at LR. If for any reason you want to return to your old position, you'd be welcome."

Jan's expression softened.

"Of course, we can't pay like they do downstate," Lailani said with a chuckle. "But they don't have these retro lunch counters in the big City like we have up here in Albany."

Jan smiled and nodded back at Lailani; she hadn't entirely dismissed the idea of working again in a close-knit community far from the drama of the big City.

Chapter 6:
Father

BRETT WAITED IMPATIENTLY for his daughter's call as he tried to relax in the Houston hotel room. He'd done nothing other than pace back and forth for the past thirty minutes. He was dying to hear the results from her conversation with Lai's former manager. The added stress was that he had to be on time at the downstairs kick-off campaign for the Houston *Sail Shape* capital fund. Looking at his watch it was clear now that he'd be late.

Houston had been the fourth camp that he had opened after Long Island, and it had taken two years of work to get it up and running smoothly. It had been fifteen years since its last facility overhaul and its age was showing.

Everyone in the know was aware that the camp's fleet of sailing boats was outdated. The fixed docks on the lakefront were also badly in need of repair; those two investments alone required eight hundred thousand-dollars, minimum.

Enrollment was down for the third straight summer as competing camps continued to poach his campers. He had finally admitted that despite his national reputation the other camps were winning.

He wanted Houston to thrive again, and the capital campaign was the tried-and-true method. The goal was to raise one and one-half million dollars.

He finally sat down in a leather side chair, willing himself to relax for his own good. Having recently started on blood pressure medication, he was determined to get off that crutch by making smart adjustments.

The challenge that he faced was his schedule. He traveled a minimum of two hundred and fifty days a year. Managing his executive directors and approving major activities at the eleven camps around the country was even more demanding than the fund-raising part of his schedule. It involved frequent onsite visits to rally staff and inspire campers.

Brett always got a kick out of interacting with the youngsters. It was the part of his job that he loved the most and the part that his executive and fund-raising efforts provided the least time for him to enjoy.

As he practiced his calming routine, he admitted that he also needed to cut back on red meat and sugar in his diet. A bit more exercise was the final component that he'd pledged to himself to achieve.

But he was encouraged; so far, his new weight reduction regimen had netted him a five-pound loss. Equally important though was following his physician's advice to incorporate a disciplined stress reduction regime into his everyday routine. He'd read that seventy-five percent of stress resulted from perception of events and circumstances. His doctor had walked him through a regime to help control his stress by altering his perception of events around him; he practiced that now.

When Keisha's call finally came through, he lunged across the room for the phone, picking it up before the first ring ended.

"Keisha, is that you? What's happening, what did you find out?"

"Dad, believe me it's complicated but the facts that we're starting to work with from Jan may hold a key to what really happened that night. Anyway, this is what the investigator was able to dig up based on the leads so far."

"First, the common denominator on the girl's camp side is a young lady by the name of Brooke Saunders. She's been a leader of whatever was going on for several years. She may have taken over from someone before her."

"Taken over what," Brett asked?

"Well, we're not sure yet. One of our people challenged her about that yesterday after cornering her in a Manhattan bookstore. She confronted her with Jan's version, including the allegation that she expelled from her group a camper named Shelley. Our investigator played it as if she possessed a lot more information than she had, trying to flush Brooke out."

Brett was doing all he could to wait patiently for Keisha's explanation to unfold.

"After the feint the investigator took another approach, demanding to know what was planned to happen among them all at two in the morning. But she got nothing, no acknowledgement, no denial, nothing. Even when she told Brooke that Kyle and Alan were likely to be convicted and serve major jail time, Brooke remained silent."

Brett was confused.

"I don't get it, not at all. Why would she be silent when confronted with the truth, or part of it anyway, by folks representing her friends? Presumably that's who the boys were, her friends. Who else could she be protecting?"

"We're missing something vital, that's for sure," Keisha replied.

"What could be so important that she stays silent in the face of one killing and two kids looking at serious jail time," Brett asked.

"And the kicker is," Keisha said," the two boys were equally mum when we spoke to them. You'd think they'd be singing like canaries by now to off-load blame and save their own skins."

"Keisha, you understand those kids mean a lot to me, don't you? I've met their folks and I've met their brothers and sisters. I know the pain they're all going through. I hate to say this, but what about a plea deal on the more serious charges. What would they be looking at if they accepted a deal?"

"They would be in jail for at least twenty years in that case, with maybe a chance at parole after twelve or fifteen. Not the best option for them, in my opinion."

The numbers stunned him; fighting was the only option.

"What else did your team learn," he said?

"Well, we finally got access to the bag that Skip was carrying that night. The boys apparently called it a swag bag. When I asked Kyle and Alan why Skip had it in the first place, they clammed up tight again. So basically, they haven't volunteered any information at all about what was supposed to happen in the middle of the night."

"Swag bag. What was in it," Brett said?

"It was the strangest thing really. There were a series of clothing patterns, maybe twenty in all, the old fashioned sew it yourself kind; but regular clothes, nothing risqué. Also included were a strange list of numbers on pages, three pages of numbers in total, long sequences. Also, there were web-based number sequences entered onto a spreadsheet. All of it was hard to interpret. We suspect that they are codes of some kind. Some might be related to currency denominations since there were pound and Euro signs as well as some other unknown symbols in the columns associated with them."

"That makes absolutely no sense to me either. Anything else?"

"Yes, one more thing, a USB stick. I had my investigator copy its content to one of our laptops when the evidence guard wasn't looking. But when we got back and tried to read it there was nothing on it but numbers and dashes."

Brett shook his head.

"I don't get it," he said.

"Teenage boys visiting teenage girls in the middle of the night and that's what's in the swag bag? Where's the beer or wine, or the cigarettes or even the condoms?"

"That's precisely what we all said. But we're getting no help from any of them."

"Keisha do me a favor, please, and without talking about what's going on back here run the USB stick and number sheet information by Joshua. Your brother was pretty good with that computer stuff. Maybe he'll have a clue."

She knew the reason why he wasn't volunteering to do that himself. The last face-to-face meeting between them at Christmas dinner turned out to be a real shouting match, all started over old, rehashed grievances.

"That makes sense, I'll reach out to him," Keisha said.

"Thanks, thanks so much. And thank the other folks on the case at your firm for supporting this. Because of that support the families of those boys are encouraged. They think you're the best attorney in New York. I told them they had that right."

"I appreciate the extravagant praise, dad, but I'll need to win some major motions in this case before claiming that mantle," she said.

"You know, my partners and I think that we'll spend a good portion of our annual charitable budget on this one. There's an injustice here worth fighting against, all of them agree with me on that. This will be the firms' major pro bono case going forward. But we won't be able to pay for the whole thing, we'll need some serious funding from the camp and the parents of the two boys."

"Don't worry, we'll raise the funds required to properly defend them."

Brett said that with much more confidence than was justified given the available free cash in his national operating budget. And his meeting with the parents of the boys had only confirmed what he'd already known—there were no extra dollars in their family budgets for attorney fees. But he was hopeful that the recently started defense fund would soon bring in donations.

"I'll check in with you in a day or so, dad," Keisha said trying to end the call and get back to the pile of work in front of her.

"Or better yet, maybe you'll get a chance to call Joshua yourself even before I'm able to reach out to him. One of you should make that move sooner or later you know."

"I agree, you're right. I miss him," Brett said.

＊＊＊

The flight to California reminded him of the many trips he'd taken there. Each one leaving him with the feeling he was arriving at a world apart, one of stunning visuals and arresting realities. The state didn't bother with the opinions of the rest of the county or the world for that matter. So enormous in size, population, and wealth, it set its own pace and its own rules, for better or worse.

And now the Golden State was trying to call the shots on *Sail Shape* by refusing permission to buy the Marin County sailing marina. The refusal was carefully disguised behind a thousand local and state regulations that were being wielded to circumscribe, entangle, and thwart the efforts of his real estate agent who had finally reached out to him for help.

The backstory was more complicated.

Jeb was the current marina owner. He wanted to sell to *Sail Shape*, partly out of loyalty and partly because he was tired after so many years of his practiced genuflection before the spoiled Marin boating crowd. Despite being a major business owner, they always treated him like a butler. The loyalty factor derived from the fact that he was the son of the original owner and Brett had known Jeb since he was ten years old. Jeb's father Clark was the man that had provided Brett the opportunity to work at the marina as a sailing instructor in the old days.

Clark believed in Brett, believed that a green horn MBA student from back east could successfully start a summer sailing program for inner city kids bussed in from Berkeley. Not only did Clark believe in him, he backed him with hard cash to set up transport for the kids to and from the marina.

Despite the backing of the seller and a solid plan, Brett was flying across country to overcome mounting local resistance. And he had an uneasy feeling that he couldn't shake, a feeling that questioned whether he was up for the struggle that lay ahead.

The thought crossed his mind, maybe the fight wasn't worth it.

Strangest of all, was the likelihood that winning approval might rest in the hands of his former protégé from many years past. He had first helped him out years ago when the kid was in high school. Now that kid was a man who'd served several terms in the California legislature, most recently representing Los Angeles County.

Senator J Broderick was also a lawyer, apparently a very successful one. Brett had figured that out quickly when J told him on the phone that he would soon term out under California law; in other words, he would be unable to run again due to term limits set by the voters. He said that he had decided to return full time to his former law firm pending his decision about running for governor. In Brett's mind being able to return to a job without applying for it was a huge indicator of success.

It was all complicated the more he thought about it, as many things tended to be in the Golden State.

What worried him more than anything was that the senator hadn't yet pledged his full support behind *Sail Shape's* efforts. He began to wonder if old ties mattered anymore and whether his former protégé would leave him twisting in the wind. He'd know soon enough, the meeting between them was set for this evening.

He tried hard to relax and practice his techniques, visualizing calmer times. But none of it erased his knowledge that very soon he would be in the middle of tense meetings with opposing forces determined to block him. He tried unsuccessfully to push back against increasing feelings of dread. It left him wondering if he was just too old for the battlefield.

He packed away his headphones and pulled a leather journal from his carry on. It was one of thirty that he had maintained over the years to record his earlier business life and his second career as founder and CEO of *Sail Shape*.

He'd brought the old Chicago journal with him because that was the most difficult camp to launch, exceeding other openings by orders or magnitude. It took four tough years to break through red tape, delays and vehement—borderline violent—opposition. His hope was that it might provide clues as well as a bit of personal spine to help him break through the problems piling up in California.

The journal was a chronological record of key events ranging from concept to final sign-off by the city. As he read through the first several pages a slight smile or frown played on the corners of his mouth depending upon the details. After fifty pages the frowns considerably outweighed the smiles as his dormant memories about the difficult slog in the Windy City were revived.

It all resurfaced—the xenophobic fear, the innuendo about the quality of the children that his camp would serve, and the utter lack of compassion, all of which had very nearly destroyed what *Sail Shape* was attempting to accomplish.

Two hours later he reached the details about that memorable dinner conversation, the one that he claimed at the time he would never forget; yet until now he had. It happened more than halfway through the process and during his third meeting with different clusters of city politicians. The mayor had positioned each of them as key stakeholders that he needed to enlist, most likely because *his honor* wanted to keep his own fingerprints off the future denial.

He was invited to join three such stakeholders at one of the city's best steak houses on Michigan Avenue. He was naïve enough at the time to believe he was making progress at the dinner as he attempted to assuage concerns about the impact of camp operations on the adjoining neighborhoods, one of several manufactured flashpoints pushed by the opposition.

Stat sheets that he handed out at the beginning of the dinner supported his argument that the camp would be a boost to the surrounding areas. There was also that one-pager for each location around the country; they told the same story— wherever located *Sail Shape* was a win-win for the neighborhood and for the parents and kids that it served.

But the paperwork didn't faze one commissioner who was methodically devouring his thirty-six-ounce steak that sat in a large pool of blood. While chewing he started firing questions at Brett about what he characterized as the competence thing. The commissioner finally admitted that he found it difficult to believe that a black owned operation could run a sailing camp by itself without outsourcing the technical aspects to knowledgeable partners. You know, he said after belching loudly, experienced white companies that did that sort of thing. He insisted as he licked his fingers that Brett reveal the names of all secret *Sail Shape* partners, or he would shut down the application.

The memories of the dinner brought the frown back to Brett's face. He shifted in his seat and stretched out his shoulder, back, and neck muscles to stay ahead of the creeping stiffness.

It was then that he remembered that long ago Chicago dinner for what it truly was, one of the few times in his life that he had called upon a higher power to help him control his temper. And it worked; he had suppressed his desire to assist the bureaucrat's digestion by cramming his remaining steak down his fleshy throat.

According to the journal, after denying that there were any hidden companies, Brett spent the next twenty minutes describing his own sailing experience and the experience of his directors at each camp. The dinner had ended with no commitment for support, which at the time was better than a turn down.

After another hour Brett paused at an entry captioned: City Council Meeting. Long forgotten images of that huge hurdle flooded back. There was nothing guaranteed about the outcome and the local betting line was that he would loose the pending vote.

After a long swallow of water, he closed his eyes before reading more. Despite the passage of years, he could clearly visualize the day of the hearing; the stuffy wood-paneled committee chamber, the white male faces of the councilmen that probed him for anything that they could later point to as the reason for their rejection, and the six hundred brown, black, white, and tan faces of parents and children who had packed the room in support of his proposal.

Suddenly remembering exactly what he needed to find he furiously flipped through several more pages before locating the stapled in draft of the closing remarks that he had delivered at the end of the three-hour meeting. He read through the text of his carefully crafted speech with a slight smile on his face.

"Mr. Chairman, Members of the Council. On behalf of *Sail Shape*, I would like to extend our sincere thank you for the time you afforded us while we were in Chicago. I understand and respect the constituent pressures that have been brought to bear on you and I know that you face a difficult decision. It's also been a challenging time for us as well."

"Allow me to share a brief story with you. It confirms my belief that we are right for Chicago, right for the lakefront and right for the youth of this city. After hearing it I hope you will agree."

"Many years ago, when I was a college freshman, I made my first visit to the Windy City. I was an ambassador for my college newspaper, a reporter, and I was here to write about the Black Muslim convention that was hosted for African American college students from around the country. The conference was held over the Thanksgiving Day holiday. My girlfriend at the time warned me against developing a big head over my selection for the assignment since no one else was detached enough from family like I apparently was to sacrifice a Thanksgiving vacation week for the privilege. Her sarcasm also stemmed from the fact that I turned down her invitation to meet her parents over turkey dinner at her house."

"For me the opportunity to visit Chicago was a huge learning experience that I couldn't pass up, it was a part of my developing eighteen-year-old self-awareness. It was the precursor that led me the following summer to Africa as an outreach student representing the United States. It was all part of my burning need to try to figure out life, to understand my personal history, and to understand what made the world tick."

"Anyway, on the ground in Chicago I took it all in back then, including long walks in the city after programs ended in the late afternoon. On one walk I got lost. I unknowingly ambled into a gang area—Crips and Bloods—and I was assaulted and robbed. But after recovering from the punches, kicks, and bruises and after reflecting on the incident and integrating a bit more wisdom, I did learn some things. Much of it was very pedestrian stuff like get yourself a map in a new city, talk with the concierge, and don't go strolling into unknown neighborhoods like a fresh-faced rube."

"But other lessons were more profound, and they helped me grow determined over the years to understand what it was about the upbringing of those three young men that attacked me that lead them to the conclusion that it was the right thing to do. As I gained more knowledge, I also began to ask what could be done to turn that around, what really works? The answers became part of my personal voyage to make a difference."

"What's that ancient history got to do with present day Chicago you're wondering? There is a direct connection."

"Six months ago, I was a holding a series of meetings at South Side community recreational centers and responding to questions from parents and guardians about our programs—what did we offer neighborhood kids and how would it help; how much would it cost, and were scholarships and meals available? At one such meeting at the end of the Q&A, a tall heavy-set black man approached me and asked if we could speak privately outside."

"After grabbing my coat, I followed him into the cold to an area adjacent to the front entrance and mostly out of the wind. The snow from a recent fall dusting crunched underfoot as we trudged along, and I quickly started to freeze up from the single digits wind chill. I remember hoping that his questions would be a short; I was determined that my answers would be even shorter."

"When he turned to face me, he pulled his black hoodie off his head. His P coat and scarf remained bundled around his large frame and his bare hands were stuffed into his coat pockets. For some reason that I couldn't place I had a slight feeling of apprehension."

"Maybe it was because his facial features were worn and old and he had a chiseled piercing look about him, about his eyes; it was a merciless look. As he exhaled gray condensation from his nose and mouth it partially obscured his dark face, but not those eyes. He continued to stare for a few more seconds before he asked me whether I recognized him. I shook my head."

"Then he reached into his inner coat pocket, pulled out a small toothpick, and placed it in his mouth. He contorted his face with the toothpick pointed sideways. That's when it hit me, that unforgettable gesture. He was the gang leader among the three thugs that had beaten, stomped, and robbed me years before. He was toothpick man, at least that's all I could describe to the Chicago police at the time. In that instance of recognition, I felt a sharp pain in the small of my back, precisely at the spot that met his steel-toed boot."

"Seeing my panic, he clamped a strong grip on my arm to stop my retreat to the community center. He stowed the toothpick, softened his features, and assured me there would be no robbery this time. He'd served thirty-five years behind bars during different periods of his life for felonies and he said he had been clean for a good while, trying now to be a responsible single father. He sincerely apologized for beating and robbing me and said he wanted to help me mobilize community support for *Sail Shape*, but only if I would commit to allowing his son and daughter to attend the camp when it opened. He offered to pay what he could but admitted that he would need help. He just wanted his kids to have that shot at something better, he said. I gave him my word on that frigid street that it would happen."

"So, councilmen, I stand before you with the same offer that I gave toothpick man and that I want to give to thousands of children in Chicago. Some of those faces are looking at you right now from the gallery. If you give me the chance to work with them using our proven approach, I'll bring brighter tomorrows to them and their families. That's my promise."

Brett nodded his head before carefully folding and reinserting the speech into the journal. He rested back against the seat.

The camps that he opened during the many years after Chicago had been relatively easy and formulaic. And that, he admitted, was only because he had bailed out and looked for properties with less opposition whenever serious challenges surfaced. Path of least resistance? Maybe. He thought back to his hearing in Long Island before Dan Quigley. He'd used some tough words and a more aggressive posture. Maybe it was a beginning.

With California he would face his stiffest test in years. So far at least he had refused to pack it in and look for an easier place to build. He vowed that he wasn't flying all the way to the west coast to capitulate. There was a major need for his program in Berkeley and he wanted to deliver, maybe one last time.

To win he would need to ramp up his grassroots advocacy and outreach, involve hundreds of parents in his efforts, and enlist the energy, commitment, and political contacts of the Senator.

And maybe he would need to write another good speech.

On the approach into LAX he looked down at the expanse of the great Los Angeles basin as its gapping maw opened to the west. To his right the majestic San Gabriel's seemed to soar even higher as the jet descended smoothly past the mastiff known as the Rim of the World. He'd done that beautiful hike from the valley floor to the Rim several times when he was a grad student.

Don't fret he reminded himself; they'll be different mountains to climb on this trip, high business mountains.

Images of great hiking trips and climbing came to mind, including a three-day mini excursion with Keisha when she was thirteen. He had helped chaperone her Girl Scout troupe up to the stunning Adirondacks. Thinking about her he marveled at the fact that she had always been the favorite of his three children over the years. On the other hand, she was there years before both Joshua and baby girl were born, so maybe it was only as simple as that.

Despite that convenient rationalization his isolation from his younger children forced him to confront the truth that his relationship with both Joshua and baby girl left a lot to be desired. Rather than becoming closer as they grew and matured over the years, he felt more distant and estranged. He had watched the walls grow over many years. Most telling, they both had fled far from home at the earliest opportunity.

Hadn't it started years ago when they were young, he asked himself, that emotional gulf. Had he been too strict with each of them, too rigid in his own views of right and wrong? How many times had they raised that very same objection with him as teenagers? How could he really deny it now given where things stand?

Was it simply his need to control everything, as they certainly believed it to be, or had it been driven by his own inner fear? Despite the private schools that they'd attended, despite the better neighborhood where they were raised, far better than where he'd spent his younger days, the city around them remained small and tough. He always feared for their safety. He knew what they didn't know, that unforgiving areas where mistakes were brutally punished were only a few miles away.

He remembered his own childhood on those Albany streets—from the neighborhood fights and his personal scraps to the bullying from kids in big families with big brothers. What had surrounded him so often back then were the mindless displays of adolescent cruelty. He and his older sister and younger brother had to pick their way through it all sticking close together, occasionally fighting together.

So often even the seemingly benign things in the old neighborhood held hidden surprises. He suddenly remembered the off-hand revelation of childhood prostitution that had confounded his young mind.

Why do all those men line up in the hallway from the fourth floor down to the first floor, spilling outside sometimes, he'd innocently asked his friend Calvin?

To be done by Sheri he was told by his grinning worldly-wise friend who was rubbing his crotch. Brett wasn't certain back then in his eleven-year-old brain what *being done* really meant, but he was certain from Calvin's smirk that he had done whatever that was with Sheri. She was just eleven herself and Brett would occasionally see her on the neighborhood streets and say hi, even after knowing about the lined-up men that she was *doing*.

All of that and much more were just beyond the front porch of his inattentive grandmother's small home where he and his sister and brother—kept together rather than split apart—had spent many years of their youth.

But times are different his kids always used to chime up in response to his deliberately vague warnings about dangers in the city. Maybe so he'd reply without giving them any specifics about what he knew and had experienced. But he was unwilling then to risk it, to risk them. As they grew older and wiser and better able to judge things for themselves and do things well beyond Albany, his approach didn't change very much.

It was clear to him, finally; he had kept too tight a control for far too long.

Baby girl was even more of a challenge than Joshua. He'd missed something fundamental between them years ago that had robbed the joy they used to experience with each other when she was a girl. He'd engaged in more sports—baseball, football, swimming, and soccer— with her and ran more races when she was small than he had with any of the others. Then one day she'd stopped sharing herself with him. It was more than adolescence; had to be he now realized.

And what about Lailani?

"Mr. Howard, welcome to the Ritz. Our entire team is at your service. I trust your flight was uneventful?"

As tired as he was, he had to admit that the manager's greeting sounded completely sincere, so he pulled in his usual sarcastic punch, using instead a light jab.

"Thank you. Yes, the flight was long but extremely uneventful, just the way I always like it."

"Good sir. Mr. Howard your room has been inspected and it awaits you. Shall I have a bellman escort you?"

"No need for that. I only have this carry-on."

"Very well; allow me to add this message to your welcome package sir, the call came in forty-five minutes ago; of course, the voice transcription system isn't perfect so please forgive us for any typos that came through."

Inside the well-appointed room he hung up his suit and spare shirts and eased his sore six-foot two-inch frame into the large corner chair. He opened the gold leafed envelope.

Dearest Brett,

We've been out of personal touch since the fundraiser in New York a few years ago. I miss catching up with you and would hope to do that while you're in Los Angeles. Forgive me for putting the squeeze on your secretary to share your itinerary. I think she matched my name to the donor list and assumed that you would want to see me.

You have my number, that hasn't changed. Call me when you can while you're here.

Ciao,

Zena

He leaned his head back and shut his eyes. Memories of his long-ago girlfriend and the smoldering passion that they had shared filled his mind. Could it have worked for them he wondered if they had stayed together, and he had pursued a different vision?

At that time they had a love affair for the ages, he admitted. And what a ball they'd had— traveling, lovemaking and planning. For several years they both believed they had a long future together.

She had looked just as stunning as always at the fundraiser when he had last seen her in person, what remarkable genes. Had it only been his imagination or did her kiss on his cheek linger for just the smallest fraction beyond what was politely necessary?

Brett thought about why he had been so hard on her both before and immediately after the breakup, cutting her completely out of his life, no soft landing. Was it fear, his own or the fact that she was a one-eighty to his own history? Yet, he'd known since he'd met her that she was different, cavalier, marvelously self-centered, rich, and often shallow.

In the beginning hadn't he loved her for it, or perhaps despite it; loved the freedom in her every fiber; that unconstrained zest of hers for life and all it offered. Also, her courage, he had loved that too; and the fact that she'd defied her family's moribund color codes that would have forbidden them being together because he was *too dark.*

So, wasn't it true that she hadn't really changed at all when he ended things; wasn't he the one with issues? And it was also clear he had never really figured out precisely why it had happened; what were the influences of each contributing factor? Was it the pressure from the takeover battle back then; that grinding struggle when cutting costs and chopping heads were all that he and the executive team could focus on? Or was it fear that she would somehow dilute his passion for social change because she just didn't care about those things?

Maybe his real concern was that he might become a mere satellite in her multi-generational black bourgeoisie orbit, despite his own first-generation professional accomplishments. Perhaps the influences of social class and opportunity were the real drivers, his inability to feel completely at ease among her freeborn black social circles.

Maybe his early upbringing had left a lasting chip on his shoulders that he could never shake.

And would they have gotten back together despite it all if Lailani had not suddenly appeared again in his life? After that he'd completely forgotten Zena. It was all Lai, and the camp startup, and Keisha and then Joshua and baby girl and more and more life stuff.

And where's that flame in his life now, he wondered rhetorically, that old, rekindled flame with his childhood sweetheart? Has it gone out completely? Were he and Lai even friends anymore?

What if Zena was offering another spark, a second chance? But even if that were true, he knew that he couldn't go back there, he really didn't want to go back there. He had to live in the now.

His resolve didn't end his ruminations because Zena's message raised an entirely different possibility. Over the years she and her sorority sisters could be counted on for at least one hundred thousand dollars annually in unrestricted operating funds; they'd adopted *Sail Shape* as one of their national charities.

After a quick mental calculation, he realized that without that chunk of money coming in within the next few weeks he'd be forced to seek additional expensive bank loans as the only way to plug the hole in the national budget.

As he considered that possibility, he grew more worried about the real motive behind her wanting to meet with him. Was it to pull the plug on the annual contribution? Had she and the other prim and proper sorority women been unsettled by the unsavory racial overtones that had propagated after the shooting?

He slowly folded her note and put it away. He leaned his head back and breathed deeply.

Part Two:
West Coast Sunsets

Chapter 7:
High Finance Sailing

JEMAL WANTED TO BE JUST LIKE JOSHUA, that's why he always called him boss. Joshua was in control, he created things, and he was brown just like Jemal was. Those were the reasons why Jemal had readily traded in his long African name for his shortened American handle that started with a J. But as he grew up to learn more about the world around him, he began to realize that his chances of becoming a man like boss were slim.

Yet he couldn't complain about his life so far. After boss and Mirra found him years ago things had started looking up. Compared to what he'd escaped from in Ethiopia, he knew that his present position and future were far better.

As he'd grown older and more adept at plumbing the web, he learned that many of his childhood friends in Ethiopia were likely dead or forcibly recruited into brutal gangs. Despite that knowledge he had harbored for a time romantic ideas that his village had survived the widespread harshness. But more recent orphans arriving from his homeland had attested that there was little left in the region of his birth. They would use native words than translated into denuded, decimated, and destroyed.

Although it varied in particulars, he understood that his story was anything but unique, despite sounding that way to the curious.

He was a young boy when he'd fled the carnage by the slimmest of margins along with his four older brothers and three younger sisters. They'd all left the village together on foot ahead of the sun. They avoided human contact and cautiously made way east to the coastal shipyard eighty miles away. They scampered through a small, jagged opening in the perimeter fence. Close to the docks, they hid inside empty barrels for safely and rest.

Noise and vibration startled them awake the next morning with huge dockside loading gaffes grabbing the barrels in which they were hiding along with dozens of others. In fear they remained hidden and silent. Once on board ship the barrels became home for the eight siblings for several weeks. Only the kindness of a South African merchant seaman who discovered their cramped hiding places kept them all from starving during the passage.

Six of them later died from blood poisoning within weeks of arriving in London. The cause was exposure to trace toxic chemicals that lined the barrels being shipped back to London manufacturers. Only Jemal and Fatima survived.

Jemal was aware enough to know that his disturbing family history wasn't completely negative and that it had played a meaningful part in his current academic success as well as his sister's. That belief had taken form as he grew older in his adopted homeland and developed his skills. His prowess in the classroom made him feel that his facility with numbers and analysis had to be in his family's DNA. To assess, to compute, and to theorize had always been effortless for him. It was the same for Fatima. Yet as far back as he could remember neither of his parents were involved in academics or business.

It must have skipped a generation he finally concluded, or maybe his parents always had the gift without any opportunity to apply it.

Whenever he thought about his mother or father it revived fading emotions from his loving times with each of them. His earliest memories were of being at home inside and safe, playing with his siblings while surrounded by the pleasing aroma of many foods.

Other darker memories always intruded.

The slaughter had happened when he was very young but old enough to retain shreds of imagery. Rapacious bandits were all over the area back then he had learned much later. They were part of a larger regional group that had invaded and ransacked many villages and towns. They would strike down and steal from the local people.

The robbery at his home should have ended immediately after his family possessions were taken from the rooms and bagged up by robbers. He retains to this day one specific memory of a mean looking man dragging a giant cloth sack filled with family possessions through his home.

Unfortunately, the robbery wasn't the end of it because his parents had hidden piles of anti-rebel literature at the bottom of a covered stowage trunk, which the thieves discovered by chance on the way out. He can vividly recall the image and sounds of the old trunk being kicked over and shattered with heavy axes.

His mother and father must have been distributing that material throughout the village and nearby towns, he later guessed.

After exposing the hidden pamphlets, the rebel leader's anger was so great that both parents were called to account stripped naked, then severely whipped for their insolence. For unknown reasons they were also hacked to death shortly after the flogging with razor sharp machetes. Before the blades struck his older brothers had covered the eyes of the younger children with their hands and hustled them outside. But Jemal had peeked through his brother's fingers.

The horrific images had been greatly dampened by his years at the orphanage among the Lutheran brothers and by his long association with Mirra and boss and others at the warehouse. He counted himself fortunate.

Fresh in his mind despite the intervening years was the first presentation that boss had delivered to him and his classmates at the orphanage. *Come to the student warehouse after class* Joshua had proclaimed to the bustling room full of immigrant and orphaned children. He'd promised them all after school snacks, computers, and books and that he would personally tutor anyone who worked hard to excel. His main promise to everyone that day was that they'd be part of a warehouse full of student brainpower from which top-tier English schools would trip over themselves to recruit.

Despite that sales talk, Jemal only heard in his young mind the promise of snacks. It was because the orphanage did it's very best to provide the basics, but snacks weren't among them. So, he and Fatima and twelve others had eagerly signed up for the program.

Beyond extra food the other thing that had attracted him was that boss wasn't Italian or German or French or even English; he was an American. Even though the strange accent made the English difficult to track, Jemal listened closely and learned all that he could. The world of mathematics, software, and computers were opened before his eyes, and he soon showed that he had a gift.

The other good thing for Jemal throughout the years was seeing the teamwork between boss and Mirra. Even when he occasionally saw them disagree, they did so without damaging each other.

Because of his long history with them he was highly motivated to research the question from boss about the syndicate banker's hidden skipper, even though he wasn't sure what a syndicate banker really was. Nevertheless, it took him only twenty minutes to determine who the bankers were holding in reserve. He sent boss an email with background information and photos about the nephew, the skipper in waiting.

But the more recent assignment concerning numbers on the spreadsheets and the USB data was much more difficult. He could decipher that the sting of numbers and letters were a sophisticated code, a key of some sort that controlled something on other computers or machines. But he had no idea where the actual lock for those keys resided, let alone the underlying intent of the algorithms.

Having hit a dead end, he was very close to giving up and reporting his failure. But there was one last thing he needed to do after school when he could use the parallel central processors at the warehouse that gave him much more firepower than his laptop. And he would run his searches simultaneously across the underground dark web.

That would be dangerous, but he believed that he was skilled enough to cover his tracks and protect warehouse servers.

∗∗∗

No one had to tell Joshua that he could learn a great deal from a detailed conversation with his father involving both critical issues confronting him in London, but Mirra did so anyway.

Your dad lived through the same kind of problems back in the day, she reminded him.

The reality that she never met Brett in person or spoke with him by phone didn't slow her down at all. Instead, she seamlessly utilized the long list of personal details about Joshua's upbringing shared over many years, some of which he'd even forgotten himself.

But he remained adamant, a discussion with his father right now just seemed too awkward and he needed more time to let the steam subside between them. That drew a disapproving stare from her as she reminded him that it had been more than two years since the blowout.

He admitted that he had deliberately passed up the chance to tap into his father's experience after leaving grad school and opting to work in London. He'd chosen then, emphatically so, to make his own experiences and to finally walk away from the paternal hand. He also shared his ultimate concern that even if he disclosed his issues to his father at this late date more than likely his father would interpret his current problems as a sign of weakness, issues that he should have anticipated and planned for.

No, this wasn't the right time. He held his ground despite the smoke that he thought he saw coming from her ears.

As an alternative he considered calling his uncle Jimmy, but he had to admit that the genuine closeness between them from years past had faded. Not out of any rancor but due to time and distance.

It was the same for his aunty Dee; her insights were very helpful when he was a youngster. As he'd grown into adulthood, however, they hadn't talked often at all.

Losing touch with family and with friends was his doing not theirs, he admitted. It was largely his priorities. But wasn't it also a good touch of indifference? Wasn't the price of great financial success measured in the number of burned relationships? He couldn't remember the source of that quote.

No. He pushed back while shaking his head. He refused to buy into that sentiment regardless of how neatly it seemed to sum things up. Not being close and not caring to be closer was different from where he believed himself to be; it was different from not being close but wanting to be closer.

In the end he reached out to his uncle Ned who wasn't a blood uncle but who was the closest thing to one. He was an old friend of his father who years ago after Joshua graduated from business school had tutored him in the fine art of banking and finance.

After Joshua demonstrated his aptitude in the London financial world Ned personally staked him, helping him and his partners raise capital from other backers to buy a seat on the exchange. One of Joshua's proudest moment's years later had been paying that eight-figure loan back with interest.

He was also mindful that Ned had been the driving force behind his father's construction of the first *Sail Shape* facility more than thirty years ago. So, Joshua guessed that he might have insights into some of the challenges that he faced with the warehouse.

Given the history between them he was also certain that Ned would keep things private.

He smiled as he called the number back in the states.

"Uncle Ned, its Joshua. I hope it's not too late for you?"

"Joshua! No! it's not too late; I was just starting to close the study here and head upstairs to relax. How've you been? I haven't heard your voice for a month of Sundays. Speaking of late, it's early morning hours there for you."

"Yes, it is, the sun is not up yet. Overall things are fine in old London town. Trading volume is much higher than last year, and volatility is down, which mean business is quite healthy. We're also in the early stages of underwriting a couple of big deals to broaden our footprint."

"That's great to hear. I'm proud of the success you've achieved. I know it wasn't easy," Ned said.

"Thanks. No, it wasn't but I had the tools and your good advice to help me, not to mention that financial stake. And Mirra is keeping me out of trouble of course while she continues to work wonders with the warehouse programs. Truth is she's grown our staff five-fold since she started. We're tutoring and developing over three thousand different students now during any given year. And before you ask, I haven't yet shared with my parents anything about the warehouse or even about Mirra. But the secrecy is sitting less and less comfortable with me, really."

As he listened Ned asked himself how relationships within families could become so convoluted, so closed. He wondered whether he and his wife would have experienced the same bewildering estrangement with their own children, if they'd been able to have any.

Joshua broke in on his reflections.

"How've you been Uncle Ned? How's that rock solid U.S. banking business treating you?"

"Truth is, Joshua, to complain would be to bring bad luck upon myself. We've been doing fine, in fact. The financial crisis that took a big chunk of the bank's growth away has faded into the past. But consequently, our underwriting and lending practices as well as those of the entire sector are much more disciplined, which is the way it should have been all along. We're also ready for any downturn, at least as much as we can be. Quiet as it's kept, I'm planning my own exit strategy.

"It'll soon be time to sell my stake in the bank, retire, and kick back."

Despite it having been some time since he'd spoken with him, Ned understood Joshua's call wasn't just for idle chatter and that it likely had a business purpose.

"So, Joshua, to what do I owe the pleasure of this surprising call?"

"Well, I could really benefit from your advice, again. Believe me, I do want to get to that place where me and my father can discuss things, but we've got some work to do before that can happen," he said, sounding more confident about the eventuality than he was.

Ned interrupted.

"And that's the good news. You're thinking about it, and you want to patch things up. You father also wants to get there, maybe you don't know that."

"By the way and if you don't mind Joshua, what the hell was that blowout between you two about? I know you've had some tense moments over the years, but what happened at Christmas dinner? Brett barely mentioned it to me. That tells me he wasn't proud of his part."

It was the last thing that Joshua wanted to talk about. But since he was the one calling for advice and counsel, he decided the least he could do was be candid.

"I suppose I may have overreacted a little and allowed old sores and scabs to push me into being blatantly disrespectful; in fact, I overreacted a lot. I'd never cursed at my father before that, although on several occasions I was sorely tempted. Basically, after the shouting started, he accused me of living in London so that I could date as many white girls as I wanted to without his disapproval."

"Oh please, tell me he didn't drag up again the relationship you had in prep school with your Scarsdale classmate?"

"I can't and he did. He hasn't lost that irrational fear that I've somehow abandoned my race and my heritage."

"It's funny, I remember him talking about that incident with you and your classmate years ago. He was shocked on two levels, you know. One, he had no idea you were bringing anyone home for Thanksgiving and two, he had no idea that it would be a white female. Truth is you really surprised him and your mother that day."

"Yeah, no question about that. I should have given them a heads up; the reality is it just slipped my mind in the rush of exams and getting ready to exit campus. But he has used that surprise to make a lot of misassumptions about who I am over the years. And yet he'd be the first one to preach that you shouldn't judge a person by the color of their skin."

"My theory is that all his animosity is driven by the fact that I didn't step into a leadership role in *Sail Shape*. Because of that he assumes that I've got no concern for the less fortunate. He thinks that all I do in London is live the high life and accumulate money. Truth is I've never been able to understand the chip on his shoulder, particularly when it comes to his interaction with me or any of his family, with the notable exception of Keisha."

Joshua could hear his own frustration level rising; he stopped talking.

Ned had listened patiently hoping that the still raw emotions would dissipate. With the pause he tried to nudge things back on track.

"Well, you've got to admit you've kept your great charitable work in London completely below the publicity radar screen; and I respect you for that by the way. But your father has no idea about the kids you're helping. It's the kind of thing that he would have done himself if he hadn't started *Sail Shape,* I'm sure of it. Tell me, did he ever discuss with you why he started the camps in the first place?"

"You know uncle Ned, I really don't remember him ever talking about it. I guess my working assumption was that it all started in Long Island, you know, around the time of my first visit to the camp during the construction phase. It was some type of inspiration on his part, I do remember him mentioning that."

"But" Joshua said, hesitating as he thought about his response, "that couldn't be the origin of the thing, could it? I was just a little kid then and things were already well underway."

"They sure were," Ned said before filling in the details.

"As I recall you were around four or five years old during that first visit; but *Sail Shape* started before you were born. You see Brett took a buy-out package after a corporate raider attacked his company. Since he was a direct report to the CEO his severance deal was substantial and like most of the other top brass, he took the money and left before the real carnage started with the restructuring. The run-up in the stock price after the takeover was announced also spiked his savings plan. He had enough to leave the corporate world and start something he believed in."

Ned hesitated; he wondered if he'd given Joshua too much background. But it occurred to him that in all the time they'd spoken over the years it had always been about Joshua or about business, not about Joshua's heritage and not about his father.

"So, he cashed out and became the founder and CEO of *Sail Shape*. That started the long process of raising public interest and investment in the venture. He enlisted a network of financial backers, including yours truly, and finally broke ground in Long Island for the first camp. He was about thirty-seven years old when he walked away to start it, only a few years older than you are now."

The idea of walking away from the business world at such a young age was hard for Joshua to relate to; it just didn't make any sense.

"But why didn't he take his skills to another company or start one. I mean take-overs aren't that uncommon—even back then— and at his level he would have been able to land somewhere else or start a venture, right?"

"Believe me, he could have landed in another high-level position or done something on his own—if he'd wanted to. But he had a burr under his saddle, long before I met him."

"And what burr exactly was that" Joshua asked, already knowing the likely answer to the question?

The touch of sarcasm behind his question didn't escape Ned's notice, he answered despite it.

"The one that drove him to initiate a structure and design that made a difference, something that had a real impact. *Sail Shape* gave him the chance to put his money where his mouth had been for years. For Brett it became put up or shut up time."

"Walking away from corporate success wasn't easy though because he'd accomplished a lot in a short amount of time. He had a string of firsts after his name. But he was itching to put into practice things he had come to believe in after many years of trying to influence change in a variety of venues. But those other efforts were mostly board position that didn't translate into the direct impact he wanted to have."

"Well, you know what uncle Ned, that's something I wasn't aware of, not at all. And it's not in his trophy cases either."

Joshua caught himself this time.

"My bad uncle Ned, my droll attempt at humor was reflexive and unnecessary."

"But you know what," Joshua said, "your explanation about what motivated him still doesn't explain the hard edges. I mean he's long been successful both in business and with *Sail Shape* after that, right? Yet instead of the relaxed confident attitude that should flow from early corporate success and a self-directed retirement, he raised us with what amounted to a cold and edgy approach to things; he continues to display that to this day. And for me it just doesn't line up next to the big-hearted motives that you just described. "

"Look Joshua, I appreciate that it's been tough for you over the years; living with a legend isn't easy. And I can understand how his driven personality would be perceived as uncaring. Nevertheless, let me wrap up the story, maybe it will help."

"Brett went to work building *Sail Shape* and I helped him with the financing. My involvement, however, was tangential to the whole thing because for me it was about returning the favor that he did for me when he spearheaded the community support effort in Albany for my commercial development project. Your father had a clear vision when he'd returned to that city after leaving the business world; he wanted to put kids on the right path, and he had the foresight to understand that my development and the jobs that it offered was a big first step for many families."

"Hold on a minute uncle Ned, I always thought that you were the prime mover behind *Sail Shape*, that your bank was the impetus for it all."

"No, not at all; the prime mover was a philanthropist from New York City, a very wealthy industrialist, I can't remember his name after all these years. Wait, it was Smith; the last name was Smith. He donated the Long Island property to *Sail Shape* with no strings attached. Wait, that's not completely true. Brett mentioned that there was an unusual string. He had to put up some type of message that was always visible to every kid in the camp; can't remember what it said though."

"Interesting, I had no idea," Joshua said. "That Smith land donation must have been epic back in the day. I wonder what motivated him. By the way, I do remember that posted message at the camp. it was a plaque that talked about pointing your helm at an honest and true course; it was from, or come to think of it maybe it was about, someone with the initials CS. I looked at it for years posted up on the boathouse wall like every other *Sail Shape* camper."

"You know, your history helps explain a lot of the lectures I received from my father—public service, reaching back, moving forward, you name it. I never really understood it all to tell you the truth, and more often than not, I bristled at it. But again, none of that really explains his steel edges, the almost paranoid approach that he took with me and BG over the years, hate to beat a dead horse over it but just being honest."

Ned could see that Joshua continued to be partially blinded by his father, that he hadn't really glimpsed the evolution of the real Brett Howard. That's difficult to do he supposed when things are kept secret. Maybe after all these years those secrets need to be told.

"You've only ever seen the man he evolved into Joshua, and that's perfectly understandable. What's invisible to you is what shaped him. I'm going to share some things with you about that process because you need to know them. And I believe you are old enough now to keep them in your pocket and to give your father space and privacy after hearing them."

"Your father's early life was shaped in the inner city just like the kids across the country enrolled in the camps, I'm certain you didn't know that. Brett had a few critical advantages though—a mother and a father that were both in his corner and who provided a stable home, and an aunt who also pushed him in the academic areas. You may have a vague memory of your grandfather Bernard, right? He was also important to Brett's early grounding. But everything was severely shaken up when Brett was seven years old, when his mother, Clara, passed."

"Yes, I do remember my grandfather, a big guy with a big voice. I can't recall my father ever mentioning Clara, though."

"You were your grandfather's favorite that's for sure. Not sure why Brett didn't mention his mother to you, unless the pain from that loss made it difficult."

"But anyway Joshua, as I've pieced together what he shared over the years, plush economic circumstances weren't part of his growing up picture. And by the way, that major distinction from my own relatively privileged background is one of the things that formed the bond between him and me; we both were convinced that we could learn something new from the other."

"So anyway, after his mother passed, his father moved him and your aunt and uncle from Boston to Albany to live with his mother since the alternatives in Boston, Clara's family, were sketchy—his words not mine. During those years your grandfather lived and worked in Boston and would drive out to see his kids every month or so."

Ned paused, but Joshua said nothing.

He realized from the silence that Joshua was essentially clueless about this part of his father's history, so he kept going.

"And that neighborhood where he grew up in Albany, Arbor Hill, was extremely marginal. He mentioned that to me more than once over the years. You may know about it, it's on the east side, about three miles from where you were raised."

Joshua knew exactly where that rough and tumble part of town was.

The gritty connection that his father had to Albany came as a complete surprise. He and his sisters had been forbidden to even go near Arbor Hill when they were growing up, but his father had never mentioned that he'd spent some of his childhood there. Why would he conceal that?

"The scars from his time in that neighborhood run deep in him, Joshua."

"So anyway, Brett's father remarried, your late grandmother Vivian, and he subsequently moved the kids out of Arbor Hill to Queens; Brett was twelve at the time. It was nose to the academic grindstone after that along with sports until he shipped out to college. But that move out of Albany as he tells it was just in time—just before things in that neighborhood took control of his future in a bad way."

Joshua struggled to connect the dots from his many years of tense interactions with his father. Based on what he'd just heard something was hidden inside his father's projected paternal image. It had to be his vulnerability or perhaps his shame from growing up in fractured circumstances; why else would he conceal such an important part of his story.

"I guess I never really tied it all together uncle Ned, because I didn't have those facts. He was always evasive about his early years growing up. Maybe that's the wrong word; selective is a more neutral adjective. His go-to stories were always about success from perseverance, about how we also needed to have those qualities without letting race or prejudice slow us down. He didn't talk about his vulnerabilities or failings at all. But given what you've just described, it's clear that he always had a personal stake in turning kids' lives around at the camps, as opposed to an intellectual passion. Turning himself around both during and after that Albany experience was very likely the first instance of success for him."

"That's exactly right Joshua; it's personal. He sees himself in the faces of those kids at every *Sail Shape* facility, both the downside and the upside potential. At times I think it makes his judgment a little subjective and suspect. Of course, he has never agreed with me about that."

"Truth be told Joshua; I've always felt that he's been unfairly harsh with you on many occasions. It was colored by a lot of his personal experiences; he always projected them at you. In his mind I think he felt that you had to make it to the top in a strictly linear fashion, no deviation and no risk taking whatsoever— because you had all the advantages. The rest of it derived from his driven approach to things. That combination in him makes it hard to transmit a warm and fuzzy ambiance but have no doubt that he loves you and his family fiercely."

"I've tried over the years to be somewhat of a counterbalancing influence, to be that supplement for you, particularly after you reached manhood. Brett and I have managed to maintain our friendship despite my occasional meddling in your life. Maybe he appreciated it from me, although he's never said that."

"The beautiful thing for me to watch is how you hit the same target as your dad involving disadvantaged youth even though you had none of the historical issues that motivated him, must be in the genes"

"But anyway, I'm going to leave the history and psychology lesson alone for now because I suspect that you called with something specific in mind. What is it, how can I help?"

"Well, yes, I do have a couple of things. But thank you for that background. It's a lot to think about, it may help me relate to him in a better way, I'm sure it will."

"I've got two big issues ahead of me, uncle Ned. The first one is whether and how to expand the warehouse. We've been very successful measured by how many kids we've boosted academically and prepared for scholarships. But at the same time, it's costing me a boatload of money and I've got no other financial investors helping me make it happen. And this is the very time that the warehouse idea should be expanded."

"The second issue involves my racing syndicate and whether I should shore up my chances to skipper our syndicate boat during the Cup challenge in San Francisco. That would mean forking in another good chunk of change, low seven figures at least. Without that I'll have to win a showdown on the water against a well-trained challenger."

"Whoa, slow down," Ned said defensively. " I'm taking a seat now and pulling over the hassock; tell me more."

As he listened, he realized that the two issues were interrelated. Joshua could probably afford to buy the skipper's position, but he would rather invest his extra capital in the warehouse school expansion.

"Look, I'll give you my input on both matters, no problem. I'm privileged that you'd ask me. But you know that your father is really the best source of advice because he lived through similar choices when he was starting out. Sure, it was a different era, but the fundamentals really never change. I'll make you a deal; you commit to contact him about this stuff before you make a real move. Agreed?"

"Okay, I appreciate that. It's a good plan, deal."

Chapter Eight:
Politics

SENATOR J BRODERICK ARRIVED FORTY MINUTES LATE at his satellite Los Angeles office. Earlier in the day at a local constituent meeting he had received complaints and some praise as well about a range of urban issues facing his district, which was the reason for his tardiness.

Spending time out among the voters, as opposed to remaining cooped up in the bureaucratic game preserve as he often bitingly referred to the Sacramento state office building, was his strong preference.

Lost in thought he walked quickly down back-office corridors on his way to a conference room. He had long since abandoned his tailored suit jacket and tie; those trappings hung in his office over a desk chair that doubled as a workday closet. He wore a monographed white shirt with JB on the cuffs that spilled over his belt that braced expensive but creaseless suit trousers above mirror black shoes. His overall appearance seemed casual— deliberately so— yet despite it he left the impression of someone who could reappear on a moment's notice completely buttoned up and camera ready.

As he approached the conference room, he made a side trip to the men's room to freshen up. Once there he mulled over how many of his waiting staffers would make the transition to the governor's mansion with him, assuming he could win the election and get there in three years. They each had their own strengths and idiosyncrasies, but they'd served him ably. The political pundits always predicted that most staffers couldn't make the leap; it was just too steep a hill. He wasn't sure though whether that was true about his team.

The pathway to California's highest political office was far from assured even with his well-cultivated popularity in many important voting blocks. Beyond garnering votes, and as he often admitted to close friends, California's sheer physical size and far-flung population centers rendered his quest for the party nomination an extremely treacherous one. It was all about raising and spending money, lots of it—for ads, to fund a statewide ground game, and to ensure constant travel throughout the state. Near the end of the next eighteen months his fund-raising machinery to support his bid would have to be up and running at full tilt.

And beyond that he had to pay his own bills and otherwise support himself during the long run up process. The biggest hurdle was the state mandate that he does not stand for reelection again because of term limit rules. That meant one hundred thousand dollars in annual salary plus an expense account gone well before the official kick-off of his campaign. While his law partners had readily agreed that he could return to the firm full time, the salary draw would be small; real income depended on his ability to generate business or win cases. Both of those activities required a big chunk of his time.

But he had salted away a chunk of savings over the past five years to help him bridge the gap.

A new impediment had appeared completely out of the blue when he received a call from Brett Howard. His old mentor and friend wanted him to step into the middle of a highly contentious marina purchase in Marin County. Although that county wasn't part of his existing senatorial district, it was precisely the kind of moderate republican demographic he would need to capture in a statewide election. Any slippage in support there could spell trouble for his incipient campaign.

Would backing Brett's marina purchase help him or hurt him, he wondered?

There was no question that the *Sail Shape* organization had carefully nurtured a positive national image for the past three decades, recent trouble notwithstanding. On the surface at least his affiliation with them would be an automatic plus. But he still had doubts about whether national cache would translate into good local politics in California.

So, he'd tasked his waiting staffers with digging into the recent thorny issues confronting *Sail Shape* back east. He needed to know what was going on that led to a young man's death within the confines of a summer camp, an elite girls' camp at that. And if that story was shaky, what was the downside potential from an affiliation and publicity point of view?

Before leaving the restroom, he stowed away his doubts and put on the air of success and confidence, becoming that take-charge politician that his team was accustomed to seeing.

"Okay folks, sorry I'm late and I appreciate you waiting," he announced as he closed the door. He grabbed a chair and spun it around, stopping it with the back facing toward his team. Sitting with his legs agape and arms resting forward on the top of the chair's cresting rail, he was ready to get started.

"They'll be many issues like this one in the future you know, last minute stuff, well outside of our day to day. Forget that I know Brett Howard; give me your best analysis, no varnish."

He looked first to his senior staffer Howie Steiner who was already putting his notes aside and preparing to deliver a well-memorized summary of his findings.

"Howie, how bad is this Long Island camp thing?"

"Senator, I'm afraid bad isn't the right word. This is toxic. It's poison. Local politicians in Long Island are running against the issue and the incumbent mayor who's up for reelection recently came out in support of closing *Sail Shape* operations down. Not unrelated I believe and closer to home, your image and favorability numbers in Marin County have dipped two points in only two weeks. Of course, your name is not that familiar to most of the electorate up there right now. But here in Los Angeles the drop is half that number among your base. We're convinced at this point that someone is financing an early whisper campaign against you. There's no question that your numbers would take a significant hit the minute you publicly stepped in on the side of the purchase, at least that's my firm opinion at this point."

"Thanks Howie; that's not good news by any means."

Left unsaid to his team was his emerging feeling that the whole *Sail Shape* issue was shaping up like quicksand—once in it you can't step out of it.

"Miriam," he said, swiveling on the seat to face her, "you dug into the underlying facts behind the Long Island shooting, right? What've you learned so far?"

Miriam fidgeted and shifting uneasily. She pulled at her skirt and blond curly hair before plunging ahead.

"Senator, the press in New York has already tried the case— without a lot of facts—in the local papers and talk shows. Of course, social media has picked all of this up as well which means that the story may soon gain national traction."

"According to most coverage there was a sexual liaison going on between the nearby ritzy girl's camp and the *Sail Shape* boys, which as you may know is full of mostly poor black kids. Finding objective substantiation to support the sensational charges, however, has been difficult so far."

Miriam glanced uneasily over at Shana, who was up next, after she said that.

"But according to the local papers senator this thing is a no brainer—inner city kids sleeping with suburban white girls. It's amazing, but the fact that one of the boys was shot and killed hardly gets any press attention at all now. Howie's right I'm afraid, this whole thing is radioactive."

He nodded at Miriam and then looked at his youngest staffer, Shana. She was well dressed and professional in her appearance as always. She was a Stanford grad who'd joined his team four years ago after a stint in the private sector. She was also his oldest link to the past despite being his newest staffer. In fact, he'd known her since she was a little girl and he was a teenager back when their families lived in the same distressed Berkeley neighborhood.

He couldn't help but notice that she'd been unusually withdrawn as she waited her turn and that her body language was signaling strong opposition to what she'd just heard from her colleagues.

As he watched her pull together her notes his thoughts involuntarily turned to the past, to those ancient half-buried memories that he'd grown more capable of controlling. Yet the ill-fated sequence of events always remained stubbornly beneath the surface, close enough to occasionally invade the present.

Long after the months of professional counseling he'd received and the subsequent passage of years he'd finally accepted that he could never hope to completely bury his memories. In fact, he was admonished more than once that to do so might imperil his health. Go with the emotions he was told by the psychiatrists and never seek to evade the impact. As he waited the past confronted him again.

It happened when he was in high school and because Shana's older sister Val along with a large group of students had staged a massive protest that ended in the take-over of the center quad of UC Berkeley University. It was a bold illegal political act at the time, one undertaken by a bunch of idealistic school kids trying to make a positive impact for their neighborhood. And he was right there in the thick of things, an enthusiastic follower.

The occupation eventually resulted in construction of a much-needed high school along with better teachers, adequate supplies, and greater optimism. Brett Howard was the guy who'd saved the bacon for him and the other occupiers. He negotiated the deal leading to the de-escalation of tensions and the end of the encampment. But it hadn't prevented the violent and accidental death of Val, one of the most vocal student leaders.

"Shana, you look a bit pensive," he commented as he shook off the memories.

"What's on your mind?"

Shana glanced quickly over at Howie and Miriam before starting.

"They already know my point of view on this one senator, I shared it after they showed me their findings earlier. When you parse out the one or two thoughtful articles about what happened at that Long Island girls' camp—articles that take the time to evaluate the known facts—I think the only conclusion that can fairly be reached is that no one really knows what was planned to happen that night, at least not yet."

She stood up from the low couch and started pacing to release the restless energy that she usually channeled by using her arms and hands to make her points.

"Senator, not one of the young people involved in whatever was going to happen has corroborated the sex ring story. And by the way, they're all very solid teenagers who were considered leaders in their respective camps. As for the kids from *Sail Shape* being poor black kids—coded meaning of that of course is lazy and dishonest— that's more BS from the rag papers. The selection criteria for *Sail Shape*, not only in Long Island in all camps, are rigorous. The campers may lack financial resources, but they are all good, motivated students with solid parental or guardian support behind them."

She sat back down, checking her notes in case she'd left anything out.

"Thanks Shana. Thank you all. This is exactly the kind of analysis I'll need around this issue going forward."

"Anything else," he asked?

By that time, he was standing up and closing his notepad.

The staffers weren't surprised that the meeting was already ending. The senator had miles to go in his day as usual.

He checked his watch. If he was going to be respectfully late for his next meeting downtown with Brett Howard, he couldn't afford any more time.

At the door he turned back and added a brief pat on the back.

"That was the kind of frank assessment that I rely on each of you for, thanks."

"Let's meet same time next week and do this again. Howie, please set that up."

"Thanks again everyone."

He'd chosen a good farm-to-table restaurant eight blocks away from the usual government eateries in and around downtown L.A. It was a place where he could meet constituents or lobbyists mostly away from the bright glare of California politics. When he arrived, Brett was already waiting at the bar. As he walked over, he could see that since the last time they had met his mentor had aged considerably and added about twenty extra pounds.

"Mr. Brett Howard," J smiled, as he placed his hand lightly on Brett's shoulder, "*Sail Shape* founder and CEO, great to see you, old friend."

They hugged and looked at one another. For his part Brett had difficulty recognizing that long ago high school kid or college kid or even the law student that he'd helped. Those previous identities were thoroughly obscured by the senator's power broker facade.

"J, you look well and totally successful. What's it been, a dozen, fifteen years since we talked in person?"

"About that long, closer to twelve. You were out here for a national meeting, an awards dinner of some kind, and I ran into you there."

"You're right Jazz, I mean J."

He couldn't help asking.

"Why did you change your old handle anyway, J?"

"That was an easy one, the polling numbers were simple to read years ago when I first ran for the city council spot. They said J was much better than Jazz when it came to projecting stability and credibility."

"I can certainly understand the rationale behind it," Brett said." It reminds me that we're all living in a political climate driven by numbers. And I'll bet those same analytics say that you shouldn't touch my *Sail Shape* issue with a ten-foot pole. Am I right?"

"That's exactly what they say. But it was a one-hundred-foot pole based on the read out today from my team."

They shared a good laugh and ordered some wine.

"Look, let's kick this thing around over dinner," J said.

"By the way Brett, I don't know if you remember that Val had a baby sister back in the occupation days?"

Brett shook his head.

"Well, anyway, she works for me as a staffer, I hired her a few years back. She's very sharp. Shana thinks there's more to what happened at Long Island than the press is reporting. I'm going to need that more, in a positive vein, to get involved. Let's discuss the young men who went over to the girls' camp that night. I need you to tell me everything about them and their families."

When they walked over to the dining room, he put his arm briefly around Brett's shoulder. At that moment a local reporter stepped out and took the photo that would splash across the Los Angeles Sentinel front page the following morning. The headline was brutal.

* * *

After leaving her message for Brett at the Ritz Zena returned the antique ivory handset to its ornate base in the corner of her library. She wondered whether he would follow up and call her back while he was on the west coast. He'd better she thought sternly; after all she was still one of *Sail Shape's* major donors.

She left the room after pausing at the drink caddy to pour a generous glass of Sherry. Sipping delicately in the hallway she placed the crystal glass on the nearby table before examining herself in the wall-mounted mirror. She smoothed her hands over her full hips while peeking approvingly over her shoulder. Turning sideways, she thrust her shoulders back to admire her chest and trim abdomen.

She grabbed the glass and took the elevator to the second floor. Unable to get Brett out her mind, she took another sip.

As she requested, the housekeepers had left the white French doors open at the end of the hallway. Beyond them was a formal terrace. Beaconed by the orange sun slipping behind the Santa Monica Mountains, she walked out and sat on a teak lounge chair facing the view, enjoying her favorite sundowner place.

The ten-acre estate was quiet now; the army of landscapers, fixers, menders, scrubbers, and polishers were gone. Only the faint blue light from the distant guardhouse reminded her that she was not completely alone.

As the internal glow from the Sherry soothed, she remembered that she'd almost reached out to him after her marriage had collapsed two years ago, a circumstance that she believed from the very beginning to be entirely predictable. But the marriage had lasted thirty years—a long stretch of make believe and shallowness. Her prediction about collapse had nothing to do with the man her husband was or later turned out to be. The fact that he could never be Brett Howard was at the root of it. She had finally admitted that to herself after the divorce decree was finalized.

Knowing that her message might result in her seeing him again alone and up close forced her to unlock a long sealed emotional vault. Within it was failure and loss and pain. They were stored separate and apart from the endless chapters of success in her life.

When all was said and done, she had chosen Brett to be her life's mate—despite his lower socioeconomic status and the pressures from her family about that— because she loved him for who he was. To her enormous shock and embarrassment, he had broken it off between them.

She had been blindsided by his rejection and by his quiet resolve when he said that they didn't share the same values and couldn't walk the same path. She was so sure that he would be back that she willingly took her leave from the relationship to enjoy a little single's stretch. But she was entirely wrong; he never reached out again.

She grimaced when she remembered their visit together to see her family at the compound in Chilmark. She couldn't blame him then for being underwhelmed by their lack of civility; she was embarrassed by it. She still remembered her now long dead great aunt who pulled her aside in the quiet of the solarium. It was all about Brett's skin tone and how it was more pronounced than the family had tolerated in the past. Aunty had pointedly demanded to know whether she had taken that fully into account.

You mean he's not mixed, and light skinned enough for you, she had replied sternly. After accusing Zena of always being stubborn and self-absorbed, aunty had withdrawn back to the game room bar.

Though Brett didn't complain she could tell that he was affected by the cool reception from several family members and friends. Throughout the visit it was as if he was preparing for a physical assault, he pulled back his normally gregarious personality while tensing to play defense.

But importantly he got along famously with her late father, the venerable Dr. Absalon Jensen, who had been very impressed with the newly minted C-suite executive. Her mother on the other hand had adopted a scrupulously neutral tone and manner, one that would patiently wait for her daughter's infatuation to blow out to the Martha's Vineyard Sea.

Zena watched the golden rays retreat behind the mountains. She slipped quickly into her cashmere sweater to stay ahead of the southern California chill.

Well at least he was sincere, she said aloud without realizing it. He had said that he wanted to build something tangible, something that would have an impact on the things that mattered. She had no idea then what he was referring to and she'd assumed that the pressures of his high-octane job were getting to him. Maybe it had something to do with those corporate raiders that were circling his company like vultures she recalled thinking at the time. Her remedy was to suggest a vacation to Paris where she told him she knew of a lovely boutique hotel in the 3d Arrondissement that would pamper them. He stared back at her blankly after she said it.

He gave her fair warning, she conceded. He talked a lot about downsizing his life and moving out of his Manhattan townhouse—the one she'd marvelously remodeled after his sailing accident overseas. Not to be deterred at the time she concluded that Paris was clearly the wrong destination and so she looked at the South Seas as a place to decompress. Again, that brought on his blank uninterested stare after she mentioned options there. Weeks later he sold Onset, his beautiful racing yacht. Belatedly, it dawned on her that something was radically wrong.

Then he abruptly ended it between them.

But it was entirely predictable wasn't it she asked herself as the warm after glow from the Sherry made it all easier to bear.

Yet, she had to admitt that she still loved him; she still loved the man that was her man before her husband, the substitute. And she still respected him for what he'd accomplished.

He had been unerringly consistent, albeit entirely too stubborn with her she believed. He was probably right about them not making it together after all was said and done. She simply couldn't imagine herself living in Albany of all God-forsaken places and listening to his endless reports about *Sail Shape's* business. But she was willing to wager that his so-called childhood sweetheart that had latched onto him on the rebound probably always listened with rapt attention.

She conjured up the derogatory imagery before she could put her jealousy in check. Let bygones be bygones she quickly reminded herself.

Above everything else she knew that Brett held the keys to helping her daughter emerge from the depression that was enveloping her.

Because of that Zena was fully prepared to do whatever it took when they met to enlist him to her cause.

***

Back at his hotel Brett kicked off his shoes and thought about the dynamics of the evening. He had to acknowledge that J was hemmed in by the negative publicity out of Long Island. He shook his head and spat the word, *politics.*

He'd never been tempted to go down that road himself. But then it dawned on him, that identical constraints were hemming him in. Fundraising, kissing babies or soothing constituents — either for a political campaign or for a 501c (3) organization like *Sail Shape*—was pretty much the same exercise.

He reached for the envelope on the desk and pulled out Zena's message. After tapping it over his index finger a few times, he decided to call her back.

"Hello."

"Hello, Zena; its Brett Howard."

"It hasn't been that long Brett; I do remember what your voice sounds like you know."

He could hear the light tones as well as her playful scolding; he could see those emotions playing on her face. She always did have a good sense of humor. Maybe it wasn't the disaster that he feared after all.

"You're right Zena, and no, it hasn't been that long since you personally delivered your generous check at our fundraising gala in Atlanta, six or so years ago? How are you? And thanks for getting in touch with me while I'm on the coast out here. My staff did the right thing."

"I'm fine Brett, thank you; free at last from a disintegrated marriage and now living the single woman's life here in Los Angeles."

Both facts caught him off guard. For an instance he wondered whether her initial contact was an attempt to rekindle something they once had. Then he dismissed the idea. There was a very good reason that they had broken it off decades ago, one that had worked for each of them at the time and since.

"I'm sorry to hear that, Zena. I had no idea things hadn't worked out. But you do sound happy, I hope so."

"Oh, I'm happy all right. I'm finally freed from competing with other men for time with my husband. Not having to do that has been liberating."

"You mean he ..."

"Yes. I mean Marshal was on the down-low for many years apparently, long before I met him."

"Jesus Zena, I'm very sorry."

His couldn't help but feel amazement that a man would trade Zena's beauty for the amorous affections of another guy. But he dragged his thoughts back to the present and tried to gradually change the subject.

"How's your daughter taking it," he asked?

"She's still in Maryland managing that development company, right?"

"Makala is okay Brett, at least so far. Thank you for asking. She still loves her father of course. But this whole thing was a shock to her, but not so much to me though. You see, I suspected it years ago, but I just refused to go there. But over the years there were too many nights out with the boys, too many boys' trips away. And then one of Marshal's closest friends was busted a couple of years ago for soliciting a drag queen, AKA undercover cop. He finally admitted it to me after I asked him some hard questions. His little group of guys had been titillating each other since college."

Brett had a hard time wrapping his head around what he'd just heard. Oddly, all he could think about was Zena's splashy New York Times nuptials announcement years ago and the over-the-top wedding and reception photos that filled two full pages of the society section.

"That's all part of why I'm reaching out to you now Brett, for Makala's sake. She needs some grounding. She may be almost thirty, but this thing has continued to rock her. It's undermined her entire outlook on men. And she's also had her own self-generated plate of stress that has resulted in career setback within her company or maybe career collapse is a better adjective. That's highly confidential of course."

Brett's mind added up the possibilities.

The hardest part of it for Zena was finally admitting publicly that Mikala had failed, because it would be interpreted that she had failed in raising her daughter, which of course wasn't the case. She had always provided her the best. Why should she be blamed because her daughter had not taken advantage of her opportunities?

But there was no other way at this point; she had to admit failure to enlist his support.

"I'd love to talk with you about it in person, Brett. And I have a favor to ask you that involves Mikala. Is it too late for me to come over," Zena said?

His brain began screaming at him that it was not only too late—decades too late in fact—but that he was a married man. Having another woman in his hotel room after ten o'clock at night was a definite no-no. But then again this was different, it was Zena an old friend and she needed to talk, needed an ear. Nobody had to be aware of the meeting, not that anything untoward would happen in any event.

"Come on over Zena."

"Thanks. I'm about thirty minutes away, I'll call you when I'm close."

She hated the night drive down from the canyons into central Los Angeles because of the steep roads that unwound for miles around her before she reached the freeway. She was aware that certain death waited on each side of the narrow strip of road in front of her.

Hadn't there been a recent fatal crash three months ago, she vaguely recalled? She slowed the Rolls Royce down.

Once in the city she reminded herself to be careful not to smash into one of those ubiquitous tent cities lurking around freeway off ramps or into the plentiful roving homeless emerging from the street shadows. She shuddered at the thoughts.

Who would have thought that he would have called her back the first evening he was in town she asked as her mind focused on Brett again. But hadn't that always been his way, focused and driven?

She peeked up at the lighted console mirror to make sure again that her hair was just so.

Yes, it had been years since she last saw him back east. And she had to admit it; he still looked good then, better than good. Had that changed?

That's got to be that second glass of Sherry talking, she admitted. Pull it together and cool your jets darling she admonished herself; this is strictly about Mikala and not about rekindling a long dead relationship.

Zena reapplied her red lipstick and dabbed a touch more perfume behind each ear.

***

Lailani had never crossed the country before. What she marveled at most as they glided smoothly over the distant landscape below was the barren vastness for so many hundreds of miles; especially after they reached the Great Plains. The mottled geography prompted her recall of odd facts from her history classes; she supplemented those with factoids pulled up from the Internet.

Remembering the health tips contained in the travel flash that Remy forwarded earlier she continued to hydrate. In time she turned back to the stack of business files covering Tony Calibri's operations. As she plowed through the data rich material she began to feel strangely elated about her current reality—flying across country alone to discuss a possible deal for her company. She placed the files back in her valise while she tried to sort through her feelings.

Despite the excitement of the moment, she could never forget how far she'd come in her journey away from those lean times when barely scraping by was all that was possible. It started with mountains of medical bills from her mother's extended cancer battle. The huge debt robbed her dad of his savings and resources. Before he even cashed his weekly night watchman's check from the stockyard, the money was committed and soon gone.

There was certainly nothing left over back then to hire a sitter for her. She'd spent the time at home and alone, locked behind the barrier of her bedroom door. Getting together with Remy and walking to and from school had been her only distractions.

But once Brett moved into her old neighborhood she was liberated, and it was great fun between them during school as well as afterwards with games and imagination. They soon became each other's favorite square dance partner in grade school despite his propensity to spend too much time stepping on her feet.

After five years, Brett and his siblings moved away, Lailani returned to being the latchkey girl with hardly any fun distractions. Other than getting safely to and from school her focus was narrowed to bringing home good grades.

That had been perfectly fine with her though, in many ways it was like meeting an old friend once again.

Reflexively she cringed and shifted in her seat as an unwelcome memory seeped in. Before she could gain control, she relived the assault against her by a drunken neighbor, a neighbor that she and her father had trusted; a neighbor who knew that she was alone in the house every night; a neighbor that she used to call uncle.

Lailani tried to push against the memory.

She closed her eyes tightly and breathed deeply, focusing on the drone of the jet engines. Unknowingly, her right hand was clenching the barrel of her fountain pen in the same way that she had gripped the handle of her hidden butcher knife that she used to stab her uncle.

She exhaled audibly when the memory faded.

Almost as if the thought arrived specifically to soothe and cheer her, she remembered her niece and the challenging years they had endured together when Keisha was her sole responsibility. Putting healthy food on the table, paying the expenses, and ensuring the best education and enrichment experiences for Keisha had been her only focus. They had made it and had some fun as well despite the lean times.

And then Brett reentered her life and the days of want ended.

Was it God's plan she wondered, or had it happened for no apparent reason?

Brett was a good man; she knew that. He was the guard on top of the wall, protector for all of them. But she missed the young man that he used to be before and right after they were married

Once he was that impetuous guy that would grab her up in a swirl and whisk her to some romantic place, somewhere fun. They needed that spontaneity in their lives again; they needed more time just enjoying each other or at least trying to.

And what about you she asked herself; was she that energetic, carefree person that she used to be; in fact, had she ever really been like that? Probably not was the correct answer, not since mama got ill anyway.

She longed to know what she could do to change the current pattern with her husband, what would make them listen to each other again, what would add some zest and excitement to their lives? She didn't have the answer. But she did have a fun idea for this trip that she'd been planning.

Thanks to her friendship with the camp secretary, she'd learned that Brett would be ending his west coast swing tomorrow afternoon and heading back east. She planned to surprise him. The idea wasn't complicated, call his cell phone from her hotel room phone—from her cell phone she reminded herself— after she landed and complain about all the travel he'd been doing lately. Then she would insist on having a few moments on his busy schedule the next morning at a local Albany breakfast spot.

She could predict his reaction. Of course, he'd agree that he'd been on the road an awful lot and he'd be apologetic for taking the present trip without letting her know exactly when he was leaving or returning. Then he'd say that he would be returning from California for most of the following afternoon arriving around midnight. Finally, she guessed that he would apologize a second time for not letting her know that in advance.

After his excuses she would spring her surprise. First, a casual mention that she was on the west coast as well for business, which she had regrettably forgotten to inform him about, was how she would begin. Then on the bright side she would mention that an early breakfast in L.A. suited her schedule just fine and she knew a spot close to his hotel. And if by chance he was interested in a nightcap before tomorrow's breakfast, all he had to do was ask and she'd meet him that evening. Lailani grinned over how mischievous it all sounded, but she quickly covered her mouth hoping that other passengers hadn't seen her.

She looked outside again as they glided peacefully over puffy orange-white clouds and the easternmost peaks of the Rocky Mountains. The drone of engines and the long flight made her doze off. But her sleep was soon broken by the captain's announcement of the approach.

After landing she was amazed at the size and sprawl of LAX. Albany's newly refurbished airport looked like a tiny regional hub in comparison. She also marveled at how efficiently the car service maneuvered to curbside to pick her up, despite the four lanes of one-way traffic. After that they flowed easily out of the airport and within minutes merged onto the highway—still referred to as the freeway by Californians she later learned.

Favorable initial impressions quickly soured when they inched along a crammed six-lane freeway for almost two hours. It was past ten o'clock when she finally checked into her hotel.

Before unpacking she called his cell phone.

"Hello, this is Mr. Howard's room, how may I help you this evening?"

The woman's voice had a carefree lilting pitch.

"Who is this," Lailani said, her anxiety rising?

She heard muffled voices through her receiver as the woman called out for him.

"Hello, this is Brett Howard, with whom am I speaking?"

Lailani's eyes filled with tears before she hung up.

Her night was a sleepless one as her emotions pin-balled among anger, self-pity, and self-doubt.

How often had he used his travel as an excuse to warm his hotel bed with some pick-up floozy? That was all she wanted to know at first.

Or maybe he had a steady relationship with someone else, somebody important to him that he meets up with in different cities; did that make him a faithful cheater?

She felt foolish and deeply hurt and she was in shock because she never believed that he would stoop so low.

She thought about all the years that she had blindly trusted him to travel and take care of *Sail Shape's* business.

After three tortured hours, the only salve that could ease her torment was a quiet repetition of the Lord's Prayer, a life-long habit. She combined that with a detailed recitation of the many blessings that she had received during her life so far.

The dual mantras provided some measure of comfort. She pulled it back together for a time before her mind started to churn again.

She reminded herself that she had known him since childhood and in all those years he'd been solid and faithful, as far as she knew. But then she remembered the enormous span of time where they had been separated from one another. Had that changed him, had it eroded his character?

He had certainly made the time back then to have at least one steady relationship and he may have had many others that he never mentioned.

Maybe deep down he had always compared her to his other girlfriend, that highborn Jensen woman. Perhaps in his eyes she never measured up to that one. Did he ever really break it off with her fully?

She thought about the innocent love that they shared as children. For a moment it made her dismiss the idea that he could be unfaithful. He was first and foremost her husband, the father of three children. Sure, the stress from both of their businesses and the raising of the kids over the years had taken a big toll. It had removed that easy mutual appreciation between them, replacing it often with indifference.

But the house was empty now. More time had been spent in each other's company. They'd made other small strides and were starting to get to know one other again, weren't they?

The optimism ebbed and flowed.

That was a woman's voice that answered his phone, her rational mind asserted sharply. Even at the fancy Ritz it was much too late for maid service, and maid service never answered cell phones anyway. What other reason but cheating could explain it?

Try as she might she was unable to reconcile why he would let the woman pick up his phone at all if he had something to hide. It could've been anyone calling; like his wife. He'd have to be a total dingbat to allow it and he wasn't a stupid man, never had been. She garnered a semblance of hope with this new line of reasoning, speculating further that perhaps the woman was a sociopath that had maneuvered an emergency meeting with him under false pretenses. Perhaps she grabbed the phone deliberately and against his wishes when he was out of the room.

But no matter how Lailani messaged the facts, nothing totally explained it away.

Exhausted, she finally dozed off at five-thirty in the morning, one hour before her wake-up call.

The absolute last thing she felt like doing at that point was getting up and getting ready to meet Tony.

But she needed to leave the mess with Brett alone and concentrate on business. Her focus shifted to the reason she was there in the first place; she rehearsed what she wanted to accomplish between yawns.

Later, while staring at her fresh-washed face in the mirror, she decided that major work was needed. She applied far more foundation and makeup than was her norm. It smoothed over the blotches and puffiness as well as some of the darkness beneath her eyes. After making sure that her business suit was smoothed and lint free, her last prop was a pair of lightly tented glasses that she would keep on during the meeting.

In the rear of the stretch sedan, she opened the window and allowed in the surprisingly crisp morning air. After they had traveled through several densely packed downtown neighborhoods neat modern architecture and meticulous landscaping started to dominate. The commercial buildings had a sunny buoyant feel about them. The contrast to the dark, gray, and pinched feeling that dominated back home was vivid.

Occasionally she would catch a glimpse of single-family homes tucked down a side street. From what she could see they were well-tended and folded back among palm trees, high green shrubs, or bougainvillea. At the same time the rising sun had started to tease out the full palate of airy colors on each block. Everything seemed bright and mostly new.

Soon enough, however, the tide of L. A. bound rush hour commuters filled the three approaching Wilshire Boulevard lanes. Not long after and despite her driver's best maneuvers they were hemmed up on all sides as well in their westbound direction.

Upon entering Beverly Hills, she asked the driver to open the other rear window. The thick traffic flow had started to abate, and the innate beauty of the surroundings fully captured her senses. By the time she passed Rodeo Drive, she had fallen in love with the vistas.

Despite the freakish traffic the idea of possibly living in California no longer seemed a scary prospect.

When Lailani stepped out of the eleventh-floor elevator she was relaxed, mostly awake, and prepared to talk business. The statuesque receptionist—AKA actress-in-waiting she later learned—escorted her into a large modern conference room. She was greeted with the shimmering sunrise enveloping the Los Angeles skyline far beyond the tinted windows.

Tony Calibri joined her minutes later. With savoir fair and masculine élan he epitomized second-generation Los Angeles success. His six-foot athletic build was trimmed in an elegant dark designer suit fitted over a tan, butter soft cotton shirt. Suede loafers facilitated effortless grace as he swept into the room full of hugs and kisses for her. Unlike one of his equally successful fellow senior citizens back east, he appeared twenty years younger. Tinted glasses and the bling of an expensive watch, bracelet, and neck jewelry reinforced his youthful air.

"Ms. Howard" he said as he smiled broadly with perfect gleaming white teeth. He kissed her on both cheeks—real kisses not the fake Euro kind. She felt a small electric tickle from his trimmed moustache.

"How long has it been, seven years," he asked?

"Eight years and two months Tony. Don't tell me your minions who prepared your briefing package missed our last encounter at the reception at John Hopkins," she said teasingly.

He smiled modestly.

That must be very well practiced, she thought.

"No, they didn't miss it; I forgot the number. And they also pointed out that we lost a bid to your firm two years after that for a lucrative Mount Sinai Hospital contract."

She smiled at the mention of that while she looked around the sumptuous conference room. The richly appointed space was designed to convey only one thing—success.

"That looks to be the only thing your company missed out on over the years Tony. Your offices are lovely. And you seem to be doing very well."

"Thank you, Lai. You allowed me to call you Lai last time as I recall."

She nodded her assent while appreciating his manners.

He politely motioned for them to move to the conference room table.

"We've done pretty good over the years," Tony said.

"I'm sure your team provided you with a complete summary. But let's go through my business strategy and then, if you don't mind Lai, I have a question or two about yours."

"But before we get started, can I offer you some coffee or tea? Maybe a mimosa?"

He smiled again.

It really was a beautiful smile, she believed.

"Just water Tony. Much too early for stimulants."

This time she smiled back, acknowledging her double entendre.

"As you say Lai. But at my age, sixty-three last April, it's rarely too early for a stimulant."

He handed her a small tray with a bottle of water and a heavy Waterford glass before mixing a mimosa for himself at the compact bar set atop a teak credenza. They sat down facing each other.

After he took a generous swallow, she could see him gathering himself. He looked at her calmly before leaning forward to start his pitch.

"Lai, it's possible that we could be working together in the future. If that's so, and I personally think it would be wonderful for both of our companies, I want to be forthright with you from the very beginning. You know my business and you know my financials. I suspect you reviewed everything a second or third time on the flight out."

She listened without affirming his hunch.

"What you don't know I'll wager is why I want to merge with your company and why I believe it would add a dimension to things around here that would make a huge difference. And for you, the big responsibility you'd have after that would challenge your management skills and require the very best."

Lailani focused on every word.

"Sure, we're a much bigger outfit," he said.

"And that would take some adjustment on your part, which I'm confident you can handle."

"As for me, I'm convinced that I need your unique ability to build and motivate a team that treats each temporary engagement that they undertake like it was their own business. The surveys that I track have you consistently at the top in that metric. If we can do that together here, I believe the sky's the limit."

"And finally, Lai, beyond the challenges that come with scale and complexity, a merger would provide you with a substantial ownership stake in the entire enterprise, stock, and bonuses.

She liked his style and listened closely for the next thirty minutes until he finished and took a second sip of his warm mimosa.

"Tony, I refuse to be flattered by those very kind remarks about what we've built back east. It has truly been a labor of love. You put your finger on the one essential element that drove Remy and me to be uncompromising—the staff that we turned out for every temporary assignment had to be motivated and had to love their engagement as if it were their own company. It is the one essential thing we always strive to achieve. Sure, the surveys that you mentioned have always ranked us most highly in those areas. But it doesn't start or end with surveys—it must be in your bones, it must be part of your faith and the whole team needs to sign up, fully committed. Those who can't commit, or who fail to live up to those principles are weeded out. There may be a place for them to thrive, but it won't be at LR Staffing."

She sat back and took a small break hoping that Tony would follow her lead. The very idea of giving up some measure of control over what she often affectionately referred to as her baby seemed suddenly to hit home; or maybe it was the lack of sleep that had her feeling a bit giddy.

Leaning back himself, he dialed his intensity down a notch.

"That's the missing ingredient Lai, the passion that you just articulated. I want that fire and mission focus in my company, and you know what, I've been moving backwards in those parameters as we've grown. I want you to teach us those lessons again. It's the key to winning the future. And I want to win that future with you as my EVP for national operations. You'd have operational authority over all businesses, reporting only to me. It's time for me to focus exclusively on long term strategy."

She was stunned by the offer, but she did her best to hide it. She hadn't expected to move this quickly or to talk about possible roles for herself. But Tony was clearly a no-nonsense guy. Long ago he'd apparently turned his charm into hardscrabble pragmatism. Nonetheless, she believed he was right about what type of staffing companies would win the future.

"First of all, Tony, I have a fabulous EVP of my own who has been at my side from day one. I'm not a one-woman band by any means. And secondly, you're a huge national operation already. Frankly, I'm not sure what it would take to move the culture of your company closer to that of my own. That's not a negotiation ploy, I genuinely don't know if it's possible."

Tony pressed a bit more, sensing that he was making progress.

"As for Ms. Remy, who I've had the pleasure of speaking with on more than one occasion, I would expect her to be your first hire after you came on board. To be honest though, my read on her is that she would be anxious about pulling up stakes and leaving New York; I could be wrong about that of course. But she could always work from your current location."

"As for the cultural transformation that's needed Lai, there are ways to assess that and to execute on a big scale like my outfit would require. But you know what, you're right to be skeptical; most people can't read the data let alone deploy a plan."

He kept pressing.

"I at least know where to start and what support we'll need. Would you be willing to come back out to California and spend a week with my operating folks combing through the details?"

She felt a flood of conflicting emotions as his question hung in the air. Working on the west coast would take her far from home. But she'd be closer to baby girl. And maybe distance was exactly what she and Brett needed right now, at the very least. Would she lose herself in a mega corporation or could she carve out her own space and make an impact? She asked herself many more questions before finally answering.

"I really do think we could work together Tony. This could very well be the next step for me. Let's sign an NDA first and share the operating details about our companies that aren't publicly available. After doing so, and if we both agree to go forward, I'll fly back in about a month and we can have several days of working sessions. What do you think?"

"I think I'm going to enjoy working with you Lai. I really need you on our team."

*　*　*

The alarm clock buzzed loudly at six in the morning. Brett had been awake for quite some time and had already finished a lengthy call with his brand-new executive director out at Long Island.

Firing the previous director who was also an old friend had been painful but necessary because Brett's internal investigation had concluded that campers had been slipping in and out of *Sail Shape's* grounds for months, possibly even longer.

So, after the termination he had a vacancy. And before he'd even advertised for the position, he had a replacement on the job and working, Zena's daughter Mikala. He realized that he had very little choice in the matter in the face of Zena's persistent charm offensive.

His cell phone rang unexpectedly, displaying an unknown international number. He answered it anyway.

"Hello Dad, it's Joshua. I'm not going to apologize for calling you so early because I know you've been up already for a while now."

Brett laughed out loud at that.

"Yeah, that's right. Things haven't changed. It's good to hear your voice son. "

Brett rushed into the next part, almost as if fearing he might lose the chance to say it in the future.

"Joshua look, I owe you an apology for that Christmas day blow up. There was no excuse for my accusations. I'm proud of you and I'm proud of your independence. Your mother and me worked hard so you could make up your own mind and make your own choices. I had no business saying that you didn't have a strong sense of your racial identity; that would be my failing and your mother's failing if it were the case. And we didn't fail in that department. Truth is, you don't need me picking at your decisions or dredging up old irrelevant issues. You won't hear that anymore."

Joshua hadn't expected anything like it; he was surprised. In fact, he hadn't been at all sure how he would start the conversation or how it would end.

"And dad you don't need my disrespect either. My language was inappropriate and very childish. I'm sorry; it won't happen again."

"I love you son, and I respect what you've accomplished. My woodiness and inflexibility have often driven a wedge between us. Believe me, I want to change that."

"We'll get better at it, dad, if we keep trying. How about we not take any more forced multi-year vacations from at least speaking to each other, deal?

"It's a deal."

"What's on your mind Joshua, I know its afternoon there, but you only called at this time because you knew for sure you would reach me. What is it?"

Straight down to business, now Joshua recognized the man on the other end of the line

"Well, a couple of issues. First, I wanted to give you the same report that I gave to Keisha. You had asked her to reach out to me about that swag bag mystery."

Brett's attention was peaked.

"Yes, that was because I know how good you are with computers. I thought you might have a hunch about the thing."

"I used to be pretty good back in the day, but the whole area has rapidly advanced since then. Now I have several students over here that I work with that are close to geniuses in the current technology. I gave the problem to one of them, he's the best."

"Any headway?"

"Yes. What I'm about to tell you is all we know so far. Keisha and her people are chasing down the details. And it will take a trip oversees to get to the bottom of it all."

"Anyway, the string of numbers was a sequence of executable codes; both on the spread sheets and within the USB stick.

He broke that down because he knew that his father was already lost.

"What that means is the numbers make other programs on a computer or other device run, no matter where that computer is situated in the world."

"Why the heck would the boys be carrying around something like that," Brett said?

"So far at least I've only got suppositions. But before I go on, full disclosure. My guy here also pulled up the information surrounding the Long Island shooting. I know pretty much what you know."

"Wow, okay, I guess it is a small world indeed, no secrets. I would have told you about the mess if we weren't being so stubborn with each other."

Joshua's discovery in London that his father had withheld from him the facts about the killing of the *Sail Shape* camper had shaken him. He'd lived and breathed the camp for more than a decade while growing up, even if sometimes he kicked and screamed not to be there. It underscored for him how far apart they'd grown from each other and made him decide to finally take a chance to break the ice.

"And by the way," Joshua added, "I wasn't just idly snooping; we needed as many facts over here as possible to crack this thing."

"Anyway, this is what we know—the executable codes were run through the world-wide-web, the underground version not what most folks use, and they terminated in Africa. We don't know precisely where yet but we're certain that it's Senegal, West Africa. And given the data flow quantities, we know for sure that it involved commercial rather than civilian communication. In other words, there were business transactions as opposed to casual interpersonal messages behind the codes."

"The process was activated periodically through the Long Island girl's camp's ISP connection, that's their computer link to the Internet. Our forensics indicates that it happened three or four times every summer for at least four years. We have that much data, but we can't be sure at present if we've traced it back to the beginning, my gut tells me no."

Brett's head was spinning.

" Executable codes, underground nets, Africa? I don't get what you're telling me Joshua and believe me I'm trying."

"That's completely understandable dad; so far, the data set is an enigma to me as well. I can't solve for what the pieces add up to."

"Keisha also sent me the clothing patterns and the sequential numbers that the young men carried that night. As for the numbers, we've confirmed that on the right machine they could be turned into hard cash without government knowledge or backing of any kind. Printing currency from code happens with the right software, ink, and paper. As for the clothing patterns, that really stumped me. But at the very least of course they could be utilized to produce the items they represent.

"Wait a minute, you said currency? How can real currency spring from codes and serial numbers outside of how the U.S. government or any government for that matter does it?"

"It's the world we live in, privately backed money that millions, maybe now hundreds, of millions of people consider real currency—which makes it real for them in their economy. Think about it for a second dad, that same belief in the bona fides of a currency is precisely what supports the value of the U.S. dollar."

Joshua realized that he needed to short-circuit his explanation because the details were proving more confusing than enlightening for his father.

"But at this point in terms of what the myriad facts mean all we have are shot-in-the-dark guesses. For example, maybe some type of personal or financial manipulation or exploitation was occurring on one or both sides of the Atlantic with those teenagers in the middle of it all. Were they victims or perpetrators; or were the camps playing different roles? Since we have a better handle on the U.S. camps, another possible theory is that the exploitation, if it existed at all, may have been occurring in Senegal."

" That's remarkable. How sure are you about all this," Brett said?

"We're reasonably sure, sixty-five to seventy percent sure about the forensics at least. My kid that chased this down is a real cracker jack with code, basically he's a computer rock star and he thinks the electronic mouse droppings are very solid. But a substantial chance remains that we're dead wrong about the big picture."

'Wait a minute, what do you mean by your kid? You haven't been holding something back from me and your mother all these years, have you?"

"I have been, but it's not what you're thinking. I'm going to lay it all out for you but not on this call. We'll need a good couple of hours at least for me to bring you up to speed on some things I've been nurturing over here for many years. I've got a big financial decision to make. You'll be at least interested, I hope."

"But like I said earlier, I believe this whole coded number thing must be chased down at the source, in Africa. I'm going to take a stab at bird-dogging that and I'll keep you and Keisha informed about progress."

"Well thanks Joshua, thank you very much."

"But right now, dad, the other issue if you don't mind taking a moment. I'm soon to be in the battle of my life on the English Channel. You raced there of course in the old days—sorry."

"Anyway, it'll be the 72-foot multihulls, the current super tech flyers going head-to-head, best out of five races. And If I win, I skipper the UK challenge boat for the America's Cup in San Francisco. I need to talk strategy and tactics with you if you have some time now or even later. We get wet in the Channel in two days."

Brett hearing that his son would soon contest for the biggest sailing prize of them all with him being completely unaware until now was a shock. That it had happened without any communication between them over the extensive preparations during the past few years really hurt. Yet he'd always known that Joshua had the guts and the feel at the helm to go as far as he wanted. His many racing trophies, the bulk of which remained at the Long Island camp, were the physical evidence of that talent.

But maybe he could provide some assistance to him now.

"Hold on, Joshua."

He reached up to his chart shelf, pulling down his old North Atlantic binder. After blowing off the dust he opened the book to the nautical charts for the English Channel; they were covered with his personal notes.

"I've got all the time you need," he replied after he placed the charts and his measurement tools in front of him.

"First off though, who are you going up against and how much do you know about that opposing helmsman?"

Chapter Nine:
Pray for Us

SHE SAT NERVOUSLY BESIDE THE TINY KITCHEN TABLE watching Sarah remove her gray habit and fold it neatly over the back of the other chair. Sarah's bracing garment, a plain white slip, was outdated even to Melinda's antiquated sense of fashion. She made a mental note to find her something better at one of the neighborhood Goodwill outlets.

Along with the single bed, dresser, and two-burner stove, the two hundred square foot space was home. A bathroom stall and shower down the hall was shared among all transients and their guests on the floor.

Melinda moved to the narrow bed, unsure of what to do next. She was free, yes; yet the idea that she could do whatever she wanted—walk peacefully to the corner or over to the park they passed on the ride in from prison, or to the Korean grocer around the corner, or just sit quietly on a bench or stoop outside—was paralyzing. The contrast to her entire world for twenty-five years could not have been starker; prison was controlling, claustrophobic, and filled with daily flashes of violence. Yet, you always knew what to expect.

She was with Sarah, who claimed to be her daughter. Melinda had to admit that the young woman certainly looked like her. Maybe Sarah was her baby, the baby girl that they stole from her.

Even the possibility of it being true triggered the pain from her many poor decisions. It also stoked the memory of the instant that they yanked her baby girl from her clutching fingers. That Melinda had changed her mind about giving her up at the last minute and pleaded to keep her didn't stop them.

But if Sarah was her daughter after all these years apart, what could she do with her now, a nun?

Sarah spread her arms, looked at her mother, and smiled after she put on her jeans and sweatshirt.

"Ta-Da," she said!

She sat down on the bed and began brushing out her blond hair.

"Sarah, your idea that we get DNA tested is a good one. That such a test is even possible is amazing. It should settle things for us, for me."

But Melinda's inner voice said that the test was unnecessary, that Sarah was not a stranger.

"From what you shared in the taxi about your search Sarah you are very brave and persistent that's for sure. But you need to know the woman who may in fact be your mother. That woman is a felon, ex-felon now, who made terrible mistakes."

"Mother, and I will call you that until proven wrong, I have already forgiven you for those sins. They are behind both of us now. This is a new day, a new start for you and me. I pray God will bless us."

Melinda stood up and walked over to the narrow window. She parted the thin curtains and looked down on the crowded city street. The steady march of cars that never ceased mesmerized her. They were all cars that she'd never seen before, modern cars of course.

She turned around and spoke haltingly.

"I don't know what I'm going to do really…I don't know what we're going to do. I must start all over you see. I'm not sure… whether that can be done."

"I will help you as best I can. You will have me to depend on while you adjust," Sarah said.

Melinda returned to the bed, sitting. Sarah looked at her mother's hands while holding them. She laced their fingers together. Then she took a deep breath.

"Mother, please tell me who and where my father is?"

"Is he alive?"

Melinda was surprised by the questions; she realized that she shouldn't have been.

"He's alive Sarah, he doesn't acknowledge you. When I found out in prison that I was pregnant I wrote him a letter and I received his reply. He asserted that the baby wasn't his and he wished me luck, two lines on a piece of paper. That was the last I heard from him. When you were born, they took you away at the prison hospital. I had already signed the papers for your adoption by the Order, but then I..."

But what if she isn't my real daughter, should I go on?

Melinda lowered her head.

"How did you know for certain that he was my father," Sarah said?

Immediately Sarah realized what her question implied; she did her best to apologize after blushing.

"I knew Sarah because I only slept with him and believe me, you weren't the product of an immaculate conception."

She stared at Sarah; Melinda's serious demeanor evaporated after the unintended joke.

For the first time they had a good laugh together.

Sarah looked at her mother steadily while squeezing her hands urgently.

"I must see him mother, even if he rejects me again. I must see him. Do you, can you understand?"

"Yes, I do understand. He'll be released from Attica soon. I will do the right thing for you, just let me think about how best to accomplish that."

Then she paused and looked Sarah hard in the face.

"You are so much like him you know, you have his eyes and his forehead, and that stubborn streak."

***

They strolled slowly down Manhattan's lower Fifth Avenue looking years out of fashion in long sleeve denim shirts and full cut mom jeans. Their destination was just ahead on the corner, a squat office building of only four floors that appeared eerily out of place among the other lanky structures that had been erected over the years. The sturdy gray edifice had been there for more than a century. The same brass lettering that Stewart remembered remained on the side and front facing walls.

Edleman Trust and Assurance

He paused and fished through his roomy pockets, pulling out his old black alligator wallet. After removing a long-expired driver's license and his social security card, he could only hope they'd be enough.

He told Chauncey to wait.

Within the safe room of the dimly lit private bank the old, stooped proprietor heard the bell ring and checked his front cameras. He zoomed in on the face of his visitor while tucking a snub-nosed revolver into his shoulder harness. He cleaned his bifocals before shuffling to the outer lobby windows near the reinforced steel door. After looking down each side of the building a final time, he released seven heavy locks and quickly ushered Stewart inside.

After locking back up the old man moved behind a mottled granite counter, turned on his banker's lamp, and looked carefully into Stewart's face.

"The last time you were in here my son you were a much younger man," he said without changing his expression.

"That's certainly true Mr. Edleman; and you were a much younger banker."

The rejoinder brought a thin smile to the old man's lips.

"I've come to close out my account," Stewart said.

He gave over his identification.

The banker squinted through his glasses at each item before holding them up to a nearby UV light.

Without a word he gave them back and disappeared into the rear of the building. Stewart sat on the worn Regency couch against the sidewall and waited.

Fifteen minutes later Edelman returned and handed over a black leather satchel.

"I have accounted for my periodic service fee withdrawals on the spreadsheet. Those never changed from our original agreement. Your interest was paid at prime plus one against your compounded funds; all as previously agreed. Consequently, your account has grown at a modest but steady rate over the years. And of course, any record of your earnings has remained off the grid."

Stewart collected the satchel and looked inside to tally the neatly bound bundles of cash. He carefully perused the spreadsheet. Satisfied, he zipped the satchel closed.

"Thank you, Mr. Edleman. Thank you very much."

As he walked down the block Chauncey fell in beside him. They hailed a cab and headed crosstown.

"Well, how did things pan out, Stewart, I see you have a cute accessory bag? But it clashes with your denim if I must say. And it could certainly use a good leather conditioner."

"Chauncey, what, you're such a stickler for fashion suddenly, and you who were so comfy for so long in prison orange."

They both laughed and opened the rear windows, enjoying the warm air and the euphoric sense of freedom.

"Whoever claimed that Manhattan air was dirty was out of their skull, Chauncey; have you ever smelled so sweet a fragrance?"

At that moment a huge construction truck towing an enormous backhoe loader pulled alongside them at a red light. The truck belched acrid black smoke across the intersection. Fleeing from the shouts and threats of dozens of choking pedestrians, the beefy driver jumped the light and lurched the massive vehicle forward.

Still coughing, Stewart leaned toward Chauncey and unzipped the black bag.

"There's a tad more than fifty thousand dollars in here love," he said quietly as he touched the bundles of cash.

"It's enough to get us started and enough to fund the lawsuit."

Chauncey was stunned. He pushed the bag aside and kissed Stewart on the lips.

***

Melinda paused to catch her breath on the fourth-floor landing while looking up at her door on the next level. She was panting as she did every day. Stairs were one thing that prison had very few of and despite two weeks of climbing them she still found herself winded.

Overall though things were much better for her today; she was anxious to share with Sarah the details of her new job at the downtown public library branch, a place where she'd often gone to read between the grind of submitting endless job applications.

At the door she tried to muster all the enthusiasm that she could over her new twenty-hour a week gig. She wanted Sarah to share in her happiness, the first step in her reentry plan. Maybe she would also help her put the modest achievement in perspective.

Inside Sarah was seated at the kitchen table. On her lap was her partially packed carry-on. An envelope and a single piece of white paper lay on the table. Melinda's heart sank as she realized that Sarah was preparing to leave.

She was acutely aware that the past two weeks had been a difficult time for her. Although Sarah was not affluent in any way based on what she'd shared about convent life, she had never wanted for the comfort of her own bed. Nor had she ever been forced out of necessity to eat at neighborhood soup kitchens or share bathroom facilities with complete strangers.

Sarah looked up when Melinda entered. Her eyes were red, and her cheeks showed fresh tear streaks.

"Sarah, what's wrong?"

Sarah stood up and grabbed the piece of paper from the table before hugging Melinda tightly.

"I knew I was right mother, the DNA test confirmed that I was right all along."

She sniffed and looked her mother in the face, and then up and down.

"The results confirmed that with a 99.1 percent certainty, we are mother and daughter," she said proudly.

Melinda felt surprise and relief and sadness and shame all together. But mostly she ached over the memories that never formed with the baby girl that she hadn't nurtured.

They sat down.

Melinda took a deep breath and started to speak but Sarah cut her off and placed a hand on her knee.

"It's okay," Sarah said. "We have the future, and we'll make the most of it. The past is gone."

They held hands as Melinda felt her own tears begin to spill down uncontrollably.

She managed to ask a question.

"But Sarah, why were you crying before I came in. Why weren't you happy? I know it's been tough these past couple of weeks, but I was just hired for a part time job; that gives me time to keep looking for another one. We'll be okay, I promise."

Sarah looked at her and nodded. She used her sweatshirt sleeves to dry her mother's tears as well as her own.

"It's not that, I enjoy the time with you. And I love hearing your story, hearing your honesty and resolve to turn away from the past and live for the future."

"No, my tears weren't for us; they were for me."

Melinda waited.

"You see, I finally called the Reverend Mother today. I should have told you that I left without her permission; I'm basically a truant and I wrongly used a convent account to purchase my ticket here. My actions were selfish and sinful."

"Well, I'll have to pay for that now. The Reverend Mother told me that she has deferred my acceptance to medical school. I must work for one year in one of the counseling programs run by the order. If I am obedient and remorseful, I may receive permission to resume my studies after that."

"Oh Sarah, I'm so sorry."

She held her daughter and for the first time, because of a report on a piece of paper, it felt different; it felt real. Then she held her away.

"When do you leave?"

"Tomorrow morning," Sarah said.

"Okay; but I must show you something important later this evening.

***

It was Stewart's night to clean up and he was taking more time. Chauncey had seriously bent the spoon, preparing a sumptuous Cajun seafood dinner using just about every dish and utensil in the apartment. After loading the dishwasher and scrubbing several prep dishes, Stewart washed and dried the remaining stoneware and cleaned the counter tops and table. Finally done, he returned the cookbook to the stack in the corner.

"Chauncey!" he shouted at the back room of their modest apartment.

"Let's take a walk. If I keep eating your cooking I'm going to swell up like a blimp. Strolls are now mandatory when you cook love, or haven't you noticed?"

"Oh, I've noticed what's up," Chauncey said as he came into the kitchen.

" Whenever I prepare a meal around here, we end up walking the neighborhood for at least ninety minutes. I realize that at the end of the day you're only protecting your figure, which of course I cherish. But I'm going to need some better walking shoes."

He smiled after that and moved in closer, his affection threatening to keep them inside for the rest of the evening. Stewart moved out of arms reach.

"Okay, busted. But there is a new Bistro over on 11th Avenue that I'm dying to try. They're reported to have some tasty madeleine cookies and other goodies, so it's not all bad news and a forced march dearest. I'm also up for a small digestif; it's really all that I can deal with after that meal of yours. So, two birds with one stone, a good long walk a small taste of sweets."

"I'm not completely signed on for that small desert option, you're not the only one watching his figure. But let's see what they have to offer."

As they strolled, Stewart couldn't shake the still-new feeling that he was finally liberated. That reality was the most amazing sensation, and it was at least as intense as the terror that overcame him when he was first locked in his tiny cell.

His spirits were also buoyed by the good news that he received in the initial meeting last week with the attorney he hired to reclaim Chauncey's property.

It'll be a real cockfight was the verdict from the scrappy, well-groomed upper-east-side lawyer. But he'd also opined that New York law was in their favor. But more work would need to be completed he had warned to properly cover all relevant legal issues.

Then he requested a twenty-thousand-dollar retainer before he could do any further work on the case.

The evening air was cool with a bracing city breeze as they made their way to the Bistro. They ambled together through the merchant-packed sidewalks and bustling pedestrian chaos of lower west midtown. Stewart was surprised again by the profusion of small shop owners and shoppers and idlers along the way, the majority of whom appeared to be Middle or Far Eastern or African or anything but American born.

They walked past the last remaining *green* space in the neighborhood. It was strewn with patches of brown dying crab grass, dust, and scattered debris. Nevertheless, many young families were playing soccer or tag with children while toddlers laughed and romped in the foreground under the sharp eyes of parents or elders. Singles and couples relaxed on rusted iron benches arranged in a large sweeping circle while clusters of chess or checker players wagered on their skills at concrete tables. The assemblage of bodies radiated out and away from a twenty-foot high, green-encrusted waterless fountain that doubled as a trash receptacle. Skaters, borders, bikers, and joggers shared the crowded paths while the homeless waited off in the shadows, gearing up to reclaim the park as their own once dusk surrendered to darkness.

This was New York City near the bottom, miles away from the fabled affluent upper echelon gloss and polished city blocks.

Stewart and Chauncey could hardly wait to move out of the neighborhood for good.

After thirty minutes they rounded a corner onto 10th Avenue and walked hand in hand among the much-reduced pedestrian flow. A few minutes later they took a shortcut down a deserted one-way street. That's when Stewart heard a vaguely familiar voice calling his name from behind. He turned around and faced two women.

Chauncey stared back at them as well and he spoke up before Stewart.

"Melinda?"

"Yes Chauncey, it's me, twenty-five years older."

Stewart ignored her and instead openly stared at the woman by her side.

No one needed to tell him who she was.

✱✱✱

Melinda gazed out at the vast enclosed airline terminal in front of her and at the scores of towering jets beyond the enormous windowpanes. La Guardia pointedly reminded her of her personal time warp, of her Rip Van Winkle existence. There was so much in the world for her to catch up on. So far freedom had only confirmed that there simply wouldn't be enough time left to do it.

Despite it all she hoped that she could have a semblance of normalcy with her daughter who was her living bridge with the past. So, she held fast against all rationality, believing that she might yet redeem something to covet and cherish; that she might somehow be a mother.

In the departure terminal they had more time to talk. Both were resigned to what had to happen. But Melinda was also disquieted by Sarah's new infatuation.

"Mother, I don't know how he could have been so certain, that really shocked me. I had prepared myself to be rejected."

"That's the only reason I was there, to support you if that happened. I think he just looked at you and accepted you."

"And he refused to have a DNA test done. I didn't expect that. I don't know what to do next, with him."

Sarah recalled that her mother needed a DNA test to fully accept her. Yet the man, her father, who denied her existence when she was being formed in the womb believed her without any scientific confirmation. Her emotions continued to swirl as she tried to make sense of everything.

Melinda had wanted to be happy for her, but she also felt as if part of her daughter was being taken from her again. She didn't want to talk about *him* anymore.

"Well anyway Sarah, next for you is paying your penance in California. And then of course you'll start medical school. I hope the punishment goes by quickly. I'll find a way to help support you financially…and help make that happen, somehow…"

She stopped talking, her failures weighing on her again. She silently accused herself of jabbering on with empty slogans.

"It will go by mother, in its own time. I'm determined to enter med school, despite the delay."

Sarah looked at her mother once more before briefly looking away. The enormous span of forced absence and the emotional distance between them made her wonder if she would ever truly know her. Would there be anything deeper than what they'd found these past weeks? Did she even need more than that now?

"Mother don't focus on how to help me accomplish things. What you really need to do is worry about yourself right now. I'll be okay. At least I've made it this far."

Without you were the words that she consciously omitted.

Sarah asked Melinda the question that had been bothering her.

"You know, my father and the other man Mr. Chauncey Smith; they seemed to be … very close friends. When we were following, they started … holding hands, I believe."

"Sarah, Chauncey and your father are a couple, they are lovers. I debated whether to tell you beforehand. In the end I decided that he was your father, no matter who he is involved with. Under New York law they can be married, and I expect that to happen."

"But the Bible says…. "

Her voice trailed off as she looked down.

"How does that happen exactly," Sarah said as she started up again.

"How would you know that your…relationship preference is…different?"

"I can't really say. I honestly don't think anyone has the full answer. My own preference has always been heterosexual. In prison that choice was severely tested over the years."

She could see in her daughter's puzzled expression that more was needed.

"But from what I've heard and read our sexuality is formed very early within us. Some say we come out of the womb one way or the other. I happen to believe that, but I don't know if anyone really knows for sure."

"Actually mother, that viewpoint is supported in some scientific journals that I have examined. My church holds the exact opposite view that we make our own choice in the matter."

"For me, I've always been at the convent. I've never dated a boy. Some were in my early classes in the lower grades. I guess I found them to be just classmates and not always serious ones at that. So, choice for me never played a part. On the other hand, strong and loving women have always surrounded me. Do you think that will influence me?"

"No, I don't believe it will, Sarah. Your heart will tell you who you love."

At that moment she realized how innocent of worldly ways her daughter was and how much she'd been sheltered within the convent. She vowed to herself to do what she could to help her prepare to enter the outside world as a student.

"I will call him from time to time," Sarah said, almost to herself.

"There's so much I want to know about him. And I can share some things about me. Will you mind?"

"No, I won't," Melinda replied, hiding the truth.

They hugged close.

"I'll get on my feet soon Sarah. We'll figure out how we can be closer to each other. Before that I intend to get a cell phone and a computer just as soon as I can afford them."

They hugged again before Sarah cued up in the TSA line.

Chapter Ten:
Baby Girl

MEAGHAN UPPED HER CADENCE CALL from the low seat at the bow of the scull. In front of her eight crewmembers sliced long oars into the water. She checked her chronograph before rapidly recalculating the crew's stroke and power output. With that done she twice marked the gap over the competitive scull closing hard on the port side.

She increased her rhythmic cadence once more in a steady clear voice.

Hearing that and pulling hard BG felt that familiar burn in shoulders and thighs as they slid past the one-thousand-meter mark. Years of disciplined training allowed her to relax her body as she increased her effort.

The scull slid forward faster.

The lead over their San Diego competitors had dwindled to ten meters. Doggedly, those women had closed the distance with a charge that started five hundred meters back.

Meagan had anticipated it and she'd saved her most urgent percussion call for the final two hundred.

catch...send...catch.... send...catch... send...

BG felt the increasing slide pulling them forward as they all dug in, rallying to the coxswain's high-tempo cadence.

Her eyes focused on the space between the shoulder blades of the crewmate directly in front of her and on the emergence there of a single bead of sweat. The cheering from thousands of spectators on both banks of the river receded into silence as it always did for her when the finish line approached.

She was outside of herself now, observing her own effort and that of her crewmates from a vantage point above the water. She held in her mind the hard-fought victory last May over Penn and visualized that her first competition for this crew would also end that way.

They slid across the finish line with a slim eighth of a boat length's lead before drifting slowly down river.

Slumping exhausted over gloved hands they cradled oars, spent legs trailing over the saxboards.

Later that night the university's alumni association hosted a grand celebration for its rowing teams from the day's competition. Nothing different about that BG thought as she remembered many similar events that she'd attended in her undergrad days back east. But there was one distinguishing factor that she had noticed about California rowing—most of the women alumni that attended booster events were only a few years older than she was. Back east the average age seemed to be eighty or ninety.

That youthful glow was suffused throughout California, which was why her leaving the Ivy-covered walls of New England had been a no brainer. She needed the new energy along with a vastly different space, one far removed from her parents. And she looked forward to much more diversity in her environment, something that had significantly declined over her years back east.

California offered her a chance to build her life on her own terms, with less concern about structuring a lifestyle to fit the expectations of others. The final bonus was the innovation embraced by some rowing programs on the west coast. They allowed graduate students to train and compete on a modified basis to accommodate classes, in BG's case medical school.

Three at a time she bounded up the broad whitewashed stairs in front of the boathouse reception hall. It was packed inside.

"BG! Over here!"

Meaghan was the one coxswain that she had admired in her years as a sculler because she didn't take undue credit for the wins like others she'd known. Meaghan knifed her small body through the crowd and greeted her with a big hug.

BG easily lifted her well off the floor before setting her gently back down.

"Meaghan, you called a great race today. How'd you know just when to pick up tempo and hold them off?"

"I wish I could say it was luck, but the truth is my boyfriend is a video photographer. He was able to acquire an index of thirty races for their coxswain and an equal number for most of her crew from various competitions. After studying that footage, I took a chance that their charge might stall a bit more if we loaded on enough of an early lead. They closed on us a lot harder than I expected, though. Credit to them."

"Wow, I've known several coxswains Meg, but no one who watched that much video. You need to take more credit for our success today, but I know that's not your style."

"Credit always goes to the rowers, no exceptions, BG. By the way, upstairs there's a smaller gathering sponsored by the Olympic qualifier crew from four years ago and a few of their family and friends. They all wanted to meet the crews separately today and congratulate us individually. Some of our girls are already upstairs. I'll see you up there when the others arrive."

"Okay."

Upstairs was far less crowded. Unlike the fifteen-foot ceilings and expansive glass panes on the main floor the second-floor ceiling height was only eight feet, below which standard curtained windows were spaced every four feet. She recognized the familiar brown leather furniture that was intimately arranged in discrete settings, all of it like the cozy spaces back east. But unlike those serve yourself buffet clubs, white shirt clad waiters in black suits briskly circulated around the room with trays of food and drink.

Several teammates as well as coaches were already mingling with the former Olympians and family; all were clustered around in threes and fours with BG's crewmates actively engaged in conversations. After introductions and several minutes' worth of pleasantries with a foursome, BG found herself speaking alone with a thirty-two-year-old cousin. The cousin, named Phoenicia, made it clear that she was sculling royalty.

"So, BG; wait, hang on just a sec darling," the Phoenicia said that with food in her mouth while holding up her large hand up as a stop sign.

In one motion she scooped two jumbo shrimp from a passing tray and soaked them with cocktail sauce.

"Hold on again dear," she said as she chewed, swallowed, and gestured over BG's shoulder.

"Waiter, stop! I'm going to relieve you of two glasses of that Champagne," she said loudly.

"Here BG, take one. Let's toast to a magnificent win and to your exceptional form and pulling today!"

"By the way," she said leaning in conspiratorially, " I really admire your spunk; not many graduate girls in the science programs make time for rowing now days. Bravo to you!"

She brazenly stared at BG's chest and hips as she encroached on the space between them.

"Thanks Phoenicia. It's pretty much class, rowing and studying. And thanks for the offer of the Champagne, but I don't drink much at all anymore, particularly during the season."

"Not to worry dear, we don't waste good Champagne," she said before she drained the extra glass and placed it next to three other empty flutes.

BG was already feeling uncomfortable around the big body of the woman. In heels Phoenicia was five inches taller than her own six-foot one-inch frame and she appeared to carry a forty-pound weight advantage.

Those physical dynamics were unsettling to BG. Maybe it was because she'd grown accustomed to always being the big girl in her crowd. Or maybe it was Phoenicia's tendency to be close in and hands on, often touching BG's body lightly with her own.

But what made her even more uncomfortable was the woman's constant habit of groping her, braille-like, with her large open palmed hands as she underscored her many points.

She was searching for a graceful way to exit the conversation entirely without being off-putting.

"BG, I've been in these damn high heels all day. Would you mind assisting my recovery? Let's take a seat on that cushy leather couch. I promise I'll be a good girl if you'll be as well," Phoenicia said as she drained the second flute—or was it her fifth BG wondered?

She couldn't believe that Phoenicia had winked at her before placing her meaty hand in the small of her back to steer her to the couch.

"I'm so sorry Phoenicia," she said as she moved the hand away, perhaps too roughly.

"I must get back downstairs and circulate a bit before I head to the dorm. But it's certainly been nice speaking with you."

Phoenicia was visibly put off.

"That's total crap dear, there's no one downstairs better for you to circulate with than the woman standing in front of you."

She moved in closer after her pronouncement and slyly inserted her hand between BG's thighs, all while opening her mouth and licking her lips.

Explaining what had happened after that to the disciplinary committee at the university had been BG's biggest challenge because she honestly didn't have a recollection. Her only excuse was that she was defending herself from assault. When questioned further, however, she was unable to convey whether she was punched or kicked or assaulted in any way by Phoenicia, beyond the initial groping.

As for the committee, they stated in their investigative findings that they might have understood a shove or even a slap or punch made in the heat of the moment and in response to any revulsion that BG may have felt at the time.

But they highlighted the thorough beating that BG had administered, along with the fact that BG had to be forcefully pulled off the women by at least five of her crewmates. The committee deemed her response grossly disproportionate.

After deliberations it was clear to them that long simmering issues below the surface were the cause. They believed that those issues needed to be professionally addressed before BG could be allowed back into the university family.

She was permitted to take her semester exams and complete that part of her academic record before her suspension. The assault and battery charges were suspended and would be purged from her record after counseling at an accredited institution. Reinstatement into medical school could occur as soon as the following academic year, assuming no further incidents.

Disposition of the matter had been carefully managed and memorialized by BG' s attorney, her father's former protégé, recently termed out Senator J Broderick.

Chapter Eleven:
Best of Five

Towering carbon fiber multihulls had gone head-to-head in four grueling matches. Each boat had won a pair with the contest remaining unresolved as weather conditions rapidly deteriorated. The two multihulls swept broad lazy circles in the English Channel while they recovered.

Race rules awarded the skipper with the best-combined time the option to break off the contest until the next day due to impending weather or to finish the rubber race match despite conditions.

Joshua held a ninety-second edge; the choice was his. Normally he would've raced the tiebreaker to leverage the advantage from his recent win that had tied the contest. But as he looked out at the fifteen-foot swells and the creeping fog bank lurking offshore to the southeast, he questioned whether momentum provided any tangible edge. The one thing that he knew for certain was that both he and the opposing skipper, plus each crew, were exhausted.

The mysterious nephew, his opponent recently out of the shadows and now known as Peter Willosby, had proven his mettle under stiff race conditions. Jemal's brief on him had been unerringly accurate and Joshua replayed once again in his mind Jemal's last words of advice.

He's a rough guy that one boss; don't be deceived by his sunny smile.

After an initial win that was followed by two straight losses before the last win, Joshua fully agreed with Jemal's assessment. The nephew was a very talented sailor. Beating him to even the match had taken maximum effort and a little luck. But as he sized Willosby up, hyper-competitive was a better adjective than rough. He made a mental note to add that to Jemal's vocabulary later.

It hadn't escaped his calculation that maybe Willosby was even better than he was. He certainly had many more recent races under his belt, and he was a certified pro. Those skills had translated into razor sharp assessments and decision-making. But if there was a weakness, he thought it might be in the form of Willosby's greatest strength—aggression.

Related to that potential vulnerability was another factor that Jemal had teased out in his research—Willosby had apparently never sailed old-fashioned monohull boats before. Being a rich kid like he was, sleek exotic fiber multihull flyers were always at his disposal. Which meant that his instincts in rough water were less developed and consequently a bit more aggressive because the full power of the ocean rarely touched his boats.

Capsize threat.

The conversation with his father pulled at his consciousness once more.

You should have the advantage over him in rough water, was his dad's firm belief.

Fine, as far as it goes, but he'd have to get a lot more specific in terms of race tactics to have a good chance in the rubber match.

Another issue was Joshua's own caution. In the four previous starts off the line, he'd lost three. While he had improved somewhat, he continued to not trust his instincts during that critical ten seconds before the horn. He'd been too plodding and conservative, he admitted. Maybe it was nothing more than rust.

He felt a damp chill penetrate beneath his foul weather gear as the wind gusted up. The shock from it reminded him of his race ten years ago off the Dalmatian coast. He had prevailed in that regatta by going with rather than against the force of wind and water, even though the modern technology promised that slicing through the heavy conditions was always the key to victory.

That's exactly the tactic you'll need here, he realized; take advantage of the rough stuff and then bend away from it like a matador.

He chuckled at his own simile before setting the helm to autopilot and climbing down. He walked gingerly across the rising and falling center deck to the big mast under which his crew had congregated. They'd already pressured up the hydraulics, checked the boat thoroughly, and finished needed repairs. The five of them were now squatting or lying down, munching on fruit and nuts, hydrating. Adding to the comfort of the much-needed break—neoprene suits were zipped down from the back shoulder and all life vests were askew.

He moved into the middle feeling all eyes studying him carefully. Kneeling, he patted his mainsail grinder on his broad shoulders and turned to his navigator, handing him back the laptop with a wink. Without seeing anything else the men were up, zipping suits and boots and tightening vests.

He radioed the starter boat and requested a set. Soon the long horn blast sounded, signaling the countdown. A few minutes later, as expected, Willosby retreated far from the start line. But this time Joshua veered off sharply with him. He came up parallel to Willosby's boat, no more that twelve inches off his beam. If nothing else, he imagined that his new tactic would cause a bit of concern in the other cockpit.

Conditions on the water had grown extreme as the wind was gusting over thirty knots. Both crews suddenly spilled wind and jibed before separating.

Seizing the initiative Joshua came about suddenly and closed sharply on the starting line, risking a foul. If his timing was right and Willosby didn't cover, he would come off the start with a razor thin lead, which happened.

Glancing at his compass several minutes later he confirmed what he had sensed for the last thousand meters—he was gradually being forced wide on the course by Wiilosby's pinching tactics.

He saw the chance to turn after spotting an almost hidden roller sweeping in and gathering steam two hundred meters ahead. Stiff wind was driving it hard yet without any of the telltale white cresting. It was entirely possible that his opponent underestimated its potential due to his limited line of sight through Joshua's boat or due to his belief that he could always ride his foils over it.

Capsize threat.

Joshua shouted commands into his mouthpiece and prepared for the hard turn to port. After he slammed the helm over, his dagger boards and foils were immediately set to slice through the building wave, which was the intended deception. The wind immediately filled his sails with a tremendous jolt, threatening to knock him down until he veered sharply off, dissipating the force.

Willosby reacted quickly to the maneuver, rapidly turning his helm right before angling back to attack behind Joshua's stern. It was a smart aggressive tactic, one that would have prevailed in nearly all conditions, except these.

Having not seen the full size of the sweeping wave Willosby had little time to bear off. The leading wedge of the twenty-ton behemoth overwhelmed his foils, barreling full on into his hull. The force quickly elevating the bow ten feet above the water as if lifting the high-tech racer into the sky for the slaughter. A stiff gust slammed hard just as the thundering torrent of seawater ripped along the entire boat length, twisting, and buckling the composite frame while ripping five crewmembers from safety lines into the sea.

Joshua glanced over his shoulder as his racer surged forward. Partially sunken wreckage appeared frozen between a fractured mast and a colorful mainsail that flapped rhythmically atop the roiling surface.

Nearby all six crewmembers floating serenely with safety lights and beacons activated.

***

Back in London he tried to ignore the persistent shoulder ache and lower back pain that were unwelcomed but expected consequences of the exhausting competition. Despite the soreness he set up an important meeting at the warehouse for the following afternoon.

His audience would be the paid staff and large group of volunteers. Many had helped him start the warehouse years ago and they continued to keep things humming. They were teachers, tutors, part time janitors, kitchen workers, security guards, mentor volunteers, and others.

He believed that it was vital to brief them about his newly formed vision to expand that included the likelihood of new construction. He felt an obligation because they'd been with him on the voyage for so long, the warehouse was part of them. He also needed to control rumors.

Louise Afford was among the first to join his team years ago. With her strong cockney accent and working-class Chelsea attitude she was a roll-up-the-sleeves worker without an ounce of quit. He knew personally that she'd scrubbed more floors, painted more rooms, and moved more furniture and boxes over the years than anyone else.

In addition to that sweat equity, he credited her with another major contribution. Years ago, Joshua had expressed his frustration during a staff meeting with the quality of the effort from the tech installers assigned to the warehouse. Louise was vocal in her support for better service and for getting the installation right for the future of the kids. It turned out that she had a knack for determining what signal configurations made sense as well as a feel for how the students would interact with the technology in the future. It was also her idea to put plenty of bandwidth up on the roof. Over the years that space became a prime meeting spot and study area, even during colder months.

Louise's spark and talent made her his greatest concern at the upcoming meeting. He believed that she would likely cast herself against expansion and against the future because she was so tied to the existing vision of the place. Her influence with the staff might undermine his efforts before he gained traction.

He understood that it wouldn't be because she wished any ill will or that she didn't want the best for the warehouse. But he suspected that she would be fearful of losing control and even more concerned over dynamic change.

He recognized that her protective attitude masked a deeper issue; a painful stripe from her culturally segregated childhood in a class bound English inner city. In her worldview it seemed that other than Joshua all the rest of the moneyed highbrow folks from Fleet Street were exploiters of the working folk.

It wasn't long into the meeting before his prediction about her reaction was validated.

Soon after he completed his twenty-minute talk in front of the entire team she stood up and rested her clenched fists on her stout hips. She acknowledged him and then she turned back to the group and spoke up in a clear voice.

"We all know that without Joshua we wouldn't be making a difference in these kids' lives. They most certainly need our help to make a dent for themselves and their families in this often-cruel world. He's a good man Joshua is and a generous soul. But I got to tell you that the other bankers surely can't be trusted to keep the faith with our kids. If we go down this road, we'll be turning the children away because they're not this enough or that enough. You mark my words; big money will corrupt our vision around here. You mark my words."

It was clear as he looked around the meeting room that her words had considerable sway among the faithful. He also knew that since her mind was set, it was pointless to engage in public back and forth to convince her otherwise.

So, he came down hard, outlining again where they had to go and why and how he wanted them all to be a part of that future. He ended with an edgier tone while looking directly at Louise. He said he would understand if some on the team couldn't make the voyage because they couldn't embrace his vision. That didn't mean they weren't special to him and to the warehouse.

After the meeting Louise spent an hour in Mirra's office. Mirra had prepared for the possibility that she would be very upset and so the tissue box was out, and Mirra's shoulder was ready.

Joshua had asked her to casually suggest to Louise a private meeting with him whenever she seemed calm enough to handle it. He hoped that by providing personal attention and an empathetic ear he could bring her around.

When she entered his office, the tears were dried but her face remained flush, and her eyes were puffy. He felt genuine compassion for her. They sat down at the workbench in the corner of his office.

"Louise, I'm sorry that I upset you in the meeting. I didn't mean to. You know how much you mean to me personally and to the warehouse. It wouldn't be the same around here without you."

The thought of that happening got her back up again and she shot him a defiant glance before doubling down.

"Well, I'll tell you this Joshua. You know how much I care for the kids and how I always will. But I can't be here to see the bankers and moneymen mess over them and make all the decisions like we were just simple folk mucking up the place. I surely can't be here for that."

She turned to face him.

"Louise no, that's not what this is about at all. The moneymen, as you call them, will work for us. They'll provide the financial structure and with that we'll increase our footprint in southern England. But we control how that happens because we're in a strong financial position. The needs are simply bigger, much bigger, than when we began."

She fidgeted a bit; the comment surprised her. He wondered whether her armor was cracking.

"That it may be Joshua, I'll grant you as much. But I've never seen bankers enter a room without wanting to rearrange all the furniture and make the place their own. Try as I might I just can't be here and see them running things that we worked so hard to put in place."

She lowered her head and paused.

Something told him to wait.

She spoke quietly.

"When I was a wee girl you know, the bankers came to my father's small printing shop. I hid under his desk and heard everything. They didn't like his financial numbers and they didn't like his message to the workingman they said to him loudly. Because he had been forced during bad times a few years earlier to take out a note with them to save his business, they acted like they owned him."

As she continued, he saw that ancient hurt resurface.

"A Socialist they called him. I didn't know the word when I heard it, but it seemed bad. They said he was making too much fuss over his workers and not driving their wages down and his profits up. They imposed changes, made him compromise, and squeezed the terms of his loan. It finally broke him. We believe that's why papa had the heart attack—because he lost control of his own dream."

He hadn't expected that. He found himself shaking his head as he experienced her sorrow. She made complete sense to him now.

And so did playing the cards that he'd held in reserve.

"Louise, in all these years at the warehouse you've given your service willingly and for no cost. That can't be easy because I know you're holding down at least two other jobs."

She was surprised that he knew.

He kept going before she could protest.

"Sure, the after-school care and the meals and snacks assist your two boys as they do the rest of the kids here. And you aren't motivated by those benefits at all because I know that you have genuine buy-in to why we're here and what our contribution really is at its core. Your time and effort to make this place tick that have been priceless to me. Thank you."

As a modest woman, she wasn't accustomed to personal praise. Her great respect for Joshua made her lower her head and come down from the high emotion.

"Thank you for saying that." she said.

"Louise, I respect your concern about change, and I appreciate you for sharing with me that tragic story about your father."

"More than anything though, I want you to be with us as we embark on the next chapter of the warehouse. I want you to remain part of us here and become a part of the other schools that will be built. And here's how. First, you will need to join the paid staff."

He could already see her starting to shake her head.

"I want you to join the paid staff Louise because you won't have time to work those other jobs anymore. You'll also be paid a good deal more than both of them combined. We're going to need all of you for a few years to come. Here's why."

"You'll be making sure that our culture, the way we do things and the way we treat the kids and each other, is not affected by the coming change. In fact, your new job will be to ensure that whether it's the bankers, the plumbers, or the grass cutters, that warehouse culture remains the same in every school we expand or open. On that issue you'll report directly to me. I want to make certain that our culture is not lost, but rather that it is strengthened as we expand. Will you do that for me?"

Louise was taken aback. He could see her thinking carefully about exactly what she'd heard. Her nimble mind calibrated the possibilities. Then he saw the realization flash across her face; he'd addressed her greatest fears—that they would become something other than what they'd grown from. And she would have the power to prevent that from happening.

She stood up and came around the bench to face him. He met her halfway.

"There's such a great need out there for what we do in this building, Joshua. You're right. I won't let you down."

He tried not to flinch when she tightly hugged his sore body.

***

Following up on his uncle's Ned's ideas as well as his father's advice about the warehouse expansion hadn't been the easiest thing. Their perspectives boiled down to a stark choice, go big and go public or don't go at all. Against his own personal preference to remain in the background, he finally accepted the reality that he had to become the public face of the warehouse expansion.

To kick things off Joshua organized a coming out party that would presage a larger national reveal.

Deciding who would be involved at this early stage turned out to be less difficult than he initially imagined because Mirra had already sketched out a plan to which he agreed. First and foremost, any potential backer had to be involved in a significant eleemosynary activity, be it youth or education related, or health and welfare related. Secondly, they had to bring to the table financial wherewithal or be able to marshal that; and thirdly they had to be squeaky clean, free of any scandal or accusations involving financial or moral impropriety. With those guideposts they pieced together a list of thirty invitees.

Surprising him, Mirra volunteered to host the kickoff dinner at their London house as opposed to his instinct for a posh local hotel or private hall. She pointed out that such venues would have been normal and uninspiring for anyone attending and probably one of at least two-dozen similar locations that they attended yearly.

She was also determined for reasons he couldn't initially understand to create an authentic and casual Jamaican meal for the kickoff at their home.

At first he hadn't been sure whether the lack of formality would work with the kind of well-heeled crowd they were hosting. But he went along with the idea because of her enthusiasm.

Later, well after the event had transpired, she shared with him that the provisioning for the meal along with the teamwork involved in its preparation and presentation had provided her a renewed connection to her homeland, which was becoming increasingly distant.

With the help of two of her girlfriends along with a Jamaican chef from east London she sourced the ingredients and spices, and they produced a bountiful feast. Jerk chicken, pepper shrimp, oxtail, curried goat, escovitch fish, and all the starches, and vegetables were displayed buffet style around the expanded dining room table.

Plates were eagerly grabbed by guests and piled high. Chewing, talking, and circulating became the order of the evening, very few folks sat down.

Joshua was increasingly delighted as the event unfolded. The energy and good feelings were exactly what was needed to build a sense of community among what he hoped would be the future benefactors of the expanded warehouse. Halfway through the event he kissed Mirra and thanked her for the ideas and effort.

After two hours and with a dessert plate in hand he moved from the dining area to the large great room in the rear of the house that had always served as a focal point for entertainment. When the guests followed his lead, he stood up from his seat on the edge of the billiards table and started.

"First off, thank you all for coming out and allowing Mirra and her fabulous team to ply you with these tasty recipes from Jamaica. This format was entirely her idea, and she deserves full credit."

Everyone applauded.

He blew her a kiss.

"I feel like I've known many of you for much longer than the brief time we've spent together this evening. It was enough time, however, to establish that we all share a common trait. You may have noticed it also as you mingled. It's that courage to look around our city, our nation and our world and recognize that with our help conditions can be healthier, our fellow citizens can receive the benefits of more education, and we can influence better lifestyles and better choices. You've all been doing that work for several years and I applaud you for it."

Joshua knew that patience was in short supply for many of his guests, so he quickly got down to business.

"In the material that I shared in the invitation you saw some things I've been busy with for many years. I've supported the work without any public or private support, and I was happy to do that."

"But now I believe is the best time to expand the student warehouse concept—not for ego or accolades—but because the needs have galloped past the resources. I'm convinced that there is more to do and with your help we can accomplish that."

William Hale was among the guests. He was a banker that Joshua had met once before during a real estate development deal as well as a major supporter of breast cancer research throughout the U. K. He raised his hand.

"Joshua, great party, and great cause. Despite my over-the-top caloric intake, I'm glad to be here. My question is jurisdictional in nature. With so many agencies targeting youth services how can you expect to carve out a more expansive footprint? Believe me, not trying to throw any cold water, but how do you plan to cut through the clutter and the red tape and demonstrate a compelling need for your approach?"

It was an insightful question; the same one he'd asked himself after his talk with Ned and his father. He'd already started to formulate his own detailed response, an outline that so far exceeded fifty pages. But as he looked out at the relaxed faces of his guests, he took a chance that the last thing they had patience for was a technical answer. He had to humanize the challenge ahead.

"Thank you, William. That's a great question. You know in the beginning, before this whole warehouse thing started, I never knew there was a need for what we eventually established; educational or social policy just wasn't my thing. I was a moneyman, a capitalist. But I guess in my blood, in my family heritage if you will, the impetus to tackle stubborn social issues had been there all along. Over time I started to appreciate that this whole voyage was mostly laid out before me, a road to take verses a road to build."

That was much too vague, he accepted that he needed to open up and share some of his private space

"Let me tell you a brief story that will connect the past to the present and to what I hope is our future together."

"About ten years ago Mirra and I were competing in a half marathon. The race ended at London Bridges. The start wasn't too shabby either by the way, over at Greenwich. But the guts of the race wound through the lower east district. As you know, it remains a sketchy area, despite the revitalization efforts."

"Now this next part is controversial between Mirra and me. She says the story stems from the reality that I was sucking wind and needed to catch my breath at one of the many tenement walk-ups that lined the course over there. But I know that wasn't it. I simply paused briefly at a stairway railing to retighten my running shoes in preparation for my big push during the last half of the run."

Those in the group who knew how swift of foot Mirra was, weren't fooled by his explanation and chuckles were heard. He joined in.

Then he became serious as the memory of what he saw beneath the dilapidated porch steps that morning replayed again in his mind.

"Underneath those stairs, wrapped in filthy painter's tarp, was a bone thin kid. He was alive, though. I wasn't sure about that at first until I looked closer; he was shivering as he slept. We learned later that the space beneath the stairs was a preferred spot, it allowed him to take a nap in relative peace and quiet away from the loud scramble at the Lutheran orphanage where he lived."

"Needless to say, our racing was done after that. We gathered him up and took a taxi back to the car. After bringing him here and giving him a warm bath and some food, we learned that he was an orphan from Ethiopia. He'd fled along with his siblings a several months earlier. All but two of them were poisoned during their illegal transit; contaminated barrels used for hiding on board ship"

Mirra felt compelled to break in at this point and tell them that he was no pushover, no charity case.

"Yes, he was thrown a lot of bad breaks early." she said.

"But he doesn't look for anyone's sympathy. He's tough and he's resilient. He would have found a way without meeting us, I believe. That's the kind of young man he is. And he's no exception; we've got a warehouse full of boys and girls who are equally tough. They're all from the hard luck neighborhoods of London and elsewhere. They just need a helping hand to pull them out of the squalor and they'll do the rest."

Joshua heard echoes of her story when she said that. It was her hard side, the one that always kept a little distance between them, the side that his sheltered upbringing disqualified him from comprehending.

But he had to finish.

"Turns out that the kid was on a waiting list for a particular school in Kensington, one of the very few that accepted his application. There were no more seats though and no other available schools across the city, except at the very elite exam schools that he was not qualified for. After learning that there were at least twenty kids in his orphanage in the same boat, including his sister, I was allowed to make a pitch to them to join my tutorial classes. Mirra and I had already launched the warehouse concept by then and we had sessions up and running."

"But I needed a much bigger space to tutor them all—both in academics and life skills. It also had to be reasonably close to where most of them lived; that's our current site. Over the years we've turned completely around the view that schools used to have about our kids. They now come to us and line up to recruit."

Triekha Semaliaa, a wealthy Sudanese businesswoman and founder of an international anti-rape organization, asked a question.

"Joshua, what I hear you saying is that you want to address both the growing academic and social skills deficits with the expansion? But there's still the capacity issue out there, right? So why don't you solve that as well by expanding the warehouse concept into a full-fledged degree-granting enterprise, eliminating much of the bottleneck, lowering costs, and attracting more universities?"

He was intrigued by the possibilities within her idea. It also highlighted the power inherent in expanding his concept to a broader creative audience with different experiences from his own.

"Triekha, that's brilliant. Thank you so much for the keen insight. We may well make that mold one day after we've funded a plan to move the current warehouse into expansion during phase one. You all saw the numbers in your materials—four million pounds over the next two years. But I promise you that more detail about the plan will come your way in a follow up package. An appeal for your personal involvement in several planning groups to drive the effort will accompany that. It's the number one priority for the success of this venture."

"But right now, we've got deserts and digestives to finish. And for those who don't want to rush back into London traffic just yet, there's a good bit of dancing to be done."

He made his way across the room to make sure he was first on Mirra's dance card.

Chapter Twelve:
Back to Africa

AFRICA.

It had always held a magnetic attraction for Mirra. It started when she was a little girl in Jamaica and her mother, aunts, uncles, and their friends would gather to socialize at the end of the day. As a youngster Mirra was not welcome to join them of course, but she always listened eagerly from her hiding place underneath the front porch.

To this day she could recall the conversations among the adults that ranged from salacious gossip to local and national politics, all the way down to the best way to repair broken plumbing. Mixed throughout it all was every manner of tall and short tales, enormous boasts, and mysterious fantasies.

On occasion someone would raise an issue about Africa. Mirra's young ears would perk up at the mention of that sonorous three-syllable word. She remembered that the boisterousness in all voices would disappear and in her young mind everyone spoke in a strange tone, that she couldn't interpret.

As she grew older, she understood that the unusual tone she remembered was one of reverence. It was as if talk of Africa occupied a higher plane, one where the surefooted cockiness displayed about local issues had no place.

In high school she started to piece more of it together. She learned the painful legacy of slave labor imported from Africa to

Jamaica. From that she made another connection to her past—that in her youth the elders were speaking about a distant and related place from which they were sure they'd all emerged, even without the book learning to tell them so.

Consequently, the idea that she would personally visit Africa left her with a heady sense of the outsized possibilities. Joshua had first broached it to her after he received the results of Jemal's computer forensics. Someone had to trace the computer connection from Long Island over to the terminus point he had casually mentioned to her hoping to pique her interest. When she didn't immediately volunteer after he described his own crowded schedule he regrouped and suggested that she might really enjoy her first visit to the continent, perhaps even more than he had enjoyed his own years earlier.

She demurred despite the tempting offer. Among her objections were the myriad day-to-day management duties overseeing the warehouse. If he harbored any doubt that she was the charge' d' affaires of the thousands of details required to feed, educate, and motivate hundreds of students each month, her detailed recitation of what that required removed any misunderstanding.

What she came very close to saying was that beyond writing checks he was well on his way to becoming a figurehead. Remaining unmentioned between them for the time being was the thousand-pound gorilla in the corner—the increasing amount of time that he was devoting to sailing.

Only after he had raised the possibility of Jemal joining her on the trip did she began to soften and think seriously about how management of warehouse business might be accomplished during her absence.

Once more she stifled her latent feelings of financial inadequacy, this time brought to the surface by the expenses associated with such a trip. Those feelings were another source of friction with the man she loved. She knew that he would pay for the airfare, lodging, and ground transportation—simply another minor credit card charge. His financial freedom grated on her even though she realized that it shouldn't.

In the end she agreed to go. Her one-week travel itinerary was driven by two important objectives—location of the region and terminus point for the transmissions from Long Island and the opportunity for Jemal to return home.

She felt strongly that he needed to establish a living bridge to his past.

Only rarely over the years had he opened a little and allowed her to see his private sadness; preferring instead to present his brave sunny disposition to her and the world. While she understood that a real connection to his homeland would always be accompanied by painful memories, she was convinced that without that anchor his future personality would be hollow and ungrounded.

An unexpected consequence of her support for his return was that she had to confront her own issues. Wasn't she as rootless as he was, just in a different way? Beyond Jamaican food and music, she asked herself, did she have any real ties to her home island?

She had long doubted whether anything at all was left for her there, nostalgia notwithstanding. Was her mother still alive; were uncles, aunts, or cousins? On occasion her dreams would suggest an answer by transporting her through time back to the listening post of her childhood hiding place. But whenever that happened, she could hear no voices from the porch, no laughter, only silence.

In another dream she would observe the profile of a shriveled bitter woman sitting alone in a straight back chair while staring out to sea. The old woman knew she was being watched but she never turned her head to look at her observer, her daughter. Sometimes Mirra would lament over the irony of the imagery— her own mother, as in the dream, continued to ignore her, just like she did when she was growing up.

Not knowing the answer about her mother's living or dying sat just fine with her, it was a harsh admission that she finally accepted after many years. Her acceptance that there was no emotional bond had provided its own measure of peace and finality. In addition to being a child of the diaspora, she was a parentless child.

Africa.

As far as she knew she had no lineage connecting her with that distant locale. Yet wasn't she about to take the pilgrimage that her relatives and family friends had implicitly wanted to experience? Would she return there with the longings and connections that she gathered as a child over the years in her secret listening place?

She wondered whether in some metaphysical sense she was returning home.

She dismissed her feelings as romantic and vague, little more than pleasant suppositions without a trace of evidence. Yet in her rational mind she was cognizant of the genetic connection to Africa deep within her DNA; it was an unbroken chain stretching back through the millennia. She wondered whether and how that ancient bond would manifest itself when she landed.

When departure day arrived, she boarded the BA flight along with Jemal, each of them feeling their own sense of anticipation. For his part and once settled in he was far more interested in solving the remaining mystery surrounding the source of the communication than worrying about what he would face on the ground. Most of their conversation included his creative speculations about what they would discover at the terminus point. She let him go on about it even though she suspected he was far more anxious over what he might encounter during the trip to his home village.

Mirra finally recognized that Joshua had entrusted her with yet another vital responsibility. She admitted that her earlier truculence hadn't made that easy for him.

She wanted to find a way to be less caustic with him at times, maybe all the time. Yet she was happy that he loved her even with her jagged edges. She vowed to work harder on her issues once back in London.

The flight was long and monotonous; despite their many individual distractions they eventually fell off to sleep. Near the end the jet glided over the Sahara, beginning a series of broad sweeping maneuvers. The dead weight of Jemal's head rolling against her shoulder blade gradually woke Mirra up in time for her to gaze down at the endless expanse of orange rippled sand.

After landing in Dakar the sun's rays against her face and exposed skin felt like fire as she descended the rear exit stairs. She would mention to friends later that her years under England's rain and fog shroud had ill prepared her for the photon-soaked Senegalese experience.

They trudged along the seemingly endless pedestrian route to the Customs hall surrounded by thousands of African citizens. With the rare exception of the European or Middle Eastern traveler they were all brown or dark-skinned or blue-black faces. The contrast to her neighborhood in central London was stark; yet it all felt familiar and welcoming to Mirra. She eagerly took it in until her ears grew flooded with the myriad spoken languages around her, none of which she could identify or comprehend.

Jemal loped along behind his sunglasses, oblivious to everything as he listened to whatever was playing through his large headphones.

Finally clearing Customs after an extensive delay, they entered a large oval greeting hall where a prearranged driver intercepted them.

"My name is Masseur Joachim Tambo Miss and Sir," he said.

He greeted them with perfect English from a blue-black face with startlingly white teeth.

"I speak French, Spanish, some German, English of course, and several local languages. I would be most pleased to be your personal guide during your entire stay in Senegal, in addition to transporting you efficiently to your hotel today."

Since he was prescreened by their travel agency that seemed like the best plan to her. So, Tambo became the constant companion for the next three days. Somehow his ancient Citroen sedan belied its dilapidated appearance and managed to survive the entire time as well.

In his adjoining hotel room Jemal unpacked a large transparent Google schematic and overlaid it with several tourist maps of the city that he'd taken from the airport and hotel lobby. He expected to quickly match the signal terminus location with a street address using GPS coordinates from his original search. But he was disappointed to learn that the terminus point was farther north and west, well away from the city center. Strangely, there was nothing on the local maps that indicated any kind of town or village there.

Jemal knocked on Mirra's door and entered with his handful of maps, his frustration was apparent.

"Well, tomorrow morning we will just have to go exploring with Mr. Tambo; I've found nothing definite. Wherever the location it is hidden or very small. I couldn't trace anything."

He smiled as he realized the implications of his comment.

"So, it has finally been confirmed," he said laughing. "Google has not mapped the entire planet, at least not yet."

Mirra laughed along with him before mentioning that she very much looked forward to being off the Google grid on the trip. But behind her laughter was concern over where they would end up tomorrow.

"Mr. Tambo will be here in at 8:45 sharp Jemal, at least that's his promise. But right now, let's go down to the lobby and get a recommendation for dinner. After we eat, I'm coming back up to tackle my London inbox."

She woke up at six to the ubiquitous blare from Moslem mullahs sending electronic prayers and announcements throughout the city. Modern technology enabled that broadcast to occur six times a day, seven days a week. The citywide audio system insured that escaping the sometimes-strident messages was virtually impossible. Thus, periodically like clockwork, the vast city slowed to a standstill as both the devout and non-devout paused and prayed multiple times during the day. Anyone choosing to evade the daily rituals remained well out of view.

The travel agent had earlier warned her against being *that woman* running alone through city streets in western style jogging clothes. The possibility of fervent rebuke against her for such a secular display could not be ruled out. So, Mirra left her workout clothes in her travel bag and hit the streets in safari pants, a long sleeve safari shirt, and a floppy sun hat that she kept low over her eyes.

She returned to the hotel in time to make sure that Jemal had made his way out of bed. When she met him in the lobby, he was energized.

"Mirra, I cross-referenced the tourist map with national geographic renderings of the area and a couple of old military maps from the hotel library."

Excitedly he spread everything out on the lobby table.

"When Mr. Tambo arrives, this is the area where he should take us. It's called the Indellia District," he said as he circled the area with his index finger.

"There are no street names out there, just district names and public places for markets and trading," he said.

"Who knows what we'll find but if we are lucky, we should find a location and computer with the same ISP address that my search uncovered. The terminus point, it's there," he said.

Tambo arrived forty-five minutes late, no explanation. After they'd piled into the back seat Mirra gave him the location. Instead of pulling away he drove a few feet outside of the hotel entrance gate and parked on the side of the driveway before turning full around to face them.

He wore his most friendly smile.

"My good friends, the location that you selected is a very poor area beyond the far perimeter of our fine city. It is way out in the country surrounded by nothing really at all. Allow me instead to show you several of our notable attractions that are much closer. These national treasures will make you marvel at our rich history here in Senegal. It is a history that goes back many thousands of years, you see."

Tambo showed no visible tension and was otherwise relaxed. His demeanor didn't suggest that there was danger of any kind if they went to Indellia; more than likely Mirra figured, it was personal profit that motivated his attempt to push them to local tourist traps.

She smiled back politely.

"Mr. Tambo, we very much appreciate your fine services so far as our guide," she said cheerfully. "But the truth is that we also urgently need to visit this location for personal reasons. Of

157

course, in that case we will continue to retain your services for the entire day. Are you able to assist us?"

Tambo calculated that a day's rental of his car plus gratuity far exceeded the kickbacks that he would earn by steering them to the usual local businesses. Furthermore, risking his future wages by continuing his objections made no sense.

"Let us go Miss. and Sir. We shall be there at fifteen to the following second hour!"

Pitted roads greeted them immediately after they left the city limits; a jarring journey through an arid countryside began.

Along the way Mirra admired the everyday citizens of Senegal through her window as the Citroen lurched forward on worn springs. Many local people were dressed in stylish modern attire while others mixed and matched modern with traditional clothing. They marched past her car window in reverse.

During slowdowns she was close enough to reach out and touch them. She marveled at their faces that resembled her parents, relatives, and friends from years past. That feeling of kinship and connectivity increased as they went by more groups. She grew convinced that were Tambo to pull over and let her walk among the people something tangible and valuable and beautiful would emerge among them all that she could not yet identify, even without her being able to speak the language.

The locals were equally curious. Who were these strangers from the big city they asked with inquisitive eyes? One thing that the onlookers wrongly appeared to assume judging from their deference was that they were witnessing high officials or even relatives of royalty.

They continued deeper into the backcountry and those that they now drove past no longer resembled the stylish dressers on the fringes of Dakar. They were plainly dressed folk in traditional village attire; but some of them still wore various assortments of western dress.

In many areas the scourge of rural poverty was evident. Nonetheless, the ordinary people continually greeted them with earnest enthusiasm and brilliant smiles.

As they traveled from one small settlement to the next everyone and everything was up and active. Painfully thin cattle accompanied by equally boney shepherds competed for space with scrawny chickens, craggy-faced goats as well as wanderers and workers.

Each village provided its own dusty pathway. Occasionally she would spot three or more backpack-laden children moving in single line formation. But moving to where she asked herself; shouldn't they already be in school?

Periodically the procession of humanity and animals was scattered aside by blaring horns from carbon spewing diesel trucks.

The ever-present bone-dry dust and burning sun baked them all.

They suddenly careened down an unmarked road that soon disappeared into dry bush. Concerned, she glanced over at Jemal who shrugged his shoulders while nodding his head to the beat of a song blaring in his headphones. Ten minutes more passed on the roller coaster road before Tambo turned sharply right and skidded the car into a ditch. He shut off the engine and swiveled around to face them, smiling benevolently.

"We are close Miss. and Sir. But the engine must rest and become cool. "

Before they all passed out from the heat, he restarted it. He gunned the motor and lurched ahead, fishtailing his way back onto the dirt road.

Before long he slammed on the brakes again as he executed a sliding ninety-degree left turn onto a narrow footpath covered by a dense lightless canopy. He roared through self-generated dust for a bumpy few minutes as dry shrubs and branches whipped at the car. After skidding around a sharp bend, he brought the car to an abrupt halt as the breeze slowly cleared the cloud away that had enveloped the front windshield.

Emerging in front of them was a squat, Moorish style building that Mirra calculated to be at least thirty meters in diameter. Nothing was adjacent to the structure—no cars, no telephone or power lines, no people.

"We are here," Tambo exclaimed with relish after turning around to face them.

"I will wait in this space for you until when you are coming," he announced earnestly.

Mirra glanced over at Jemal with a look that asked whether they really wanted to step out of the car in the middle of nowhere. But Jemal was already gathering up his things, visibly excited. She didn't get that at all.

"Look around," she said softly while pulling on his arm. "I don't think this trip was worth the time."

He turned to her as he grabbed the last of his belongings.

"This is the place; I know it for sure!"

"How in heavens name do you know," she asked as she scrambled out of the car behind him?

Moving beyond Tambo's line of sight he held her elbow and gently turned her to face the far side of the building. Then she saw it, a small almost invisible micro satellite dish attached to the lower lip of the circular roof.

"This is the terminus point; it matches my GPS estimate. I don't see any power lines so they must have a heavy-duty battery set up inside or maybe a diesel generator somewhere on the property. A battery could be charged up with periodic plug-ins to vehicles. Or it could even be charged with hours of hand cranking," he said.

"I'll vote for laborious hand cranking," she said almost to herself while studying at the isolated structure.

"Well, let's see whose home," she finally suggested.

Before they could knock the door was opened; a slight brown-hued man in his fifties bowed deeply at the waist. He showed a bald circle on the crown of his head as he did so. His priest's collar was the only white on otherwise dusty black attire.

"Good morning pilgrims! Welcome to our humble chapel! Come in, please come in," he intoned in mellifluous voice.

As the kindly priest ushered them inside as if they had dropped by for tea, the building anxiety that Mirra had kept bottled up dissolved.

Beyond the small entrance hallway, they approached an enormous circular space that apparently served as a great room and prayer center. The large domed ceiling area above the room was unsupported by beams. Leading away from the room were two hallways set apart at a forty-five-degree angle; they disappeared into the shadows.

Moving into the center they saw many carved African sitting stools neatly arranged in a circle. Among them all was an enormous leather-bound hassock. As Mirra looked at it closely she could make out carvings of biblical scenes on its sides.

On the far outer edges of one half of the room a dozen or so additional stools were haphazardly set against the wall. Set apart, a six-foot long wooden crucifix with a coal black stick figure of Christ impaled upon it adorned the opposite wall.

The priest gestured for them to be seated in the center. Then he sat down on the hassock and smiled again.

"I am Father Simone. Welcome to our humble school."

Mirra was skeptical, where were all the students?

After introductions he served them bottled water.

She spoke up.

"Thank you, Father. We are perhaps your most unusual pilgrims today. We have traveled here from London. We have come to solve a great mystery."

"Ahh," he exclaimed as he sat back on the great hassock.

Was that a flicker of concern that just crossed his brow, she wondered?

"You have traveled a far way indeed," he replied. "If I can, I will help you solve your mystery. I would be most honored."

He placed his small rough hands over his heart and bowed his head slightly.

She looked at Jemal and nodded. He quickly took his bag from his shoulder and pulled over the closest stools, forming a scalloped but mostly flat surface. After that he neatly arranged the clothing patterns along with the USB transcription documents and the coded spreadsheets.

The priest starred at the collection for a moment, then he leaned forward and touched each of the items, almost tenderly. He lowered his head and crossed his heart after mouthing a silent prayer.

When he looked up, he had tears in his eyes that he tried to blink away.

"I can only thank God for your arrival," he said in a chocked voice. "Our Lord must be praised."

He continued with renewed energy.

"You see, for many months our connection had been broken and some believed that we'd been forsaken. There was talk that the evil one had devoured our good works at last. I prayed for a miracle. The children also believed in the miracle, and they have kept the faith. But I must confess at times my faith lagged."

He smiled.

"And now you are here. Thank God. The children will arrive in thirty minutes. They will see with their own eyes again that God answers prayer."

"Father Simone," Mirra said, "we may or may not be the answer to prayer. But the truth is that we came because we have no idea what any of these objects are used for."

She said that as her right hand swept over the motley collection.

Her voice grew more strident.

"Father, one of the boys who was apparently involved in the effort to send these things to you by computer link was shot and killed. Two other young men are on trial and could spend decades in jail. And that's just the tip of the iceberg. The young women who assisted them have been insulted and ostracized. And many good people who have helped others for a long time will also suffer."

"Please, tell us what's going on here so that we might help them all."

The priest was stunned; he leaned back for a moment after her hearing her words and gathered himself.

"This is a most terrible thing. How could it have happened in America? When we put in place our secretive measures it was designed to protect the children here in Senegal. Indeed, in the early days of our program one of our children was detected and chased by a repressive mob—one supported by the government at the time. That child died by throwing herself over a cliff rather than submitting to capture and torture."

"After that tragedy it was imperative for us to operate with the utmost secrecy, including moving from our original location in the city center. Our American friends always kept our existence hidden to shelter us from harm. But I never imagined that they would be the ones in danger."

Then the priest's facial expression relaxed, calmness settling over him.

He stood up and gently clasped Mirra's hand. Then he reached out for Jemal.

"Come with me my dear new friends," he said softly.

"Let me show you the things that the young people from America have brought to us over many years."

***

The flight from Dakar to Addis Ababa was more than eight hours. Despite being aware of the flight time in advance Mirra marveled at the sheer vastness of Africa and how most history book descriptions failed to convey that. She also knew that once they were on the ground, they would enter a world completely apart from the one that they'd just left. Ethiopia was yet another sovereign nation on a continent with few unifying cultural traditions. It was also home to cultures that were far more ancient than anything that had existed in Senegal.

Putting aside her musings she woke up her laptop and reopened the email that she'd asked Jemal to send to Joshua. As she reread his bubbly letter she was inspired again by the amazing courage and generosity of the young people in Senegal and those in New York.

Dear Boss,

I am writing you this note from a desk at the terminus point in Senegal.

The mystery of the Long Island camps has been completely solved by Mirra and me. You sent the right detectives!!

The students in both camps in the U.S.A. were involved in an international charity effort that had been ongoing for many years. It was essentially kid-to-kid, no U.N. agencies, no government big wigs, and virtually no adults. I want to run this from the warehouse when I get back! I'll call it Kid-Genius!

Here's how it works

On this end in Africa there is a desktop computer, a 3D printer, several old Singer sewing machines, and a small metal smelting machine. There's also a bank account controlled by Father Simone.

Basically, the things found in the swag bag allow the kids in Senegal to create clothing for sale and use electronic currency that is beyond the government's control. That currency has value in many rural and urban areas and allows them to fund their sales network. But they must be careful, so the currency transactions are concealed for safety reasons.

The profits from the operation are used to support orphanages as well as other health and education related needs ignored or underfunded by the government.

The computer connections began many years back, it's hazy exactly when. Then four years ago a wealthy U.S. kid named Brooke visited the region as part of the worldwide tour they she and her family were taking. She wanted to do something more, so she took over the effort and expanded it.

And I almost forgot, the reason that the U.S. kids were doing everything at two o'clock in the morning was simple: they were working with the kids in this time zone and keeping a very low profile in the U.S.

Kid-Genius!

Signed your top detectives,

Mirra and Jemal

(BTW, CONGRATULATIONS ON YOUR RECENT RACE WIN!!!)

Mirra closed her laptop and smiled. She could still picture the happy faces that they'd left behind at the church. The kids—or should she call them miniature charitable workers—that arrived that morning were amazed to meet their benefactors from America, or so they had all assumed.

Watching them all crowd around as Jemal upgraded their aging software with new programs from the web, what other conclusion could they reach? Despite their denials the children kept thanking them and touching them and singing to them and hugging them. One perky young lady became Mirra's favorite; Jemal teased her that it was because she had met herself from the past.

The most emotional thing that Mirra had ever done in her life was leaving the children behind.

Jemal plunged from high elation in Senegal to deep despair in Ethiopia and he'd only been in his home country for two hours.

The descent started at their first stop after leaving the airport; it was the address they'd received for his home village after speaking with several people. They were told that it was situated one hundred miles away. Beyond a general location no one could offer any details about the place. Yet the journey there felt more like a three-hundred-mile ordeal because the roadways appeared to have been deliberately gutted.

What greeted them when they arrived was far worse.

The driver gingerly steered into what was previously a large gaping village square; it was now layered with debris. He circled slowly. Passing through the apocalyptic scene they saw only desolation extending well beyond the outer limits of the square.

Stinging blasts of dust-laden wind buffeted them as they toured; they lowered and secured hats and covered their faces with bandanas.

Stumps that were once supports for scores of village houses had been severed down to knee height by wind and seasonal rains over many years. Scattered some distance away were crumbling withered shells of what may have been ceremonial or municipal facilities. An apparently more affluent section of the village had been reduced to rows of barren cinder blocks surrounding open geometric spaces.

Scores of razor-sharp corrugated and pointed construction shards scrambled together frenetically throughout the deconstructed landscape. They seemed to gyrate within the swirling winds at times, lifting and twirling yet always remained within the village confines as if refusing to leave home. As the lethal dancers roamed back and forth across the village, Jemal kept a constant lookout while he wandered the area on foot searching in vain for some sign of his former home.

Worried, Mirra finally reclaimed him from a makeshift seat on a pitted cinder block. Before leaving he filled a plastic water bottle with lifeless dirt as his only keepsake.

Next stop was the headquarters building for the administrative district. They needed answers.

Following a dusty two-hour ride, they finally approached the one-story barrack-like structure. Dozens of people sat scattered over the grounds outside with their belongings, waiting. It appeared to Mirra that they must have been waiting patiently for days for something that only rarely showed.

A long cue of citizens waited to enter the building.

Jemal jumped in line straight away with the crowd of local people and endured another ninety minutes while lethargic clerks attended to the business of the multitudes. Having spent considerable time in government cue lines over the years Jemal was nevertheless dismayed by the complete lack of responsiveness from the civil servants. He saw anger frequently boil over from those ahead of him who finally made it to the counter.

When his turn came, he showed his papers and British passport and asked where his extended family lived. The clerk casually looked at the documents and without explanation left the counter. He returned twenty minutes later and patiently explained that he could be of no assistance. As Jemal asked more questions the clerk's English abandoned him entirely and he only shook his head. Eventually he gestured at a preprinted sign, the offices were now closed.

Jemal left the building completely frustrated. When he described the experience to Mirra she rubbed his tense shoulders and tried to cheer him up. After that the driver gingerly pulled out of the parking lot being careful to avoid hitting any of the people who were sitting on the ground, waiting.

At the hotel Jemal released his angst by scouring the web, searching for any clues that he might have missed before.

He found nothing.

Eventually needing fresh air, he walked over to the airy hotel lobby. Yet despite the cooling breezes there circulated by large ceiling fans he continued to feel as if the country and its secrets were deliberately suffocating him. A large glass of coconut water provided by the friendly kitchen staff helped calm him down.

He sat in a quiet area enjoying the drink and watching the high mountain ranges beyond the open entrance doors. The afternoon sun had suffused from the highlands, spilling all the way down into the lobby. He became relaxed and walked to the front doors to take in more of the panorama.

That's when he was sure that he saw someone signal at him from the end of the long entry driveway that slopped down from the front of the hotel. He put aside his drink and looked again with both hands shading his eyes. He saw it again, from a man wearing a khaki uniform. But the man quickly vanished.

On a hunch he stepped outside onto the veranda. A good bit farther away he saw the same person. It was clear that the man was beckoning to him this time before he disappeared behind a line of parked lorries.

Jemal casually walked in that direction for a few minutes with his hands in his pockets.

He spotted a narrow footpath leading away from the roadway and followed it for about one-hundred meters before reaching the base of a large tree-covered incline that led up into the foothills. He stopped and glanced back over his shoulder; the hotel behind him was no longer in sight and he was struck by the stillness all around. Unsure of his goal and feeling isolated he started to turn back. At that moment someone emerged from behind a large balboa tree off to his left. It was the clerk from the administrative office who had given him the runaround.

"Mr. Jemal, please forgive my rudeness during your visit today. But we are under strict orders from the very top to be of no assistance to inquiries such as your own."

The clerk walked closer.

"So, it's true," Jemal said. "The rumors about the government's policy. They continue to hide the truth about the massacres."

"I'm afraid it is true, all of it. But some of us believe that your quest and that of many others who come home to this land in search of family should be honored," the clerk said.

"Do you have anything that could help me?"

"Yes. Your extended family and many other villagers were relocated many years ago to the Natali district. That area is well north of the capital, on the banks of the Ubezi River. Some of your cousins and other relatives may still be there; but I cannot say from personal experience. And we have no updated records, you see."

The clerk looked down for a moment before saying anything more as if he was ashamed.

"I must tell you that all villagers who were relocated had to change their names as part of the resettlement program. It was for their protection; or so it was said by high-ranking ministers."

The clerk's frown betrayed his true feelings.

"The name of your kin would now be Hasnadi, according to the records that I searched."

The clerk nervously jerked his head around looking for eaves-droppers.

"I must go now my brother," the clerk said quietly. "I cannot put my family at more risk; may Allah be with you."

"How can they do that Mirra, just move people away from their homeland," Jemal said while pacing?

"How can they get away with treating human beings like sheep or goats"?

She could only shake her head.

"Then to just let the home village rot and disappear. Everything is decaying as if it never happened."

He plopped down on the chair in the corner.

"It's inhumane Jemal," Mirra said. "And it's unfair, no question about it. I'm so sorry. But let's not give up quite so fast," she said as she discharged her familiar role as comforting big sister.

"Were you able to find out anything about the Natali district on-line," she said?

"Yes, I located a few things. The Ubezi river region is a completely different ecosystem. It's several hundred feet below our elevation here. It is an ancient floodplain area but there was no information about what the people in that area are like. I really think that my relatives were sent there to be forgotten, or worse."

He stood up and started pacing the room again.

"Jemal look, I know you're upset, and I completely understand."

"But let's examine the positive side for a moment. We've got the name of the area where your extended family was relocated and we have the name of your kin, the government name anyway. That combination means that we can complete the other reason that we came here, doesn't it?"

"And by the way, I called the front desk while you were doing your research. They can have a car for us at 5:00 P.M. Even though it's quite a ride, I say we go out now and look around."

That settled him down quite a bit, but he stayed on his feet.

"Thank you. There is good news of course. I don't mean to be so agitated. It's just that for years I swallowed as best I could any memory of my family and my village. It was easier than thinking about it. But now, now that I'm so close, the memories of those times...."

He sat down on the bed with his head in his hands.

Mirra walked over and gave him a big hug.

"Jemal, you know what, I'm going to miss you this fall when you start university. And you'd better stay in touch," she said as she poked her finger into his shoulder.

"And I expect you to come back and visit us regularly on your semester breaks. That'll help keep the younger students motivated. Face it, you're a role model alumnus now, like it or not."

"Don't worry about it, no problems really, I'll be there," he said as he focused his energy on his alma mater.

"Some of the students will work on the Senegal charity project with me. I'm not letting that process stay offline when I get back home. If boss agrees we'll adopt Kid-Genius! as the official warehouse charity and since we won't have the same issues that the New York kids had, we should be able to expand it quite a bit."

"I don't think you'll have to worry about Joshua's support," Mirra said."I'm sure he will agree that it'll be a tremendous project for the warehouse; one loaded with lots of positive learning."

She glanced down at her watch and saw that time was getting short.

"Look, I'll meet you in the lobby in thirty minutes. I've got to clear some things that came in from the staff before we leave."

On the ride to the village, Mirra's anxiety over where they were heading increased after she failed to see any road signs or other markers for over an hour. It took another forty-five to reach the outer boundary of the Ubezi river region that was designated by a small, faded road sign. They left the high mountains and plateaus far behind and were mired in the thick mud of the flood plain as the driver gunned the truck to keep them moving. He seemed to know where he was heading, and he stubbornly wrestled the wheel over the rutted single lane roadway.

The driver yanked the wheel hard left, the truck bounced off balance away from the thick undergrowth and onto an elevated crushed stone roadway with much better traction. They continued toward a wide outcropping of emerald, green bush that stretched for a thousand meters before seeming to blend in with the sky. A few moments later they turned right onto a smooth unpaved pathway that gradually descended back down to the riverbank. Within a half-mile's distance and set well back from the bank, three-dozen round thatched houses appeared. As they approached, they saw all houses were randomly spread across a large tree-less clearing and elevated upon supporting poles.

Jemal stood up in the open safari cab and surveyed the area as they moved in closer. What was missing was immediately apparent, people.

He hesitated and then looked down at Mirra. Maybe the villagers were away at the market or to fish or hunt, he suggested.

She could tell that he didn't believe it.

She stood up and looked more closely. She pointed out that in addition to their being no people around, there were no small animals or other livestock and no signs of farming or subsistence.

The driver turned sharply down a wide dirt path filled with large rain puddles from an earlier downpour. At the end of it was what they could only imagine had once been an enormous livestock coral.

Jemal glimpsed a sudden movement out of the corner of his eye in the open window of one of the houses. He whispered to Mirra who casually looked back and saw the same motion.

"They're hiding from us, but why," she said?

"They must be afraid for some reason."

"Maybe if we get out and walk around that'll show them that we're not goblins," she said smiling.

They told the driver to wait.

They walked together along the narrow passageways that snaked around and between the village houses, passing an irregularly shaped structure every few meters. Within fifteen minutes they had crisscrossed the entire settlement—still no sign of life. By that time the heat and humidity weighed on them like a water-soaked steam blanket; they were drenched.

Jemal finally lost his patience. He cupped his hands over his mouth and shouted.

"Hello, Hello, I'm Saliamonadiak Hasnadi."

"I was born near Addis Ababa seventeen years ago. I have come here from England to find my family. Hello!"

He repeated the greeting and waited for several minutes. Hearing no reply and thoroughly disappointed, they were about to return to the truck when they saw movement at the end of one of the muddy paths. A male village elder was slowly approaching. Several other villagers joined him on the flanks dressed in mixed traditional and western style clothing. The chief, robed in traditional garb reserved for royalty, carried an ornate, carved cane.

He stopped several feet away. He measured Jemal through hooded eyes set beneath thick, unkempt eyebrows. Despite the oppressive heat his dusty brown skin was completely dry while Mirra and Jemal continued to drip.

Satisfied, he spoke.

"Welcome son of Hocknosandi, you have been away a very long time. Welcome home."

The voice was deeply resonant, as if it were amplified.

171

The chief had used Jemal's real family name, not the made up one provided by the government.

The other members of the entourage applauded, and everyone started to smile and laugh. Seemingly from nowhere dozens of other animated villagers had emerged

The chief spoke again.

"Son of Hocknosandi, you must forgive us for we are a poor village and cannot greet your return with proper ceremony. We grow no crops here and we butcher no animals. We depend upon the canned goods delivered by government truck."

"But thank you for visiting us. We now bid you good day, farewell, and safe journey."

Once again, the villagers applauded, smiled, and clamored.

Then the chief turned and began to walk away with the others in tow; the welcome ceremony was over.

"Wait a minute," Jemal erupted. "What about my relatives, my cousins, where are they?'

The chief turned around.

"They have all passed on my son; they reside among the great tribe of the ancestors. You are the last of your bloodline."

Jemal was stunned.

"But how can that be, how can they all have died, that's, that's impossible?"

It was clear from his sour expression that the chief was unaccustomed to being questioned. For some reason he made an exception.

"It was the river sickness. Over the years scores have been taken. We that remain may have the covering. No one has been claimed for many months now. But we are few."

Jemal couldn't process what he was hearing; instead, he started talking, saying anything to prolong things.

"Do you need more medicine? We can help with that. Where are the closest hospitals? What are the signs of the illness? Let us talk to your doctors. We have a safari vehicle that you can use if you want to."

One of the attendants to the chief moved in close and spoke quietly into his ear.

The chief turned to Jemal after that.

"We have seen no doctors over the years. We have only our local medicines. But their strength is weak because the herbs in this land are different from our ancient herbs in the high valleys. What medicines do you offer to us son of Hocknosandi?"

Jemal turned to Mirra and whispered. She nodded her head.

Excitedly he told the chief that they would provide the village all the medicines that they traveled with from London. They were very powerful, he promised.

Mirra added the specifics.

"We have penicillin, percocet, codeine, morphine, prescription strength Ibuprofen and acetaminophen, loperamide, and a few others."

Mirra also knew that their medical bag was back at the hotel. Even If they left immediately, they couldn't return until tomorrow. She was certain that no one would travel on the roads that far from the main city so late at night.

She spoke up again.

"May we ask chief, why you would be interested in medicine if the villagers with river sickness have all died and those that remain have the covering that you mentioned?"

Once again, the elderly leader consulted his entourage. A lively discussion continued for several minutes in the native tongue.

Finally, he turned around.

"Because we have one girl child who is ill. She has been sick for many weeks. Her sickness follows the path of the other villagers before her. Yet she has lingered much longer. Perhaps your medicine has more power."

Mirra followed her instincts. Since she and Jemal had already endured the full barrage of WHO shots for Senegal as well as Ethiopia, she was unconcerned.

"Chief, may we see this young girl? If we can help, I will send Jemal back to the big town to return tomorrow with our medicine. We will leave that medicine for you and your village."

This time the chief didn't consult with his team. He gave orders and two assistants took them through the maze of houses. They arrived at a diminutive structure set far back among the bordering trees. Inside was dim and musty. One of the attendants lit the candle at the entrance.

They could see the sallow-skinned girl lying on a thin straw mattress against the rear wall.

She was asleep and wrapped in white sheets. She could have been ten or eleven years old, although her severe loss of weight made it hard to tell.

A small wooden crucifix had been placed on the low bedside table. Next to it—perhaps as an insurance policy—lay a native talisman containing tightly wrapped roots and special herbs bound with a dark leather cord.

Mirra knelt and touched the child's forehead. From experience she estimated that the fever was at least one hundred and three degrees. Sitting lotus style on the straw mattress, she cradled the girl in her arms before looking up at Jemal.

"The penicillin might help break this fever. If you take the truck back, you could return at first light and be here well before ten. Be sure to use the same driver, say firmly *same fare, double tip*," she said, handing him a wad of local currency.

"And don't flash this around in front of anyone."

Jemal looked worried.

"But Mirra, I promised boss to be with you everywhere and keep watch, shouldn't we leave together," he said?

"I'll be fine here. These are honest village folk. They'll take good care of me. Go, it may save this one child. Even though she's unrelated to you," she said as she stroked the young girl's cheeks with the back of her hand, "she may remember some of your relatives and be able to speak about them and share their stories. They would live in you through her words."

"Joshua would agree with the plan," she said firmly after seeing Jemal's hesitation.

He thought about it for a moment and then nodded before heading back to the truck.

She continued to hold the girl close after asking the escorts to bring plenty of hot water, clean sheets, and soap. When they returned, she washed the girl's face and chest after loosening the tightly wrapped encasement. Before the escorts backed warily out of the room, she instructed them to reattach the mosquito netting and open the two small windows.

Moments later the young girl opened her eyes. Mirra smiled at her.

After removing two Ibuprofen tablets from her purse, she helped the girl swallow, making sure that she took in plenty of water. The child's eyes showed life before she fell back to sleep.

All Mirra could do after that was hold her close.

Jemal was anxious, he barely slept. He finally dozed off at four in the morning. Ninety minutes later he was awake again and getting dressed for the return trip.

Grabbing the medicine bag and his safari hat he headed to the lobby. The driver would arrive in one hour. He walked back to the rear of the dining area to see if the kitchen was open. The hotel cooks had long been there; they freely gave their new young friend from London a large sack of fruit and fresh baked bread for his village.

He couldn't stop thinking about what he'd seen the day before. It continued to eat away at him that a whole village was left to fend for itself without the things that made them what they were. What kind of world is this he asked himself? Had he been sheltered from the worst of it by the good brothers at the orphanage and friends like boss and Mirra and Louise?

He knew the answer.

Sitting alone in the lobby he sipped coconut water while staff came and went around him busily preparing for the coming day. He railed at himself for how naïve he had been for so many years and he vowed that no longer would his sometimes-petty gripes about not having enough extra pounds or the latest video game or software occupy any of his thinking.

Consider yourself from this day forward to be very fortunate, he said silently as he leaned back into the couch and propped his feet up on the wood carved lobby table.

Seconds later an audible snort and sharp glance from the nearby housekeeper made him sit up straight with both feet on the floor.

The safari truck arrived sixty minutes late, by which time he was highly agitated. Then he remembered his briefing notes about the country—unexplained delays of that magnitude are common.

The journey into the countryside revealed a completely different aspect of things than the day before. This time he enjoyed the sounds and fragrances and vistas and even the glimpses of enormous termite mounds.

As they slipped and bounced farther along the route he began thinking about a plan for the little girl after she recovered. He would most certainly incorporate her into his Senegalese Kid-Genius! group. Why not? She would be his eastern-most distributor in Africa. He grew excited about the possibilities the more he thought about it.

All it would require was a second sat phone over which he could direct a high-speed link to her location. They could easily pay for that subscription cost from London. The purchase of the phone along with the laptop, sat dish, sewing machine, smelter and 3-D printer would unfortunately double his overall budget; but many more sales were guaranteed. He sketched in his notepad the outline of his expanded business plan that he intended to share with boss once he got back home. Mirra could help him finish it he conceded after he discovered several tough logistical issues.

The truck skidded to a jarring stop before he jumped down with the medical kit and the food sack. He could feel himself being secretly observed by reticent villagers as he walked over to the small house.

Still shy he said while shaking his head. But wait until they get connected to the worldwide web and the kids start selling clothes and bringing in real money to the village.

That was when he realized the big flaw in his plan. With only one child in the village, there were no others to comprise his sales team. He was wrestling with that when he entered the sick girl's house.

Mirra was seated against the back wall. She held the girl in her arms like a precious bundle as she slowly rocked her and quietly hummed.

He looked down; the girl's face was completely covered over, and her small body was bound up tightly again in the white sheets.

The native talisman, herbs, and roots askew, was crushed between Mirra'a fingers.

Part Three:
Turbulence

Chapter Thirteen: Camp

BRETT CLOSELY WATCHED HIS OLDEST DAUGHTER'S facial expressions. For the life of him he couldn't understand why he saw no joy or elation or even satisfaction.

"Keisha, the information from Joshua nails this thing, doesn't it? I mean the kids were involved in charity, a great cause. We've got the back up for that now. The police are going to drop all the charges, right?"

They were at her law firm in downtown Albany facing one other across a conference room table. The wood paneled walls around them were covered with portraits of the firm's long-dead law partners. The stoic white faces peered down as if they too were awaiting her response.

Her delay rekindled the anxiety that Brett had lived with before receiving the details about the Africa trip.

She leaned forward and rested her elbows on the table.

"It's just not that straight forward, here's why. You've got to factor in that the police shot an unarmed young man, a young black man. They've taken a beating in the court of public opinion and protests around the state and nationally have become increasingly more vitriolic—including flashes of violence—as the investigation into what happened drags on. In self defense the police will continue to demonize Skip and the other young men; in fact, I expect that campaign to intensify."

Brett was having difficulty processing it. Despite knowing the extent and depth of Keisha's experience firsthand, he pressed ahead.

"But all we need to do is to publicize the evidence from Senegal. I mean the campers were doing tremendous things over there. That must count, right?"

From her restrained expression he knew that he was missing a key set of factors and he finally realized that he needed to shut up and listen.

"It does count, of course it does dad," she said.

"But the criminal justice system requires more. We need evidence to counter the charge that there were illicit sexual liaisons occurring at the girls' camp. That's criminal activity regardless of how many good deeds we can demonstrate. And let's not forget about the underlying trespassing charges; the camp was private property, clearly marked as such."

"Well didn't Lai's other information help? That young lady from the girl's camp, Shelley, the one who had the abortion; did your team ever get to the bottom of that? My kids couldn't have been involved; I'd stake my reputation on it."

Keisha realized that she had to take some of the emotion out of the conversation, she shifted gears to something more familiar to her father, a business footing.

"No dad, we haven't chased down those facts, unfortunately. The truth is that we've had to be careful where we spend our legal and investigative resources. Detectives and experts aren't cheap in New York. My firm is already advancing hundreds of thousands of dollars against this case. And believe me, we don't begrudge that. But at the same time, we just can't afford to chase down every lead."

Brett pushed back from the table and walked over to the large window that framed another overcast Albany afternoon. The city was on the cusp of a drenching shower; he'd felt that when he walked over earlier. He looked far out to the horizon where his old stomping ground remained. At the very least some of the dirty Arbor Hill streets would get a needed wash down.

His mind drifted to the years that he'd spent on those thoroughfares as a boy, crisscrossing back and forth on one childhood quest after another with his friends. On most adventures they ran everywhere at half or full speed, covering large swaths. They were convinced that they were the fastest kids in the city, a fantastic belief nurtured by a steady diet of action figure comic books

Brett turned back to face his daughter; he had to be as candid with her as she'd always been with him.

"Look Keisha, I know that what I've been able to pay so far is well short of what we should be contributing. Truth is we've been struggling to raise additional money for the defense fund. Negative publicity has slowed our efforts. And even though the folks shouting on the protest lines have provided huge moral support, they haven't responded strongly to calls for donations. And if that wasn't bad enough, the negative publicity has jumped clear across the country and threatens our plans to buy a California marina."

He sat back down and slumped in his chair before he explained the California issue.

"My recent trip out there to get things moving, a total disaster. After a local paper splashed a picture of me on the front page with a headline claiming that I sanctioned late night panty raids by my campers, it caused an uproar."

He looked away shaking his head.

Keisha looked at her father, sympathy and love in her eyes. He would always be that special man who'd entered her life suddenly and changed it completely thirty years ago. All she had back then were memories of her mother's funeral, her aunty Lai's patient nurturing, and her birth father's weeks long absences.

Despite his having aged so much over the years, she easily remembered the tall dashing Brett Howard in his dark blue suit and blinding white shirt.

Keisha was confined at the time to an in-patient psychiatric facility in Manhattan. She was recovering from a traumatic incident that occurred while she played outside in her neighborhood. Doing well, her doctors had allowed her aunt Lailani to take her to visit some of the tourist sites in Manhattan.

The one that Keisha was the most excited to see was the Empire State Building.

But Keisha got stuck in the glass-enclosed turnstile at the entrance to the famous building. Her aunt tried in vain to pull her out but instead they both ended up inside of the rotating entrance like two country bumpkins from Albany.

Brett appeared from nowhere to slow it down, pulling her out and then her aunt. Keisha could still picture them in her mind facing each other after the rescue as well as that look on her auntie's face when she recognized that it was her long ago childhood friend.

Keisha had always wanted to find her own knight in shining armor, but it hadn't happened yet. She'd resigned herself to believe it probably never would. But at least she found a great father.

"Dad," she said, pulling her mind back to the present, "we'd love to reverse the damage by waving a magic wand, believe me we would. It's just not that easy. But we're building the defense with a measured approach. It may not seem splashy, but I believe that we're going to be effective. And by the way, we'll manage the timing of expenses as best we can; don't worry so much about that. We just need to be wise."

Brett sat up.

"I know you all are doing a good and professional job. I haven't lost one bit of confidence in you or your team. It's just that my political contact in California was crystal clear that we had to win the case here or at least make significant strategic gains that we could publicize if *Sail Shape* was to have any chance to purchase the marina out there."

"Not to sound sarcastic," Keisha said partly out of frustration, "but your California advisor sounds like a genius. I suppose he also has tons of legal experience as well to back up his prognostications."

Brett was careful to position the next part in a way that didn't signal any lack of confidence.

"Well, the guy that I was photographed with out there is a senior partner at a law firm in Los Angeles. And he's admitted to practice in New York State. By the way, he was the lawyer that helped baby girl settle her issues with the university several months ago."

"Interesting," Keisha said, as she considered the different dimensions of her father's comments.

"He certainly got baby girl the best deal possible under the circumstances. By the way, she did send me a draft of the proposed final settlement to look at just in case, it was well drafted. So, I take back my snide remarks. I'm sure that your west coast attorney friend has a very good understanding of the challenges we're facing in this case," Keisha said.

"I think he does. And he's made me a very unusual offer. He'll travel here along with a paralegal. He'll spend several days with you on the case under your specific direction and see if the added resources can get the facts out. All expenses associated with his time will be absorbed by his firm."

Keisha sat up straight.

"Who is this person really dad, and why would he do that for you, for us?"

"His name is J Broderick; I always called him Jazz when he was a kid. That name still slips out occasionally. Many years ago, when he was in high school J and a group of students took over the Berkeley campus as part of a protest effort to get a new school built. I helped them out back then when I was a grad student out there. The new school was completed and Jazz, J rather, was in the first graduating class at the new school. Over the years I've helped him with recommendations, advice, and on a couple of occasions, tuition money. I think he's just paying me back."

Keisha nodded her head.

Her irritation was completely gone now. She knew exactly what was motivating the California lawyer, it was heartfelt gratitude. She looked across the table at the man who had adopted her when doing nothing would have been the safest choice. She felt truly blessed.

"Dad, the sooner you can get him here the better. There are a series of critical depositions coming up that include solving the issues surrounding the young lady who received the abortion. I could use another seasoned lawyer with me."

"I'll call him this evening. When we last spoke, he said he could be on a plane within a couple of days."

The following morning Keisha entered the Albany convention center garage and took a parking spot next to the elevator. At the end of a long day and evening of meetings as this one was sure to be she wanted her car very close late at night for that extra margin of safety.

She gathered up her things and walked over to the meeting rooms.

Long drawn-out staff meetings like this one promised to be were a fact of life and she had never missed one. Except for those rare executive sessions which were closed-door partners' only affairs, her entire firm met off-site every other month, excluding only secretaries. She was quietly lobbying to change that. Her argument was simple: when crunch time came and everyone was pulling back-to-back all-nighters on a big case, could they get it done without secretaries?

She was prepared for the fact that today's meeting might be edgier than most because business was getting harder as the recession strengthened and clients were demanding more savings. Every law firm in the city was laser-focused on cost cutting and profitability. So, she expected questions about her cases, and she was equally interested in the productivity of her fellow partners.

So far at least no one who mattered was questioning the fact that the camp shooting case was turning out to be a bigger than anticipated charitable investment for the firm. But third-party bills continued to accumulate and payments to help cover them from her father and the parents of the two boys were lagging. Nonetheless, her firm still had a strong balance sheet, she didn't anticipate any serious pushback.

Just in case she was prepared to give a spirited defense if that happened since her passion about the camp case was a prime reason that they had undertaken the defense in the first place.

Her confidence in her firm stemmed from their decades long pro bono advocacy for social justice. It was a primary reason she'd chosen them in law school. Or more accurately, they had chosen her, basing their decision on the clerkship that she had with them during her second year. When they invited her to interview for a permanent position, they'd asked about her career goals. She was clear that she wanted to work on criminal defense litigation and domestic abuse cases. As it turned out they'd been looking to expand in those areas. They even allowed her to work for two years in the DA's office before joining them, which helped hone her trial skills.

She saw the Lord's hand in it all.

Yet despite her confidence in the firm's moral compass, she never revealed to her partners that she'd been a victim of violence herself when she was a young girl. It was because of her personal pain that she felt an extraordinary commitment to use the law to help the vulnerable.

As she won more cases as a young lawyer, helping to build the firm's reputation as well as filling the coffers, everyone naturally assumed that her motivation was like their own—the love of winning and the love of generous compensation for doing so. She was fine with that misassumption. In truth, the financial success allowed her to take on more cases in pursuit of social justice since those cases generated modest fees at best.

As she walked up a central translucent staircase Keisha ran into Stephen Whalen, a black law clerk who had worked with her on a matter the previous year. Stephen was a third-year law student set to graduate in the spring.

In the old days he would have already had his permanent employment lined up. The business downturn changed all that. She knew that he still held out hope that his good work at her firm would eventually land him something there. She had learned that wasn't going to happen. But Stephen hadn't been told the bad news yet. She didn't agree with that decision, but it wasn't her call.

"How've you been Stephen," she asked cheerfully, masking her foreknowledge.

"I'm fine, Keisha. Thanks for asking. But fine is probably an overstatement," he said with his usual self-deprecatory sense of humor.

"Truth is I'm trying to get involved with something substantial at the firm where I can put up some decent hours. The drop off in available work has been noticeable. All of us clerks are a little worried. By the way, if you need some assistance on the Long Island matter let me know if I can help. I went to camp there when I was ten and eleven, before my dad moved us to Philly. I remember your father, Mr. Howard. He was a good guy—despite being the big boss."

"Small world indeed," she replied. "If there's a need on the case, I will definitely call you in."

Walking away she felt a chill that made her shiver and gather her silk scarf more tightly around her neck and shoulders. It wasn't the ambient air temperature she realized; it was the chill of financial insecurity that she was feeling vicariously for Stephen. She had learned recently that his college and law school debt totaled almost two hundred thousand dollars; now he would face that mountain of debt without a job.

Inside the large meeting room partners were huddled together in small groups while others were talking with younger lawyers or sitting alone in front of laptops. She took her usual seat down front and unpacked.

Matters during the early morning sessions involved long-winded updates about significant cases that generated major fees. After that were administrative and space management items and she would never understand why those things were important enough to occupy ninety minutes of agenda time.

Following the thirty-minute buffet lunch Bill Harpin— son of the firm's deceased founder—asked her for an update on the Long Island litigation. After her response she realized that his question was merely a pretense because he launched into a long-winded soliloquy about the dangers of daughters, fathers, and sons working together. Since Bill was also the grandson of an eminent attorney, he had a basketful of dos and don'ts and he sprinkled family stories liberally throughout his remarks. Other attorneys and paralegals zoned out.

Keisha listened closely, however, and tried to follow his drift. Even though he hadn't mentioned her by name she was convinced that he was obliquely questioning her objectivity on the Long Island case and whether she could protect the firm's investment, wherever the facts might lead. She had to respond.

"Bill, I appreciate your concern and I respect your perspective. The question of objectivity is vital. It's the foundation upon which we all must build our cases. And I think my record at this firm supports my skill at being able to discharge that obligation. The evidence in the Long Island case points to an injustice, I'm convinced of that. Our firm's reputation is also on the line in the matter. But you know what, when I expose that injustice our client's and our own reputation will be just fine."

Bill seemed satisfied. He sent her a generous smile across the big table. And besides, he was doubly happy since he'd been able to hold court before the entire firm once again.

Before the dinner break, she briefed her partners about the soon-to-arrive California lawyer and paralegal. Warding off any objections she mentioned that he was also licensed in New York State and that he would work entirely under her direction.

$$* * *$$

Remy closely watched her best friend.

She was concerned because Lai had always been so steady and consistent. But now there was something going on below the surface, making Lai appear pensive and distracted. Was she still jet lagged from the California trip?

They were finishing up another long day at the office, this time in preparation for the upcoming quarterly close. They'd learned long ago that running their business profitably depended on laser sharp focus against revenues and expenses. They both knew that only after all of that was under control did you have a chance to build something successful.

After the operational review they took a break before Lailani spent the next two hours covering every aspect of what she'd discussed with Tony Calibri. Then they exchanged ideas about the strategic advantages and drawbacks to any combination with his organization. Between them they had always been able to see through to the bottom of most issues, but this one was proving to be a challenge.

Together they'd successfully grown their startup company from scratch into a million-dollar business. But despite that topline number, profits had remained modest given the high New York operating expense and tax burden. They didn't see any reasonable path to expanding further on their own. But the right deal would solve that problem.

They also talked about the follow up visit that Lailani had agreed to with Tony once the NDA was in place. Lailani wanted Remy to be in California with her at that time to dig through the details. If the deal still made sense after that the next step would be to talk specifically with Tony about structure, price, and timing.

At first Remy was anxious about the trip, mostly because she'd never left the east coast let alone spent five hours on an airplane before. Yet the more Remy listened to her friend's vivid descriptions of the sunrise, colors, and different vibe out west, the more she became enthralled with seeing it.

When they talked about the business aspects of any possible deal, they always ended up back at the same question—why Tony would really be interested in their small regional business. They even considered the possibility that he harbored a sexual attraction to Lailani before they dismissed that as a nonstarter. After all, he'd made no move when she was right there in his world, alone. In the end they accepted his original pitch that the management and motivational style that they'd cultivated over the years was the reason.

After they had covered every angle, Lailani paused and looked away for a moment. Then she walked over to the corner of her office before looking back at Remy.

"Would you like a cup of tea, Remy? I think I'll have one."

After turning on the carafe she finally said what was on her mind.

"Remy, there was something else that happened when I was in California..."

Whatever it was Remy could sense that it wasn't good and that her friend had been completely shaken.

After Lailani described her call to Brett's hotel room and the woman's voice Remy understood why she'd detected something just a little off in Lai's tone of voice after she'd picked up her telephone message confirming the completion of the meeting with Tony.

When she finished the story Remy's reply was as real as she could make it.

"Girlfriend, I've known Brett for many years, almost for as long as you have. Don't forget that I was watching him from a distance as your best friend back when we were kids, just to make sure that he was on the up and up with you. And he was then, and he has been as far as I know for all these years. I have a hard time believing that he just suddenly flipped."

Lailani nodded absentmindedly as she finished brewing the tea.

She had to admit that Remy had made some goods points, as usual. And she also remembered that Remy had been very wary back when they were kids about the new boy in town named Brett Howard and the attention that he was lavishing on her. But that was way back then, what about now?

"Remy, I've thought about that call from every angle I can think of. Sometimes I excuse it, sometimes I condemn it, but the one thing I can't do is erase the fact that my husband had another woman in his hotel room late at night."

Remy nodded before she responded.

"I can't understand why that would be the case either, Lai. But I've never seen Brett as the kind of man who would go on the road and have some hussy in his bed. I mean let's face facts; he travels more than two hundred days a year, right? And he's been traveling for what, the better part of twenty-five, thirty years? Guaranteed you would've come across something before this that made you suspicious, believe me. You know as well as I do, men just aren't that careful. They always slip up."

That made sense: she was encouraged. Never had she come across anything at all that made her suspicious. Nor had she ever once felt that the relationship problems between them over the years were caused by infidelity.

She placed the tea service tray on her desk and sat down.

"Okay, then tell me, why would a woman answer his cell phone late in the evening when he's three thousand miles from home? Business meeting?

He sure doesn't work those kinds of hours around here."

"I honestly don't know. And I agree it looks bad on the surface. But I don't believe that he would wait until he was in his mid-sixties to start cheating on you."

"I don't know if he cheated before Remy, I honestly don't know."

She shook her head and sipped her tea, trying to hold it together.

"We've been so separated from each other the past few years…"

Remy saw the tears.

"We don't love each other like we used to. We don't make love. Why wouldn't he find it elsewhere?"

Remy came around the desk after grabbing a handful of tissues; she hugged her friend and dabbed at the tears.

"Lai, let me tell you something, not being as intimate with your husband as you were in the past is a whole lot different than believing that he's cheating on you. And yes, I speak from experience. My own Don Juan left the building several years ago. Sports in various flavors get a whole lot more looks at my house that I do. But you know what, I can see him watching a game or a sitcom at home and still know that my man loves me. Not that I wouldn't want him to show that love more amorously and more often by the way."

The humor brought a smile to Lailani's face.

For a while they engaged in the same impish laughter that bound them together years ago as children.

"The Don Juan's may indeed be outside stumping around and looking for the entrance," Lailani kidded. "But they'd both need to have a big spotlight shine on the real front door in order to find it."

They had a belly laugh at that one.

Finally turning serious again, Remy needed an answer.

"Have you asked Brett about the woman, Lai?"

"No. I think on one level I'm afraid of the answer. And on another level, I'm afraid that I'll lose it if he admits to me that there's someone else."

"Well, you can't have it both ways; you either want to know or you don't, right?"

The pensive expression returned to Lailani's face, she nodded.

"Here's an idea girlfriend, rather than checking with him about it initially, which you know you need to do at some point, you should check other sources. Have you talked to J in California? Brett may have gotten together with him on the trip. Did you look at Brett's itinerary or his calendar?"

"No, I honestly haven't done any of that. I've just been sick over it. Come to think about it, Brett mentioned in passing that J is coming here to work with Keisha on Kyle and Alan's defense. Maybe I could ask him then."

Lailani set her cup and saucer on the tray.

"And you know what else, Brett keeps an old-fashioned calendar in the study right on his desktop. I suppose I could check to see if anything …unusual is entered on it."

"Those are both good ideas Lai; better than assuming the worse too early. And when's J arriving?"

"He'll be here Tuesday afternoon; I'll mention it to him when I see him. Those were great ideas Remy, thank you."

Remy was happy that she could provide something to lighten the anxiety that Lai had kept bottled up. Despite the worry lines on her friend's face, she always saw the young Lai, that seven-year-old girlfriend whose house she rushed over to so many times. Lai always had news to share back then about the new boy, Brett, who had moved into the neighborhood. It was always good news, at least until the last time.

She could still recall Lai's girlish voice and breathless tone: He's kind of quiet and reserved she would say as if entrusting Remy with a profound secret, he must still be sad about his mom.

Remy would share her own opinions as she got to know more about him and whenever Lai allowed her to get a word in edgewise.

On another day, one of several years of happy days for her friend, Remy remembered Lai's description about how Brett had prevented Flintroy, the class bully and groper, from dancing with her during square dance hour.

Brett is tall and skinny, Lai explained seriously and patiently as if Remy had never seen him in person before; but he walked right up to Flintroy in class and said to him very quietly, Lailani won't be dancing with you today or in the future. Wasn't that brave of him Remy, Lai asked her with wide eyes?

Lai and Brett were inseparable, and Remy was sometimes jealous about him spending so much time with her. But he had always treated her friend with respect, so she was okay with it.

Then the last day came. Remy remembered when Brett had suddenly gone missing. He just disappeared and Lai had learned from his sixth-grade teacher that he and his brother and sister had been moved far away. Completely by chance, like a chapter from a love story, they met again twenty years later.

Where are they now, those lovers from the past, Remy wondered; how will they even end up?

"Starting with J is the best approach," Remy finally responded. She sipped her cold tea she put it down before gathering up her papers.

"You've known him longer than me Lai, but J always struck me as a straight shooter. But you know what, he does have that super polished veneer that he wears on the outside. It's almost funny, in the few times that I've met him he appeared to be on stage, like an actor about to give a dramatic presentation or something?"

Lailani nodded and laughed.

"You obviously know him almost as well as I do Remy. I suspect though, different from you perhaps, that underneath his smooth glossy exterior he's basically just a highly polished individual."

They cracked up together.

***

Income and cash flow statements from each *Sail Shape* camp around the country were stacked in a neat pile on the bare restaurant table in front of him. The thought popped into his mind that all that was missing was a nice red manila folder to place them in—it would match the red ink that was leaching from the strained budgets.

The humor didn't lighten Brett's mood.

But it did underscore why he'd set up the emergency meeting today with Ned Jensen. If anyone had ideas about righting the ship and staying afloat, Ned could be counted to give them up without the sugar coating.

As he waited, he looked around the small restaurant and wondered how many times it had been remodeled since his first meeting with Ned back in the day; probably half a dozen remodels he guessed. Patch and paint he observed, if only it were that easy with things involving the humans.

Right on time as usual Ned slipped through the front door and eased his long frame into the booth. They shook hands. Brett thanked him for coming on short notice.

"Good to see you Brett, what's it been three years now since we saw you guys down on the Vineyard?"

"That right and that was the last time wasn't it, over at Clarence and Virginia's party in Oaks Bluff," Brett said.

"Yup. I'm glad you called me; your timing was perfect. I'm in town anyway for three days to roll over the financing for the Broadway Street mall. Believe it or not the old girl requires another capital infusion for a big spruce up. This is the third one since we broke ground three decades ago. But that mall has paid us back many times over. And of course, as you're aware, without it the so-called Albany renaissance wouldn't have happened."

Brett understood Ned's impact on the community; maybe he hadn't shown his appreciation as much as he could have over the years.

"You know what Ned; you deserve much more credit for what transpired over the years in this town. Sure, a ton of urban issues remain, and I appreciate that you like to keep a banker's low profile, but you were the key driver back then when very few around here really believed in urban renewal. And to think it took a bomb thrown into your local office to turn the tide of opinion to support the mall."

Ned flinched at the mention. He understood that Brett was only making small talk before moving to the real reasons for the sit down, but he would have much preferred that the arson story remain unmentioned.

"Yeah, I'll never forget that whole calamity," Ned said after a delay. "It was by the narrowest stroke of luck that my office staff escaped injury, but my God…those innocent bystanders …"

Ned shook his head as if to clear away the memory of attending what felt like endless memorial services and funerals.

After seeing Ned's pained expression Brett regretted bringing the whole thing up.

"At least there was some small vigilante justice for the families of those innocent bystanders, Ned. The guy who built and planted that bomb—Shaka was his name— was killed years later in prison by a cousin of one of the victims, don't think that is widely known."

"Look Ned, sorry I mentioned the whole thing."

He collected the papers in front of him and held them up.

"I sent you this in an email earlier today, I doubt that you've had a chance yet to digest it, but it's worse than I thought after I ran the latest numbers. If this rate of loss keeps up for six months, I'm going to have to lay off half my management team."

"I did look them over and carefully," Ned said.

"Waiting six months would be a big mistake in my view. I think you've got to start layoffs much sooner, like next week, starting with your core team of long-service executive directors. That's where you'll reap the biggest cost savings. One director managing three camps minimum must be your future model."

Brett wasn't at all surprised to hear the prudent—albeit harsh—advice. He was thankful for it. Over the years Ned had proven to be a loyal and reliable colleague as well as a wise uncle to Joshua. But there was no way he could implement his recommendation without destroying the credibility of the *Sail Shape* brand. There had to be another way.

"You know Ned, if this were just about making widgets and profits, I would follow your advice in a heartbeat. But it's not just a business. You understand better than most that we're about changing the trajectory of kids' lives."

"An on-site, fully committed executive director forms the essential core of our brand. They instill the character and the discipline; they're the visible role models. You've heard me say it countless times, we attack two things that knock these children out of the box once they leave school at the end of the academic year—idle time and lack of motivation. How can I accomplish that with an executive director shuttling among three camps and never getting to fully know the campers?"

"Believe me, I understand the mission and I believe in it," Ned said leaning forward.

"You've made a difference over the years in the lives of thousands of kids, no doubt about it. But if you can't pay your bills or pay your staff, you're dead in the water. Your labor expense is your biggest nut. With benefit and salary savings, you can cut that expense by at least a million annually."

Ned gave him the rest of the grim picture.

"Slashing your operating expenses gives you a chance to salvage most—not all—of the bigger facilities. And by the way, I believe that the California deal should be placed on the back burner, maybe permanently."

Brett stood up and shoved his hands in his pockets before walking over to the far wall and leaning back. He replayed in his mind his firing of Hershel shortly after Skip was killed. Hershel was a longtime friend. His firing was for cause, for negligent supervision of campers. Yet it was difficult and emotionally draining to fire a man whom he'd known for fifteen years, a friend with two kids in private school and a wife pregnant with a third.

What Ned was proposing was altogether different; it was a mass firing squad. Could he line up and shoot two thirds of his directors for no reason other than prudent budget management?

And his campers, wouldn't they receive a vastly degraded experience after the fix was put in place. For parents and guardians, they would receive far less than they expected when their campers returned home without that needed, daily hands-on supervision from a strong camp director.

So, when all was said and done everyone would pay up because the CEO, the founder, couldn't make it happen, because he couldn't do his job.

The more he wrestled with it the more it sounded like the excuses he'd always heard in his previous business life. In big business the messages were wrapped up in shiny accounting foil but inside they carried the same truth about failed leadership—we couldn't t get it done so you're going to have to pay the price, you're fired.

No, not here he vowed.

He positioned his objections to Ned differently, however, taking himself out of the equation.

"Here's why we can't do it like that and salvage anything Ned," he said holding his arms wide open.

"My national donor network would completely dry up if we shrank from the field. And getting them back would be well-nigh impossible. Other organizations would use our setback to steal our mission and our donors. We're no longer the only game in town anymore."

"But didn't you imply in your email that fundraising was way behind plan. Isn't the drain happening now; aren't your donors already heading for the exits?"

Brett knew it was the case, but he refused to acknowledge it again.

"The glass is half full the way I see it, it's the way I must see it, Ned. We're getting some good investigative results in the lawsuit, and I think we have a chance to gain an acquittal for those two young men. If we're able to hold on and do that, the positive press would leverage the camps again and fundraising should bounce back. There's real smoke certainly, but I refuse to panic unless I see the fire."

"Okay Brett let's assume that's true. The reality now though is that you've got a rapidly growing operating deficit to cover until then. How do you propose to hold on?"

"I'll need a loan from your bank Ned, a sizeable one to tide *Sail Shape* over. I'm willing to pledge two million dollars in value on the Long Island property. You'd also have priority over any other debt."

"How much leverage is already on that land," Ned asked? His tone was non-committal.

"Some of the equity is backing various loans and notes used in recent camp expansions. Two million more is earmarked for the California purchase. And then there're seasonal operating budgets that must be covered with lines of credit until fundraising catches up. But substantial equity remains, more than sixty percent of the recently appraised land value."

Ned pushed back a bit and stretched his neck and shoulders. He changed the subject while simultaneously running the financial numbers in his head.

"By the way and on a positive note, I was happy to hear from Zena that you hired my niece as your replacement director in Long Island. Mikala's always had a first-class financial mind. She could be a huge asset for your organization as you take an ax to costs. Not that I'm being critical of your financial acumen by the way," Ned said with a smile.

"Tell me," Ned said as he narrowed his gaze, "when exactly did Zena put the squeeze on you to hire Mikala? She was a little vague when we talked about how it all happened."

"She called me while I was in Cali believe it or not. She left the sweetest message at the hotel and ended up dropping by for a late-night chat. I thought she was planning to cut off her sorority contributions. I was having heart palpitations until she made the pitch for Mikala."

Ned was curious about how strong that pitch had been; he knew full well the persuasive powers of his first cousin, especially when she wanted something badly. He let it go.

"Like I said, my niece knows her numbers, she was Phi Beta Kappa during her undergraduate years. Zena always updated us with news about her successes over the years. But Mikala's had to deal with some heavy weight family issues in the last couple of years, including her parent's divorce as well as her own personal issues. She kept those things mostly under wraps for some reason, it affected her health I suspect. But I think her hire is a good move for her and for you."

Ned shifted forward in his seat again.

"Let me be frank my friend, I think I can get the board to go along with a secured loan to keep *Sail Shape* afloat. I still have that much clout as the bank founder, even though the board knows that I'm serious about retirement. But the paperwork will have to be airtight. And we'll have to have first position, well documented with no air holes. And unlike previous years, outside of this transaction we won't be able to make any additional gifts to *Sail Shape*."

Then he added the stinger.

"And finally, we will have to call our note and foreclose if any payments are missed."

The stiff terms were sobering but they represented more than Brett dared hope for. They were a risk that he was willing to take because they provided a chance to bounce back.

"I get it Ned; believe me I do. We'll do the due diligence and sign the deal up tight. I wouldn't ask you if I didn't believe we'd come out of this thing in good shape in the end. But we'll have to go through rough weather to get to the calm."

Ned nodded back, hoping that he was right.

***

In the back seat of the taxi J closed his laptop after finishing the last of the interview notes that Keisha emailed.

He took a few minutes to show Shana some of Albany's famous landmarks as they approached the downtown exit.

"It's a small city compared to mega New York; but being the capital, it still has broad statewide influence," he said.

Shana looked out at the city's expanse; she was happy to finally be there with him.

He pointed at the front left window as they approached a fifty-story office tower.

"That's our destination."

The trim receptionist, one of three in the foyer, ushered J and Shana into a large conference room immediately off the lobby. Before long Keisha Howard joined them.

He was impressed. After reading her bio he'd expected a more matronly lawyer, probably because of the gravity of so many of the cases that she'd taken to trial. But she was the opposite of that; he decided on the spot that stunning was the appropriate adjective.

He and Shana stood up as she walked toward them.

"Thank you so much for coming, J" she said as she extended her hand.

"My father has said nothing but great things about you."

"Brett always did exaggerate," he replied.

They both knew that wasn't true.

"As we discussed on the phone, Shana and I are here to pitch in for a few days at your direction. Truth is, I wouldn't be doing what I'm doing if it hadn't been for your father; so, it's a privilege for me to do what I can to help."

He stepped slightly away from Shana.

"Ms. Keisha Howard, allow me to introduce you to Ms. Shana Richards," he said formally.

"Shana, allow me to present Ms. Keisha Howard."

Keisha made a mental note about his highbrow formality along with his buttoned-down appearance; stereotypical California laid back was not what she'd be receiving from Senator J Broderick. It made her curious about whether he had kept his tie and suit jacket on for the entire flight across country.

Out of the corner of her eye Keisha glimpsed the long shapely legs displayed beneath the paralegal's tight skirt and high hemline that was level with the lip of the table. What surprised her more were the six-inch high stiletto heels. They helped explain why she felt like the shrimp in the room standing before them.

"Pleased to meet you, Shana."

"The pleasure is mine Ms. Howard."

"Keisha is perfectly fine, Shana."

She smiled to put the young woman at ease.

"Thank you both for crossing the country to pitch in." she said as she motioned for them to be seated.

"The truth is we've been starved for adequate resources. As you are likely aware J, they are ridiculously expensive in this state. And remind me again to follow up on what we discussed briefly; I'd be more than happy to share with you how we're approaching this thing as my firm's major charitable initiative."

J nodded.

Then Keisha got down to business.

"I imagine that you've both read the case files that I sent, sorry for that massive data dump. It's a complete look at where we are so far, however. The information from Africa was, of course, a big help but under New York law it's not enough by itself to win an acquittal. I'll get to that later."

"Let's talk first about the young lady named Shelley. Her deposition is on the schedule and she's the key to solving the entire case, in my opinion."

"Before I question her under oath," she said while looking at J, "I need you to solve the mystery surrounding her and the real reasons that she betrayed Brooke and those young men from *Sail Shape*."

After four more hours they wrapped things up. Keisha had the receptionist call them a taxi before she headed back to her office.

Fighting jet lag, the two lawyers met for dinner in the hotel lobby after working separately in their rooms for hours. Because J had more calls to return, he vetoed Shana's suggestion to work together after dinner to plan the best approach for Shelley.

Chapter Fourteen:
Revenge

"SO, EXACTLY WHAT'RE YOU GOING TO DO NOW STEWART? And please don't take this the wrong way, but how can you just assume that she's your daughter without due diligence?"

Chauncey had grown increasingly agitated over the whole thing during the past week and his patience was shot.

"You know what," he said being unable to restrain himself, "when you were watching the nun that evening, I was watching Melinda. Frankly, I think that she'd try any trick, including religion, to get you back."

After blurting that out he was forced to recognize that he was too jealous to think rationally.

Jealous, raging queen, he confessed to himself.

His angst over Melinda burned again like an old wound with the scab ripped off. The original scar happened years ago when he learned about Stewart's secret affair with her and his plan to give her a bigger cut of the spoils than he and CY would receive. That it happened before his own relationship with Stewart didn't matter in the least.

Melinda was a dissembler, that much was clear. Her willingness to take more than him for far less contribution to the plan proved it.

Everybody else knew at that time, including the prosecutor in the case unfortunately, that it was really his contacts and his initiative and risk taking—not hers, not Stewart's, or Cy's —that was largely responsible for them coming so close to extorting five hundred million dollars from Taurus Corporation.

Stewart broke in on Chauncey's internal fuming.

"Chauncey, I can look at Sarah and see that she's my own. And after talking with her it's plain to me that she's got guts and more than a little cunning. Otherwise, she would've never found her mother or me. From where do you think she got those traits? Be honest, when you saw her, didn't you see the strong resemblance?"

"Yes, she looks like you, I grant you that; not that those things can't be faked by the way. But let's assume she is your daughter, what now?"

"Truth is love I honestly don't know what's next. But I do feel something for her. I feel a closeness that's hard to express in words. We've only spoken once since that first meeting. But somehow deep inside me I need more contact with her. Can you understand?"

His heartfelt words only served to reignite Chauncey's anger, causing him to blurt out something that he would regret.

"Fine, I get it. You should try to learn so much more about her then if you feel so strongly. Why don't you go out to Cali and visit? That would allow you both to catch up on old times, very old times, right? And it would give me a chance to finally redecorate and get this depressing little apartment in order. "

Hearing Chauncey's license for him to travel west made him suppress a smile.

"I just may do that, love. There might be some very cheap fares out there," he said already knowing the answer.

"It may provide me an affordable two- or three-day jaunt out to her habitat without spending a fortune."

Stewart laughed at his own pun.

Chauncey was grim.

***

Back in California, Sarah endured a monotonous sameness within her personal purgatory; it somehow kept her going. She'd grown fond of the old three-story Victorian building that was now her place of work and residence. The historic structure had been converted by the order into a mental and spiritual health treatment facility providing social services for a range of female offenders attempting to reintegrate.

Sarah's working hours were long, seven to seven six days a week with Sundays off. Normally she would see as many as twenty women daily, each of whom would have benefited from more of her time and preparation. Over the life of the facility most women had been unable or unwilling to complete the requirements; the failure rate remained above seventy percent.

The specific needs and demands on Sarah's time were many and varied. In the first weeks after she completed her counselor certification courses, she worked with several categories of women, including the homeless, those arrested for stealing drugs or food or both, recovering crack addicts, and many partially healed alcoholics. She also counseled women who seemed better suited as residents at long ago closed mental asylums. Instilling self-confidence, discipline, and faith into the women had proven to be an elusive goal at best. But she and the other sisters tried hard to accomplish that.

At the end of each day, she returned exhausted to her small room in the basement to eat dinner, which was usually ordered from neighborhood takeout vendors. After that she'd return any calls before prayer. Her activities had to be finished before lights out.

She earned one additional afternoon off every other week as personal time.

As tough and resolute as Sarah was, she realized early on that she had a long year ahead of her. She was determined to survive it. Strangely enough a source of hope and encouragement had come to her in the person of her father who recently called her again.

Despite her initial reluctance, when speaking to him she'd developed the same affection toward him that she had thought was only reserved for her mother. That had been a complete surprise. At one point she wondered whether his gender was influencing her in any way. His manner of speaking and thinking and even his deep tone of voice was different and more interesting than anything that she had been exposed to before. But their talks had been mostly superficial.

During the recent call she told him that she wished she might see him again; her desire was blurted out before she'd even thought about it. Or had he suggested the idea previously, she couldn't remember?

With scant variation her daily routine persisted—up every morning at 5:30, cold shower, prayer, a brisk thirty-minute walk, and then up to the counseling hall to grab an armful of files and a muffin before back-to-back meetings.

Her first session this morning at seven would likely be a complete nonstarter because the women at that hour were generally half asleep, uninterested, hostile, or all three. But today as she glanced down to the file, she thought that her first meeting might be different.

Why would a judge send a medical student here?

As she approached the door she found the answer—assault and battery.

Despite her anxiety she straightened her habit and entered.

***

The Reverend Mother had long ago released her anger over Sarah's headstrong and dishonest actions. Among her students over the years Sarah had proven herself to be the most resolute and resourceful, accomplishing the near impossible. As a result, she prayed earnestly that her exile would pass quickly.

The world needs more stubborn committed and holy doctors to wage war against sickness, she said aloud as she fingered her olive wood Rosary beads.

Suddenly remembering an earlier message from the headmistress where Sarah was serving, the Reverend Mother returned the call.

"Sister Grace, may peace be unto you."

"And unto you Reverend Mother."

Never one for small talk, the Reverend Mother went straight to the point.

"I received your message Sister Grace regarding Sarah's request to meet her father when he visits next week from New York. I think it would be a fine idea. I'm not concerned about her overstepping that small freedom. In your message you indicated that the meeting would be manageable. You have my permission to arrange it properly as you see fit. Go with God, Sister Grace."

Sister Grace was convinced that the best meeting place would be at St. Phillip's Church located not far from the counseling facility. There she would keep Sister Sarah surrounded by priests and nuns from the order, just in case her criminal father harbored evil intentions.

Sarah waited quietly in her space on the mahogany pew. She'd been allowed a sixty-minute reprieve from counseling duties, and she intended to use her time wisely. From her zippered inner pocket, she removed the list of seventy-five questions that she'd written out in cursive. She needed to hear his answer to each one.

She rechecked her list while uncertainty surfaced again. Would she ever really know him as a father; would his answers bridge the enormous gap in time between them; would they be good friends? As anxiety increased, she pulled out the narrow bench in front of her shins and knelt to pray.

Stewart arrived at the address and was startled when the soaring church complex loomed before him. Then again, she is a nun, where else he asked?

He found his way through the gaping front entrance and took a seat on a pew near the middle of the naive and waited.

His eyes were drawn to the carved vaulted ceilings, to the stout cedar beams, and to the immaculately rendered stained glass panes. Within that imposing frame vast frescos, tapestries, and the mesmerizing gravitas of Catholicism confronted his Jewish sensibilities. Having never been a temple-going Jew, however, the feeling of alien strangeness quickly passed along with his nausea from the acrid odor of frankincense.

Looking ahead, he idly wondered whether his daughter was among the forty or so nuns quietly gathering within the front pews. Minutes later two dozen or so left the group and filed silently to the rear of the church

Sarah stood up from her prayers and looked back to the long narrow vault of the church. She easily spotted him while he continued scanning the sanctuary for her.

She approached with her head bowed in prayer while peaking up every so often.

"Father, thank you for coming."

She had surprised him despite his mental preparation.

"Well, thank you for inviting me, Sarah. This is strange for me," he said, looking around.

"It really is," he said. "I must confess; not in the Catholic sense of course, don't call a priest over.''

She smiled at his joke.

He wanted to hug her, but he held off— unsure of himself, a rare feeling.

"We can sit over there off to the side father; it will be mostly private."

They shared a pew and turned to face each other.

"Sarah, I must tell you this straight away now that we're face-to-face again. I didn't believe your mother years ago when she said she was pregnant. The idea of having a child was so…alien to me. I was just thinking selfishly, stuck in my own needs, and living with the fear of a long stretch behind bars. I shut the possibility of you out completely. I'm sorry. I know that sounds weak."

She was relieved to hear it and encouraged by his openness. He'd answered her most important question.

"I thought about you often over the years father. I wondered what you looked like and why you had abandoned me. I think I even may have hated you for part of that time. Men are supposed to be the head of the household, which of course we never had and part of me blamed you for everything. But I became determined to find you; out of anger at first. Along the way during my search, I forgave you."

Stewart looked at her with wide-eyed wonderment. That she had come from his seed, was a living part of him, was difficult to grasp. He had to remind himself that his feelings were unique to his circumstances and that fathers usually met their children first as babies rather than waiting until they reached their twenties.

"We can't salvage the past Sarah. That makes me hugely sad. There are so many times that we simply will never be able to share. But you know that reality also makes me determined to redeem the present. What can I do for you or with you? Do you need any help?"

"I very much agree with that. The past will remain the past and we can never change that. It saddens me also that we've wasted so much time that cannot be reclaimed."

With a trace of disaffection, she answered his other question.

"I have everything that I need right now. Thank you for asking."

"Would you mind if I asked you some questions, father?"

"Go right ahead, ask away."

She unfolded her paper and methodically began going through her list, often scribbling notes in the margin.

Even though he hadn't anticipated a rigorous interrogation, Stewart patiently answered.

After fifty minutes she looked down at her small watch. She put away her notes and looked at him. She decided to finally ask the question that had been on her mind since the day she first saw him.

"Father, I don't want to pry, so forgive me if it seems that I am, but how did you know that Mr. Chauncey Smith and you were...well that you would be so close."

Instinctively she lowered her head.

"It's okay Sarah. I'm glad you asked and perhaps I understand a little why you would be curious. Let's just say that Chauncey and I have a commonality of spirit. It took me longer than him though to understand my own needs and desires. Chauncey had figured that out for himself way earlier. I would say that I finally decided to follow my heart and let go of convention."

He stopped there because he was unsure of what lay ahead between them.

She almost asked a follow up question; but she was running out of time.

"Thanks for letting me ask you about so many different things. I appreciate your honesty. I also can tell from your responses that you are very bitter about the past. I have no way of understanding that. But I know that we are only made whole if we forgive those who have transgressed against us. Your feelings of revenge against those that you perceive wronged you will work against you and may well destroy you," she said.

Stewart couldn't help himself; he lost his patience as he always did upon hearing the moralistic absolutes spewed by organized religion. He responded more harshly than he intended.

"I can't really expect you to grasp my feelings or my decisions. Your life has been mostly sheltered from the economic unfairness and manipulation by the ruling class that I mentioned in some of my answers. You see, the world around you and its constant comforting allusions to democratic freedom and religious pluralism is a phony lie, one created by the extremely wealthy few. Organized religion has always been one of the greatest enablers of that lie."

"The truth is that the very few at the top allow the rest of us to view only enough of the real underlying picture to keep us striving—working hard, saving, slowly advancing, if at all. Now they've allowed legalized drugs and marijuana to cloud things over even more; keep the masses drugged up and happy; they won't see the strike-out pitch coming, let alone strike three. And all the while in plain sight that same privileged few covet the vast portion of the spoils for themselves because the population is hypnotized by specious entertainment, tribalism, sports, or religion."

Stewart lowered his voice, but his agitation increased.

"You need to know that I'll do what I must do to level this warped playing field that we exist within. I refuse to be petted on the head and lied to like I'm ignorant about what's really happening in this country, in this world. I'll take back some of what's mine—steal it and yank it away just like the robber barons of old—the ones that everyone worships today after their Madison Avenue makeovers."

"Chauncey and I deserve that much after all the time that we spent in the pen. The lawyers will do it for us."

He smiled broadly, trying unsuccessfully to soften the hard blows.

Singed by his anger, Sarah stood up and backed away from him.

She waved goodbye weakly before running to the rear of the church from where Sister Grace and many others had been keeping a watchful eye.

The following day Sarah used more than half of the call with her mother to talk about him and share her concerns about his plans for vengeance. Melinda was torn between wanting to support her daughter and her understanding that being at the bottom of the economic ladder was a crushing burden, one that often lead to envy and poor choices.

She chose to say nothing and listen.

Sarah used the rest of the call to talk excitedly about the tall woman that she'd counseled who'd been suspended from medical school.

"She's a good person mother. She's not Catholic but from what she shared with me so far, she was raised in a Christian home where faith and belief were important. I think that's a big part of her make-up even though she doesn't admit to it. Her name is BG."

"It's amazing to me Sarah that you would be counseling someone who was admitted into the same medical school where you were accepted."

"We'll be enrolled together next year," Sarah replied excitedly.

"We would have been in the same classes if we didn't each have our own issues to sort out. So anyway, I'll only be a semester behind her. And she's even offered to share her first semester medical books and labs equipment with me for no cost. That'll save me at least two thousand dollars."

"What about her family; where're they from and what do they do for a living?"

"They're from Albany, New York. BG's father runs a national kid's organization from there as I recall her mother heads a medical company of some type. They're African American. "

"That's wonderful Sarah, I'm glad you've found someone your own age to share your feelings with. But I suppose your relationship is less as friends and much more as patient counselor, right? How often will you meet with her?"

"Well, she must complete three hundred hours of counseling, so we'll be meeting three times a week for the rest of this year and a good chunk of next year. She also must take specialized counseling sessions during that time as well. Those are taught here by the nuns that have advanced degrees."

"The funny thing about our session mother was that we clicked right away. Unlike most of my other sessions, BG wasn't intent on trying to pull the wool over my eyes. And guess what, she was feeling sorry for herself at one point. So, I said wait a minute, before you complain anymore, try this family history on for size."

"After she heard my story, she started looking at the brighter side of things."

"That's wonderful," Melinda said cheerfully, even though she felt the sting from the remark. "Relationships are a precious gift, I'm happy for you."

"I'm going to say goodbye now Sarah before they cut the line on us again."

"Goodbye mother. God bless."

"Thank you, Sarah"

After Melinda hung up, she couldn't quite put her finger on what was troubling her. There was something about BG's family that Sarah had mentioned; something ancient that eluded Melinda's recall.

Chapter Fifteen:
London Bridges

HAROLD GUIDED THE BLACK SEDAN through central London's fog bound streets with the skill of a thirty-year professional. His focus was interrupted when he thought he heard his employer ask him something. He checked the rear-view mirror only to see Mr. Howard deep in thought and staring out the window.

What the hell are you waiting for?

Joshua had asked the question out loud without realizing it as he continued to wrestle with the same issues involving Mirra.

He knew that she was smart, committed, gorgeous, and that she loved him as much as he loved her. He never had to worry about his back around her. While occasionally she might display indifference about what they meant to each other, from personal experience he knew that she was fierce in her devotion. She would always do what she thought was best for him, regardless of the consequences for herself.

Then why shouldn't they tie the knot he asked as his mind churned the question again?

Because it takes two to Tango he replied responding once again with the same answer.

He flicked off the AC and opened the rear window enough to let in some air along with Knightsbridge street sounds. It was early evening as they passed a few of Mirra's favorite shops, ones where she had occasionally dragged him inside while they were out on a casual stroll.

He smiled as he thought about her; then he suddenly remembered a recent dust up between them. It happened after they'd arrived at a posh Mayfair address for an over-the-top soiree sponsored by the CEO of Platinum Investment Group.

Mirra's devotion and her intense protective nature were on full display then.

The hostess was the CEO's wife, his third and last, he would often proudly remark. She was stunningly statuesque, well over six feet tall. She also wore the latest fashion and bobbles from haut courtier Parisian houses. Chiseled Afro-Asian features and alluringly applied makeup rounded out her dazzling appearance. She personally greeted Mirra and Joshua in the reception room of the grand estate after they arrived.

It became playful repartee with her from the first introduction. He found her to be quietly charming, friendly, and hyper attentive to his every word. She quickly felt like a trusted friend, or so he believed. She summoned her head butler with the snap of her manicured fingers and instructed him to by-pass the checkroom to secure the coats within her private quarters. Since they weren't expensive items, Joshua had interjected that the special arrangements were much appreciated but completely unnecessary. Her rebuff was as smooth as the silk fabric that caressed her firm torso and hips; he could only accede to her wishes.

He smiled to himself again because he could still hear Mirra's sharp warning after they stepped into the gaily festooned ballroom to mingle with other guests.

Joshua, that woman is a polished professional whore, a slut, nonetheless. Her husband still has no idea, I suspect. She's in disguise apparently but her plan tonight is you. Simply for practice she'll want to clamp her snares—and her other well utilized equipment—onto you. Once you are in her web, she will determine how to exploit you. When she comes back at you later with the innocent request to escort her to her quarters to check on the status of the coats, I fully expect you to decline, come find me, and admit that I was right.

He remembered looking at Mirra back then as she squinted her eyes and squeezed his forearm. He nodded his head in agreement but only to appease what he assumed was misplaced jealousy. She didn't take his condescension lightly at the time.

Her prediction was confirmed, however, when the lady of the house approached him from behind thirty minutes later to suggest in a quiet voice whispered into his ear that they venture to her quarters to check up on everything, an invitation that he politely turned down.

Mirra was gracious after his confession, saying that she had confidence that he would have found the strength to resist the professional charmer even if he had ended up alone with her in her boudoir.

For his part Joshua was grateful that he hadn't been tested.

Why shouldn't he get married, he asked once more? Hadn't it been more than long enough to decide about Mirra, about each other? Hadn't they both kept their commitment to be faithful?

Deep down he knew that the marriage gene was in his own DNA. His images of a couple living, working, and apparently loving together were as old as his being. Two parents, a marriage, and one household, it was natural, right?

And that was why the seemingly perfect arrangement for some guys—shacking up in style with a beautiful, committed woman like Mirra with no strings attached—was sitting less and less easy with him.

Of course, he was aware that her circumstances growing up weren't anything like his own. On the rare occasions that she would open to him about her past, he had trouble even empathizing.

As she told it her father who by now was long dead of liver disease was a gigolo who had seeded a large swath of Jamaica and the Caribbean with his children. But he'd raised and nurtured none of them.

She derisively referred to him as that charming island rake, meaning someone who laid his head on all the willing and not so willing female pillows he could appropriate. Apparently, her father had plenty of money during his hay day, real hard currency from his work as a merchant seaman. Returning to port for him was essentially a long drunken party scene. She mentioned that occasionally he would make a brief stop at home.

He would toss a fistful of money at the kitchen table. The toss was usually way off, and he would stagger over to raid the refrigerator after that. Mirra recounted that her most vivid recollections were from peeking around the corner and watching him during those times.

The exclamation points to her father's irresponsible lifestyle emerged a few years ago when she met for the first time a grown half-sister in London at a Jamaican ex pat function. The woman was born on an island two hundred miles from Jamaica. Yet she had described Mirra's father to a tee as they casually chatted about childhood experiences.

Though the island rake had used a different last name, after comparing notes with her half-sister there was no doubt that when his ship was in that port he'd sired another set of children. But he was no more nurturing to his family there than he was in Jamaica.

Mirra had once shared with Joshua that she always wondered how many other families there were.

Joshua had abused her candor a few years back by joking that if he gave her five minutes with any other Caribbean woman, they would both know each other's entire life history and perhaps be related as well. She was angry after that, and he learned his lesson about how sensitive she was over her upbringing.

Her mother also contributed to the early scarring process. From what little Mirra had mentioned her mother seemed to have hardly missed the island rake when he was away. She had a well-timed rotation of male companions. But she made sure that none of the men touched her children. As a child, Mirra heard stories about the mysterious disappearance of one of them who had tried to ignore her mother's rule.

The only other thing that mother did well in Mirra's eyes was her strict insistence that her children bring home top grades.

As Joshua learned the full contours of Mirra's story over the years he accepted that the mother and father concept meant an entirely different thing to her. Hugs, genuine affection, and pep talks were unknown phenomenon in her life. Despite his own frequent objections to how he'd been brought up he damn sure knew that he had involved parents and that they were committed to him and his sisters.

Lack of a nurturing upbringing had left Mirra with an occasionally defensive edge. He believed that it was a kind of emotional damage that would make her pull away when he wanted to be closer. At times he wondered whether she was capable, without a model from her past, of being committed to him in the manner that he'd always assumed would be normal between spouses.

At the same time, he recognized that there was an amazing emotional depth within her as well. He'd seen ample evidence of her caring and selflessness over many years in the way she treated the children and the staff at the warehouse.

In the end he decided to try to create the outcome for both of them that he held in his own mind and imagination, because he loved her as she was and wanted their commitment to each other to be formal in nature and permanent in duration.

Time to man up and ask for her hand in marriage he finally concluded. If she says no, just deal with it. And anyway, he asked himself how long was he going to keep that engagement ring hidden before she accidently found it during one of her redesign-the-townhouse frenzies?

It was also time to come clean with his mother and father. They needed to hear about his love and commitment for her; after all, she was their future daughter-in-law.

He leaned forward.

"Do me a favor Harold and stop over at that little specialty shop across the street from the Herod's main entrance. This is a day for sweet treats and flowers for the lady of the house."

***

Jemal had never been as busy in his life as he was now at university. The awards and back slapping from his graduation ceremony and after party had faded well into the past. At Oxford, none of his previous accolades mattered. He was merely one among three thousand entering freshman. And everybody around him seemed to be as bright or brighter than he was.

Yet despite the extant pressures, he had followed through on his idea to revitalize the African charity work utilizing the warehouse as his base. Boss had supported him one hundred percent just as Mirra predicted.

The Senegal mission children continued to strive and were on track to double sales. A favorable national election had also resulted in less concern over government suppression in the future.

It hadn't taken him long to solve the distribution challenges posed by his eastern most outpost, the isolated Ethiopian village. The old chief had turned out to be his principal ally as well as a shrewd negotiator. The chief had leveraged the bounty of left behind medical supplies to gain acceptance for the plan from other trusted chiefs in the region.

The reticent adults in the village had also stepped up. Once again, they were in touch with the outside world. They proceeded to build a corresponding adult and children's network. They received in return a renewed sense of hope from serving as extended family for many of the children from other villages.

Yet despite those fantastic results Jemal had started to wonder if he'd bitten off too much with Kid Genius! The reality confronting him was that he was fighting for his academic life at Oxford.

But whenever he thought about quitting and turning the whole thing over to one of the seniors back at the warehouse, he would remember the faces of the kids that first greeted him at the Senegalese mission. And there were the periodic updates he'd receive from them about how the business had been growing. Occasionally they sent him personal emails to keep him abreast of their comings and goings.

Because of it he persevered.

At Oxford the primary challenge facing him was one he hadn't expected, his own inner drive to succeed. His occasional feelings of malaise and disorientation made him fully appreciate that Joshua, Mirra and the rest had provided an emotional buffer and the needed motivational encouragement against the reality of his true social and financial position.

That he was a poor orphaned kid with relatively few advantages in life very rarely crossed his mind when he was in London. His mind and body were fortified.

At university, however, there were no daily trips to a safe space after school and no words of encouragement or challenge to get him psyched up and to keep him engaged. And despite his scholarship and reasonably comfortable financial circumstances, for the first time the full scope of economic disparity and generational privilege were revealed to him as he observed the astounding wealth and resources of some of his fellow students.

He had earnestly sought to branch out and build a personal network to help him integrate into university life. Some time ago he'd signed up for the computer club and the math club; both were supposed to be good contact and support groups based on what he'd heard during orientation. He did the same with the science and history clubs. All the groups had aggressively marketed their advantages to incoming freshman at the festive orientation sessions.

But he hadn't received so much as a peep back from any of them after he hand-delivered his applications. He'd stopped waiting.

There was one group that did accept him; they were all members of his advanced software class. Their eyes had gleamed bright together at the assembly hall when Oxford faculty had issued its annual technology challenge to freshmen, especially when the faculty mentioned the grand prize of fifteen hundred pounds for each student on the winning team.

In Jemal's eyes it was a fortune.

The team he ended up joining was comprised of five other freshmen.

As chance would have it, they were all standing close to one another during the faculty announcement. All had been top math and science student at their respective high schools. Most of them were immediately filled with hubris at the possibility of placing first.

Some of them had started yammering out load that the university should just assign the prize to them and spare the rest of the students wasting time. That self-confident attitude was contagious and soon several of them suggested joining up together to form a team. The only common denominator at that point was brainpower and openness to working with others from different backgrounds.

Fifty separate teams—Oxford's best and brightest science and math freshman— were assigned a question from the panel of cyber and computer professors. Judging criteria promised to be rigorous. All solutions and proofs would be due in sixty days. The teams would utilize every bit of their spare academic time to complete the project.

Or just maybe Jemal later admitted he'd joined the team because of a shy pretty student from Liverpool. He had seen Wilma raise her hand to be a team member before he had decided to raise his own.

They were a talented and eclectic group, feeding off one another's energy and brilliance and the reality that they each had serious plans for the cash.

Jemal had finally found his much-needed social lifeline.

At the end of another exhausting day of labs and classes he was on the way back to his dormitory. Passing by the student union he noticed a vibrant flyer taped to the glass door. The green, gold, and red colors lured him and the message on the face of the brochure struck a chord.

If you love and miss the real Ethiopia as much as we do, join us for a celebration this evening!

He'd been exposed back in London to several Ethiopian parties. Yet the underlying social messages from the hosts were just suspicious clutter to him at the time. He'd often joke with his high school friends that they should be wary of malware trying to infect their software. It was the way of politics he'd always comment.

One thing that he had figured out in high school was that the social slogan shouters shared a common trait—recruitment. Join my intellectual gang of protestors or my boots-on-the-ground army. Those strident enticements had never appealed to him, maybe because he was largely ignorant about the real passions and issues boiling below the surface.

His dismissive attitude about politics had been tempered by his trip back home. He'd seen first-hand the impact that those running the country could have on ordinary people.

But as he looked again at the lively messages within the colorful brochure there were no political slogans or attacks against past or current government policies. It seemed to merely be a wonderful opportunity to celebrate.

On a whim he called Wilma to see if she would join him at the event since they had spent many hours working together in the lab and had gotten along. Jokingly he promised her good food and good music with the added benefit of his culturally enriching presence as a native son of Ethiopia. To his great delight she accepted. They met outside of her dorm dressed in the Oxford freshman fall uniform—jeans, sneakers, sweatshirts, jackets, and umbrellas for later.

He had no problem holding forth about his interests and passions while they strolled across campus. Wilma on the other hand was quiet and borderline shy. He had to draw her out with humor and word play. Later he got her to admit with a nod that she was as lost as he was on the vast campus.

At one point he turned to her with a serious expression. He opened up, sharing his happy memories about when he had received his number in his admission package last spring along with names for all three thousand freshmen in the class. Everyone was listed by academic rank in the documentation he said, which had greatly surprised him. He was ranked seventh in the class, he modestly admitted. He asked her whether it was true that her class rank number was eighteen hundred and fourteen as shown in the paperwork. He was certain that there was some error because after personally witnessing her first-rate work in the lab it didn't make sense.

Seeing the predictable embarrassment on her face he cracked up; he pointed at her while backing away and laughing even more. Wilma joined in but she was already plotting a creative way to pay him back for his clever little ruse.

As they talked more Wilma shared that she was from a middle-class family, the middle child of two teachers. Nothing remarkable about that she said, maybe other than being lucky to inherit a good chromosome set from them.

What was her most exciting thing in life so far, he asked?

Delivering the valedictorian address to her class, she answered quietly. That was awesome.

Her modest way of mentioning it earned Jemal's respect and admiration.

Wilma was speechless when Jemal revealed more about his personal life and explained the real reason he was in England without any family except Fatima. It made her suspect that his sunny outward demeanor compensated for his painful past.

Just before they arrived at the cultural center, he asked her quietly how it felt to have the very same mother, father, sister, and brother all throughout her life. She shrugged her shoulders and said that it just felt normal. She thought she saw a flicker of sadness when he turned his face away from her before leading them up the stairs to the party hall.

Lively music spilled through the open doors to greet them. Inside the entire area was suffused with displays and the aroma of vegetable stew, lamb, plantain, Doro Wot, and many other dishes that Jemal recognized. Wilma noticed from his posture how it all visibly lifted his spirits even before he turned and told her happily that he couldn't wait to taste everything.

To Mirra's senses the aromas were blended but he took the time to explain the characteristics of each one. With her appetite peaked she looked forward to skipping the evening blandness at the freshman dining hall.

Yet despite the growing holes in their stomachs, they were drawn to the many elaborate booths throughout the main hall. Every nook and cranny were decorated with artwork, easels, and visual presentations. Scientific, technological, and military displays were especially prominent. Every display that they passed told the story of ancient and modern Ethiopia. They laughed and joked with each other that only true nerds would look at anything else before raiding the food tables.

Food stations lined along the far-left wall were doing a vigorous business. As they approached, they noticed that at least half a dozen other tables were stacked with liquors and wines. Each one had wait staff present that were pouring drinks freely for anyone who approached, which seemed odd to them given the drinking age restrictions on campus.

Looking around Wilma estimated that at least four hundred students were present. Most were in groups of four or six and everyone was having a wonderful time. He had never seen anything like it before.

They finally cued up in the food line and before long started serving themselves ample portions from the wealth of choices, piling plates high. Afterwards they both accepted a glass of wine and moved gingerly out of the main traffic flow while carefully guarding their gastronomic treasures. Jemal was feeling pretty good about his hunch and the reality that the event had turned out to be perfect. He was happy as well that Wilma seemed to be having a great time.

Very little conversation happened between them as they focused on their plates.

That they were both teetotalers was soon apparent. Neither one of them drank more than a sip of the wine. Wilma placed her glass discretely aside and she caught Jemal trying to conceal his glass next to a napkin holder. She joked with him about it, and he smiled back, confessing that the wine was much too strong for his mind.

When they finished, they spent several minutes lamenting that they would revert to cafeteria meals the next day. In protest they toyed with the idea of packing up another huge plate of food to take with them. But without refrigeration the plan didn't make sense.

"Maybe dry ice from the lab," Wilma suggested with a furrowed brow.

He realized that she was serious.

They talked about the challenges involved with accessing the lab after hours and quickly constructing a divided small container for the dry ice and food. Then they recognized the necessity for spiriting it all away without attracting attention at the lab or from anyone around them now.

Before they could fashion a solution, a loud rousing cheer erupted from the other end of the hall. They pushed their empty plates aside and along with everyone else around them headed in that direction.

Scores of students were ahead of them, the atmosphere was electric. A band with a male and female singer had set up on the other side of a parquet floor. The rhythm and vocals had many couples up and dancing. He asked Wilma if she wanted to *cut a rug a*nd to his surprise she grabbed his elbow, and they made their way to the middle of the floor. Her movements were athletic and graceful, and he found himself staring at her compact and curvy figure more than once. She caught him shyly giving her the once over a few times. She wasn't reluctant about watching his moves either as he gyrated his long thin frame to the beats.

The more they danced the more they realized that they didn't recognize anybody else around them or even elsewhere in the hall for that matter. As far as he could tell from complexion, facial features and dress the crowd seemed to be all Ethiopian or east African students, except of course for Wilma. Maybe it was just par for the course given the enormous size of the campus, he guessed.

It wasn't long before he spotted several tall men in the distance over Wilma's head. They'd entered from a side door in a loose formation. Each was outfitted in an old-fashioned pea green military uniform. They methodically made their way to the front where an elevated platform had already been moved into place. After the troop was positioned around it the music stopped and a spotlight illuminated the stage.

Everyone in the hall pressed forward.

A tan-skinned nattily dressed adolescent with sharp bird-like features stepped into the spotlight. There were huge applause and cheers. Wilma and Jemal joined in with the clapping without having any idea who he was.

The hall grew very quiet after that. Almost in unison everyone clasped their hands together and bowed deeply from the waist. That only lasted a few seconds before the boy man bowed his head ever so slightly in reply.

Then he started to address them in slow measured tones. Even without a microphone his voice was deeply resonant and powerful. Despite his young age, it was apparent that he was a well-practiced speaker.

Wilma and Jemal listened carefully to the words that were at first very inviting and welcoming. He praised the students and he praised Ethiopia. He said that he looked forward to attending future events celebrating *his* land.

After that the speech veered off course. Harsher terms were used to describe the current government. He spoke forcefully about reuniting *his* sacred land with the rule of the people and their rightful leaders. Everything he said evoked cascading chants and cheers of approval. Just to blend in Wilma and Jemal offered their own approbation, but it felt awkward because they had no idea why what he said was such a big deal.

Before long the boy man started his final push. At first his phrases were highly optimistic—united together, advancing peace and prosperity, feeding the poor and dispossessed.

But the final part of the talk burned both of their ears. The young prince began to speak forcefully about racial purity and bloodlines and heritage. He continued in a higher pitch as he declared himself and his words ordained by the gods of Ethiopia. Then he boldly proclaimed that he was indeed God in human form before raising his right hand into the spotlight where it seemed to shimmer and glow. By then he appeared to have thoroughly hypnotized the crowd that watched him slack-jawed.

The boy man began to stir and chant, speaking in a singsong manner as if possessed. He called out the stain of white Europeans on his land. They alone, he claimed, had exploited his country's wealth, and corrupted its current leadership. As the crowd grew more frenzied, he cried out for a global, God-inspired, blood purge of all white Europeans and their kin that had profited from the exploitation, no matter where they may be found. He repeated that call, following up with a chilling slay the white devils chant that was aped throughout the hall.

A throaty roar went up from everyone around them after they had feasted on the phrase for several minutes.

Wilma and Jemal on the other hand were conspicuous behind frozen faces. They had no doubt that their phlegmatic response to the messenger of hate would soon out them to the mob.

It occurred to Jemal that maybe the prince had failed to notice Wilma. Or maybe he had noticed and didn't care at all about the possible danger into which his words may have placed her.

Casually moving away, they made their way to the back of the hall and quickly escaped using the rear stairs.

Once outside Jemal looked at Wilma sheepishly and mumbled his apologies for bringing her to something so unfriendly. Maybe he was just grasping at straws, he admitted.

Wilma said that she could very well take him to the same kind of *party* back in some of the neighborhoods of her hometown—"hate was just hate," she said

"It's just blind bigotry, nothing more Jemal. I know you meant well."

He looked at her and nodded, still in shock. They headed home in silence.

Halfway to the dorms she reached out to hold his hand.

Jemal was excited about his return to the warehouse to see his favorite adults along and his Kid-Genius! crew. Over the past three months he'd been able to recruit seven students. Even though he had orchestrated the whole thing from Oxford, he much preferred seeing them in person.

He was also looking forward to seeing the gang at the Lutheran orphanage, including the brothers who had tried their best over the years to keep his personality boxed in and tamped down. But most of all he realized as he gathered the last of his things into his shoulder bag and zipped in his laptop, he would miss seeing Wilma every day.

She'd left for Liverpool that morning.

Darkness was settling over the city when his bus arrived in London. He transferred to the underground Tube and rode it out to the closest warehouse stop, choosing not to check in at the orphanage first. Mirra had promised to have Harold drop him and Fatima back there after the get together.

He'd taken the same route on the Tube for many years. But this trip that had him returning as a university student felt different. He knew that for all intents and purposes he looked the same; but he sure felt like things were altered inside of him. He wondered whether the kids would treat him that way after seeing him in person. As he thought about it, he figured it out—as long as there were snacks at the party his physical presence would be mostly unnoticed.

After leaving the station he started the two-mile walk. Darkness firmly controlled the run-down neighborhoods at this hour. Despite that the shroud of night the squalor was more noticeable to him, more ominous. As he trudged along through narrow streets and back alleyway shortcuts it dawned on him that all he'd seen for months before were the beautifully tended gardens and soaring gothic architecture of Oxford and its surroundings. This is definitely not that he noted, picking up his pace.

The already chilly temperature was dropping; the cold was reinforced by moisture that would soon turn into London fog. Windows along his path were closed tight and heating units were cranking. With disgust he inhaled the arresting smell of cigarettes, warm ale, and piss, all of which were stronger near each dank tavern that he passed. They seemed to dot almost every corner, with few patrons hanging around outside tonight.

The last shortcut was a deserted half-mile cobblestone cut through that snaked past the rear entrances of uniformly shabby boarding houses. From them spilled the muted sounds of children playing, coughing, arguments, and televisions. Before him the path was lined on both sides with head-high bush and overgrowth. The dense surrounding shrubs always gave the route a claustrophobic feel.

He was surprised as he walked along that nearly all the pole lamps that hung stiffly above him every few meters were burned out, leaving large pools of darkness rather than light along the path. It forced him to slow down and pick his way using the muted glow from tenement windows. He grew irritated that the city hadn't taken the time to replace the bulbs.

Glancing up he saw that the glass had been shattered, leaving ominous jagged shards stabbing from the edges of the metal fixtures. Every lamp that he passed had suffered the same fate.

Destroyed not burned out, he wondered why.

As he tried to figure that out, he heard heavy footfalls from the bushes off to his right and the only thing he was certain about was that they were closer and louder. Flying bodies barreled into him before he could react. slamming him hard to the ground. His legs and arm were hemmed up by vise-like grips. Before he could cry out his mouth was stuffed with an oily rag triggering a gag reflex. As he choked and coughed the tightening of thin strips of plastic bound his ankles and wrists. His briefest glimpse of his attackers was cut off by a foul-smelling, dirt covered mask yanked roughly over his head.

While laughing and panting, two beefy skinheads repeatedly smashed their weight down on top of Jemal's prone body, driving his into the concrete. Others cut his bag from his shoulder and rummaged through it.

Breathing had become impossible now without sucking more dirt into his lungs. Gagging repeatedly, he was passing out.

The last sounds that he heard were the roars of celebration from the plunder of his shoulder bag.

$$***$$

After receiving the call about Jemal's emergency room admittance Joshua quickly pulled up an online hospital schematic and located the floor and nurses' station where he was being treated. Shortly after that he was on the phone with the supervising nurse until he arrived at the ward. By that time, she was more than happy to pass him off to the physician.

And now for the third time he was calmly stating his requirements to the attending doctor and demanding an immediate response.

The doctor started to waiver under the pressure, but he continued to object that moving Jemal all the way across town to

Kensington Memorial was out of the question given the hour. He conceded that it could be arranged very first thing in the morning. Nevertheless, Joshua persisted, even threatening to have the hospital's certification reviewed by the district magistrate for medical accreditation. His ability to mention that official by name got the intended result. He and Mirra peeked into the crowded ward and watched the sedated teenager being bundled up for the move.

Jemal's transfer and admittance had long taken place by the time they completed the paperwork at the old hospital to authorize it. Harold later dropped them off at the entranceway of the new facility. Jemal was awake but groggy when they entered his private room and rushed to his bedside.

"Jemal," Joshua said with a big smile trying his best to appear cheerful, "what've we always told you about dramatic entrances; your return from university was over the top."

He looked up drowsily. His forehead was bandaged, and part of his face was obscured behind a thick gauze wrap that partially concealed two neat lines of stiches high on each jaw. His eye sockets were puffy, yet his eyes seemed otherwise undamaged. But his cheeks were badly swollen and apparently scraped raw beneath the gauze. The left arm was encased in a big fiberglass elbow cast that was supported by a well-wrapped sling.

Nevertheless, Jemal was defiant.

"Boss, I had to be sure to capture on my return everyone's attention. It's just my way, you know this."

Mirra leaned over and hugged him, gingerly avoiding the plaster contraption. She sat on the bed and hugged him again while Joshua squeezed him lightly around his shoulders.

Despite his embarrassment at being fussed over, he hugged back with his good arm.

That's when Mirra noticed that his hair had been shaved completely off in the back.

"What happened to your head, Jemal," she asked while patting the area gingerly?

"It's shaved clean back here; were you hit with something?"

"No, the ruffians decided for some reason that I only deserved a half skin-head haircut, I don't plan to be around for them to apply that other half."

He shifted heavily in the bed; they helped him sit up higher.

"The doctors say I'll be in this fiberglass prison for six weeks until the break heals. And of course, you both must sign it before leaving," he said that as he struggled to raise his cast up.

"The good news is that the damage to my face won't need anything beyond the stiches and time. The Doctors say I was fortunate to escape with only this."

"Damn lucky, indeed. What were they after, other than mindless mayhem," Joshua said?

"I think they were searching for the laptop all along. Once they ripped it out of the zipped inner pocket the last thing I remember was hearing the cheering."

That worried Joshua, a lot.

" We're definitely going to have to make some changes to our security to keep the kids safe on their way to and from the warehouse. Most of them travel with one of our loaner laptops as you well know."

"Were you able to give the police any description of the thugs," Mirra asked?

"Only that there were at least five or six of them, skinheads. And the fat ones who crushed me must have weighed sixteen stone apiece."

Jemal suddenly noticed Mirra's left hand and ring finger that she seemed to be holding slightly levitated away from her body as if it were powered by some invisible force field. He grabbed at it and held it high up while feigning blindness from the ring's platinum setting and diamond luster.

"My God," he exclaimed with theatrical drama, "what have we here; booty from the Jewel House at the Tower of London, no doubt?"

Mirra blushed before plugging him back.

"Not at all; we only got engaged several weeks ago because we had to make certain that you had truly left town for school; only then did Joshua felt comfortable spending money on extras."

Jemal looked at them, turning serious.

"Congratulations to both of you."

"Ms. Mirra is a great catch boss, and you're not bad at all either."

He smiled through the gauze as best he could. After that they filled him in on how they'd reached the decision to get hitched. At the end Jemal said light-heartedly that he would remember the learning in case he ever faced a similar situation in the future. The comment caught Mirra by surprise because as long as she'd known him girls had never been on his radar. She wondered what was going on up at Oxford.

After a while Joshua couldn't help turning back to what was on his mind.

"About the warehouse Jemal, you know first-hand that the entire area around it has been in a tailspin for years. With that in mind Mirra and I recently met with an exploratory committee that will help us expand the facility—new space for us, construction jobs for the community, and maybe a kick start for the whole area. We're also thinking seriously about going public to site other schools in southern England. But none of that matters if we can't solve the safety issue."

As he heard himself explaining the plan to Jemal he realized that his favorite kid from the old days had grown up into a young man, one fully capable of digesting complicated planning and perhaps also assisting in the execution.

"That expansion will take some really big bucks right," Jemal asked?

"Yes. Eventually we'll need to pull in north of three million pounds," Mirra said.

"But that'll take some time," Joshua said. "Right now, we're still biased toward our current space. Yet we may be forced to move the location to get the footprint that we need. And after what happened to you, we have to deploy some kind of transportation option to get the kids safely to and from in the short term."

"It's sounds huge and exciting." Jemal said while he tried to sit up straighter against his softening pillows.

"Unfortunately, I'll be in university during the early part of it. But you can count on me for support, particularly during the summers. But remember, the old building has one advantage that's hard to replace."

"What's that," they both asked simultaneously

"It's located where the real needs are. All I had to do was take the Tube and walk to the place—there in forty minutes. Please don't go too far from the blight with your expansion plans. The kids that need help the most could be shut out."

They would heed his warning.

"A little lower please honey; I think I pulled it two days ago when I was doing those Tai lunges with my trainer at Albert Hall. This may finally teach me a lesson about getting on board fads."

He had been kneading her lower back muscles for thirty minutes while she lay face down on the massage table, keeping the same pressure and rhythm despite his cramping fingers. Rolling her thin workout top higher, he extended his strokes to the scapula.

"You're tight as a drum sweetie. I'm going to add a little more oil, but I think a warm Epson salt bath might be just what's needed before bed tonight."

Painfully, she shifted over on her side and looked up at him.

"You're just trying to get me worked up thinking about what might happen after the relaxing bath Mr. Howard, aren't you?"

"Well forgive me if that's my preference love," he smiled slyly.

She rolled over completely to sit up and hold him despite the tightness.

His arms supported her.

Moments like this made her happy that he was her man and she had been trying for a while to make sure that he knew she was, forcing herself to cleave away the occasional acerbic blasts that he didn't deserve.

But at the same time, she had been feeling increasingly anxious of late, something inside didn't feel right. After dismissing the cyclical calendar explanations and eliminating pregnancy as a cause, she was stumped. Whatever it was it had caused her to endure several evenings of fretful sleep. At least she hadn't awakened him.

On top of everything else she'd confirmed that she was carrying around a slightly elevated temperature. Her anxiety had been there for several days, and now dampened her desire to make love.

She finally realized that it had to be her disquietude over his upcoming schedule that was causing the symptoms.

Is that what true love means, she asked herself— am I experiencing premature separation anxiety? You fall apart when you know that you'll be away from your man for an extended time.

"Joshua, I knew that the Cup races in America were going to take a big piece of your time, but I honestly didn't think you would be gone for three whole months, and quite possibly longer than that."

"I'm sorry honey, I should have explained it more clearly. I did mention the time commitment over a year ago, but I'm not surprised that you don't recall that slice of the discussion. Basically, it's a three round competition, three months all in give or take. There's the first round series against the other UK syndicates; that will take several weeks. Then the open competition against other national challengers following that— taking three, maybe even four weeks. And we've got to prevail there, of course. The winner goes on to challenge the Americans which could be decided in as few as four straight race wins, less than a week."

"I remember it vaguely; you did explain all that to me, I'm sure," she admitted irritably; but she honestly couldn't focus her mind and remember it at all.

She scooted her hips forward to the end of the table and gingerly encircled her raised legs within her arms. She rested her chin on top of her knees.

Then she pulled him over, holding his hands as he faced her.

"I guess I just forgot, that's all. In my mind it was going to be you and your crew going to San Francisco to challenge the Yanks. I just had this erroneous belief that the whole thing would be over in three weeks. But you did walk me through the intricacies, I must have only half listened, sorry."

She reached out and touched his clean-shaven cheeks; she smiled at him bravely.

"I'm going to miss you terribly darling, and with this steep price you'd better win over there," she said wistfully.

"You know," she said, "we've never had a separation this long, a whole quarter of a year apart."

"And by the way, how can you leave the trading floor here for that amount of time? Won't your business suffer," she asked knowing how weak her objection sounded?

Joshua heard alarm bells go off; where was the Teflon armor that she always carried? Where was that casual indifference that occasionally signaled that she would make it regardless of the two of them being together?

"My business issues are the easiest part," he said.

"I can manage the trading desks using high speed links from San Francisco. I'll just operate in the local time zone here, which means a ton of late nights for me in the U.S. And don't forget, my London team is very seasoned. They understand my brokerage philosophy and they're well incented to execute it."

He moved in closer, gently messaged her shoulder blades as he hugged her.

"I'm also concerned about our extended time apart," he finally confessed.

"I'm not happy about it. You've got to come to the states with me. We'll find someone to run the warehouse and work with the fundraising folks on the building expansion. We can lease a small place in the Bay area. Deal?"

She gently pushed him back to arm's length while shaking her head.

"No deal honey. Finishing the planning and managing all the logistics are way too much for any fill-in manager. I've got to be here. Louise certainly can't do it all; you know that. And more importantly, each of those kids depends on us as a lifeline—both academically and emotionally—they need to see one of us here and involved during the front end of the transition. It's going to be a stressful enough change for them Joshua. I'm got to continue to be one of the stable factors in their lives."

He could feel her armor returning; he must have only imagined the kink. But even though he knew she was right, being away from her for so long wasn't an option that he wanted to accept.

He sat on the end of the bench with slumped shoulders. What she said was true the more he thought about it. It certainly would be a huge change for the kids without him even though he hadn't been an in-class instructor for several years. It made him question whether his whole desire to race for a damn gold-plated cup was one giant slice of self-indulgence. Was it worth risking the essential continuity that he had built up over the years with the kids?

"Hey honey," she said as she moved into his arms again, cradling his face in her hands.

"Don't think for a moment that I'm not supportive of your goals. You've got nothing to apologize for. Racing is in your blood; it's what you've always done."

He smiled back weakly.

"You're a good skipper," she said sincerely. "You're going and you're going to win. We'll manage on this end; and with the streaming video cam from your boat the kids will practically be there with you whenever they want to check in."

He hugged her tight for a long time. He'd needed that, her endorsement of his quest. He knew that she hadn't given it lightly.

"I love you," he said softly.

He kissed her long and slow and drew her in closer as his hands moved to her hips.

"But Mirra, darling, I do need you over there with me for some part of the time. Promise that you'll carve out at least a week, maybe two, and join me? We can't afford to become indispensable to anyone but each other—the kids will survive with the help of Louise and the team. She's really the original English nanny, as you well know. There's no better continuity than her."

She kissed him then pushed him gently back to arm's length. She was sterner than she meant to be.

"You'll be fine there, and I'll be fine here. Three months apart will fly by. Let's not over romanticize it, okay?"

It wasn't what she wanted to say at all. Seeing him in America if only briefly would have been wonderful. But deep down without fully understanding why she had already decided that it shouldn't happen.

Joshua always called it her prickly heat. She'd serve it up to him occasionally. It was an emotional barrier between them. Maybe it was there for her protection.

"No problem then," he said. "We'll make the best of it on each side of the pond. But you will miss me a little won't you," he asked?

She answered his question by pulling him in close again and with the rising heat from her body.

He gently removed her top and workout pants. She inhaled his fragrance as it mingled with her own. Then the surprising spasms rolled through her. She grabbed him closer, pulling at his waistband.

She caught her breath when he lifted her up like a ballerina in his arms before cradling her and kissing her fully on the lips.

She felt the firmness of the table beneath her back as his weight pressed down.

Chapter Sixteen: Premeditation

STEWART HAD ALWAYS FOUND THE LAWYERS he'd known early in his career to be a separate breed, different in both temperament and orientation than other business colleagues that he worked with. Overlooking their peculiarities, he had granted them a place among the necessary components needed to get deals done. Often though, their advice was hedged or timid. Nevertheless, they invariably expected an equal level of compensation as the other bankers and dealmakers; it was wishful thinking to which he never acceded.

So, at best the legal eagles were uneasy allies.

At this follow-up meeting with his attorney Leonard Salzman the last thing he wanted to hear was a song and dance about the chances for a favorable outcome from the lawsuit against *Sail Shape*. But that was exactly what he was being told as he sat impatiently in a richly appointed law office on West 57th Street. He started to worry about what value his twenty-thousand-dollar retainer was buying him.

"The truth of the matter is Stewart you correctly analyzed New York Trust law while you were in prison," the lawyer said dryly.

"Well, that's good to hear counselor," he said. "I had plenty of time to do that you know, a quarter century worth of time."

Leonard allowed himself a smile. He still wasn't accustomed to or comfortable with representing an ex-felon. But money was money and clients were harder to find now.

Leonard chose to deliver his next bit of advice in the simplest way possible.

"There is indeed a serious weakness in Carleton Smith's revocation of the trust document. But for our best case we need another witness. Otherwise, I must tell you, New York judges might reasonably rule against you."

Stewart was growing more impatient. But he calmed down, determined to get this right.

"So Leonard, what you're saying to me is that I need a witness who was aware of Carleton Smith's intent toward Chauncey at that time?"

"That's exactly right," Leonard replied while taking off his dark-rimmed glasses and smoothing his unruffled hair.

"You look as if you might have someone in mind, Stewart."

"I might know just the witness. Let me confirm that and get back to you."

"Good; now we need to talk about pressure points on the other side to force a capitulation and settlement before trial. I'm assuming that you're not wed to recovery of the actual real estate out on Long Island and would instead take a multi-million settlement?"

"Not a penny less than thirty million Leonard. That property—land alone— has got to be worth north of fifty million dollars after all these years."

As he said that he recognized that he would have to manage Chauncey's huge disappointment over not getting the actual land back.

"Perhaps it is, we'll know soon enough when the title search and appraisal come back. But equally important are two pressure points that our research shows might force the other side's hand and earn you a lucrative settlement."

"The first is a civil lawsuit against the camp and Brett Howard personally. We have a plaintiff; they're the parents of a girl that was at the girls' camp and who was hustled out before the *Sail Shape* boys arrived. The family wants to file a big money case claiming negligence and emotional distress. Their daughter was apparently quite distraught over missing her last couple of fun camp days because of the evacuation; of course I'm sure she was distressed about the shooting as well, I'll recommend that they add that to the complaint."

Stewart thought he saw a slight smile on Leonard's lips before he said the next part.

"Their attorney, a close colleague of mine by the way, will keep us in the background. Brett Howard will never know that in negotiating with either one of us any settlement price will include compensation for the other."

Stewart was encouraged, the strategy made perfect sense.

"That's what I wanted to hear Leonard, an aggressive approach. Get that other lawsuit filed ASAP. But you said there were two pressure points."

"I did, the second one is more…subtle. We've discovered that Howard is attempting to make a big purchase in California. He wants to buy out an existing marina and turn it into another *Sail Shape* operation. Pressure point number two Stewart is that you consider letting the dogs loose in idyllic Marin County."

"What's that mean exactly counselor," he asked?

Leonard finished cleaning his glasses and walked over to his standup desk next to his wide office windows. He opened the gray horizontal slats and looked down at the constant parade of stylish pedestrians and expensive cars along the broad street below.

He replied without turning around.

"It means that we need to put the fear of God into the white citizens out there. They've got to feel that the last thing they need is an invasion of poor urban kids to threaten the purity of their wives and daughters."

Stewart started to ask a follow-up question about exactly what type of activity was being contemplated but decided that not knowing was the safer alternative.

"Leonard, that idea is also very sound. Take whatever action you feel is necessary. No need to consult back with me."

***

Melinda couldn't figure out what he was up to. Out of the blue he had called and asked to meet, claiming that it was important and that it involved Sarah.

She still had a hard time accepting the fact that he was interested in Sarah's wellbeing even though she had long ago admitted that she couldn't really blame him for his denial of paternity. The fault was entirely with her back then.

In those days her distorted image of herself was that of the airy and brilliant party girl with an Ivy League MBA. She lived the high life on both the west and east coasts, a lavish lifestyle financed by her windfalls from scamming gambling casinos. What better way to utilize her business acumen, she would boast to close friends?

Her point of view was why wait for paychecks and stock options and savings when she could cash in immediately. Her lucrative casino hustle had made perfect sense—until she was busted and banned from them for life.

Her approach to things in her youth had always been loose and free, never letting the grass grow. She believed in her dreamscape imaginings that she would always float through life like a princess on a cloud.

Relationships with men were another one of her fantasies. Always keep them guessing was her mantra. So, she'd never let on to Stewart that she was in effect a monogamous woman, his woman. Instead, she projected the illusion of the carefree single girl, the brainy ingénue with men to spare. Admitting that she really loved him would have been a sign of boring conformity. She believed that it was better to play the role and let him think that his affair was merely one of her interests. It also made the sex hotter at the time for both of them.

Consequently, there was no surprise when he gave her the cold shoulder after she told him she was pregnant.

If she'd been honest, if she'd told him early on in their relationship that he was the only one, he would have accepted her pregnancy as his own child, she believed. Things would have been so much different for Sarah, despite the fact that her parents were convicts.

But what the hell could he possibly want now, she wondered irritably?

Heterosexual relationships were a thing of the past in his world; that much was clear. So, the meeting couldn't be about them or what they had in the past. Maybe it really was about Sarah.

She agreed to meet him at the same Manhattan breakfast spot where they'd hatched their ill-fated plan to kidnap, drug, and extort Chauncey's father. It was only an hour and thirty-minute walk from where she lived now.

After arriving she went to the back seating area. The place looked the same except for a couple of coats of the same tan paint over the years. Stewart was seated at the exact table where they'd all brainstormed together. Her memories of the four of them hunched over and scheming brought back the painful headline about Cy's savage murder. That's when it struck her that Stewart had only arranged two other chairs around the small table. The fourth chair was leaning against the wall. Chance? Not with Stweart's calculating mind, she wagered.

"Hello Stewart, I'm sorry for the early time; I suspect you're not yet one of the working stiffs like the rest of us."

"Hello Melinda. Good to see you again," he said as he rose quickly to his feet and gave her a small hug and the obligatory air kiss.

"Please, have a seat. Can I get you a coffee, anything else," he asked?

She detected too much accommodation in his tone of voice, which made her wary.

"No thanks. I'm good. I'm a working stiff ready to charge into the library and rustle those books together for another exciting day in the literary world; a world ruled over by librarians anonymous. I might even get to answer a question or two from a bibliophile seeking that rare soft cover edition of War and Peace, the one with the extra strong binding."

He laughed at her sarcasm. But her comment about working stiffs was his opening; he exploited it.

"Melinda, not only will I never plunge into the nine to five world again, but I'm also going to restart life soon as a multi-millionaire."

She was visibly surprised because she remembered that by the time they'd all been sentenced their respective families had disinherited them. Not that she had a lot coming from her tightwad folks anyway.

Now Stewart had her complete attention; she couldn't resist asking him how he planned to accomplish that.

"Did you skim some money from the original plan? How did you get away with it? And what about our share?"

He casually looked around before responding, holding onto his reply for maximum effect.

"Unfortunately, the answer to that question is *no*, so there is no share for you or anyone else. But I did manage to retrieve a small rainy-day fund that I personally stashed away years ago, well before our little scheme. Not enough to make a life with mind you, but enough to extract a life from those profiting from my demise."

She felt the blast of bitterness with his answer. It snapped her back to the present and why she was there in the first place.

"What're you talking about? And what's this got to do with Sarah; isn't she why you wanted this meeting in the first place?"

"It was indeed. It's about Sarah. And I sincerely regret that I blew you off years ago and never acknowledged the possibility that you were pregnant, with our child. I just didn't think it was possible. You had several others."

"Stewart don't obsess over it. I don't hold it against you. We both missed so many years with her. But still, she's quite a young lady and she got there entirely without either of us."

"She certainly is that, and I want to stay in touch with her. Though after seeing her recently, I honestly don't know what I could add to her life at this point."

Melinda kept her jealousy over that to herself.

"Stewart, why did you want to meet? What's really going on?"

He looked casually around before lowering his voice.

"There's a strong chance, according to Cy before he was killed, that Chauncey and I will take back at least thirty million dollars. The plan is to reclaim the Long Island property, or rather money from it, that Chauncey's father, you remember him of course—Carleton Smith— left in trust and then donated away after Chauncey was arrested."

The memories came flooding back to her, the drugging, the kidnapping, and the vast deceptions. Was he proposing to step into another quagmire?

"The case is already pretty strong," he said, reading her expression.

"To make it stronger you could testify that you heard Carleton mention his desire to have Chauncey inherit that property and that he intended him to have it despite what his wife wanted, that's all you have to say."

Melinda was floored.

"What! Are you serious," she asked, raising her voice?

"You want me to lie again, to get skewered by another one of your mislaid plans? The last one cost me twenty-five years in jail."

He gestured at her to pipe down before leaning closer.

"Think about it Melinda." he said with his mouth inches from her ear.

"Your part in this is minor. No kidnapping, no drugging, and no identity theft this time. Those were criminal acts. And yeah, you paid the price as we all did. The plan went way south, and I take responsibility for missing the critical loose end that caused that. But the truth is and as you no doubt recall I only missed it because dear Chauncey unknowingly allowed his old man to spy on him for years, thus pushing us into a rushed backup plan. But you have to admit, we were very close to pulling it off anyway; very close to a five-hundred-million-dollar payday."

He flashed a quarter inch gap between his thumb and index finger before sitting back in his chair.

Suddenly Melinda needed fresh air; she didn't want to be there in the restaurant, not with him. Wasn't she at risk by the very act of meeting with him, an accomplice of some kind? Instinctively she looked around for cameras.

"Don't worry," he said calmly.

"This place didn't have cameras back in the day and they still don't have any."

He leaned in again.

"Look, all you need to do is swear to those facts. It's a no brainer: Carleton Smith is long dead and cold in his grave along with his pretentious wife. They can't call you a liar. And Chauncey is in on the plan. Even if the judge doesn't believe your testimony there's no jail time here. That's it, that's all you need to do. In exchange for that you get a five million dollar cut in cash."

She was stunned and revolted, but she couldn't help being enticed. Five million dollars; she was bringing home two hundred dollars a week now. Without her subsidized living arrangements and food stamps she would be homeless and starving.

What if the plan failed like the last one?

But he was right she believed as her mind began to tumble the possibilities. Her role would be minor, a footnote really and without criminal activity, even though she'd be a liar again. With the money she'd be able to move to California. She could be near Sarah and support her in medical school.

But didn't it boil down to lying all over again, going down the same old path one more time?

"I don't know Stewart; I don't think I can help you here. I'm trying to tow the line. The last thing I want is to get back into any kind of trouble with the law."

He easily read the lack of resolve behind her words and pressed harder.

"Look, there's no potential trouble with the law, that's the beauty of this thing," he said.

"Remember, this is a civil case. You're not subject to jail. And again, who's going to contradict your testimony anyway?"

Melinda couldn't help running through the risk calculations again in her head. He was right; it involved virtually no risk.

She rationalized and caved.

"Ok, I'm in. But this is the last time I walk down this road with you. Don't even bother to ask in the future. Okay?"

"Good. And sure, this is the last fling we'll take part in together."

"I'll be in touch soon with the exact wording that you'll need to memorize before the deposition. Just lie low for now and don't mention this to anyone. That's really your only hurdle. Testifying in the court case will just be repeating what you say at the deposition. You can do this, and you'll be well paid."

Relieved, he sat back and pushed away from the table, watching her.

"Do you need any cash to hold you over?"

Before she could answer he pressed ten folded one-hundred-dollar bills into her palm.

She squeezed it.

Part Four:
Fulfillment

Chapter Seventeen:
Manhattan Truths

WAITING FOR SHANA TO BRING HER FILES and notes over to his hotel room he was questioning whether having her with him on the east coast had been a smart idea; not that she was anything other than bright, highly motivated, and extremely hard working.

But the by-product of the trip so far was that he had spent far more time around her than in the past when short briefing sessions on issues was the norm. That additional proximity made it difficult for him to overlook the fact that she was a highly poised young woman. He'd caught himself staring admiringly at her on more than one occasion.

Shana had also started to dress in ways that seemed designed to attract his attention, beginning with the departure flight from Los Angeles when he noticed her thighs because her skirt was nowhere to be seen after she sat down and strapped in for takeoff. He'd never noticed the scant formfitting outfits and very high heels that she now wore every day without exception. It was almost as if being on the east coast had freed her from previous constraints.

Or maybe, he tried to rationalize, she considered the east coast trip work but also a bit of a vacation. She was a young woman after all, and he realized that fashion and glamour came with that territory. Nevertheless, it had become an unwanted distraction.

But what could he really do about it? He'd been around long enough to know that bosses simply didn't comment about personal dress to female colleagues, period.

He thought back to when he'd first hired her onto his Senate staff several years ago. Basically, it was out of a sense of loyalty to her big sister Val as opposed to his immediate need for a third staffer. Or was it out of guilt?

Shana was only old six years old when he first met her, and she had quickly become his tag along baby sister. Whenever he stopped over to see Val Shana found a way to be around, following, watching, and listening to everything that her two favorite teenagers were saying to each other. It was cute when she was a little kid, although occasionally it was seriously annoying.

They were meeting in his hotel room that evening because he didn't have an accessible office in Albany at that hour. His goal for the meeting was to hear her summarize two days of field research into the Brooke, Shelley relationship. He was surprised but appreciative that she had offered to come by his room to brief him in advance rather than presenting everything the following morning at Keisha's firm.

As he watched Shana prepare her files and notes the not-so-subtle fragrance of her perfume filled the space between them.

Finally ready she swiveled around, crossing her ankles before moving the foot high stack of files onto her lap.

They only partially concealed her short skirt.

"One second," she said sounding flustered as she shuffled several folders.

"I want to put this stack in chronological order in case you want to examine a source document."

"Okay, ready; this is a composite summary of what I've gathered from my telephone interviews with five of the girls who were at that ritzy camp—modestly called Camp Summit by the way—over various times during the summer. They were all more than willing to spill the beans after I told them I was a reporter for an Ivy League publication writing about camps for the best and brightest."

"Yes, I know," she said in response to his skeptical expression, "that's a small stretch but they were under no compulsion to speak with me, so I think I was inside the lines. Unfortunately though, it didn't work on Shelley, she hung up on me."

He wasn't certain about her ruse, but he put his questions aside for the moment.

She leaned slightly forward over her notes, resting her elbow on the stack to keep it balanced. She held a notepad in her other hand that served as her crib sheet. The awkward position caused her skirt to ride up higher.

He looked away abruptly and grabbed his own leather notepad as she started.

"Most important in my view everyone I spoke with had a great deal of respect for Brooke and really looked up to her. The girls that knew Shelley said that she started off that way as well. But she got the hots for Kyle, one of the young men who was scheduled to visit from *Sail Shape*. Two of the girls confirmed that because Shelley had bragged about her intimate relationship with him, a nonexistent one from everything I've learned so far."

"Then Shelley went rogue after she received an email from Brooke about the rendezvous that copied Kyle. She contacted him separately a couple of days after that and tried to set up a time to meet with him alone. Somehow Brooke found out, probably from Kyle, and then Brooke disinvited Shelley from the planned meeting."

"Okay, that's very good work," he replied.

"But most of it we know from other sources, right? Did you learn anything else; what about the abortion that Shelley received?"

Nodding her head Shana pulled out another sheet from the files and leaned back a little in the chair to quickly review it, she had to spread her long legs wider apart to balance the folders.

"The abortion was directly connected to Shelley's pregnancy, of course."

Shana blushed and smiled nervously after she said that.

"And her pregnancy resulted from a secret visit to the camp by her boyfriend eight weeks before the shooting. I use the word secret very loosely since all the girls knew about the visit and the resulting romp between them in one of the cabins. The problems for Shelley were three-fold: she and her boyfriend didn't use protection, parent's weekend was approaching, and she was starting to show. She couldn't see her mother during parent's weekend without revealing the bump."

Shana decided that her makeshift lap platform wasn't working. She put the stack of files on the desk and swiveled back around to face him, crossing her leg high on the knee.

"I'm sorry Shana, I lost you there for a minute. What was the connection between the abortion and the legs; strike that, I mean between Shelley's abortion and Brooke?"

Shana continued as if she hadn't heard the mistaken reference.

"Shelley basically had no other option than to shut the camp down. In her mind it was the only way to hide things. At that age kids just don't see the forest for the trees. That what she planned to do might cause significant harm seemingly never entered her mind. I really believe that her secondary motive was to get back at Brooke, but so far, I can't confirm that."

Shana re-crossed her legs while pulling lightly at her skirt.

J kept his head down and scribbled in his notebook

"Shelley left the camp the week before the shooting and had the abortion completed in Manhattan days before parents' weekend. Not sure yet what her cover story was with the camp or with her mother, but we do know that she spilled the beans to the Summit camp director about the secret meeting involving the *Sail Shape* boys at some point. Although we're not sure yet exactly what she told the director."

"Her father paid for the abortion by the way. He'd long ago been estranged from her mother. Whether the mother is even aware that it happened is anybody's guess."

"Wow," J said as he looked up, "not a close-knit family at all, huh?"

"Absolutely not," Shana agreed.

He summarized back to her what he'd just heard to make sure he had the key points.

"Along with the facts about the charitable work in Africa that Keisha documented, I don't see a conviction in this case," he concluded.

"I'd be happy to see Keisha Howard alone tomorrow and go through all of this detail with her," Shana offered. "You'll have one less tedious meeting on your schedule."

"No thanks, Shana; but I appreciate you offering to do that."

"Keisha and I already have an early evening meeting set up for tomorrow. Some of that time will involve my getting to know how her firm approaches pro bono cases; they are miles ahead of us in that area. In the interim I would really appreciate you summarizing your notes and transcribing your interviews. If you can deliver them to her in the afternoon well before my sit down that would be ideal."

Shana's jealously over the cozy working relationship that he had developed with Keisha Howard over the past few days had grown so much that she could barely conceal it anymore.

"I'll make sure she has everything well before your meeting," she said flatly.

He was surprised that it was past eleven o'clock already. He looked over at Keisha; the head was still down, buried in a thick evidence binder. He had developed great respect for her legal skills, intelligence, and work ethic during the past week. And as important as the *Sail Shape* matter was to her, he was also aware that she was lead partner in three other pending cases at her firm.

And his day one assessment about her attractiveness had only been reconfirmed the more he'd been around her. Yet as he thought about that he decided it was really her inner depth of spirit— of which he had caught several glimpses —that was the real driving force behind her beauty. She had a quiet courage and inner drive that belied bluster and hubris, traits so often associated with successful litigators. Instead, her modesty and focus reminded him of that old expression about still waters running deep.

Slow down a tad buffalo soldier, he warned himself. Stay focused on the work at hand and remember that she doesn't flash that wedding band and diamond ring because she's starved for male companionship.

But as he considered it more the intriguing thing was that she had never mentioned a husband…or kids for that matter. At his firm back home women partners and associates always mentioned their second full time job if they had one when they were working late, raising the family.

Most of them would leave the office at some point during the day or early evening and attend to one or more domestic matters. They'd invariably return for the late-night slog. But as far as he'd seen, she never excused herself from the work; start early, stay late, no let up.

Which was why she was a complete enigma.

Maybe she was divorced or estranged he speculated optimistically. He figured she might be thirty-six, maybe thirty-seven, and certainly no more than forty. If she had kids, he calculated that with law school and her career they couldn't be more than five or six at this point, max.

Keisha glanced up from her binder and caught him staring.

"What's on your mind senator," she said, a light smile playing on her face? "You've either had a major revelation about this case or I've got a prominent zit on my forehead."

He was light on his feet, sidestepping the question.

"I'm sorry. It's not you, or this case for that matter," he said moving aside his binder.

"I was just thinking again about what an incredible coincidence it turned out to be that both of us have Brett as our connection point. Of course, you see him differently; he's your father after all. He was a big brother to me when I first met him in high school and later, both a mentor and friend. Truth is, he helped me get on track and continued to help during the years after that whenever I needed it. His advice, or as I call it the head food, was the best thing. That allowed me to develop focus on my own goals and priorities after high school—as opposed to my old default position, following the crowd."

She moved her file and rubbed her eyes; it was welcome break. She ruffled her fingers through her hair and pushed back from the table.

Looking over at him she decided that maybe she could open a little. After all he wasn't a bad working companion. And he hadn't once tried to hit on her, she realized.

"It is unusual, that connection to him that we both share, J. Brett is the only father that ever cared about me. My biological one never felt like I was more important than his booze or his women."

Okay, that's enough sharing for today and that came out more bitter than it should have, she admonished herself. She hoisted her internal privacy screen back up again and deftly changed the subject.

"Brett told me that you were quite the firebrand during your high school years senator. Did you really occupy a college campus in California," she said in disbelief?

"Crazy as it sounds, that's precisely what we did. However, he supported us anyway despite our Berkeley style radicalism. My role in it, other than following the group, was a minor one."

He searched his memory during the brief pause; he didn't remember Brett ever mentioning that Keisha was a stepdaughter in all the years he'd known him. But he wasn't surprised that he'd never referred to her as such.

"He also mentioned the shooting of your friend by a SWAT sniper; it happened after the occupation had been resolved he said, during a celebration?"

"Yes," he replied. "It did."

Despite the decades that had passed since the shooting he could still see Val lifeless on the grass. He told her the rest of it.

When he finished Keisha shook her head, she regretted bringing it up.

"It took a lot of counseling for me and for the other kids who witnessed that to finally put it in a place where it couldn't damage us. Funny thing is that Shana, she's Val's baby sister, looks so much like her that I'm often reminded about the past even when I don't want to be."

"Oh really," Keisha replied, with more relief in her voice than she intended.

"I didn't know that connection," she said. "So that's why Shana's at your firm. To tell you the truth, I thought there was a bit of a love interest there, at least on her part. It seems to me that she worships the ground you walk on."

"Love interest," he said disbelievingly?

"Not at all. Shana's very bright and she's a hard worker. You're probably misreading her loyalty that she always demonstrates. You see, she was a staffer on my senate team before I hired her at the firm as a paralegal; she's a very good one by the way."

"But I guess she did sort of look up to me when she was little. And of course, over the years I continued to assist her and her family whenever I could."

Keisha wondered how he could have possibly missed the young woman's amorous interest in him. Shana all but wore it on her sleeve, and even more than that on the very high hemlines of her tight-fitting dresses.

She shifted gears to lighten the mood.

"By the way, my father occasionally refers to you as Jazz. What's that all about counselor? Don't tell me you're a musician in your spare time."

He laughed and shook his head.

"I went by the handle Jazz when I was younger. It started when I was a kid listening to my father's extensive jazz collection; I'd dance around the house to swing tunes all day long when he or my mother would allow it. But you know how it is, we enter college and law school and we've got to begin getting serious. And running for political office was the kicker. So, it's been J for many years now."

"Well, personally, I like Jazz better; it has a soulful ring to it."

She added a generous smile to her endorsement.

The good vibes so far encouraged him; it was the first time they had ventured outside of the narrow work mode with each other. Why not probe a bit deeper?

"What about you, you caught me staring and I admit that my reply was a head fake. But you know what you are a mystery, never mentioning your husband and kids and all the while putting in the grinding hours here. That can't be easy on you."

His question forced her to challenge herself and rethink her near obsession with keeping her life private. After all, they did share a genuine connection, and they were becoming friends.

"Truth is, there's no husband and there certainly are no kids," she said with a slightly embarrassed look.

She raised her left hand to show the big rings.

"This is a red stop sign that I was forced to adopt against your species. It works maybe ninety percent of the time. For the other ten percent that view these as an invitation to bed down with a married woman, I have a collection of rebuffs from mild to severe that I use. I just didn't have the time anymore, J, for the endless banter and the lewd solicitations that men feel obliged to spew, it's too much."

He nodded his head in agreement before walking over to the corner fridge for two more waters. He needed the break to mask his elation over the fact that she was single and available.

Several months ago, after many years of unsuccessful serial dating, he'd finally admitted to himself that he probably would end up being single for life. Despite trying for several years, he hadn't met anyone who was a real partner, someone who shared his values and looked at the future in a similar manner. For the most part his dating pattern had yielded a succession of very attractive but very young women with much different priorities. But had he found the right woman he would have been more than willing to give up the overrated bachelor lifestyle.

Thinking about Keisha, what impressed him was that she was completely genuine. And she was the closest thing to being drama free that he could recall when he thought about the women he'd dated over the years. She had even come clean about the rings, showing remorse over the deception.

The more time he spent around her the more he believed that there was just something different there. She was self-assured and she had depth and complexity. He wanted to get to know so much more about her.

After sitting back down he looked directly at her and began with a somber tone.

"Keisha Howard my fellow counselor, that you've removed yourself from the race, the race for companionship, is a cause of great distress to me. I may be forced to file an appeal to have that decision overturned by the highest court in New York."

She chuckled at his high-strung humor.

"The truth is I haven't permanently removed myself; at least I don't think so. I'm still shy of forty for crying out loud."

She noticed that he didn't flinch at all upon hearing her age, so different from the others.

They laughed together again.

"Then you're waiting for Mr. Right, I suspect?"

"You want to know the sad truth? Mr. Right would have to be a shrink," she said.

"You mean a real shrink?"

"Definitely. I've got issues you know. I finally had to admit that to myself. My biological father warped my senses about men and what they were all about very early on. He robbed me of trust. If it wasn't for Brett's steady influence, I would have tanked years ago."

"Is your father still alive?"

"I think so. To be honest it's been many years since I've seen him. Last I heard he was on skid row in the Bowery district— lower Manhattan."

"I'm curious, why did you ask me about him? Why would you care," she said.

With those questions she realized that her privacy genes were rearing their heads again. They had made her an expert over the years at deflecting questions from curious fellow professionals or from the gratuitously nosey.

"I asked because he sounds like a demon from your past, your father does. One thing that counseling did for me after that high school tragedy was show me that I had to confront the demons, make my peace in some way, then put them aside or at least learn to live with them. That's not easy to do."

She looked at him closely; she accepted that his concern was real. And she knew he was right. She had to confront the demon called her father at some point and she'd always avoided it.

"That's good advice counselor, thank you, I mean that. But you know what, it will be hard, real hard for me after all these years of shoveling dirt and trying to bury things."

***

Shana was awake at five o'clock in the morning; she hadn't slept solidly that night. J had been out so late that she had dozed off in her new silk nightgown while leaning back against her door. Her plan had been to wait for him to unlock his door when he returned; then she planned to peek out briefly to show a little of her gown before waving goodnight. Instead, she had ended up splayed out and asleep on the hard hotel room floor.

Now she sat on her bed and fretted.

What could he possibly have been doing with that woman was the question eating away at her? In her agitated state she couldn't consider the possibility that they were working for most of the evening.

On the other hand, and knowing well his tendencies, she was certain that he would have no amorous attraction for Keisha Howard at all given her advanced age. Since Shana had been on his staff all he had dated were women in their late twenties or at most very early thirties, none of whom had lasted long she noted with satisfaction.

Smugness that her presence near him over the years had contributed to his dissatisfaction with his dating partners was quickly replaced again by worry. She was certain that there was no way that all his time last evening could have been taken up by legal matters.

She was convinced that he must have fallen under Keisha Howard's spell. It all made sense to her now given last night's meeting; she must have insisted that J not bring her so she could lure him in to be alone with her.

She thought about sharing with J the research that she'd gathered about her— no prominent social or family lineage, no online media profile or other meaningful web presence, no public affiliations with organizations other than the Bar, no record of involvement with men in any venue, civic or otherwise. Shana was reasonably certain that she was a closet lesbian or even trans, despite the huge fake wedding rings. All of it caused alarm in her mind because if those facts were made public along with the woman's shameless wooing, it could end up damaging J's campaign back in California. And it could also threaten Shana's future with him.

Obviously, Keisha Howard had no clue about what it had taken for J to get this far, a step away from the Governor's mansion. Shana was certain that her own contributions to his success over the years had far outstripped anything that Keisha Howard could provide at this late date, even if she was a law firm partner.

Growing increasingly determined to break the woman's grip on him her protective instincts went into overdrive as she wrestled with the best way to proceed.

With the predawn light slowly seeped through her windows she had to struggle to shake off her fatigue and think clearly. They'd be flying home to California the following day she recalled; she would have him all to herself again. In that case maybe she shouldn't share her research. He might hold it against her in some way for digging into the woman's personal life without his permission.

The recognition that they would soon leave Albany together settled her down. She also recognized that despite Keisha Howard the trip so far had been a success.

Before leaving California, she had realized that the trip east alone with him was her best opportunity to change things up and let him see her in a different light. The hardest thing had been keeping her plan to herself, which meant that her girlfriends couldn't be trusted with her secret, even though she really wanted to tap into their experience. But nonetheless she had been able to develop a strategy to make him see her differently.

And it was clearly working; she had confirmed for the first time yesterday that he wasn't able to overlook the fact that she was mature and desirable, despite his best efforts at trying to ignore her. She smiled as she remembered his slip-up about the 'abortion and the legs;' her own legs had finally captured his eyes.

Despite her decision to follow her carefully laid out plan she realized that she needed to figure out very soon how to let him know that she was the only one who truly understood him and who cared about him. He needed to know that she was the only one left who had loved him from the very beginning.

Encouraged, she walked over to the full-length wall mirror. She tried hard to see herself as he would see her, and she wanted to improve any area that might be more pleasing to his eyes. She touched and inspected her calves, thighs, and hips. Diligent running and a strict diet had kept them trim and toned. But she had no time for a run today.

Instead, she raised and lowered herself on her toes repeatedly until she felt the swell in her peaked calf muscles. For another twenty minutes she tightened and relaxed her butt and worked her ab muscles until the burn was severe. When done she lifted her nightgown and watched the rippled bulging in her thighs as she ran through dozens of half squats and high kicks. She held a vertical stretch, elbows to the floor for three minutes

She was breathing hard with the sheen of sweat over her body making her nightgown cling.

After stretching and limbering her upper torso and arms, she began pushing her body away from the wall using only her fingertips for several vigorous sets. That had always trimmed and toned her shoulders and triceps. She felt the familiar burn in her pectoral muscles by the end of the fifteen-minute set. Finally, while breathing hard she bent forward and encircled her ankles between long fingers, holding the position for minutes.

Sweating freely now, it would have to suffice for today.

She stripped off her wet nightgown and turned to briefly admire her profile in the wall mirror before hitting the shower.

Afterwards she went to the corner desk still wrapped in a towel to turn on her laptop. That's when the emergency notices from the court monitoring service loaded into her inbox.

What's all this?

After a quick read she had the answer, two new civil cases had been filed in New York courts. The first named Brett Howard and *Sail Shape* as defendants. It was a negligence case stemming from the trespass. The second case had been filed first. It was in Suffolk superior probate court and sought to reclaim the ten-acre plot of land on which the Long Island camp was located. She knew right away that the second lawsuit could be far more damaging.

She forwarded both notices to J knowing that they would mean more of his time being spent in New York in the future, without her.

Because of that she felt a growing urgency; she had to make him view her as the best and only choice for him when they returned to California, no more holding back she vowed.

***

He had only been home a week before hell broke loose. A mysterious home invasion was all over the morning news up in Marin County and the local police had no suspects. It was clear from the evidence at the crime scene that whoever carried it out was a supporter of *Sail Shape's* proposed marina purchase. The neighboring community was extremely upset, and political pundits were carelessly fanning that anger.

Shortly after the story broke a longtime political consultant that J had utilized for years called him saying they needed to get together.

They met at the City Club that was located atop a sixty-story Los Angeles office tower with commanding views of the mountain ranges that rimmed the basin. It was where L.A.'s movers and shakers often met for a drink, a meal, and business. As J waited for Chad Pendleton to arrive, he thought about their long collaboration together that began fifteen years before. It all started at a networking event organized by the L.A. Chamber of Commerce.

Chad had mentioned to him during their friendly get to know you conversation that he was impressed with J's presence and with what he characterized as J's likeability attributes. Those intangibles were essential to a successful political career, Chad stressed. Later in the conversation, just for fun, Chad postulated a possible track for him if he was at all interested in politics. He suggested an initial term on the city council or zoning commission, a term or two as a state assemblyman, and after that a term or two in the senate. He predicted that J could run for governor at that point with a damn good chance of winning, assuming no intervening scandals or disasters.

Chad's predictions over the years had been dead on.

Before his recent involvement with Brett Howard J was certain that the path to the state's highest office was firmly within his grasp. But he increasingly understood that it was now no longer a sure thing, as bad news seemed to attach to everything his former mentor was involved with.

His entanglement with those issues was going to sink him; that was the bottom line. The two most recent lawsuits were bound to cause even more fallout. And now he had to manage the negative publicity from a home invasion. He would need to make hard decisions very soon to have any chance of salvaging things.

He didn't expect the meeting with Chad to change that conclusion.

Chad arrived on time and well dressed in upscale SoCal digs that included an unreconstructed designer suit, a draping black LV shoulder bag, and crested silk loafers. An open neck hot pink cotton dress shirt set everything off. Although hardly obvious from outward appearances, Chad hailed from a family of conservative Republican numbers men—they were the political pros who told you before the election how many points you would win or lose by and why.

After shaking hands Chad got down to business.

"J, thanks for meeting me like this on such short notice. Hope you've been well."

J nodded.

"We received some polling back yesterday. It was disturbing to say the least. I sent you those early this morning. Then we picked up the wire headlines about the home invasion. So, my quants back at the office estimate a five point down tick from the numbers that you have."

"Thanks Chad. Yes, I did receive that data and I'm glad we're sitting down. I'm the one who's been out of touch during the past few weeks. I've read all the newspapers and on-line coverage about the home invasion. What do you know about what really happened up there near the marina?"

"I've got some connections inside the sheriffs' office, so this info is strictly confidential—at least right now. But you know how it is, the key points will be leaked by the local prosecutor well before any indictment is handed down, assuming they apprehend the felon."

"And those leaks might help sink your campaign before you even announce."

He was growing anxious because Chad usually wasn't so dramatic. He steeled himself for more bad news; he wasn't disappointed.

"Anyway, here's what I'm being told by my sources. Last night at 2:05 A.M. an alarm company in Mill Valley recorded the trip of a residential window security mesh. The home is walking distance from the marina that you're trying to buy."

"Anyway, alarms at that time of night get an immediate armed response but by the time the security firm and police arrived the intruder had vanished; there can be a 10-to-15-minute delay in response sometimes, the bad guys know that."

"What was left inside in the house on the living room wall was a giant street painting. Basically, the house had been tagged on the inside. The only good news is that the family that was home wasn't harmed. They were sleeping in the private wing of the property at the time, and they locked themselves into a safe room after the alarm sounded."

Chad paused briefly as if he were rethinking how he would deliver the rest of the story.

"As you know J that tagging stuff usually happens out-of-doors, ninety nine percent of it anyway, and in urban areas primarily. In this case the mural splashed across the wall was maybe twenty feet wide and as high as the fifteen-foot ceilings. It was an edgy looking red, black, and green collage of a sailboat. And beneath it there was a red-lettered inscription."

J had a sinking feeling, but he had to know.

"What did it say?"

"It said: Vote Yes for the *Sail Shape* Camp."

He shook his head.

"Chad, I get that this was vandalism and a brazen act, and maybe a little over the top enthusiasm for our purchase, but why the great alarm on your part, why the connection and concern with my campaign?"

"That connection and concern is already being made in the local community up there my friend. The result of it all will be a spate of editorials and other negative newspaper articles. They're being written as we speak, believe me."

Chad reached into his bag and held up a photo of a pleasant looking white family of four that J didn't recognize.

"You see, J, the couple who owned the home have two teenage daughters. It doesn't matter that nothing happened to these young women. What really matters is that something could have happened. This whole scenario will stoke local fears and anxiety already at the surface. There's major concern about bringing city kids into the community and exposing the neighborhood to urban issues. You know what I'm really saying, right?"

"Yeah, I get it. You don't have to spell it out."

"Look" Chad said while sitting forward.

"Even though it may be late in the game you've got to distance yourself from that east coast litigation, senator. And I say that already knowing that you're probably planning to get involved more deeply, right? But you really need to walk away from it all or you won't even get out of the gate in the governor's race."

J shook his head, as if instinctively recoiling from the decision ahead of him.

"That's a hugely difficult thing for me to do, Chad. Friendship and loyalty are on the line. Without my help, particularly given recent developments, I would have to watch an old friend and mentor slip below the waves."

"If you want to be governor that's what you'll need to do. And believe me, I'm not making light of that decision."

"Maybe you're right. You know I respect your insights. But there's also the truth. Underneath all this litigation is the truth and I think finding out what that truth is could be another way to win."

It was brave speculative talk; he recognized that as he listened to his own words.

He was aware that he was playing a losing political hand and that he had to fold it sooner rather than later.

After sleeping on it he decided that the only way he could limit the damage was to pull out of the fiasco completely. At the end of the day the raft of new problems had nothing to do with him, he concluded. They were unfortunate circumstances for sure, but they were not his circumstances or his cross to bear.

He'd have to see Brett in person and just tell him that he was done, he owed him that much. Would his old mentor understand, would he recognize that his mentee was following the same advice that he had imparted to him in high school—set your own course based on your beliefs rather than following the course of others?

He would later wonder if his choice for a face-to-face was merely procrastination because telling Brett on a phone call was really all that was needed; same result easier to accomplish.

Before flying back east he planned to load as much intelligence about the new litigation into his briefcase as he could. He would leave that trove of information with Keisha and her team; it would help a lot.

Shana had taken the lead and pulled together all the data. They finally got together in one of his firm's smaller conference rooms after nine that evening.

When he walked in, she was standing in the corner head down tapping on her cell phone. Seeing her reminded him how relieved he was after they returned from Albany because she had abandoned her provocative east coast outfits. Tonight, was no different; she wore a conservative gray waist jacket over a blue silk blouse buttoned almost to the top. And her full cut dress fell well below her knees. But he noticed that she was wearing those six-inch heels again for some reason, the ones that elevated her right up to his height.

"Shana, we've got to stop meeting like this."

She looked up, smiled, and walked over to the swivel chair at the conference room table to wake up her laptop. He smelled a subtle fragrance of perfume in her wake.

"If we stop meeting like this," she said over her shoulder "it'll mean that you're not billing sufficient time and I'm not getting the hours that I need to pay for my overpriced downtown apartment."

"You're right, billable hours drive us all."

"Like I mentioned yesterday," he said to her back, "I'm flying to New York tomorrow. It'll be my last trip. This whole thing is threatening the primary goal; I can't let it do that. Leading change at the state level—if I'm elected—has got to remain my top priority."

She was encouraged to hear that, just like she'd been when he told her to pull together all the files and research for transfer. But she remained skeptical that he would walk away from the effort, especially since he was going back east where he would be alone with *her* again. She stuck to her plan.

"I know it's a huge problem for you and a difficult choice," she said as she rotated around to face him.

"I agree with your final decision, continuing would very likely cripple your campaign," she said before turning back.

"We've worked up all the facts and law in the negligence case to help them get on top of that one," she said over her shoulder.

"And our estate lawyers took a good look at the merits of the land case at my request. I have the key finding for us to review tonight."

He interrupted.

"Wait a minute Shana, slow down; how did you manage to get them to do that? We haven't even set up the billing priority on that matter yet. Those guys won't touch a case unless there's an active, funded client matter that they can bill."

She swiveled around again and flashed a radiant smile while she smoothed out her dress.

"Well, I do have some pretty good powers of persuasion that worked like a charm."

He returned the smile, but he wondered whether she meant something else.

She stood and dragged a fat accordion file binder in front of her from the middle of the table. It held five manila folders that she quickly unpacked, spreading them out evenly. J impatiently moved in to examine the file tab names just as Shana turned around to face him. Their bodies bumped firmly while their lips brushed lightly.

"Excuse me," he said quickly, as the fruity taste from her lipstick jarred his senses.

Shana was shaken by the contact, but she quickly regained her composure.

"This is the backup that you'll need on your flight to Albany," she said calmly.

"The whole thing is indexed in this reference file; we'll email two last minute memos to you tomorrow," she said while removing a paper from the folder near her briefcase.

"The reference tab numbers on this sheet correspond to the document sets. They are bound together internally just in case you have an accidental drop. We'll put the whole thing in a carry-on rolling suitcase for you later."

"Thank you. That's exactly what I'll need. This will go a long way toward helping Brett's defense."

She glanced at him before staring down at the documents. After taking a deep breath she sat down.

He took a seat on the opposite side and waited.

"I think that we should review the summary that I prepared in the land case point by point this evening," she said confidently.

"As I said, it's the more dangerous of the two in my opinion. It should only take thirty minutes. The rest you can review on the flight."

As usual he was impressed by her efficiency.

"Perfect. Do you have a copy of that for me," he asked while reaching for it?

"Well, no, I don't, I thought we could both refer to this one index sheet together," she said.

"I'll leave this with you to take and print one out for myself later. But come to think about it, I won't need to since all of this is for the Harpin firm."

He nodded in agreement but remained confused about how they would share the sheet.

With effort Shana dragged a heavy leather chair closer to her own. She centered the index sheet on the table between the chairs. Then she positioned a yellow pencil and note pad in front of each chair.

He came around and grabbed a seat.

"Let's get started," he said eagerly.

Methodically she began reviewing the known facts. It wasn't long into her presentation before he was convinced that there had to be some other motive behind it.

"We're going to need a complete work-up on this plaintiff," he interrupted.

"Strike that. They will need to get that done back east. Something's going on below the surface, isn't it? This thing has a wealthy billionaire father disinheriting his son, while the father was living, but then again not really. The son, what's his name, Chauncey Smith, is alleging it was all a plan to produce a result twenty-five years later. It's bizarre, I don't buy it."

"Funny you should mention that. I've got preliminary data about the son—an ex-con by the way—right here," she said while placing the document on top of the index sheet."

"It's compiled solely from what's available online."

He leaned in and started reading.

She had placed it slightly off center, just a couple of inches to her side so that as he angled in her direction his trouser leg contacted her full dress beneath the table. She slowly lifted the material and softly draped more of it over his leg as he focused on the document.

Shana gently rolled her chair closer while he devoured the report such that his already close upper arm lightly touched her own. Again, he failed to notice and added even more contact from his side as he focused solely on the research document.

After a few moments Shana inched her chair a tad closer making the slightly increased contact between arms and legs seem entirely natural.

Before long she shifted her arm behind his chair, seemingly to provide additional room. Within minutes after that she inched slowly forward, softly resting her chest against his shoulder.

The increasing heat along the length of his body finally jolted him. He sat back quickly after realizing the cause and looked at her.

She was confident when she spoke.

"J, I don't want you to go back east, I can't stand the thought of you there without me. I can pack everything up and ship it to her. Please, stay here with me."

He didn't know what to think or how best to respond as he took in the full extent of what had occurred. Then he remembered that telling conversation with Keisha about Shana's hidden feelings. Keisha was right, he'd missed it; over all the years with Shana, he'd missed it. Now he fumbled for a solution.

"Shana, we go back a very long way. I was so glad when you agreed to join my senatorial staff years ago. You were terrific. And you've been a great paralegal at the firm."

It sounded lame even to him; he had to be tougher.

Shana seemed calm and composed as she steadily looked back at him. He noticed for the first time that her eyes and brows and face were fully made up and that her quite long lashes seemed to be reaching out to him along with her capturing gaze. He hadn't seen that look before.

"But you can't be anything else to me, Shana. I love you, I love you like a sister. I want to see you succeed. This isn't the way to do that," he said gravely.

"I'm not a little girl anymore you know, haven't been one for a long time," she responded immediately.

"I'm a woman. I hope you can fully appreciate me for my attributes now, in the present moment."

She calmly crossed her leg high on the thigh after rolling her chair back from the table. With a deliberate gesture she swept her full dress back from over her knees. The fragrance of her perfume wafted at him.

He didn't know what to say so he stood up and walked to the other side of the small room while shaking his head.

270

She looked thoroughly unflustered watching him squirm even though it seemed to him that the room temperature in the space had spiked by ten degrees.

"Shana look, we can't get involved in anything outside of our working professional relationship, it's as simple as that," he said after approaching her from the side.

She swiveled in her chair and stood up near to him full on; her face was level to his own. She wore a light inquisitive expression as if she were pleasantly ignoring his every word. She appeared to be slowly moving closer, which made him back slowly towards the corner of the conference room before continuing.

"That would be completely wrong," he said as he struggled to find the correct response to her infatuation while sparing her feelings.

But he could see in her demeanor and body language that she wasn't deterred in the least. She now stood shoulders back and wide-legged, lightly resting her hands on her hips. She was growing more rather than less comfortable with each passing moment. She slowly stepped two feet closer and now partially blocked his path with her arms crossed and long legs crossed at the ankles.

Then he remembered where he had first seen that defiant mannerism. Shana was demonstrating the same headstrong posture and attitude that she would throw at him and Val years ago when she was little. Not taking no for an answer, she would always try to follow them whenever they would leave the house, sometimes having to be carried back after sneaking out behind them. They often had to come down very hard verbally on her to change her mind and get her to stay put at home. Usually that elicited more than a few tears and sniffles.

He had to use a similarly harsh approach now.

He began by taking great pains to explain that some relationships were defined and limited by forces larger than themselves. The relationship between them he counseled had long ago been defined as one based on friendship, loyalty, and trust; trust between them and trust with Val and her parents.

Shana's defiant, seductive posture immediately changed after she heard her sister's name. He noticed.

He took several more minutes to define the dimensions of that trust and the mantle that it placed upon him as a man. The years that it had taken to build the legacy with her family and with her he said firmly couldn't be suddenly turned into something else after all these years. In fact, he continued, doing such a thing would demean and corrupt every trust that had been placed in him over the years, including Val's trust, which still lived all around them.

He could see the increasing doubt in Shana's eyes. She sat down and rested her hands in her lap.

His firm rejection was cathartic, it seemed to release Shana's long pent-up emotions.

"Why can't you just see that I love you so much," she finally asked with pleading eyes?

"What's bad about that, about our happiness and future?"

"Don't you realize that we were meant to be together, that you've always been special to me? What's wrong with admitting it to each other? The age difference between us doesn't matter anymore; I've been a grown woman for a long time you know. Why shouldn't we be happy and in love? I can give you all of me, everything you'll ever need; more than any of the others. You won't have to search anymore, J."

She waited for his approval, for some sign that he understood.

It didn't come.

She began to grow desperate because she didn't see anything in his face that showed his love. Where she had expected tenderness and caring, she saw only coldness.

She already knew that her plan had fallen apart even before he destroyed it completely.

He sat down on the other side of the table.

"Shana, think about it for a moment, we weren't meant to be together as you claim. Don't you see that? I was Val's friend? That's all. I was just a good friend, not even her boyfriend. And we were all kids together even though I was several years older than you. The fact that we were there, that I was there around you was only circumstantial, nothing more. I was merely an older boy that you formed an attraction to when you were a little girl. Anything else is just a fantasy, something that you've held in your head for all these years. I'm sorry but you've got to face it."

As she took in his cruel words, she accepted that she would never have him.

Her giant miscalculation was apparent now; the self-absorbed plan that she hatched had been misguided and naïve, it was inside her own head. It dawned on her that not once had she ever shared her feelings or plans with anyone else, not with friends or family or mentors. They might have helped her avoid this moment, she realized.

She grew desperate to come away with something, she had to release her errant dreams and try to salvage a friendship. Unable to look at him, she spoke in measured tones with her head bowed.

"I'm very sorry, J."

"This was stupid; it was dumb, sheer desperation on my part. I tried to make something happen that wasn't meant to be, and I now realize that. When I would try so hard to picture us in my mind as...as lovers, it only happened rarely. Now I understand why. You're just too much of a big brother to me. I respected and idolized you for that. I guess I've always loved you for it, as a little girl and now."

"I'm so sorry. But I had to know how you felt about us, about a future together."

She continued to study her hands.

As he watched her, he saw the resignation and the sadness and he wasn't immune. He was reminded of the long journey that they both had taken since Val's death, apart at times and together. They were family and he loved her dearly. And she was right; she had grown into a beautiful woman during those years even though he was the last one to notice. He felt an enormous tenderness for her at that moment. But he suppressed his emotions and keep his distance.

Shana dried her eyes, determined to pull it together. She reached for her own personal file folder and placed a second copy of her summary sheet in front of him, smiling sheepishly.

"I did happen to find a second copy," she said as her voice cracked.

He smiled back. "All right, what've you got?"

At the end of the thirty-minute briefing he had a complete picture of the case. He pushed away from the table and stretched.

"That was perfect Shana, thank you. Are you sure you don't want to pursue that night law school opportunity you were considering? You'd be good and you'd be successful."

"That would mean a lot of time away from the office, J."

"But maybe now," she said as she smiled bravely, "I'll reconsider it seriously since you've completely shattered my fantasy world."

He smiled back at her, hoping that everything would be okay.

She turned away to pack up the files.

Chapter Eighteen:
Ships Ahoy

JOSHUA HAD TO ADMIT that Mirra's idea that had him landing in New York and surprising his father out on Long Island was a pretty good one.

Why not stop over there for a night on your way to San Francisco, she urged. She reminded him how long it had been and that he'd get to surprise his father at the camp.

Seeing his hesitation, she added a kicker—wasn't it his race strategy against Willosby that allowed you to be in the skipper's seat, and don't you owe him a personal thank you for that?

Well not exactly, he'd countered. But he had to admit that his father had first mentioned the capsize threat. After thinking it over he conceded that those early ideas had helped to generate his final race tactics leading to the win.

And besides he admitted, it had been much too long since he'd seen him in the flesh.

Mirra was happy.

He flexed his quads and stretched his Achilles tendons in the first-class cabin seat, finishing up a stationary routine to get a jump on the coming stiffness from the seven-hour flight. As they swept high over the eastern edge of the Atlantic the monotony of the engines started pulling at his consciousness; he nodded off even before his sleeping pills kicked in.

He dreamed about his two trips as a little boy to the Long Island *Sail Shape* camp in the year before it opened. In one surreal scene his mother seemed to be pulling him back to Albany, stretching his small body like miles of thin brown taffy while he held stubbornly onto the camp gate, Gumby-like.

In the second colorful dreamscape he was a diminutive construction worker who toiled along with his dad and the full-size contractors to finish the camp. It was real work just like everyone around him was doing even though he was only two feet tall.

Other scattered scenes followed where he was a courageous sea captain who commanded a huge sailboat; he always sailed it fast.

Later he found himself cruising close to shore but this time standing at the stern of an itsy-bitsy vessel. He was shouting at campers back on the docks that his dad owned the entire ocean. Then the wind shifted, and he drifted helplessly out to sea.

The final dream sequence was less exciting and nowhere close to his actual experiences. The setting was his adolescent days of innocence when he had imagined himself to be a rich kid. He was on stage pitted against classmates in an exciting jeopardy-like contest. Even though he had picked the category it was clear to the host and everyone else that he was struggling to score any points trying to demonstrate that his father owned a wealthy fleet of boats and vast lands.

His classmates, however, didn't have to choose a category and simply racked up the score by yelling out of turn that their fathers owned shipping companies, airplanes, and giant factories that employed thousands. Points for all contestants appeared on a huge scoreboard, Joshua continued to have a bagel next to his name.

The frustration from being shut out literally woke him out of his dream.

Still agitated and groggy he adjusted his seat to full recline and grabbed a wool blanket before clicking back in.

Moments before the sleeping pills dragged him back to dream land, he cued his classical music playlist and refitted his ear buds.

Professor Warren H. Foggle looked up at two hundred of the newly admitted business school students arranged neatly above him. They were seated within Wharton School's newest high-tech fishbowl. In front of Foggle a digital chart projected student headshots and location onto a backlit dais. It also displayed their hometown and a summary undergraduate record. It was quite an upgrade from the old days when Foggle relied on voluminous loose-ring binders crammed with papers and photographs.

By the middle of every semester, he prided himself on being able to call on any student by name without the aid of the summary information. He could also remember where they were from as well as their undergraduate major. Years ago, he'd stopped memorizing GPA scores because they were so similar.

For his first class of the semester every student was allowed fifteen seconds to give a quick talk about themselves. Foggle secretly recorded a plus, a minus, or a neutral mark next to the student's name when they were done.

Students unable to keep it brief while providing a cogent insight about their personal story—usually more than a third— received a minus mark. Most marks were neutral for those that followed directions. A small number—fewer than seven percent— were rated plus based on Foggle's opinion about the student's self-awareness and candor.

The secret grading system was the underpinning of a regression analysis that Foggle had calculated for his seven thousand students over the past twenty-five years. With ninety-seventh percentile accuracy his system predicted each student's probable academic distinction in business school. After many years of collection, he finally published his trove of information, masking student identities. Despite knowing that knowledge about his process would corrupt his data set going forward, Foggle was proud to add yet another publication to his vitae.

Joshua Bernard Howard stood up after he was called upon and looked down at the professor. He admitted that his academic record at his undergraduate Ivy League school had been unremarkable and blamed himself for that. In closing he said that he hoped to make a significantly better showing over the next two years because of the lessons that he had learned about himself.

Foggle placed a plus mark next to his name.

Joshua wasn't being falsely modest about his undergraduate performance. He was simply admitting that his 3.57 college GPA didn't reflect his best effort at all. While he had seriously pulled it together his junior and senior years, the earlier semesters were steeped in sailing regattas, parties, and numerous girlfriends.

It was only after his mother's unannounced visit to campus during his sophomore year and the intense embarrassment that caused him among his social circle that he'd stepped back and realized that maybe he did have a stake in directing his own future. That had been Lailani's purpose.

But the almost two-year period before her surprise visit were raucous and often steamy.

He smiled at the cascading images as he slept.

Sheila was from Virginia and in his opinion the hottest junior on campus. Even though he was a freshman at the time his frat buddies goaded him into approaching her one evening at the Friday cleanup party. The gathering was one more excuse for less serious undergraduates to get an early start at weekend partying.

Rumor had it that Sheila was easy but picky.

"It may appear as if I'm being overly formal Sheila but actually my role this evening is largely in an official capacity, as a guide you see." he offered with mock seriousness as he handed her a cold beer.

Lovely Sheila wasn't impressed yet by his freshman pickup line; but she decided to play along because he was cute.

"Well Joshua, and by the way is that a shortened version of Joshster," she asked?

Then she purred her double entendre without waiting for his reply.

"Actually, I was looking for a personal tour of the fraternity assets. Can you get up for it," she asked sweetly.

Sensing an opportunity to be with an upper classman he put his half-finished beer on the wooden coffee table and extended his arm in invitation.

"Sheila, you are soon to be in the best of hands. Let's start on the lower floor, in the lockable game room."

His frat house tour didn't extend beyond the game room, but the evening between them continued until 5 A.M. when he finally made his way from her single back to his own bed. Later, he eagerly described details about his exploits to his fellows who listened with rapt attention. The incident established his reputation as a significant player in the undergraduate dating game. An almost endless rotation of coeds followed Sheila along with less than stellar grades.

What are you doing here mom, why didn't you call?

He had asked that while quickly collecting his latest girlfriend's scattered personal items from his bed and his dresser, including her birth control dispenser. But Lailani had already spotted that and much more in his disheveled and smelly living space.

"Joshua, Joshua, excuse me. My name is Samantha Jones."

He heard her pliant voice vividly as his subconscious mind veered back to graduate school.

"I thought your remarks to Professor Foggle were uncharacteristically modest, at least for a Wharton man," she said.

He turned around to see the loveliest cinnamon-brown face ever, exceeded in splendor only by the generous curves of her body. And she was smiling at him.

"Thank you so much Samantha. You're from Texas right. You're an equestrian. I liked your bio in the class summary."

She was flattered that he'd recalled her personal details from among the other two-hundred students. Their intimate six-month relationship was vastly more settled than he had become accustomed to in his college days. Samantha quickly consolidated her living space with his and they became a serious couple in their spacious and sunny graduate apartment. Samantha also had immense academic talent and a 4.5 college GPA. He hadn't yet become accustomed to a woman who was smarter than he was, so he had to poke.

"Samantha," he whispered sweetly in her ear after a morning of intimacy, "tell me dear, how does one accumulate a 4.5 GPA when the maximum grade point in college in 4.0?"

After posing the question he eased his long body next to hers under the beige sheets and messaged her taut abdomen.

"Actually Joshua, the technique is quite straight forward—extracurricular activities."

Then she grabbed him firmly between the legs.

"I see," he said while reciprocating the grab and rubbing her lightly with the open palm of his other hand.

"It sounds like a form of frontal grade inflation if you ask me," he said.

He liked the settled life, at least for a while. They carried on like husband and wife until he got tired of playing house and Samantha faded, pushed away by his claustrophobia.

Then Mirra and all things Jamaican drifted lyrically before him.

The music was rising to crescendo though strangely it wasn't Jamaican reggae at all he realized as his closed eyelids rapidly blinked. Instead, it was the lovely Baroque style of Vivaldi, violins peaking.

Suddenly all was disrupted by the gravely captain's voice announcing landing at New York's Kennedy Airport.

***

On the long ride out to *Sail Shape* he continued to think about the past.

He suspected that his rendezvous again with the camp that was once his circumscribed playground was the reason.

He remembered an ancient source of tension with his father, one of many in high school. It happened because the answer to what he had assumed was a simple yes or no question at Thanksgiving dinner had turned the meal into World War II. He never thought his dad would fly into a tantrum over his request to spend the upcoming Christmas break with his best friend's family down in Bermuda. Surely his father knew about the place and how safe it was because Joshua had seen several Bermuda Cup sailing trophies around their house.

Being fifteen at the time, tall for his age as well as a varsity athlete, he hadn't anticipated any problem with the request because he'd be safe enough, particularly in Bermuda, which was why he had already assured his friend that he would be there for the week. But rather than a yes, he got another lecture about keeping the faith with the less fortunate and investing forward into the futures of those without advantages. He politely interjected that he didn't see any connection between that and what he wanted to do over Christmas. That was when he got the emphatic no without further explanation.

He shook his head in the back seat. He really had no clue then about what his father was getting at, how could he? Uncle Ned's gloss on the whole thing had pretty much put those years in proper perspective for him—his father's actions were most likely driven by a nagging concern for his safety, never expressed. The micro lectures from him about social consciousness were sincere but secondary and they didn't always fit the circumstances. It was that disconnect that had often confused and frustrated Joshua.

All he knew at the time was that most of his friends at boarding school were heading out of the country to exotic locations during school breaks while he was always heading home to Albany of all places. It was embarrassing and it chafed as he grew older. There was a time when he thought his father was a cheapskate at best or a sadist at worst. Shouting that accusation during a later argument between them predictably lead to more rather than less tension.

It was pretty much a standoff during his last year of prep school as they both tried to stay out of each other's way when he was home. His mother had become the de facto conduit for communication. What kept him going in those days was the knowledge that all he had to do was get away to college, far enough away to escape from under the thumbs of his old man.

But what about the last dozen or so years, he asked himself? Hadn't he been imitating his father's footsteps, unconsciously perhaps? Hadn't he soaked up all that chatter about helping others through the process of osmosis? Despite his history of denying it and asserting his own independent vision about things, he finally conceded that the warehouse full of poor and disadvantaged kids back in London was the affirmative answer to his questions.

He glanced over at the passing mile markers on the expressway; they were making great time.

"Driver, our exit comes up next; you just go right off the ramp and east from there; we'll be at *Sail Shape* in thirty minutes."

When they approached the camp it was pitch dark. Several safety lights at a good distance away dotted the interior of the property. He told the driver to turn off the headlights before they started the quarter mile drive to the main circle, then he lowered his window. The insects had quelled all noise and settled in for the night. Beyond the buildings ahead he could hear and smell the vast ocean breathing. The sound of its rhythmic undulation and the thick salty taste in the air seemed to welcome him home.

Rows of cabins were set back among the trees as they drove slowly up to the main circle. Farther west but invisible, a similar cluster accommodated the girls.

Being inside the grounds felt like an old glove, albeit a smaller one. They pulled forward quietly and kept well away from the winding driveway that fell off to the right. At the bottom was his dad's cabin tucked away among the trees near the docks.

After tipping the driver and grabbing his sea bag he walked quietly across the sandy path back to the driveway. On the way down to the cabin he knelt and peeked through the trees. He could see the floating docks illuminated by yellow safety lights; beyond them were the familiar lines of sailboats floating in parade order. The safety lights didn't ring a bell: must be add-ons, he surmised. Looking closer he spotted a couple of outsized boats among the fleet, at least forty footers, and realized that the old fleet had been replaced, of course.

He heard his father stumping around inside before he rapped loudly on the cabin door.

His father's raised voice wasn't welcoming.

"It's past lights out sailor, you're supposed to be in bed. We'll handle your question at first light."

Joshua was enjoying this. He rapped louder again this time and faked a few sniffling sounds.

The door flew open and just as Brett was preparing to blast the unfortunate camper that he'd assumed was either homesick or afraid of sleeping in a dark cabin, he stared at his only son.

"Joshua!"

The surprise had worked; they hugged for a while.

Brett backed up and eyed him suspiciously.

"Was your mother in on this," he asked squinting?

"Not really. It was Mirra's idea. She sends her best and looks forward to meeting you and mom in the flesh at some future time. But of course, I had to let mom know and apologize for not stopping up in Albany. How've you been dad?"

" Well," he replied as he hesitated before deciding to be straight about the current challenges, "the truth is it's been a slog on this end. We're involved in three lawsuits now, two as a defendant. But your sister is making progress for us in all of them."

"By the way, you remember Jazz don't you, he was the young man that I helped through college and law school; you met him many years back at a *Sail Shape* awards ceremony."

Joshua shook his head.

"Well anyway, he's pitching in the support of his west coast law firm to bolster Keisha's efforts. So, we've had to lawyer up for sure. It's money that should really be spent on infrastructure and equipment for the camps. But we're holding our own, at least so far."

Then he remembered the help that his son had provided last year.

"Remember that report from Africa that you sent to us about what the kids were doing that night at the girl's camp?"

"Sure do."

"Your mother also had an old contact that added more evidence to help us. The case could possibly be dismissed if things continue to go well. But anyway, enough already about our troubles on this end."

He looked Joshua and smiled, happy to see him.

"Hey, aren't you supposed to be in Frisco now competing in the pre-Cup regattas?"

"First race is in three days; I'm all set and I'll be early."

No, he really wasn't, and he knew it. Against his better instincts he chose to share a bit of his ongoing anxiety.

"But you know to be perfectly honest my palms have been sweaty. As many races as I've had, there's something different about the tension around this one. It's more than the reality that it's a grueling three-month pressure cooker. I think it's because there's so much other life stuff that must be put on the back burner. And lest I forget, some of the best skippers in the world are gunning against me for the same prize."

"But anyway," he said changing the subject, "it's great to see you again, dad."

"Joshua, I'm happy you came through. I 've missed you."

He put his arm around his son's shoulder for a moment and thought about what he had just said, he couldn't remember a time since before adolescence that Joshua had been so open about his feelings.

"It's really no surprise you know that you're on edge about the races. In fact, if you were cool, calm, and collected you would either be a robot or be completely ignorant about what you're going to face out there in the Bay."

As he looked at Joshua he wanted to say more, he wanted to be closer than they were before. He tried.

"It'll be big boy racing that's for sure. And as good as you are Joshua, you'll have to contend against pros that were racing for money when you were just getting serious about your life. Truth is, I wish I were thirty years younger and that I had the skills to be on crew for you. But I'm not and I don't."

It was the first time that Brett had articulated what he'd known for many years, Joshua had far eclipsed his own sailing skills; he was the better skipper now in the family.

"But you've got what it takes Joshua, you always had it. You'll be just fine out there."

They both had the same thought running through their minds; they couldn't recall the last time that a compliment had been exchanged between them.

The truth was that they were both a bit uncomfortable with the mutual candor up to this point. Lack of practice in the space, like lack of practice at anything, was the reason.

Momentarily Brett withdrew into his familiar emotional shell, averting his eyes. Then he instinctively pointed to the far side of the room, to a small space where he had bonded with his son years ago before the tension exploded between them. It was a mock navigation station that had been built into the corner of his cabin. Unlike real onboard stations, it had a second chair that he utilized to provide individual tutoring to the more promising skippers during camp sessions. Joshua had sat there many times when he was a boy.

They sat down together again.

The brief exchange about his feelings had been about as far into genuine emotion as Joshua had gone with his father. It was shallow, but it was the best that he'd managed to do since he was a boy.

He took another stab at breaking down the barriers.

"Look dad, I called baby girl before I left London to let her know I was coming. The way she tells it she's been a bit of an unintentional family switchboard over the past year or so, spilling all kinds of beans. She fessed up after revealing that you and Mom were having some…relationship issues of late. Is everything okay?"

Brett hesitated before responding, resisting an easy defensive reply. His son was a man he reminded himself, he'd long been a man.

"No, actually things aren't okay between me and your mother at all," he said.

"We've had our stress and strain over the years, and it's taken a very big toll. I know I need to get better to change that, I really hope it's not too late. But the last issue was a matter that may have destroyed her trust…in me."

All Joshua could do was wait for the rest because he was feeling completely lost in the new emotional space between them.

"You see, I was in California on camp business—we're trying to open a new facility out there, it'll be the new flagship one day if things go as planned. An old friend, someone who your mother understood I had dated for years before your mother and me reconnected—you know most of that story—well anyway, your mother called me at the hotel and Zena, that's the woman, answered my phone. Turns out your mother was also in Cali on business, and she planned to surprise me."

He studied his father's face; he'd clearly heard what he said but for the life of him he was unsure about what it all meant. Had his father been caught cheating? Yet at the same time the whole explanation sounded like a denial. The confusion was swirling in his head when Brett broke in.

"Joshua, believe me, I had no designs for cheating on your mother then, and I still don't have any. Zena had come to the hotel to plead the case for her daughter, a young woman who had faced serious emotional issues of late. Zena was only there to ask me to give her a shot in the *Sail Shape* organization, a chance to start at the bottom running this camp and then to help me with the budgeting issues nationwide, if she worked out."

He was relieved until he realized that what he'd just heard contained a significant ambiguity—if his father hadn't cheated by design was it more of a spontaneous cheating; or entirely not at all? Or maybe he was just reading something into his father's explanation that was otherwise harmless. It was apparent to him now that getting real with his father was loaded with potential fallout. Yet he preferred it to the superficial conversations that they'd had in the past.

"Did you explain that to mom," he finally said?

"I did, but I think it added another piece of erosion between us. I shouldn't have allowed myself to be put in the situation in the first place. It was just that Zena is a major donor to the camps, has been for many years…we're talking close to a million dollars just in the last ten years. I felt I owed her a personal meeting."

"I think I understand now. Can I do anything to help you and mom…?"

Joshua's voice trailed off because the words and what they implied sounded so weird.

"Don't worry, I'm hoping that we'll work it out. I'm just trying to change some of my ways a day at a time, which should help things."

"So did you end up hiring the daughter?"

"I did. She's about your age and a decent sailor, certainly good enough to supervise staff conducting the water activities. She's also a very good businessperson and I can use that expertise. Hey, by the way, can you turn out for the morning muster meeting tomorrow at seven?"

"Sure, I 'm not flying out until one. I wouldn't miss the opportunity to chow down on camp food again for anything."

They both laughed.

"Great. I would really appreciate you addressing the kids. It doesn't have to be a long speech by any means. What a surprise it'll be for them to hear from an America's Cup skipper. And by the way, most of them already know who you are because they see your old trophies and photos in the case every day at the mess hall, some have followed your webcasts."

"I'd be happy to greet them but between you and me I'll only be that Cup skipper you mentioned after I win some races in Frisco."

Brett smiled, glad that his son had remembered one of the old maxims that Brett had shared from Bernard, his own father—don't count your piglets before they're born.

During his ten-minute speech he looked down less often at the scribbled notes he was holding, instead keeping his focus on the three hundred inquisitive faces in front of him. He directed his comments to as many pairs of eyes as he could. They'd all been laser-trained on him the entire time.

Halfway through the talk he had remembered himself as a young boy out there in the hall just like them, listening to speakers that his father had lined up for the summer. But he realized that most of the kids in front of him didn't have the same financial advantages that he had when he was their age; many also didn't have that constant head food at home and elsewhere to help them hone an early perspective on life. Socio-economic circumstances for most were sometimes sketchy despite the support they received from committed parents or guardians.

He wanted to find a way to bridge that divide and leave them with something solid. He thought about the problem in the back of his mind while delivering his talking points.

The solution came after he remembered some of his conversations with his long ago camp mates as they all sat around the fire or when they relaxed at night in their bunks. Many had always bemoaned the peer and family pressure that they received when they left their neighborhoods for *Sail Shape* or after they returned home. Some even tried to hide the fact that they'd been away to a sailing camp in the first place.

Joshua thought it was so stupid at the time and he used to tell friends exactly that; why wouldn't they brag about attending a camp like *Sail Shape*? But over the years he had learned quite a bit more about class-based assumptions and misdirected jealousies. They often quelled intellectual curiosity, dictating a conformity among those that needed exactly the opposite.

He put his outline in his pocket and tried to capture that complex idea in a way that the girls and boys listening to him could understand. He took the risk that things hadn't changed that much since he was a kid sitting out there.

"You'll hear many folks, including some of your own relatives, talk down to you about your experiences here at *Sail Shape*," he said.

"They'll point out how bourgeoisie—uppity—and white the sport of sailing is and how it makes you less genuine to be involved in it. They'll talk about how you should be spending your summer in a real sports camp playing football or baseball or running track. Don't believe them. But do believe that they're thinking small. We're thinking big here at *Sail Shape*."

He could see in many faces and head nods that his words had struck home.

"My fellow skippers," he said as he raised his voice after turning off the microphone and leaving the small stage, "don't be mad at them either, they can't show you a place that they've never seen."

"And above all don't be defensive about your experiences here."

"You know why? Because the ones criticizing you have never been on-board ship with us calculating the rough waves and wind or riding out a threatening squall ripping through the rigging. They don't know about the demands you face to put brains and muscle and urgency into every turn of your boat during a tough regatta. They certainly don't know what you've learned about shutting out fear and leaning hard on your own courage and skill and that of your crewmates while underway."

"Don't forget, you are learning the same skills here that are used on the high seas, hundreds of miles offshore. I also learned those skills, right here; I still use them every time I'm at the helm."

He could see that his message was resonating. He walked over to the area where the campers were seated and gave out a few high-fives and daps before finishing up.

"Instead of being ashamed when that stuff comes your way from home, lean in and continue to focus on your skills here and on your grades in school. Above all, focus on the quality of your friendships. Make sure they're based on honor and honesty and that you and your friends are building each other up and not tearing others down. Remember that message about CS on the bronze plaque by the boathouse. It gives each of us a mission— point your helm to an honest and true course."

"When I leave this afternoon for Frisco, I'll try my best to win when I get there. But just like you I know that victory is in the effort, it's in the trying, it's in the sacrifice. Do those things and the victories come."

"Good luck and fair winds to each of you."

"Thanks for listening."

The campers jumped up and erupted in loud cheers and shouts, most were standing on their chairs clapping.

Listening to him from the far corner of the mess hall, Mikala was extremely impressed; she hadn't expected to be. He was a banker after all. And both black and white she'd spent more time than she wanted to remember in their professional company. Not a lot of emotion or passion—except for accumulating money— in that crowd.

But this banker was something else again, she thought. He certainly wasn't like the others. Walking across the mess hall to thank him she studied his face more closely while he talked to Brett. Had she met him in the past, she wondered? He looked so familiar, handsomely so.

"Joshua, thank you for that," Brett said while patting his son on the back.

It was the first time in seventeen years that he had heard his son speak publicly. It was a painful reminder of many missed opportunities.

"That was great for the kids," he added. "All eyes were on you for the entire talk. Do you know how difficult that is to achieve?"

As Mikala joined them Brett made the introductions.

"Joshua, I'd like you to meet Ms. Mikala Jensen, our new Executive Director. Mikala, this is my son Joshua Bernard Howard whom I've mentioned occasionally in the past."

"I'm very pleased to meet you Mikala," he said smiling broadly."

"The pleasure is mine, Joshua," she responded, returning his friendly expression with her own.

Then she turned serious.

"That was a very thoughtful speech. It was just what they needed to hear. You put your finger on it exactly; oftentimes they hear misassumptions and narrow thinking. On behalf of the camp, thank you so much."

He hadn't expected to meet someone so striking. When his father had mentioned her financial background, he'd just assumed she was another burned out executive looking for a career change. She was anything but burned out; she was drop dead gorgeous. And talk about small world and one degree of separation; she was his uncle Ned's niece. When his father had mentioned that he wanted to kick himself for turning down Ned's invitation several years ago to join him at his family's big reunion in Manhattan. He would very likely have met her much earlier.

"Thanks for the kind words, Mikala. I was trying to make a personal connection and give them something that helps when the doubt and doubters creep in."

Since neither one of them had taken their eyes off the other, Brett felt that he needed to break the trance.

"Mikala, Joshua has an hour or so before he heads to the airport. Why don't you both get to know one other and I'll fill in for you at the boathouse briefings."

He turned to his son.

"You know the drill; we have three regattas set for the morning."

"Nothing changes around here, does it dad?"

"Want to grab a Cup of Joe Mr. Howard," Mikala chimed in pleasantly.

"Nothing would suit me more Ms. Jensen."

＊＊＊

Twenty minutes into the conversation two things about her were apparent to him, she detested bland camp coffee as much as he did, and in her role as Executive Director she was in way over her head. Sure, she'd sailed a fair bit on her own over many years; seamanship wasn't her challenge she admitted. But she went on to explain that directly running an organization with as many moving parts as *Sail Shape* was a huge step up from anything she'd done in the past.

"But I'll tell you this much Joshua, being able to interact with and influence the quality of the camper experience is a huge benefit for me, even though those young innocent faces that constantly refer to me as Ma'am or Director Jensen sometimes make me feel much older than I would like."

He was impressed that she enjoyed rubbing shoulders with ordinary campers. Yet as he listened more it was also clear to him that his father had really hired her for the financial skills.

Inevitably the conversation turned to the world of finance since they each had earned an MBA.

"Tell me Joshua, other than giving inspiring speeches how do you remain energized and engaged with the real world which is vastly different from money and finance. I just found that to be very hard to do after several years."

"It is a hard thing to accomplish, no question about it. I think it helped that I'd developed the ability to compartmentalize very early on, probably a boarding school thing. I just had the capacity to work in discrete areas of activity that were unconnected. I didn't even think about whether there was something underneath it all that implied a deeper meaning."

"As I grew older and thought more about it there was a bit of coherence to the frenzy. Finance satisfies that controlled gambler instinct I suppose, sailing of course feeds the physical and mental competitive streak that most of us have, and I do some things on the side with kids back in London. My dad mentioned that you were also a prep school baby, so you've got a good idea about that as well I suspect."

Mikala nodded but something in her eyes suggested to him that she hadn't experienced the balance that he was talking about.

He couldn't help but notice how easy and enjoyable it was to talk with her, almost as if they were old acquaintances. And she seemed to be laser focused on him, listening carefully to his every word.

"You know Joshua, that's a great balance that you struck. I had that to some degree at one point. I think what lead to a kind of accelerated burnout for me was shifting to focus solely on work as I climbed the ladder higher. But isn't that exactly what the pundits tell you to do?"

He nodded in agreement.

"Ninety and one-hundred-hour work weeks back-to-back, year after year; vacations that were really akin to just taking my office on the road, that finally did it for me, or to me. And of course, it didn't leave a lot of time to develop and nurture meaningful relationships."

She paused for a moment, wondering if she was sharing too much. She decided to shift the discussion to a lighter footing.

"By the way, congratulations to you. Your father whispered to me secretly before we left the mess hall that you were recently engaged. Do you think that meant that he had a trust problem with us?"

He smiled and responded playfully.

"I don't know any reason why that would be, do you?"

They laughed.

"You know, I do admire that you're engaged despite all the hectic things going on in your life. Your fiancé must be quite a woman."

He didn't quite know how to respond to that. It would have been a complicated answer because his relationship with Mirra had so many dimensions and so many emotional levels. So he replied with sincere thanks and steered the subject to the upcoming races in San Francisco.

They ended talking about her career change plans and the possibility of an expanded financial role for her with the other *Sail Shape* camps. She conceded that she was looking forward to giving up her current position for that opportunity if it worked out. Managing a dozen sailing instructors plus staff and the facility itself was beyond hectic, she confessed.

He hated to end their pleasant and rambling chat, which had taken longer than an hour but seemed to have lasted only fifteen or twenty minutes; but he had to catch his flight.

As he walked back to grab his bag, he found himself missing the quiet tenor of her voice. He couldn't put his finger on why there was such a pleasant familiarity about her, it was just below the surface.

Suddenly he regretted not having asked her for her contact information. What could possibly have been wrong with that— other than your engagement, his conscience asked him?

But his father would certainly have her number he realized, ignoring the cautionary voice in his head.

Before landing in San Francisco, he thought that he finally figured out exactly what it was about Mikala that had so strongly attracted him; it was an intense familiarity of feeling between them, an empathy almost; and strangely, there was this familiar sense from her physical presence. But weren't those both sensations that would normally be felt only between a man and a woman who were committed and close to each other, like he was with Mirra for example?

Yet he'd only just met Mikala, how could it be like that.

He finally had to admit that given his many years away from the singles scene his instincts at reading and reacting to women were suspect at best.

After their chat Mikala had walked slowly to the docks to rescue Brett from acting race director duties. As she thought more about her enjoyable conversation with his son, she felt the tug of a powerful premonition. It stubbornly refused to yield despite her every logical objection. It left her with the overwhelming impression that her first meeting with Joshua Bernard Howard had been a perfectly timed and intricately coordinated event. But coordinated by whom and how, she had no idea.

She spent most of her free moments that day thinking about it. After dinner and end of day activities she was no closer to a solution when she returned to her cabin that evening.

As predictable easterlies kicked up offshore and thumped noisily against her cabin window, she tucked her chilly legs under the covers and leaned back against her pillows. She grabbed a few folders from the bedside table thinking that she could finish proofing the recently completed camp-wide physical inventory report.

But it had been a long day and she tired quickly. Pushing the papers aside, her thoughts drifted back to Joshua. She racked her brain, she'd seen him before she was certain of it now; but when, where?

Then it hit her like a lightning bolt; everything made sense when she connected his face with a seminal event from her childhood. As a little girl, she'd accidentally discovered her mother's hidden trove of photos taken with a long-ago mysterious lover. He was the spitting image of Joshua. But it wasn't Joshua; it was his father, Brett. Now her rapid-fire hiring sequence at the camp made perfect sense.

When she applied for the open position, she was completely unaware of her mother's earlier amorous involvement with Brett. And of course, he no longer looked anything like he appeared back when the photos with Zena were taken. Coyly, her mother hadn't admitted to anything beyond a passing mention that they were old acquaintances.

But he was obviously much more than that, which is why she only sat for one interview and was hired so rapidly, without so much as a background check or a drug test.

She smiled thinking about her childhood discovery of that treasure trove of photos; she was nine years old and romping around the house. Except for the maids and two private guards that manned the security gate inside the enormous estate, she was alone as usual creating fun ways to entertain herself.

She'd been playing tennis—hit off the wall style—in the family game room. She was retrieving one wildly smashed shot from behind a heavy settee. Precariously balancing prone along the top of the couch, she braced against the back wall. When she lunged to the floor to reach her ball behind the couch, her shoulder pressed hard against the lower wall causing a hidden Velcro seal to release. A small secret door popped inward. She inched the bulky couch far enough away from the wall to crawl into the space. In the near semi-darkness, she found and removed a thick photo album. She remembered thinking after she first opened it that the pictures were just placed loosely on the album pages, unlike the other books in the house where each photo was carefully mounted in its own special place.

She sat lotus style, arranging all of them on the floor. The resulting collage startled her. Her mother was smiling and seemed to be very happy in each one. And there was a man that she'd never seen before who was in each shot. He was touching her mother in most and kissing her in several. They looked like they were made for one other, so much in love. But the man was not her father; that was the one thought that seared her young mind.

She never mentioned to her mother that she'd found the album because she was very afraid of falling out of Zena Melody Jensen's good graces, something that even to this day was not a wise strategy. The secret of the hidden man became a heavy burden to carry. With the passage of years, Mikala forgot all about the album.

She thought more about her pleasant chat that morning with Joshua and her heart skipped a small beat. She realized that in other circumstances, in another dimension, she could very well imagine herself in his arms, smiling and equally as happy as her mother had been with his father long ago.

The reality of her recent failures quickly dissolved her fantasy.

The truth was that she was formerly engaged, but no longer so. It had taken many months for her to be comfortable admitting that and accepting the judgment from others that came with it.

It was her mother who had conveniently invented the idea that her enormous set back should be labeled burn out. Mother dearest had correctly assumed that it was better than telling the outside world that her high-achieving daughter had been deceived. It was certainly much better than telling everyone that her fiancé had been captured by networked security cameras after hours at his job while he deflowered his secretary atop a bare conference room table.

Not to blame oneself was the stoic mantra ingrained in her throughout all the therapy sessions. He was the bad guy, not her. But she also accepted that she'd been terribly naïve, she'd been raised in a bubble and had been easily blindsided.

Her mother's cover story had at least been half right; she was recovering from a type of burnout; it was relationship burnout and life burnout. As she sipped her warm lemon water and thought more about those painful days, the key lessons remained.

Her therapy had exposed the artificiality of the socio-economic cocoon woven around her since childhood. From church to school to camp to dates, it was always the usual group, the just-like-me crowd. They were preapproved, they were largely bland, but they were most importantly safe.

God forbid if she ever asked to go to a party or attend an event with someone outside of that group, not a chance in hell of it happening she had learned. So being a good girl and wanting to please, she accepted things.

As she set her cup down, she suddenly remembered Mickey who so long ago had been her first clumsy attempt to break away. Her heart still ached after all the years for the boy for whom she had developed a fever-pitched puppy love.

Where he had come from was a mystery. But he was suddenly a member of her Sunday school class, dropping in from God knows where; unlike the others who had always been there. Mickey was thirteen, same age as her. What struck her the most, besides his shoes, was his chocolate brown color. She couldn't remember meeting anyone before who was brown like he was. He also had holes in the bottom of each of his shoes. She saw them even though he tried hard to hide them, she didn't care.

Maybe he'd ended up in her class due to the special grace of some high Anglican missionary outreach to the inner city she had speculated years after it was over. Or perhaps he'd been adopted by one of the families in the large affluent congregation. She didn't know and she never found out.

Mickey was interesting, opinionated, and bold. She was extremely impressed by him the first time they were around each other. He came right out and told her while looking into her eyes that she was a star. What did that mean she asked him shyly? Mickey said it meant that she was hot and smoking, just like the sun.

She thought that his handle for her was just perfect, a star. She also liked him because he was patient and he paid careful attention to her emerging adolescent feelings.

The puppy love romance carried on for many Sundays. He would always find a way to be next to her in Sunday school and later during church when she sat away from her parents. But after service he would make himself scarce for some reason. On more than one occasion she almost asked him if they might meet at some time during the week for ice cream of perhaps hot chocolate. But she never did.

One Sunday morning he was no longer there. She wandered throughout the enormous church complex searching for him but there was no trace.

It was only by chance years later that she learned bits and pieces. Apparently one of the jealous boys in Sunday school had sent an anonymous note to her mother. In it he'd described the sins into which Mikala had fallen and the *dark* spell that Mickey had cast over her.

There were rumors that her mother had taken matters into her hands with a vengeance. Apparently after her pointed call to the pastor of the church, poor Mickey, and he was very much that, was sent packing away along with his several siblings and grandmother. The ostensible charitable plan of the church was abandoned to make peace with an influential family.

At the time it happened she only knew that Mickey had been torn out of her life and that her mother may have had something to do with it. She was at a loss over what else she could do because she had no idea where or why he had vanished. Yet she failed to ask any questions of her mother or anyone else and she meekly accepted her fate without protest.

Or was she intimidated in some way to accept the result?

Whatever the reason, the incident became an indelible marker for her future conformity.

Much later her fiancé emerged from the safe list of families. Without her even knowing it he'd been preloaded and preapproved since the days of her cotillion; her mother had shared many of Mikala's secrets with him behind her back. It was no wonder that his conversation and all his allusions and frames of reference for their future together seemed so familiar and safe to her. She mistook his calculated well prepped wooing for true feelings.

That he loved the company of other women—whether freely given or violently forced—wasn't that big of a deal her aunts and grand aunts had secretly confided to her after the discovery. Give him a second chance they pleaded; he'll find another position. At least he's been caught and punished, and you won't have to fret about another woman anymore, they assured her; it was a blessing they pointed out.

She demurred; she had sensed the monster hidden behind the façade on several occasions, even though he tried hard to conceal it. And she had figured out that over the years she had likely been spied on and betrayed. Her obstinacy over it all was disappointing to the many guardians of legacy within her family.

During her therapy she decided that she needed her life back; or better yet that she needed to find out what her life was on her own terms.

On the work front she was determined to find a way to spend less time trying to scale the corporate ladder because it became the ultimate catch twenty-two, the harder she chased after success and satisfaction, the farther from her grasp they moved.

Sail Shape came along right on time and was exactly what she needed. The staff had accepted her, and she believed she'd already been able to make a small difference in the lives of many of the boys and girls.

Maybe she shouldn't be so quick to move into another role after all.

Yawning, she pulled her covers up and shut off her light.

Before falling asleep she thought again about whether there was a kind of predestination involved with meeting Joshua.

Or was it only her loneliness?

Chapter Nineteen:
Testimony

KEISHA HAD JUST FINISHED READING A SUMMARY of testimony from a witness in the lawsuit that contained good and bad news for her side.

The good news was how easy it had been for her investigator to gain Melinda's Smith's confidence.

They simply stated that they were working on the trust litigation and that they wanted to reconfirm her testimony in the case—all totally true. Nothing had prevented Melinda Smith from asking whom the investigator worked for.

It signaled more good news—the other side's litigation budget for the case was bare bones. Otherwise, they would have spent the time and money to prepare their witness for such tactics.

But the bad news was huge—the substance of Melinda Smith's testimony provided the extra weight upon which a judge could rely to rule against her father.

In Keisha's experience the only way to survive the impact of such damning evidence at trial would be to have facts of her own about Carleton Smith and his wife.

Knowing that her trial instincts took over. She decided to find that evidence herself in Hartford, Connecticut. Two former servants for the Smith estate had been in nursing home residence there for more than twenty years. If anyone had potentially helpful information, they might.

Background on them was virtually nonexistent since they predated the Internet by decades and had lived solitary nonpublic lives. All she could be sure about was that Alfred and Wilemina worked at the Smith estate for at least fifty years before they retired. They were there long before Chauncey Smith was born; they were there when Chauncey Smith's scheme to defraud his father blew up; and they were at the estate when Carleton Smith suffered a massive stroke.

Apparently, they had both left employment at the same time, shortly after Carleton Smith was declared mentally incompetent by a judge. Keisha's investigator had sniffed out rumors that the two servants were actually fired by the wife.

Keisha's hunch was that an involuntary dismissal, if it had in fact happened, might cancel out the slavish loyalty that some service staff had for the super-rich. But if the domestics ended up supporting Melinda Smith's version of events, then it was better to know that sooner.

The drive from Albany to Hartford took her eight hours in heavy traffic. Nonetheless, she managed to receive calls and place them, participate in teleconference meetings, and send and receive emails and faxes—all while driving.

Again, she vowed to herself that after the trip she would cut out those distracting and dangerous habits and focus her attention entirely on driving.

One of the emails that she received was from Jazz who was arriving the following afternoon; she smiled when she saw his politically correct name, J, pop up in her inbox. She clicked on his message with anticipation; he'd sent a list of possible questions for the two domestics. She decided to integrate some of them into her own list. She was impressed because it wasn't all hammer and tongs as so often served up by her male litigation colleagues. He'd used his inductive reasoning skills to anticipate and counter setbacks that she might experience during the questioning.

He had also reinforced her belief that the only goal for her at the end of the interview was that she came away with something that might help undermine the thrust of Melinda Smith's testimony; and that it would likely be something indirect.

Despite his legal tips she was a little sad that his email was all business without any hint of a personal message for her. But she would see him tomorrow and that made her happy.

As she neared the outskirts of Hartford, she received an urgent update from her firm about the Long Island shooting case. The prosecutor had reached out to strike a deal—offering a reduced term for each boy down of twelve to fifteen years with possible early parole in exchange for a reckless endangerment and trespassing plea. While that was a major improvement, she realized that it was still akin to a death sentence for their futures.

Convinced that the time was right to drive a virtual truck into the prosecutor's office she emailed back a strong counteroffer.

Keep you damn eyes on the road she warned herself after drifting over the centerline; the rest can wait. She forcefully closed her laptop.

Then she remembered the strange way that Jazz had ended his email—that this might be his last trip east due to his announcement for the governor's race. He said that it made his continued involvement in the case doubtful.

But as she thought more about it that didn't square with his earlier comments. He'd told her three weeks ago that his announcement was still several months away, closer to a year. And he'd been guns-a-blazing on the cases. She wondered if the negative publicity and political heat had gotten to him.

Staying in the litigation wasn't an easy choice for him, she recognized. Had he decided to resolve things by retreating to California politics and pulling away from everything else? Yet he hadn't struck her as someone easily turned from a challenge. But she had to admit that she didn't really know him all that well despite their collaboration.

Most of all she wasn't certain what was really beneath that smooth polished veneer that he always displayed. In the end she guessed that he'd probably walk away and that she'd have to carry on without him.

Glancing frequently at her GPS, she navigated the last mile to the nursing home before driving slowly into a neatly groomed suburban-looking neighborhood within the heart of the city. A large stately colonial residence confronted her when she rounded the next corner. Oddly it was nestled in the shadows of three gleaming white commercial structures that were evidence of Hartford's once thriving insurance industry. The house was set back at least one hundred feet from the curb. The colonial's street address on the sidewalk mailbox matched her GPS input so she parked in front and walked up the plant-lined path.

Probably the palatial home of an insurance CEO in the good old days, one of his several residences she speculated as she approached the large red door before rapping the heavy bronze doorknocker.

A tall trim nurse greeted her. She wore a traditional starched white uniform along with the white stockings, shoes and cap. Keisha thought that those ancient symbols had long been abandoned to multi-colored pants suits designed to conceal or obscure participation in the profession. The crisp spotless uniform reminded her of aunty Lai's starched whites that she had always admired when she was a girl.

She kept pace as the nurse briskly led the way while chatting amicably. While they walked down several corridors to the interior of the structure, she didn't see any patients. She had assumed there would be scattered groups of seniors in various states of health. Equally strange was the absence of odors of any kind. Although she hadn't been sure about the facility disposition, the gleaming Spartan environment that surrounded her certainly wasn't expected.

They marched down another extended corridor beneath spacious skylights, it led to a separate wing that was hidden from street view and that terminated at an open sitting room. In the corner next to an enormous bay window that overlooked an English garden were Alfred and Wilemina.

Both had warming blankets wrapped around their shoulders and legs. They appeared much frailer than the file photos she had seen. But their matching electric powered wheelchairs were shinny and new. She noticed empty fine China teacups on a nearby colonial coffee table.

They were alert and both looked up at her when she entered the room. She remembered that they were ninety-seven and ninety-eight years old respectively. She could only hope and pray that their mental agility and recall had survived.

After introductions the nurse left. Keisha asked if they would mind if she used a digital voice recorder and they both said, *no not at all* at the same time. She got the distinct feeling that neither one of them knew what a digital voice recorder was. She discretely placed the thin device on the table.

She described the lawsuit. It was a long explanation but an essential one that provided context and signaled the importance that their accurate recall would have on the case. Then, after they both nodded their heads in agreement for the umpteenth time, she got down to the essence of her visit.

"Our investigation revealed the decades long service that each of you provided to the Smith household. You were in service to Carleton Smith and his wife long before their son Chauncey was born, if that correct?"

Alfred waited for Wilemina to speak, but she nodded at him to go on ahead.

"Counselor"

Alfred began in a thin voice that she had to listen to very carefully.

"We both knew everything about the goings on at the Smith estate. That was our job."

Wilemina's voice was loud and clear as she added on.

"And we took pride in doing our jobs well."

"Thank you both for that. What I would like to know is whether Carleton Smith was opposed to his wife's desire to disinherit her son Chauncey after he was arrested for kidnapping and drugging?"

"Mr. Smith gave that boy everything, even after he became a man,"

Alfred declared after coughing up spittle to clear his throat.

He leaned forward and raised his boney right hand from under the blanket.

"But that boy was ungrateful. All he wanted was more—more cars, more money, and more leisure time at the Long Island property."

Wilemina chimed in.

"Chauncey had always been a selfish, ungrateful child since the time he was born; fact is even in the womb he was selfish, quiet as it's kept. And he didn't have brothers and sisters around to learn how to share, you see."

"Truth be told," she added "his parents spent so little time with the boy that CS just continued to grow up that way. Nothin that I did in all those years around him made even a dent in his selfish soul."

Alfred cackled at that and nodded his head vigorously before speaking up again.

"We knew what was happening out on Long Island because we had to get that property cleaned up every time per strict orders of the lady of the house. We'd send a girl all the way out there by car ya see, just to clean up after him and them other young mens that he always entertained."

Wilemina shook her head and closed her eyes while sucking her teeth, as if remembering the details. Then she finished Alfred's thought.

"But that Chauncey, he liked it out there, private it was ya see; just him, his men friends, and the ocean. My girl always said that cleaning up out there behind them was a chore, a real chore."

Keisha didn't care to know any more about it at all and she was alarmed by what she was hearing. She was becoming convinced that advanced age had ravished the mental faculties of both. They seemed to comprehend her questions only partially and then they rambled head long down broad irrelevant avenues.

She tried a more direct approach.

"Would Carleton Smith do something that his wife objected to; would he hide the fact that he didn't wish to do what she wanted?"

WIlemina took the lead this time.

305

"Mr. Smith didn't hide from nothing. He was used to getting his way, yes he was. But he did love his wife; in between all that sleeping around with other women, I suppose he did."

Wilemina closed her eyes with a pained look and shook her head; more teeth sucking followed, leading Keisha to conclude that she must have personally witnessed or perhaps even personally experienced things.

Alfred began to nod in agreement before he covered up his hand under the blanket.

"Aint that the truth," he offered absentmindedly.

He repeated the phrase to himself three or four times. Then he added a completely unrelated fact.

"The wife wanted us out and gone from the Westchester mansion soon after Mr. Smith was stroke stricken. Gonna hire one of the modern services with modern people, she said. Mr. Smith was real weak back then, yes he was. And she had all them lawyer mens take him to the judge. We found out the judge was on her side cause Mr. Smith couldn't say nothing. Not long after that the missus gave us five hundred dollars cash apiece for our fifty years of service, yep ten bucks for each year. She even offered up a little bitty smile when we was headin out the door, luggage in hand."

"But seemed like she didn't know till after Mr. Smith passed and the will was read that he'd already set up a iron-clad trust to take care of us good!"

Wileminia added the kicker.

"Ya see, the missus learned from the will readin that we'd be the only ones here in this big white house. We don't want for nothing, all the help we need. Joke was on the wife, yes it was; two black folks livin in a big white house with modern help!"

"Mr. Smith had also given away that Long Island place to a Black group a few months before the stroke; it was a big surprise for the missus and she was in a rage over it. We think the one-two punch of it all moved her early into her own grave a year after he passed."

Alfred cracked up after she said that and was joined by Wilemina. They laughed so hard that Keisha grew concerned for their frail health.

Alfred abruptly stopped laughing and uttered an apologetic sentiment.

"The Lord gives and the Lord takes away, and I suppose we should honor and not mock the dead. Lord, forgive us."

Before continuing, Wilemeina nodded solemnly.

"Mr. Smith always got done what he wanted to get done," she opined.

Keisha tried to get things back on track.

"Did he ever mention in your presence that he would disinherit Chauncey?"

Alfred again.

"I heard him say many times counselor that he'd been too soft on that boy."

Willemina nodded in agreement and added some more.

"Yes he did counselor. Mr. Smith knew he'd been soft on CS and it wasn't hardly any good for no one. Have to let him sink or swim was what he kept saying during them court days with Chauncey. Sink or swim; he said that a lot. And CS went on ahead and sunk into prison, yes he did."

Keisha spent another thirty minutes trying to angle something else that might help her case. In the end she concluded that she had a tape mostly full of generalities. But in her gut the portrait that the lawsuit painted of Carleton Smith—a timid man afraid to disappoint his wife's desires—didn't square with the independent minded and manipulative alpha-male revealed to her by the two nonagenarians. In fact, her strong impression was that Chauncey's kidnapping stunt to extort him had been the last straw—a personal affront—that drove him to cut CS completely off.

Which meant that Melinda Smith's testimony and the lawsuit that it supported was a lie.

***

Theo Madrian looked around his three hundred square foot print shop and admitted that if his business was to survive he needed to go out and find a big headline. Printing only serious stories about important community issues hadn't helped his bottom line.

He was among the nearly two-dozen struggling community newspapers in Berkeley that distributed their newspaper free of charge. His revenue derived solely from ad placements. While most of the local small businesses had supported him with paid advertising for the past three years, with his declining distribution that might soon change.

Since working as assistant editor at the student newspaper in high school his dream had been a paper of his own, one that served a vital community need for relevant and topical news. A four-year journalism degree to get him there had been his original plan. But with average grades from an undistinguished high school and no family resources, the nearby two-year community college was his only viable option. And now, as his paper continually failed to make a meaningful profit, his dream to return to college for his B.A. was on hold as was his personal life after deciding that dating was too expensive a habit on top of falling revenues

On a positive note his recent series about youth engagement in quality extracurricular activities during afterschool and summer months had received dozens of favorable comments.

He followed up those articles with a light piece about the *Sail Shape* purchase of the Marin County marina. He teased his readers with a question about whether that might be a good venue for youth who found themselves restricted to their Berkeley neighborhoods during the summer. He promised them more about the camp in future articles. But soon after that was published the home invasion took place and the hysteria that ensued made him delay a planned follow-up story.

But Theo was convinced that an overnight camp in easy busing distance from the dangerous conditions that many kids faced in their neighborhoods during the summer made a lot of sense. As he thought more about it he shuffled through the pile of papers on his cluttered desk and pulled out something he remembered reading in a national publication.

"If we make the effort to attack the twin anvils that hold our kids back during the summer—idle minds and lack of motivation—they will be much more successful. When opened our new *Sail Shape* camp in Marin County will do just that." Brett Howard, Founder and CEO

That made perfect sense to Theo because he'd covered so many kids over the past three years that had ended up in trouble simply because they had nothing better to do and no positive activities to engage in.

He thought about the home invasion again. The circumstances had always seemed fishy based on the facts reported in the papers over there. The obvious flaws were the tagger's use of blocked lettering as opposed to free-style and the fact that nothing was taken from inside the home. But none of the articles found that to be strange.

He also remembered that silly message supporting the *Sail Shape* purchase. In his opinion the syntax was much too mainstream for any self-respecting urban tagger. Most important of all though, there was no signature or bragging rights emblazoned on the work. That just didn't happen.

When he finally posted his thoughts about it all he'd received more than a thousand likes and several detailed comments supporting his point of view. But a number of comments criticized him for ignoring the fear that the invasion had caused the family. Black or white, no one deserved to have his or her living space violated they pointed out; he agreed with them in his reply.

He walked over to his workstation and opened his social media links as he continued to ponder his diminishing future in the newspaper business. They showed week-to-week downward trends that were exactly the reverse of what he'd pledged to accomplish three months ago.

So, at the risk of bringing up old news he posted a new message about the home invasion. After all he reminded himself as he typed the post, this is about hits and engagement and the home invasion had drawn his greatest number.

Am I the only one that finds it strange that there's been no follow up and no closure in the Marin County home invasion case? Don't we all deserve competent police work?

He pushed back in his desk chair and watched the likes, dislikes, and comments populate his pages. The likes were outnumbering dislikes by about five to one. Nearly all of the positive comments agreed with him in one way or the other.

But one strange comment from a reader called Hand of Justice stood out; it was unusually hostile. It pointedly warned him to let the matter drop and admonished that old news was cold news. It went on to threaten that Theo might find himself joining cold news as a cold case in the future. As he stared at the comment it just seemed to be a huge outlier; no other post had criticized the very mention of the issue let alone followed up with a death threat. He did something then that running his small business rarely afforded; he clicked on the page of Hand of Justice and examined his site.

The usual family and friends photos along with numerous pseudo-wisdom quotes were displayed, but strangely not one selfie. He was about to leave the page when his eye was drawn to the large collage of vivid photos; pretty good stuff though all seemed to be phone shots. One was a picture of the wall that had been tagged during the home invasion.

He assumed at first that it was just lifted from the newspapers. But as he examined it more closely he thought that it looked slightly different from the image that the police had released. He went into his archived database and pulled it up; they were identical, except that the Hand of Justice shot was taken from the left side of the image rather than the right.

He realized at once the implications of his discovery.

Hand of Justice had to have been at the scene, he'd taken a shot of the wall with his cell phone while he admired his handiwork.

At first, he was tempted to send his conclusions to the police and walk them through why Hand of Justice had to be the one. But the more he rehearsed that scenario in his mind the more he realized that the police and many others had no vested interest in finding out who perpetrated the actual crime since no one was injured.

He decided to use social media. He created a multi-week contest for his print edition and for his web sites that boldly claimed that he had solved the home invasion mystery without the police, and he challenged his online and print audiences to be the next to solve the crime. They would win a five hundred dollar cash prize for the effort.

In his wildest imagination he couldn't have predicted that his circulation during the contest would explode. He also never imagined that his ad revenues would climb by three hundred percent. His social media was so hot that he hired a part-time journalism student from a local college just to keep up.

It tuned out that several members of the police force had been monitoring the website for clues and they'd used Theo's leads to identify the fake online account of the perpetrator. The home invader turned out to be a local tagger who'd been hired by an unidentified man from New York.

Police made a quiet arrest one day before the grand prizewinner identified Hand of Justice.

The positive news from the arrest signaled that it was the best time for him to publically renew his support for the *Sail Shape* camp. He decided to run a series of investigative articles about the camps across the country that would also serve to counteract any lingering negative press coverage in Marin County about the east coast lawsuits facing the camp. Getting ahold of someone who could speak knowledgeably about what was happening in the legal cases turned out to be a big problem. Reaching Brett Howard for a telephone interview was impossible.

He took a chance and pulled up all of the on-line court filings in the New York litigation. To his surprise there was a west coast law firm based in Los Angeles on the case in addition to an Albany firm. He assumed that the Albany firm was affiliated with Brett Howard given that the papers were signed by an attorney named Keisha Howard.

He recognized senator J Broderick's name as the other attorney involved and he wondered what connection could possibly have influenced the senator to be involved with the cases given the reliable rumors that he would soon announce for the governor's race. One thing was clear, however, his chance of getting an interview with the senator was virtually nil in light of all the pending activity. But perhaps someone else in the Los

Angeles firm who worked on the New York matters might be reachable.

After a convoluted explanation to the law firm's receptionist where Theo employed some of the practiced charm that he had mastered over the years when digging into stories, she finally put him through to a paralegal named Shana Pierce who was reluctant at first to speak even generally about the lawsuits and the prospects for success. But gradually he was able change that and convince her to talk about each matter.

Nevertheless Shana was careful to stay within the confines of what had been filed publically in the cases and to limit her opinions about where the cases were headed.

But Theo at least had something to work with.

"Well Shana I can't thank you enough for taking the time out of your afternoon to accept my unsolicited call out of the blue. You've given me a great overview of where things are. I've got more than enough to begin my planned series, but given the sensitivities I would be reluctant to publish anything for fear of compromising the cases. Maybe we could collaborate and if you wouldn't mind you might take a look at my drafts to ensure that I stay on the right side of the lines?"

By that time Shana had lost her earlier frostiness with him. In truth anything associated with the east coast litigation had made her sad and angry in alternating waves. But Theo's enthusiasm about the advantages that *Sail Shape* would have for Berkeley youth had won her over.

But she also liked hearing about his newspaper and his aspirations for it. She found him to be quite inquisitive and clearly talented. And he was the first newspaper editor she'd ever spoken with personally. And more than that, he had a good sense of humor and a self-deprecatory style, both of which had helped chip away at her irritability.

"It would make good sense for us to review the articles before publication, Theo. My boss, senator Broderick, should also be involved in that. Can I depend on you to email me any drafts as you complete them?"

"Certainly; that's a great offer Shana and I accept. I also had another idea that I hope you won't find too forward on my part.

The independent black newspaper association is holding its annual convention in Los Angeles next month, the 6th, 7th and 8th. Loads of contacts and info that are invaluable in my business will happen over those three days. I'll be there for two out of the three days. Maybe we might get together for lunch and go over a draft article together in person."

He held his breath, hoping that his offer wouldn't be considered a rude come-on. But if she considered it a normal come-on he was fine with that since it was.

By then Shana had already pulled up three articles and photos about one Theo Madrian from Berkeley, CA.

Hmmm, not at all bad looking; business owner; not married; and definitely not rich or famous.

Maybe lunch would be fun, she concluded as she closed the pages.

"That would be nice Theo, I look forward to meeting you in person."

"I feel the same way, Shana. I'll call you to confirm the week before. Thanks for helping me today, I believe these articles will help *Sail Shape* and help the kids in Berkeley after the camp is opened."

When she hung up the phone she had the strangest thought, she hoped that J would decide to stay in the lawsuits after all, at least until after her lunch with Theo.

✳✳✳

Waited for her in the conference he'd yet to decide how to explain that he would be withdrawing from all of the New York litigation. But at least he had determined to share that conclusion with her first before telling Brett.

How do you say I quit he asked himself? How do you walk out at a critical juncture and leave your team under resourced?

That he had to walk away, had to abandon the cause was his only realistic play if he wanted to be a viable candidate for governor. It was a hard decision he rationalized, yet one that would allow him to make a bigger difference later on.

Nevertheless, it wasn't sitting well with him particularly now that he was on the ground in Albany.

In fact recent polling results seemed to be breaking against that decision. Since his meeting with Chad his favorability numbers were trending up. The litigation was also starting to turn somewhat in their favor along with two recent positive press stories.

But none of it was enough to make him change his mind.

He was fidgeting with a yellow paperclip when his internal debate flared up again. He felt compelled to try and convince himself again that he had already contributed enough such that his efforts wouldn't really be missed. In lawyerly fashion he mustered his best arguments.

In his estimation the shooting at the Long Island camp seemed unlikely to result in convictions—unless the prosecutors wanted to risk being embarrassed at trial. They didn't appear to be that stupid and they would likely accept Keisha's counter offer since more delay hadn't improved their chances.

Second, the lawsuit against Brett for negligence was a bit of a stretch, particularly given that there were no physical injuries to any of the girls at the camp. Yet the possibility of damages for emotional distress was still a risk. So the case still needed substantial work.

Finally, he calibrated the facts in the suit to take *Sail Shape*'s land. There was no denying that a tough slog lay ahead there. But at least the research that he was leaving behind would lighten the load and the costs.

All he'd done he conceded was confirm that he was abandoning ship but not at the worst possible time. But his conscience reminded him that it certainly was the most favorable time for him. And by the way it tweaked him again, forget about any possible future romantic involvement with her, she'll understandably turn away from you after you quit.

Just when he was feeling completely condemned she swept into the conference room, intense, beautiful, yet clearly worried.

"Don't tell me," he said looking up at her with a wry smile, "there's been another lawsuit filed right?"

"No, I actually wish it were something that simple. It's my father, my biological one. You see I took to heart your pep talk that maybe I should confront him, get the demons out in the open. So at the end of a search using several different sources I found him. He's still in the Bowery but now at an in-patient facility for recovering addicts and alcoholics. After a few conversations with his doctors I assumed that he was doing okay, sober and off drugs for about a year."

"A few minutes ago they called to tell me that he had a setback. They call renal failure a setback nowadays," she asked before nervously answering her own question?

"The last time I checked the medical literature—which was right after I hung up the phone—it said that the consequences might be fatal."

"That's terrible; I'm very sorry to hear it. You're right to be worried though, renal failure is no joke. But at least you've located him and have been keeping tabs on him, that's good news; otherwise you would have no idea what's happening. Have you been there to see him or have you spoken to him yet?"

"No and no. I've been intending to talk with him on the phone but it just never happened. I actually tried to go to see him several times. You know, just get on a flight, take a cab and see him…it's not like he's going anywhere or like I need an appointment. But something seems to always come up at the last minute, maybe it's more than procrastination."

He got up and walked over to her, placing his hands lightly on her shoulders.

"Hey, we've got a forty-eight hour window before the motion hearing. Let's fly down to the City. We'll go by to see your father together. It's not like we won't be working on the flight down and back."

As he said that he heard his rational mind screaming at him that it wasn't true, that he should take back the offer immediately, that he was done and soon heading back to California.

She looked up at him. Despite herself she'd already begun to see him as a man as well as a good lawyer and it was becoming increasingly more difficult for her to erect the professional separation. She was confused by her new feelings and also slightly terrified that she was thinking about him in that way.

"That's very nice of you but I certainly couldn't …impose on you like that."

"Nonsense counselor. You already said your father has taken a serious turn. Would you really want anything to happen before you've had a chance to see him?"

She knew the answer was no. It made sense to go and just get the visit over with.

"Okay then, let me have my admin book our tickets for later this evening, if you're really up for it. She'll get us a hotel room, two rooms, and we can go by and see him in the morning and fly back here tomorrow afternoon. Thanks, thank you very much."

"Now you're talking. But before we get too ecstatic about that I've got about two hours of briefing material to go over with you."

On the short flight he pretended to read a thick legal brief as he reclined two seats over from her. But inside he was wrestling with how and when to tell her that he had made a final decision. Was there a better time and place than another? Maybe when they returned to Albany. Giving her the news now while she was making an emotional pilgrimage just didn't make a lot of sense to him.

But how disingenuous would it be to tell her later? You spend twenty-four hours together and not mention one word about where you've landed, that you're pulling the plug?

He thought about doing it right after she visited her father, before the return flight. Yet he had no idea how emotional the long overdue meeting between them might turn out to be. And then what, drop the hammer on her while she's trying to sort through everything?

He mocked himself.

Umm, excuse me, would you like a tissue, what a tough meeting that was between you and your dad? And oh by the way, I'm going to abandon Brett and the camps and you, have a nice day and make sure to keep in touch.

The word abandon resonated in his mind; it became a vortex pulling in self-indicting memories and questions.

Abandon

Wasn't that what happened long ago with Val? She worked; he played; she died. And for the many years after that hadn't he abandoned all semblance of the passion that inspired him and his classmates to occupy that college campus in the first place. He'd chosen safer roads for himself since those days, the bland and proper. Hadn't he fully abandoned the courageous activist's road that Val had blazed for all of them? Wasn't he merely a follower, both then and now?

Hadn't he used Brett in the years after that, not to help him forge a path forward but rather to help perfect his path of least resistance?

He'd even abandoned his own name, opting for the politically correct and focus group tested alternative.

He spiraled into guilt and didn't realize the pitch of his descent until he triggered that lifeline of psychological counseling that always seemed to help—you didn't abandon your friend Jazz; her death was a tragic mistake by a police sniper. There was nothing you could have done to change what happened, nothing.

Get it together he counseled himself; the situations then and now are completely different.

But were they distinct, he wondered? Wasn't there an analytical bridge between the past and the present? Wasn't it his own inconsistency, his own malleable persona? And hadn't that been demonstrated throughout his adult life where he'd settled for the comfortable veneer of probity above all else?

Pushing back he recognized that he had been in the middle of the fray on occasion, advocating aggressively on behalf of his district when called upon. Yet for the vast amount of time ever since high school hadn't he only played defense while looking every bit the part of the heroic combatant?

Vestis virum non facit, the Latin phrase came back to mind from his junior high class; clothing does not make the man. Hadn't he forgotten that lesson?

No. No, none of that's true he protested, dismissing his own charges. He'd done a raft of good and made a difference in many areas. He had tried to do the right thing; but yes, he wasn't perfect.

Echoes from his ancient counseling sessions gave him one more lifeline to grasp; you control your own future Jazz, never yield that job to the past.

Managing to get more of a grip he kept the depression at bay. Yet he realized that he had to get out of his own head and quickly. Talk to someone, to her he thought as he glanced over— about anything but the past.

He put his binder aside and looked back, her head was still buried in a file, and as usual she laced her fingers slowly through her curly Afro.

Her reached across and lightly touched her arm.

She looked at him and smiled.

"Keisha, did I ever tell you why I actually want to go through the tortuous gauntlet of running for governor?"

"Well no, in fact you never did. I always thought it was because you were a masochist like the rest of us lawyers; don't we all have to admit to that on the law school application? Going into politics is clear proof that you can't be cured."

They shared a good chuckle.

"I'm sorry for the levity," she apologized.

"I would very much like to know why you'd run for governor of the great state of California?"

She focused her hazel eyes on him while she settled back and waited to absorb his every word.

She looked so gorgeous like that he realized, but he maintained his concentration.

"Well, first of all," he said with a grin, "if I tell you, you must be prepared to be the first lady of California."

She smiled and raised her eyebrows as she listened for more.

It occurred to him that she didn't say no.

He cleared his throat.

"Okay, I'm getting serious. And this isn't from some slick campaign booklet...we'll produce those in about twelve months."

"I want to be governor because I believe I can effectively lead the state. It's a state of astounding diversity, a state with huge problems on the one hand and enormous potential on the other. My record in the Assembly and Senate and even earlier has proven that I can work with different constituencies and build coalitions to tackle the important issues facing all of us. We've got to stop wasting valuable time, we've got to start cutting through gridlock and doing what matters. I've always been able to accomplish that with people who want change—in high school, back in college and in the business and political arenas."

She listened; occasionally she nodded her head in agreement. As she did so she thought about the brief time that she'd known him and concluded that he did have those abilities and that he was an influencer, a leader. He had even been able to move her to see her father, which she admitted was an extraordinary achievement. In that moment she finally made up her mind about him.

He had substance and depth beneath the politician's veneer that he frequently wore. And his involvement in the lawsuits—despite the political pressure that he must be feeling—meant that he had guts as well.

Her active listening encouraged him; he abandoned his talking points to reveal more about himself.

"You know what, I'm a bit of a fish out of water in Cali, a black Republican in a vast pool of liberals and progressives. Primarily that's due to my stance on economic issues. I'm convinced that opportunity for all can only be gained by economically empowering folks, freeing them by removing roadblocks in front of their dreams and letting them go for it; in real estate, business, and other fields. Those are the hard battles we have to take on and win. Patting people on the head and promising to take care of all their needs is a false hope, hasn't worked yet."

"And it's where I fundamentally differ with the other side of the isle," he added.

"Don't get me wrong," he clarified.

"My personal points of emphasis don't mean that rights and causes don't matter. I just think there is more leverage and a stronger future in the economic arguments.

She thought about it. She had felt her nose scrunch up a little at the mention of the Republican Party. Yet as she considered what he said she didn't disagree with him on the economic arguments so long as fairness was part of the equation. She made a mental note though about his political affiliation. Her small crowd was strictly comprised of democrats and independents. She wondered how he would manage at socializing with her friends. He'd do just fine she decided.

But hold on there she admonished herself and don't get ahead of things with him; he's just a friend.

"I've never really thought about it quite that way," she replied.

"But do consider that not everyone on the democratic side of the isle is a blind supporter of the welfare state."

Her raised eyebrows signaled that she included herself in that skeptical group.

"Exceptions noted," he acknowledged.

"So that's it in a nutshell, that's my sixty-second elevator speech. It's the message that I've got to deliver to millions of Californians to earn their trust and their vote."

He shifted, moving his long legs from under the seat in front of him, stretching them out beneath the middle seat. For a moment he turned away from her.

Maybe he'd gotten a bit too amped up about the coming campaign, he worried. Would she understand his positions or treat it all as hubris?

"Thank you for sharing that with me, Jazz."

She smiled; she hoped that he wouldn't mind her using her preferred name for him.

"It was enlightening. Your passion for the position came through loud and clear. I think that you'd make a good governor given your varied background. Without a doubt, if I were a California voter you'd have my support senator," she said pleasantly.

She looked down for a second as she considered whether to place another part of herself with him.

"Do you have any idea why I really want to see my father after all these years," she asked?

"Well no, not really; in fact not at all based on our previous conversation. From what you've told me he was a cold fish, basically unconnected to you and your mother and sister."

"That's it exactly. And his indifference continued unabated after mother passed. Aunty Lai adopted me soon thereafter and within a year she'd married Brett. My absentee father was completely replaced from that moment forward. But the more I've come to grips with it the more I realize that our relationship shouldn't have ended like that."

She thought she saw compassion in his eyes or was it confusion.

"The reason I need to see him is to tell him that I've released all my anger and disappointment. That took me many years to arrive at you know, decades. I carried so much hurt and resentment for so long. But over time I began to see how strong addiction can be and eventually I understood that some folks don't have a chance; they just sink to the bottom as if bound up in chains. But my analysis of it all had just stopped there years ago. It's why I appreciate the push you gave me; who knows how long it would have taken me to see him without that, if ever."

She had to make sure that all the layers were disclosed.

"Don't get me wrong, "she continued.

"I'm not letting him off the hook; a lot of the choices he made were deliberate and mean spirited. They scared all of us. And yes, there was violence. My sister and I would sit huddled in our room and listen to the blows."

It's just that my views on the whole thing have softened; my faith helped me get there in a big way. So maybe my visit will give him some peace in his current condition. If not peace, then a sense of closure on our dysfunctional past."

Once again, she looked away and paused. She appreciated the fact that he had said nothing yet in reply, that he was a good listener.

"You know, there's another related thing," she offered after finally deciding to reveal her long hidden secret.

He wondered what could be next.

"When I was a girl, soon after my mom passed, I was assaulted by a mentally ill man in my old neighborhood. But he had been sane enough at the time to set a trap for me when a group of us were running around playing a hide and seek game. He caught me alone and pulled me through a door into a dark basement."

He watched her close her eyes and exhale.

"Fortunately, I received the professional help then to deal with everything. But according to the physician that I spoke with at my father's facility he still screams about it in his sleep. So you see, he remains tormented about not being there to protect me, even though I was able to protect myself during the years that followed."

He didn't know what to say after hearing it, a very unusual circumstance for him. He reached for her hand and held it.

It made him think how easy it was to form misassumptions about someone that you didn't know well. He'd been guilty of that with her because she always appeared to be so polished and in control. Yet she was as human and vulnerable as he was. They both had unique pain to carry.

He needed to lighten the mood, perhaps to lighten her burden as well, but he wasn't sure how. He said the first thing that came to mind.

"You'd like California, you know," he said while smiling. "I'm certain that you would."

She looked at him, not daring to ask what he meant by it.

Chapter Twenty:
London Sunset

PREPARING FOR ANOTHER PREDAWN JOG, he laced up his running shoes at five in the morning. He was alone which was his daily routine in San Francisco. Running was a medicinal necessity, providing that needed endorphin boost that allowed him to operate at a high level on very little rest.

He missed Mirra even more after so many weeks apart. There hadn't been any post adjustment phase where he had grown accustomed to her absence. Occasionally when his separation anxiety spiked, he felt as if she'd sent him away deliberately, that she'd exiled him for reasons she wouldn't share. When he coupled that with the fact that she continued to reject the idea of visiting, even for a brief time, it just didn't make any sense and he would question whether what they had together was going to last.

But he would always recover his senses during those down moments and assign the proper responsibility for his anxiety—he was the one on this quest; he was the one chasing after the Cup; and he was the one who left her back home in order to do it.

Oftentimes near the end of his hilly and chilly 5 k tempo runs through the Presidio, Russian Hill, and Hayes Valley, his lows were replaced with incredible highs. On occasion he imagined that he might even beat her when he returned home for those much-missed and flat Hyde Park runs together. Well maybe not beat her he usually admitted, but at least give her a better go than in the old days.

Needing to hear her voice before heading out he reached for his cell phone. It was early afternoon London time, so he hoped to catch her having a late lunch.

Just like the previous three days there was no answer and her voice mailbox remained full. Something tugged strongly at him, something wasn't right.

He hit Jemal's speed dial button and waited.

"Hello boss, how are you?"

He detected far too much stress in his voice.

"Jemal, what's the matter with Mirra and don't BS me; I already know something is very wrong."

Jemal was relieved to finally tell everything that he'd been holding inside, the words poured out.

"She started to get sick a few weeks ago, boss. She said it was just a small fever, but it didn't improve and now she's in the hospital. When it started, she ordered everyone not to worry you about it because of your racing. She said that everything would work out fine. Later on, when she lost a lot of weight she said that you would be okay where you are; and that she had already taken care of the future. It scared me. I didn't know what she was talking about, nobody did."

"God damn it Jemal," he heard his voice rising.

"When's the last time you saw her; what do the doctors say, get me her primary physician's address and telephone number; and I want the home number as well. Damn it, why didn't someone reach out to me?"

He was fast developing a pressure headache; it radiated out from his forehead and pressed deep into the back of his cranium. He slowed down and willed himself back to calm.

"Jemal, I'm sorry I swore at you. Forgive me, there's no excuse for that."

"What do they think is wrong with her," he asked as calmly as possible?

Jemal hesitated for a moment before plunging ahead.

"I haven't heard anything in days, I feel cut off out here from everything. But when we were in Ethiopia at the village several months ago there was a child that she stayed with during the whole night."

Joshua couldn't stop himself from cutting in.

"I know all that, she told me. The girl had a fever, also had severe malnutrition, right? She died while you went to get medicine. What about it? What could that have to do with Mirra?"

"The young girl had severe malnutrition, yes boss, but that was from the sickness alone as there had been enough food provided to her. She had river sickness. Mirra may have it; at least I think so. She was eating fine but she mentioned to me on the phone about a month ago that she was losing more weight. When I was speaking to Louise after that she had joked with me that if Mirra kept working out as hard as she was, she was going to waste away before you got back home."

Joshua heard himself screaming, again.

"Boss, boss please slow down. Yes, I tried to explain this to the doctors, but they don't hear me at all. They've never heard of river sickness, so it doesn't exist for them."

"Jemal, how much time do you think…?"

"Not very long; you must come home quickly."

The unique aspect about so many London buildings he thought distractedly as he walked along after Harold's lift was how old they looked on the outside but how very modern many were on the inside. Unlike his experience in California, London and indeed most of Europe had found a way for the past and the present to coexist without a zero-sum war between them.

Crossing through the spacious reception area beneath the enormous, vaulted ceiling he wondered how many times this prewar, Baroque inspired shell had been renovated. Then he remembered his research; the structure had been leveled during WW II due to its proximity to No. 10 Downing Street. It had been completely renovated twice after that.

He signed in at an unattended reception desk. Immediately after that a heavy-set male nurse who had been leaning against a far wall intercepted him and escorted him down a well-lit hallway. He found it odd that that the nurse was wearing a jacket despite the comfortable temperature. Without saying a word, his escort left him alone in an empty anteroom.

Dr. Stockholm arrived five minutes later and greeted him with a limp hand wave and no introduction. He was a short slightly built man with immaculately coifed hair. He wore black-rimmed glasses that dominated his face and weighed down his nose.

Stockholm spun around in a military-like manner and walked rapidly to a far corridor; Joshua fell in by his side.

The destination was intensive care; Stockholm had muttered that without turning his head. On the way Joshua noticed that the hospital was empty, just like the lobby. When they finally reached the ICU a small collection of functional furniture occupied a ten-foot square space in front of the entrance. A half dozen elongated windows covered with ill-fitted light blocking curtains surrounded the enclosure. They moved quickly through the entrance and marched down a glistening white corridor while passing dozens of closed doors and abandoned nurses' stations.

After rounding a corner, they were confronted by three bulky special-forces troopers who had been leaning casually against the opposite wall while cradling automatic weapons. On their feet in a hurry, they eyed Joshua warily as he and Stockholm moved past.

What's that hell was that about he mumbled out loud as his pulse rate slowly returned to normal. Stockholm was unfazed and remained silent.

Must be a V.I.P. patient or maybe a prisoner on the floor he rationalized as he tried to make sense of what he had just seen.

Finally, the doctor stopped and turned around to face him in the middle of another barren corridor, one that reeked of pungent antiseptic.

"Mr. Howard, I'm Dr. Stockholm. I'm pleased to meet you. I understand you've come a very long way."

Already impatient with the belated pleasantries and increasingly suspicious over his surroundings, he managed to suppress his strong urge to shout that he wanted to know immediately, right then and now, about Mirra's condition.

"Doctor, thank you so very much for your care and attention for her. Please tell me how she's progressing. And of course, I would like to see her as soon as possible."

Stockholm removed his giant glasses, cleaning them thoroughly with a soft cloth produced from his lab coat breast pocket. After an extended pause he looked up.

"She is stable Mr. Howard. Her vital signs have finally leveled off. We are providing her with added hydration and nourishment, intravenously."

He waited for more, for something that would provide a sliver of hope. But Stockholm had stopped talking and was fidgeting with invisible dust on his sleeve.

"Doctor, when will she begin to pull out of this? And what exactly is the diagnosis, you didn't say?"

He asked that while managing to keep his voice steady.

"Mr. Howard, you see that's the strange thing about this case," Stockholm said as he finally looked up with magnified eyes.

"We've never seen anything like it before. Our expert team conducted the standard battery of blood and toxicology work. Nothing. Then we called in a second highly renowned panel, same result. At this point we've hit a brick wall. We have no diagnosis, let alone a prognosis."

"Is this some form of river sickness," Joshua asked, hiding the desperation in his voice?

"She was in west and east Africa several months ago. I'm sure you're aware of that."

"Yes, we are aware of her precise travel itinerary within Senegal and Ethiopia. The truth is that if this is a form of river sickness Mr. Howard, it is a strain that the western world has never encountered before, an isolated strain thank God. We must keep it so."

"So far, our best efforts have only prevented her from…slipping over the edge. Yet we don't know how long the current stabilization will last."

Mounting despair and dread gripped his chest. He swallowed hard before finding his voice.

"Doctor, I must see her."

Stockholm removed his glasses once again and cleaned them thoroughly. He looked up while his left eye twitched.

"I'm afraid that won't be possible Mr. Howard; since this…. illness is so evasive we have out of necessity invoked the national health protocols."

That's when Joshua lost it.

'What? What does that mean exactly? What kind of protocols are you talking about? If you don't take me in there to see her right now, right this second, I'll have her removed from here."

He pulled out his cell phone and started to hit Harold's speed dial button.

Stockholm reached for Joshua's wrist and slowly lowered the phone.

"I'm afraid that won't be possible Mr. Howard. You see, because this sickness is a danger to the entire city of London as well as to Great Britain as a whole, your fiancé has been isolated and quarantined. No one may see her in person until that is lifted. That also includes me I'm afraid. Those restrictions are backed by English force of arms. You passed some of that on your way in. Even the nurse in the outer lobby was Special-Forces, heavily armed."

It killed his anger.

He closed his eyes and pictured Mirra as a prisoner inside the walls; isolated, alone, sealed.

Think; he forced himself. He looked at the physician and managed to speak calmly.

"But doctor, if no one can attend to her how is she being cared for?"

"The protocols mandate strictly robotic care under these extreme circumstances which are the most unfortunate, I'm afraid. As a treating physician I certainly know the power of human touch as a healing agent. We haven't had access to her for three days now."

Think, think; there must be a way to get past this.

His mind raced, then he had an idea.

"Doctor Stockholm, do you have audio-visual equipment in the room with her?"

"Well not exactly, but of course we keep a careful watch on her through a small observation portal. And we have her connected to the usual battery of monitoring devices for blood, pulse, and vital signs along with back up dialysis and cardio equipment, if needed."

"Okay, but do you have a separate observation camera in the room right?"

"Yes, of course."

"And that camera is hard-wired to the network here in the hospital, right? The network is WI-FI capable; I assume.

"Yes; we use encrypted WI-FI in the hospital, and it is available in the wing where she's isolated. But I'm afraid the picture quality is primitive. And we haven't used the microphone set up for the many years that I've consulted here."

"Okay; thanks. Then what I need you to do, please, is have one of your robots take my cell phone into the room and brace it near her pillow, cell camera pointing at her. Before that I'll need your passwords and the IP address of your video camera network. I can hack your network and program my phone to run the audio and video signal. She won't see me, but I'll see her, and we'll be able to talk."

Seeing Stockholm's reluctance, he added one thing more.

"You can sterilize or even destroy my phone after it is removed from the room, if need be."

Stockholm looked at him and started to take his glasses off again before he suddenly stopped.

"Yes, we can certainly do all that Mr. Howard. Come with me."

"Mirra, Mirra, wake up darling. Wake up love its Joshua."
Nothing.
He tried several more times before turning to Stockholm.
"That bot, can it be manipulated to nudge her awake?"
"Why yes, the bot is fully functional."
Stockholm reached for the control module and began punching codes into the panel as he swiveled the joystick.
The bot rolled smoothly to the bedside and then bent over as if it were taking a bow.

She stirred after it tugged on the blanket several times.

Joshua called her name again, her eyes opened.

"Turn your head to the right sweetheart; turn to the phone."

She slowly moved and looked at it; he saw her face for the first time in weeks, small, sunken, pale. Her eyes were filmy and unfocused.

He choked back tears.

"Hello Joshua, hello honey."

The voice was weak and raspy.

How long had she really been spiraling down like this? It couldn't have happened in only three days. But he put off questioning Stockholm, for now.

"I'm here with you darling right outside the room; but I can see you. They won't let me come in until you're better love. But I'm going to be here until then, don't you worry."

She seemed to draw energy from his presence; he believed that she was visibly getting stronger now that he was near.

"I was dreaming about you, about us," she said. "We were together in America, talking to each other. It's so good to be near you again, Joshua."

Her speech was halting, yet he still felt her spirit.

"How is your racing going honey; are you winning," she said?"

"Yes darling, we're doing well," he said that even though it was the last thing he wanted to talk about.

"When I left, we had two races max remaining in the current round and a final round after that. If we win that we challenge for the Cup. There's been a little slippage in the schedule."

"But Joshua," she objected, her speech seemed to falter.

"Will they...penalize you for coming...to see me? I didn't want that."

"No darling, I'll return and race. There's plenty of time for me to be here until you start feeling better."

He willingly lied.

She looked into the camera and blew him a kiss before her hand fell limply down.

"Joshua, I want you to return to San Francisco and race now; you must practice... with the crew to be ready..."

She started chain coughing from the exertion. Stockholm rolled the bot over to her bedside after it collected a glass of water from the meds table. She managed the straw and took in lots of fluid.

Mirra turned back to the camera and smiled at him. That lifted his spirits.

"I won't be getting well darling, I'm sorry. It just wasn't the plan for us, I don't know why. But you must believe that I'll always love you and that… I've taken care of the future."

He watched her features soften, her thin frame seemed to slowly absorb into the sheets and blankets around her.

The transformation startled him. It couldn't be happening.

"That's not true, darling. You'll get your strength back. And by the way, I'm more ready now to take you on during our morning runs. I've been kicking well you know in Frisco, running all those bloody hills. You'll see when you're well and we're back out in the park."

For the last time he witnessed her living spirit in the faint edges of her disbelieving smile and in the effort she used to raise her index finger and slowly move it from side to side.

"Joshua, I loved you so much. Thank you for believing in me, for wanting to be…husband. That…."

She paused again before whispering.

"Will always mean…"

Chapter Twenty-One:
Bless Us

SARAH WAS BESIDE HERSELF; a burst of optimism had lifted her mood to start the day. She wanted to go outside and skip along the sidewalk like a child. Instead, she took the stairs two and three at a time from her basement room.

Several months ago, she had no one except the older nuns and her convent sisters in her life, for which she always gave thanks. Now she had a mother who she was beginning to understand as well as a father, even though he remained more of a mystery. But at least he had professed to love her like a daughter.

And now she had BG.

How should she think about her?

She's more than a very good friend. She's more like an actual sister really. However, Sarah quickly recognized that she'd never had a blood sister for comparison purposes.

What do you like, no love, about her? She quizzed herself as she poured a cup of coffee and watched the clock steadily move to 7: 00 A.M.

For starters she felt as if they shared so much in common. Then again as she considered it more, she had to admit the truth, their lives growing up had been totally different.

But our lives are such an open book to each other now, she said out loud without noticing.

She wondered whether that kind of emotional sharing was permitted in counseling sessions. Thinking back to her training courses she couldn't remember if it was covered. It was too late to change things now anyway she cheerfully declared.

What impressed her most was that during all their sessions together BG was open and candid about the pressures on her in the past to be someone that she wasn't. She remembered a story that she had shared about her high school junior prom, one of many examples. Her mother and father had gone all out for her back then and she wore a lovely gown with cape, shoes, corsage, and the like. She remembered BG saying jokingly that she would have willingly donated the outfit to charity and worn something much simpler, like jeans and a sweatshirt.

Her mother had carefully selected her date from the local church because BG had failed to identify anyone on her own despite the months of pressure to do so. Her date was a good boy and a regular boy she admitted. That meant that in addition to attending the prom he wanted to have his dessert after it was over. In his adolescent mind BG was that item.

She explained to Sarah that they were sitting in the young man's car in front of her Albany house when he reached over, grabbed her, and planted a big kiss on her face. Because she was startled by that BG said that she had used a right hook that she learned from her big brother to knock the boy unconscious. But she said that she honestly couldn't remember throwing the punch.

Later, after the ambulance, the hospital, and the arrival of the boy's father to drive his son's car home, BG sat in her father's home office with an ice wrap on her knuckles trying to explain what happened.

That meeting didn't go well, apparently. Her father couldn't understand why the boy's desire to steal a kiss after the prom in front of the house verses in a park somewhere had resulted in a knockout punch. He was very unhappy. For her part BG said that she really didn't have an explanation at the time. All she could say was that she wasn't interested in boys. Her father heard her say that for several years but he figured that when she became a teenager he wouldn't be able to keep her away from them. But that hadn't happened.

The story prompted Sarah to reflect on her own life. It dawned on her that she'd never really been interested in boys either, not that her convent upbringing provided many opportunities for her to meet them. She was twenty-five years old now and it occurred to her that no boy or man had ever kissed her. Should she share that with BG, she wondered?

After finishing her coffee, she walked to the conference room for the first appointment. She hoped that the day would fly by because her mother was landing from New York at ten o'clock that evening.

She had so many more questions to ask her mother about life.

They sat next to each other on the low single bed in Sarah's windowless room.

"I should have fessed up before my flight Sarah, I'm sorry. I was just so ashamed, Stanford business school to ex con. I should have admitted that I'd spent two years here earning my MBA. And so no, this wasn't my first plane ride to California, not by a long shot; even though I falsely lead you to believe it would be."

"Mother, there are very few secrets anymore. Some of the articles I discovered about your trial mentioned that. The good news is that I have some of your smart genes in my DNA, along with my father's I suppose. I'll certainly need them all for med school."

Melinda looked at her, surprised.

"I guess I keep forgetting about this new future that I've joined. Be patient with me."

One thing that she hadn't forgotten was what had been troubling her since her deal with Steward to testify.

"Please let me ask you some questions about your friend BG if you don't mind, Sarah. First, how's she doing?"

Sarah instantly brightened.

"She's doing great. My work with her though is general verses clinical in nature, I urge her to share her feelings. So far, we have an open and honest relationship and that seems to have helped."

"We also have several advanced counseling courses at the center. They've helped her too, I believe."

"She knows that at some point she must talk with her parents. She wants to travel back east a few weeks from now to do that. Apparently, her dad is involved in a big legal case that's coming to a head and she wants to be there and show her support. That in and of itself is a huge change for her."

Melinda looked down and said something under her breadth that Sarah didn't quite hear.

"What was that?"

"I said I'm happy for her Sarah, for BG. I know you're both grown very close."

"Sarah, what did you say her last name was again?"

"Howard."

"She's from New York, right dear? Upstate?"

"That's right. She's from Albany."

"Did she ever tell you specifically what her family did for a living? Trust me, I'm not being nosey without good reason."

"Well, okay. Her mother runs a temp agency in the medical field. Her father is the founder of a group of sailing schools around the country. I think she said the original one is on Long Island somewhere; it's called *Sail Shape*."

Melinda's worst fears were now confirmed; she was involved in a case that would destroy the family of her daughter's best friend.

"What is it, why so many questions about her?"

After coming clean Melinda stopped talking. She knew that whatever faith Sarah had in her would be shattered. She waited for Sarah's reaction almost as a child awaits a spanking.

"I really can't believe that you agreed to get involved in a scheme like that."

Sarah's voice was shrill.

"Whether or not it involves BG's family is beside the point; the scheme is steeped in lies. I thought you were repentant, I thought you learned something during the past twenty-five years behind bars—you said you had! But now you both are at it again. And you're going to destroy an innocent family."

Sarah bolted from the bed over to the door. Staring back at her mother, she felt her loyalty to BG overwhelm the nascent feeling that had emerged for her parents. She confronted Melinda once more.

"You can't do this. You can't lie; you can't start the same pattern all over again. Don't you understand that the money won't help you, that you'll get tripped up somehow, maybe even run afoul of some obscure criminal rule. And my father, the same lies, the same deceit; prison didn't teach him a single lesson. He carries his bitterness around like a trophy."

"I wish I hadn't found either of you," she said!

Melinda remained seated on the bed as if glued down. All the justifications that she'd constructed in her mind had collapsed. She was guilty, an ex-con who hadn't learned a thing.

She finally replied with her head down.

"I'm so sorry Sarah. I was wrong and selfish and stupid. There's still time, I'll do my best to make it right, I promise you."

***

BG hung up at the end of a long call with her mother. She had gotten caught up on way too much family business and had disclosed more than she intended about her own.

She finally understood why her brother had been so unreachable. She'd thought it was the sailing until her mother described Joshua's telephone call that she received about Mirra's death. She guessed that he had called her for comfort and prayer. They were things that she excelled at.

How very sad, she thought. She'd never met Mirra in person but from the few times that they chatted on the phone over the years she had formed a bond with her. No question about it, they would have grown even closer if Mirra had lived and married her brother.

She remembered Joshua's excited call from London when he proudly announced that he'd popped the question. He was so up back then, and BG was overjoyed for him. Mirra had grabbed the phone and expressed both surprise and ecstasy that the proposal had happened. They had chatted together like sisters for at least an hour, which must have cost Joshua a small fortune. The fond memories made her remember a poetic phrase from her English

Lit class in college; it was about life being so very short and true happiness being even more fleeting. But she couldn't remember the writer's name.

During the call with her mother, she listened to her mother's several pessimistic comments about her father. He wasn't doing that well—health issues worse, two more lawsuits, and the California marina purchase in serious trouble. She also heard in her mother's tone that she was struggling mightily—and unsuccessfully—to remain close to him.

That her mother openly criticized him was the clearest sign because BG had never heard her speak about him like that before, so negatively and seemingly shutting him out. It forced her to think more about her own relationship with her father, how she'd essentially done the same thing but for different reasons. But dad wasn't her enemy; she had finally recognized that during her counseling sessions. And he didn't deserve all the emotional indifference that she had shown him for so many years.

So, she had passively listened to her mother's criticisms while refusing to join in.

Despite it all mommy dearest seemed to be holding up okay in other areas. BG heard the excitement in her voice when she mentioned that she and Remy were several months away from closing the deal that would merge LR Staffing into a huge company. She said it gave her the chance to spread her staffing philosophy nationally. When BG asked her where she would work from after the merger was closed, her reply had been telling.

Far away from here baby girl, I'll be in California, closer to you.

Then as an afterthought her mother had instructed her not to mention anything about the upcoming move to her father.

But what about you her mother had finally asked before hanging up? She was curious about why BG had been so out of touch and how she was coping with being away from medical school, and how the counseling sessions going; all of it asked in one run-on question.

As to why she'd been out of touch she replied that it was a combination of withdrawal and focus on her own life, trying to get better. She didn't mention that she had increasingly grown tired of the typical mother-daughter conversations between them, a lifelong ritual that covered everything but the most important things.

She also mentioned that the counseling sessions were helping, which was partially true. She shared that she was making good progress toward completing the requirements mandated by the judge as prerequisites to her return to medical school, also mostly true. And she spoke some about Sarah but deliberately not in a manner that conveyed the depth of the friendship that they had developed.

But what she kept hidden was that deep down inside she was far from happy even though her advanced counseling sessions had fully exposed the reasons for her wounded self. Yet, at the same time, they'd avoided any discussion about how she could accommodate her present disposition into a balanced and healthy emotional state in the future.

The diagnosis had been that living with her inner conflicted feelings was the cause of her volcanic explosions recently as well as in her past. So far so good with the analysis she'd believed when she heard it. But no prognosis had been forthcoming other than to pray earnestly about it. That proposed cure hadn't helped her at all, either in her past lives or recently.

Tough questions raced through BG's mind near the end of the call. Should she tell her mother about the drawbacks of the counseling? Would her mother be capable of taking it all in given her fulsome religiosity? Most of all, would she be prepared to accept the remedy that her youngest daughter, her baby girl, had finally started to believe was essential?

Despite great uncertainty she made a life-changing decision, acknowledge and confess the truth that she had suppressed since she was a pre-adolescent.

Mom, I'm simply not like most girls you know, I've never been attracted to boys or to men. I've met someone here... and she's wonderful. If she'll have me, we'll be together for life.

At first, she didn't believe that she had actually said that out loud; she must have only imagined saying it.

Lailani had responded, however, and what she said was a shock.

"I'm very happy for you baby girl, that you've embraced your true self. I'm heartbroken that we were never supportive of you as you struggled with identity. It was hard for us but that's no excuse. We could have done so much better raising you, understanding you, and accepting you for who you are at your core."

As she listened BG experienced what felt like a gradual weightlessness. She found herself having to listen very closely to her mother's words, clinging to each one, which seemed to keep her anchored and not floating away.

"My personal failure to do that was made worse, not better, by the one thing that has given me strength throughout my life, my faith. In the end though I just couldn't accept the orthodoxy anymore that preached that you had a choice and that who you were at your innermost was subject to a switch that you could willfully flip on or off. I had planned to share this with you in person when you came home, but now is best."

"Baby girl, please forgive us, forgive me; I'm so sorry."

She thought that she heard her mother crying softly. But all she could do was listen and wait and hold on.

"You know," Lailani said after a moment, "your father wants to see you very badly. He understands more now, and he loves you the same as he always did. He said he's looking forward to throwing the football around with you like he did so often when you were young. He put some air in that old beat-up, dirty thing last week."

"Come home to us soon, we need you here. Bring her with you. We want to meet her and welcome her. I love you."

In that remarkable moment as her mother's words continued to resonate, she felt the weight of the years lift from her shoulders. She believed for the first time that maybe things would be all right and that she might be okay. She was free now, wasn't she?

Sitting quietly after the call she continued to gain confidence and shed doubt. In time her thoughts returned to Sarah, she would have to share her real feelings with her as soon as possible.

***

Lailani didn't want it to be an emotional confrontation. On the other hand, she had grown tired of pretending that everything was going to work itself out. *Make it a quick conversation without drama,* she decided; Brett would have to adjust.

They sat next to each other in the old Adirondacks on the broad wraparound porch of their Albany home just like they'd done over many years before. He sipped lemonade while she had her iced tea.

Another generation of children ripped up and down the streets playing hard at Ring-O-Levio. As she watched the frantic bursts of energy, one team streaming away dead set on evading capture by the other, her mind's eye conjured images of Keisha, Joshua, and later baby girl running wildly through the same neighborhood playing the same game. Everybody knew it was the most fun game ever.

She was convinced that the best player ever at the game was sitting right next to her. She could still recall the many inventive escape and capture routes that he always seemed to devise when they were children together over in the old Arbor Hill section.

Looking at him she decided that the only way to begin was to share what was on her mind.

"There are some things that I've put off speaking to you about Brett. This is as good a time as any."

He could hear the anxiety in her voice; it signaled that the talk was going to be a serious one.

"What's on your mind, Lai?"

"Two very much related things really, one of which I've carried around for a good while now and the other that happened several months ago when I was in California."

The California reference surprised him because he couldn't remember her mentioning that she'd been there.

"First, I was out west to see Tony Calibri. You remember him of course. I should've told you that I was going. Tony pitched the possibility of buying LR Staffing several years back as I'm sure you recall. Well, I went out there to follow up with him on a phone call that he placed to Remy where he expressed interest again. I didn't mention that for two reasons. First, I wanted to surprise you while I was there—you were on the west coast at the same time—and second, I knew based on what happened years ago that you'd be opposed to my considering any possible deal with him."

As he thought about it, he had to admit that she was right about his negative reaction in the past. Why the heck did she need to combine with another company when she'd grown her own business without anyone's help? Yet, as he remembered more about those days it was part of his usual pattern of exchange with her, always pontificating and leaving her silently disappointed.

Were his negative opinions about a possible deal back then substantive objections or simply knee-jerk reactions? Much more of the later he admitted, much more of his well-honed reflex to dictate what and how things should be done.

It was one of the things that he was trying to change.

Then he remembered the strange call to his hotel room in California from a woman who had asked for him and then hung up, according to Zena. He shifted uncomfortably and took a long swig of lemonade.

"Was that your late-night call to my hotel room, Lai?"

"It was, yes. I called to surprise you and to meet you for breakfast before heading back east. The real shock for me was the woman answering the phone."

She looked directly at him.

"Have you been cheating on me?"

She held her breath.

"Cheating on you, Lai? No, I haven't been cheating on you. That's never been my aim. But yes, I did exercise bad judgment in that circumstance out there. The woman who answered the phone was Zena Melody Jenson; you remember the name, I'm sure. She insisted on the meeting and basically invited herself over that night. It was all about her daughter Mikala when she showed up and her need to have a fresh start. And that's the only reason I hired her to run Long Island for me; because of loyalty to a longtime supporter of the camps."

Lailani reached for her iced tea. Strangely she had felt no flush of relief after hearing his explanation.

But she certainly remembered Zena Melody Jensen and she understood the woman remained a major benefactor; and that she was his ex-girlfriend.

Pushy and self-absorbed were the descriptions that fit her to a tee. Over the years Lailani couldn't keep count of the number of citations, awards, and public praises that Brett and *Sail Shape* leaders had showered on her in absentia at any number of awards dinners; all because Ms. Jensen expected it. She could easily imagine her pushing in on him to exploit her exalted status.

Zena Melody Jensen wasn't a woman who threatened her marriage, though. She simply couldn't imagine Brett rekindling anything with her at this late date given the fundamental differences in life outlook between them. But that's him she thought as she considered it more. What about her; had she ever gotten over Brett?

Lailani couldn't understand why she continued to feel so coolly neutral after hearing his denial, neither happy nor sad. Had she used the possibility of an affair to justify her own plans? Was it the excuse she needed to break away and live her own dream? Or had there been something too matter of fact, almost too practiced, about his explanation that left her with doubts over whether he was coming completely clean?

"I'm relieved to hear that," she finally replied, trying her best to sound sincere.

"I've gone round and round about it for too long. I didn't want to believe the worst, but I couldn't ignore it."

'Lai, we've got our share of issues and I'll admit that I own most of them. There have been too many years where my priorities were outside of this house; the kids absorbed the lion's share of what was left over. But I haven't given up on rebuilding what we had between us."

She'd heard that speech. In her mind she wasn't sure anymore whether rebuilding was possible. In her spirit the long passage of years had left an empty space, something had gone missing.

She sat up straight and put her glass down before facing him.

"The second thing I need to mention is that I'm persuaded that pursuing the Tony Calibri opportunity is the right move, I should have told you sooner. Remy and I have grown LR Staffing as much as we can. We're a very good regional company. But to expand beyond that is too much of a stretch. It would take a lot of capital, much more than we could invest on our own. The right merger would provide a viable pathway and Tony's company provides that opportunity. We are going to take advantage of it."

She paused. Tell him the rest.

"It will require that I relocate to California in my new role."

She watched him, trying to read his face, and waiting for the outburst full of objections.

Brett was surprised by it all, stunned. He leaned back as the full import of her words sank in. His mind drifted forward to a future time when he would return home to an empty house.

But why should his comfort or discomfort be a driving factor in what may be best for her, he asked himself? And she's long had the talent and the smarts to work out what's best for her own business, even if he was the last one to realize it. He should have kept out of it years ago; he vowed to keep out of it now.

He would have to adjust to the west coast time zone he realized as he thought more about the new future, speak with her late at night after her own long day. But she'd be closer to baby girl which would be good. They could keep an eye out for each other, bond again, and be safer together.

And she would be happy.

He reached for her hand.

"I think it's a wonderful idea, I'm happy for you Lai," he said masking how much he would miss her.

"You deserve to take LR Staffing as far as you can. Other than staying out of the way, what else can I do to help you," he said.

***

She was anxious and unsure, emotion that she rarely experienced together. She realized that coming out to her mother was a walk in the park compared to her plan to share her feelings with Sarah.

But damn it, why should the two things be any different she asked herself while waiting at the restaurant for Sarah to arrive. As she thought more about it the differences were almost paralyzing.

The most obvious difference was that while she'd mustered the courage to tell her mother the truth, she had done it on the telephone and without realizing that she'd spoken the words out loud. Also, that three-thousand-mile physical separation was a great safety net. If she was rejected or condemned on the call she could've just hung up.

But here in a very public space everyone might be looking if things went south.

And what if she'd misread Sarah's concern as something that it was never intended to be, she worried? Just because they had spent time in the counseling sessions sharing their feelings about things and planning the upcoming academic year that didn't mean that Sarah was genuinely interested in her as a person, as a lover.

But they'd also talked about being roommates. Didn't Sarah know enough about her life now she fretted; how could she be unaware that her straight life was largely an illusion? Why would she still want to be roommates if she knew that?

She glanced at her cell phone. It was already twenty minutes past the agreed upon time and no message had come in.

What if the nuns changed their minds and Sarah wasn't allowed to leave for dinner after all? But wouldn't she have called in that case?

Fighting back stress she grabbed her water glass and almost drained it. Then she leaned her head back on the banquet seat and slowed her breathing. She closed her eyes and visualized a successful evening.

"BG, are you sleeping? I know I'm a little late but only a tad. I'm so sorry."

She opened her eyes; Sarah was smiling at her and she wasn't wearing the habit. Instead, her blond hair was down to her shoulders, and she wore a casual beige top and faded jeans. She couldn't believe how beautiful she looked.

Impulsively she stood and hugged her. Being more than a head taller, she enveloped Sarah completely in her arms, lifting her high off her feet.

She may have only imagined it, but it felt like petit Sarah had returned her hug with equal force. If that were the case, it meant that Sarah was squeezing back even more tightly.

"No, I wasn't sleeping, silly. I was just trying to relax, practicing some of my sculling techniques."

"And I was also listening to my stomach rumble at the same. Let's look at the menu before it gets too late, I hope you're hungry."

"Speaking of sculling," Sarah offered cheerfully after sitting down, "I really want to see you row this coming season. I know nothing about the sport, but you'll tutor me right?"

"You bet. If you're going to be cheering me on, I want you to know what I'm doing right and when I could do better."

"Would you like a glass of wine, Sarah?"

"Sure, but you should know that I'm pretty much a one glass and done type," she answered while playfully feigning passing out.

"Don't worry, I'm not going to ply my counselor with wine and try to take advantage of her," BG said smiling.

"Well why not, I wouldn't mind that at all," she said.

BG was caught off guard. Was Sarah's remark candor or was she only joking in her usual rapid-fire way? The anxiety returned as BG realized that despite her plan for the dinner, she still hadn't figured out how she would convey her true feelings. Maybe that comment was an opening.

"Let's order and then for sure I want to follow up on that provocative remark of yours."

They laughed, each of them anxious in their own way to move beyond the present into the unknown future.

BG waited until the waiter left the table before speaking.

"You look quite different you know when you don't have your habit on. That's not a complaint at all, but you do look truly wonderful in civilian clothes, I love the look on you."

Sarah was flattered by the compliment. It made her feel alive and desirable. Instinctively, she stroked her hair.

"Thank you, BG. I decided at the last minute to change into this. When I first received permission, I don't think Sister Grace had this outfit in mind; I still had to wait until all the sisters were in their rooms to slip outside. You know, I've worn the habit and bonnet so much over the years that I feel naked when I'm in regular clothes. I guess I'm looking forward to the change of not having to wear them in med school. Street clothes 24/7 BG," she said grinning and holding up her wine glass.

For the life of her BG couldn't figure out if Sarah was just being innocent or whether she was being coy with her. The reference to feeling naked without the habit and bonnet was so suggestive and it reminded her of something that her old sculling mate Katie might have said back in college. The more she thought about it the more it stimulated her to the point where she had to excuse herself to cool off in the restroom. After rinsing her face and checking herself in the mirror she returned to the table, believing that it was now or never.

"You know Sarah, I did a brave and equally stupid thing recently. I told my mother that I was confronting my differences and embracing them. I told her that… I'll never be the daughter that she and my father tried to force me to be, that I was going to love… in my own way."

Sarah interrupted when she saw her friend struggling.

"That's wonderful. It was so courageous of you. But I wouldn't call it a stupid thing. Why do you?"

"Because during that call I told my mother something else. Something that I now realize was not my prerogative to mention all by myself."

"You see, I said that I 'd found someone that I love, someone who I hoped also loved me and that wanted to be with me. But I 'm not sure if she…feels that way about me."

"That's wonderful, so what are you going to do now BG? What will you change?"

346

Those weren't the words that Sarah wanted to say from her heart. Instead, she had instinctively fallen back on her counselor's training; she'd been thrown off stride by BG's confession.

"That's a very good question. It's certainly one that I should have anticipated from my counselor/confessor. And of course, it's one that I haven't yet really thought through."

She sipped some of her wine. Sarah did the same.

"But you know, my mother was happy for me. She said that my dad seems to get it finally, to get me. That was a shocker for sure. Most of all she apologized for not supporting me during my early years. She was genuinely sad; I think she was crying. She wants me to come home to visit with whomever I love."

She looked at Sarah and released a long slow exhale.

She glanced down for a moment, knowing that she had to continue.

That's when Sarah reached across the small table with both hands, encircling BG's strong hands in her own. She squeezed them lovingly.

"I want to be with you," she whispered. I want to love you and I want you to love me."

BG took the napkin from her lap and dabbed her moist eyes.

"You will go with me won't you, to meet my family back east," she asked as she tried to contain her emotions?

"Yes, I will; I'd love that. But I'm still struggling with my own imprisonment. Don't forget that I 'm in a Catholic order. It's much more conservative with its constraints than what's out here," she said with a gesture toward the room. I wish I could say our future together will be smooth sailing, or rowing."

BG nodded her head knowingly.

"But that's far from the case, my love. Will you be patient with me while I work my own issues out in the order?"

They clasped hands again, this time beneath the table.

"You know I will; we'll pull on the oars together, no matter what the future throws at us."

Chapter Twenty-Two: Sunrise

IT HAD BEEN TWO WEEKS since he presided over her memorial service and the event was just as she'd directed it to be—a celebration of life among her friends. He discovered her instructions back at the London house; they were neatly folded under his running gear. After that discovery he wondered how long she'd known she wasn't going to pull through.

The question always stirred his guilt.

But she had also left another folded message in a separate envelope; one that he had reread so many times that he could recite it from memory.

Joshua, my sweet man, my lover,

We shared so much together. So many moments, a lifetime of them, will always live between us. I so wish I were fully there with you now.

Forgive my roughness at times, dearest. They were my demons; your devotion allowed me to hold them at bay.

You must go forward now, without me.

And make another part of us so happy when you do.

I have acceded to it.

And remember love, take me with you into your reverie, release me there when it's time.

Forever,

Mirra

Repeating her precious words to himself brought him no closer to understanding them.

He was beginning to plan for his flight back to the U.S. He would fly straight into to San Francisco; that was the plan until he spoke with his mother. She wanted him to stop over in New York first. The stress of the trial, she explained, was beginning to hugely affect his father.

No matter how hard he tried to imagine that scenario, it was an impossible thing for him to visualize. Sure, his father had put on too much weight, at least based upon the last time he saw him. But so what, he was almost seventy.

In his head and despite his many disagreements with him, his father remained the rock of the family, the founder with the plan. As Joshua had started to expand his own vision and enlarge the London footprint of the warehouse the sheer audacity of his father's dream thirty years ago—even bigger back then by comparative standards---had given him a new respect. It was something that he simply couldn't appreciate before as a boy or even much later. It was why the image of his father buckling under pressure from the current issues was impossible to accept.

At the end of the call, he didn't commit to his mother to come home.

Among the number of items that he needed to finish before leaving was a stop in at Oxford where there was business to settle with Jemal. He needed to make one last attempt to erase the festering guilt that the young man carried since Mirra's death.

After being notified Harold was excited about the drive. Once underway he navigated at high rev speed along the winding motor routes leading to the storied university; that was just his warmup. Next, he erased the numerous sharp switchbacks and roundabouts at rally pace before finally shifting down to third gear to tour past meticulously manicured grounds, stately country homes, and storybook mansions.

The idyllic scenery reminded Joshua of the great minds that had studied at Oxford long before and who had viewed the same pleasing background, albeit at greatly reduced speed; minds like Bacon, Frost, Hubble, Hawking, Bhutto, and so many more. That eminent list of names caused him to chuckle as it occurred to him that the university now had to accommodate one additional great mind, that of Saliamonadiak Hocknosandi.

He wondered whether anyone was left up there that still thought Jemal's university admission was some kind of one-off accommodation for east African orphans. If so, he suspected that Jemal's first place prize last year in the technology competition had temporarily stilled those prejudices.

But after Mirra's memorial service Jemal had withdrawn from everyone. The kids at the warehouse, his biggest fans, had hardly heard from him and Joshua had trouble reaching anything but his electronic shield—voice mail, text, and email. But the few replies had been cryptic and evasive.

At first, he thought that it had to be the big crush of academics at the highly competitive school. He'd known all along that despite how well prepared Jemal was to succeed, many of his classmate had even better preparation that started long ago before they were admitted, including ample resources and knowledgeable family input.

He remembered the conversation that he privately had with Jemal near the end of his raucous graduation party. He had told him to fight like hell to stay on top of things at university and that he was certain that he could do that. Smiling back at him confidently, Jemal had responded with one of his characteristically cocky assurances.

But the call that Joshua recently received from a young lady named Wilma, whom he had to assume was Jemal's girlfriend based on her obvious emotional attachment to him, changed everything. Wilma had lifted Joshua's private number from Jemal's mobile. She called later that evening and pleaded that it was urgent that he come out to the campus to talk with Jemal because he was drifting away from everything and everyone.

Joshua glanced out at the pristine grounds just before they started edging their way into the beehive like heart of the central campus. Wilma had said that Jemal would be at his Slavic history class at Beaverbrook Hall.

Harold nudged the sedan close in by the side gate of a vast, gray Gothic building and shut down GPS and engine. He half turned and nodded.

After stepping out Joshua tried to be inconspicuous while walking down to the front sidewalk and into the main entry gate that led up to ten-foot-high oak doors. But there were curious stares from every passing student. If he harbored any thoughts that his thirty something year-old self would ease unobtrusively back into the college scene the looks said otherwise. Maybe it was only his conservative clothes, he speculated.

Before reaching the building, he veered off the path to his left. He waited several feet away, leaning casually against the front facing façade of the structure. With his profile view of each student that exited it wasn't long before he spotted the thin, angular frame of his protégé with a heavy backpack slung over his shoulder.

"What's a friend have to do now days to make personal contact with someone who's very special to him," he asked as he approached Jemal from behind.

Jemal spun around.

"Boss, I'm sorry," he said looking down. "I should have returned your calls."

Jemal quickly slipped on his sunglasses.

"It's just been hard to say anything," he said. "What can I say? I blew it, you told me to take care of her and I didn't...I didn't."

Joshua grabbed his right elbow and steered him down the walkway before they crossed to the expansive green lawn that blanketed the central quad.

They said nothing and he well knew that his normally voluble student couldn't formulate a word if his life depended on it. Only walking and fresh air and green space could settle him down and prevent the eruption of the feelings that he'd been carrying.

He grabbed Jemal's backpack and slung it over his own shoulder. Jemal was so lost in emotion that he didn't notice.

They kept moving, finally reaching the east end of the main campus where they scrambled together to the top of a high bluff. They sat on a low stone bench behind an ancient military parapet composed of thousands of small gray boulders. The structure afforded commanding views of England's lush green fields in the distance.

Joshua realized that had to get something started so he used his only hook.

"Did I ever tell you that the day after Mirra died I went for a run in Hyde Park? You remember how we always used to get in a 5k every morning that we could?"

Jemal nodded, staring straight ahead.

"Well anyway, I was feeling low that morning. In fact, it was by far the lowest that I'd ever felt. So, I forced myself to get dressed and head out for a run the park, even though my mind screamed *no*."

"Guess what? Mirra had folded a couple of notes into my running clothes; she knew my habits and she knew that I'd run the day after she died. The first note was about how she wanted her memorial service handled. I followed those instructions to the letter; we all celebrated her life together, didn't we?"

Jemal nodded again then lowered his head.

"But the second note that she left was a personal one for me and for all of us that were very close to her."

Stretching the truth about the note's content was the only gambit that he thought might work.

Jemal's natural curiosity and his love for Mirra made him look up and remove his sunglasses.

"She left us some much-needed advice that allowed me to put her life and death into perspective. And it also eased a great deal of my pain. You see, she knew she was going to die a long time before any of us did. She was aware that she wasn't coming home from that hospital, alive. She understood that she was going to die when you both were in Africa when she gave her love and her warmth to that isolated young girl. It was her gift to the child you see, given so that the child would pass away knowing that she was loved by someone who cared deeply about her, without reservation. Mirra held the child all night until you returned with the medicine, didn't she?"

"But boss," Jemal said, "why would she do a thing like that if she was already aware of the danger to herself; why?"

"I can only think that it had to have made profound sense to her at the time. You see that sacrifice was deep within her being and part of what she aspired to be—a nurturer, a giver of optimism, and a companion. It's the space where she found the greatest fulfillment even though she didn't have all those things growing up. We can only respect it and honor it in the way that we live our own lives. But in fact, it's not unlike your own gift to the kids at the warehouse, right?"

Jemal wasn't sure what he was hearing, his confusion showed before Joshua explained.

"You give of yourself, don't you? You willingly share your energy, love, and loyalty with the kids. Believe me, I know how difficult and isolated it is for you up here. I know how competitive it is and how you're seen by some as an outcast, not worthy of entry into their private little clubs and associations. But you overcame it all and kept your spirits high; that's not easy. You also find the capacity and spark to give your gift to all the kids at the warehouse, to inspire them, even though you could use your energy and time to study and compete up here."

He saw a glimmer of recognition in Jemal's eyes.

"Not only that but you've given your gift freely to the kids in Africa by continuing to run the charitable work over there. I know how challenging that's been for you and how much of a drain it is. But you set up two networks that are making a huge difference."

"Mirra was so proud of you Jemal; she always was you know. She understood that you had what it takes long before I did."

Jemal stood up slowly and shoved his hands into his pockets. He looked down at his scuffed boots for a long time before speaking.

"I've been a coward boss, living in self-pity. I haven't spoken to the kids at the warehouse in more than a fortnight."

"I know. They all miss you. Thank God they're very busy and the academics keep them focused. Look, you must grieve, it's natural. We all must grieve, and it's not over. But you can't blame yourself for Mirra's decision."

Jemal looked at him quizzically.

"Boss, how did you find me here on campus?"

"Well, someone who apparently really loves you and was worried sick called and asked me to come. You are very fortunate to have a woman that loves you like that."

If his dark completion had not concealed the blushing Jemal would have turned beet red.

His face lit up with a smile.

'Wilma is very special to me. We are going to finish Oxford together and then complete our PhD's. She is quite bright you know. Boss. She is scary smart. You must come with me; I want you to meet her."

They scrambled down the embankment and walked back laughing and joking.

***

Joshua knew that by this time the syndicate had lost all patience with him; they were entirely justified. He had been away from Frisco for almost a month. He'd missed critical regattas designed to advance his team and fine-tune the boats for the heavy lifting against the Americans. In his absence, though, his crew kept winning.

The lead bank had already advanced a sub-rosa submission to the board to permanently replace him with Willosby. He'd been tipped off about it by two of his old board friends. The critical vote on the issue would happen in three days. He could break the expected tie and defeat the bank's move, but he had to be at the syndicate meeting in person to vote. After that he had to be back in Frisco, ready to race.

Before his mother's most recent plea being at the docks with his crew ready to race had been a sure thing. But now with a possible multiday stopover in New York, all bets were off. Unsure about what he was going to do, he purchased an expensive open ticket. Immediately after the syndicate meeting adjourned Harold drove him out to Heathrow.

On the flight over he thought more about his mother's urgent call. Sure, he got that she was very concerned. But on the other hand, why wouldn't his father show some signs of stress under the circumstances. But he had always managed a steady helm through pressure packed conditions. The most extreme situations were at sea where Joshua had watched him react calmly under duress many times in the past.

He braced another pillow under his lower back and eased further into the wide seat. As he relaxed, he thought about his teenage years; the days when he'd sailed a lot with his father, times when the tensions and challenges were the most extreme. He remembered one occasion when his father invited him to join his crew for the Bequia, St. Vincent regatta, senior division. It was a surprise reward after a successful summer camping season where Joshua had overseen all sailing instruction for middle school campers.

As a sixteen-year-old he was psyched by the opportunity to sail with the old guys that had crewed for his father back in the day, the guys who had won so many regattas together. The treat had partially erased the fact that he hadn't wanted to be in camp at all that summer.

As he recalled they'd gotten off to a horrible start out of Admiralty Bay, dead last. And that was completely his fault since he had forgotten to tie off the mainsheet stopper knot. That would have prevented the line from running out of the winch and stalling the boat.

But his father didn't panic; they raced harder.

After navigating the tricky routes through the many small islands along the course the fleet had to head across that infamous eggbeater channel called the Bequia strait, a two-hour ordeal with stiff winds, cross currents, and steep rollers.

To this day he could feel the force of those ten-foot waves and the 30-knot blow. Everybody on board had been anxiously awaiting his father's signal to douse the big genoa headsail like the other boats and throw up the storm jib.

But his father didn't panic; the signal never came.

His father continued to wrestle the big wheel all the while maintaining a good line. He had also stretched the course dangerously wide to maximize boat speed. His calculation then was one that Joshua now knew well—greater speed over a slightly longer course could mean victory.

At the end of the race and despite the lousy start they secured a remarkable second place finish, a silver cup.

No, his father wasn't one to buckle under pressure. But maybe the stress of the litigation was getting to his mother. And perhaps the fact that she had only recently arrived back at the trial and had just three days before having to fly right back home to California was part of it as well.

Was a trip to the courthouse and a one or two-week wait there necessary he asked himself again; should he sacrifice everything he'd worked for during the past four years?

After he landed a strange urge pushed into his consciousness; he had to call Mikala, right away. The odd thing about it was that there was absolutely no reason to do it. But the thought kept agitating his mind along with the recollection that he had her number since he had asked his father for it the last time they talked. If he were to call her, he imagined that it would be a pleasant chat between them, like it had been the last time.

Then he realized how awkward that conversation would be given his personal circumstances. He firmly rejected the urge.

But his mind seemed to independently locate a convenient and persuasive workaround to weaken his resolve.

He was reminded that Mikala would be wrapping things up at *Sail Shape* in preparation for the season close. What better source for a second opinion about his father than from her; she was probably in touch with him daily. He couldn't recall the act of dialing her number as he continued to think about his objections; but he suddenly heard his phone connecting. Did he accidently dial that?

"Hello"

"Hello Ms. Mikala Jensen, it's me, Joshua Bernard Howard, without my father's permission to speak with you this time."

"Joshua, why hello, how are you? What a very pleasant surprise! Yes, we'll have to be very cautious without your father's blessing to converse."

Given her lighthearted reply he was relieved that his attempt at humor had worked.

Mikala heard herself mouthing the cheerful words but in fact she didn't at all feel that his call was a surprise; she wondered why.

"Let me first say Joshua, belatedly, how sorry I was to hear about her passing, your loss. Brett mentioned it to me, please accept my condolences."

"Thank you. She was an amazing woman. What we had together was…very special."

After he said that Mikala said something very unusual.

"I understand that she contracted an illness when she was at a village in the Indellia District, in Ethiopia. It was near the end of her multi-day excursion that spanned the width of the continent."

Her remarks sounded almost clinical, and they were precisely accurate, yet her tone was somber.

"Yes, that's what I think happened. It's the only thing that explains her symptoms really. However, the doctors had no accurate diagnosis before she passed," he said.

As he thought about Mikala's comment he was puzzled; he was positive that his father didn't learn those details about Africa from him; so how could Mikala possibly know them?

"It was incredibly brave of her to share her life so selflessly with that sick young girl," Mikala said. "Along with your sorrow you must be so proud of her, as well. "

What surprised him more than the emotion in her voice was that she continued to speak with such certainty about the facts.

Nevertheless, what more could he say now about the whole thing he groused as his emotions from losing her forced him inward again. After his talk with Jemal he had sworn off playing nice over it, had refused to be drawn into discussions just because people felt compelled to ask him gratuitous questions about Mirra's death.

Why the hell should he allow himself to be pumped for information that would later merely be a part of someone's cocktail party conversation anyway, he wanted to know? They could never understand what he was going through, what he lost.

And even now, why should he have to make small talk with Mikala about it? It's not like she and Mirra were friends or even acquaintances. They'd never met, never spoken.

The truth was that he was only now beginning to get through a whole day without thinking about her. And this would no longer be one of those days.

Yet the fact that Mikala seemed so emotionally invested in the circumstances was confusing to him the more he thought about it. Or was she merely feigning concern to be polite?

Then it hit him hard, how could she have known that it was a girl child that Mirra cared for; he hadn't been that specific with his mother or his father or anyone else for that matter. He was certain that he'd only mentioned that Mirra had most likely gotten ill sometime after the trip. He had been deliberately vague because no one really knew the definitive cause of her illness and he didn't want to cast an aspersion at Africa without solid evidence.

Searching for an answer he speculated that maybe he had shared more detail with his folks at the time and had simply forgotten; perhaps that was it. He probably just wasn't thinking clearly then or now for that matter.

"How are you really doing, Joshua," Mikala asked quietly, drawing him gently back into the present?

"It's only been four weeks since the memorial service," she said.

"That is so little time, isn't it," she said?

Without speaking he mouthed the answer; yes.

But she seemed to have heard him, nonetheless.

"It must be so very hard for you now to accept continuing without her. It must be so challenging to look forward when you feel so alone, when you know that distance apart from her cannot be easily closed."

"But that aloneness won't be your future Joshua, I'm sure of it."

Mikala's voice felt like a comforting balm, it covered him completely and broke the tension, it eased his anguish. She seemed to be right there next to him, holding him.

He had to accept her concern as heartfelt; her understanding and empathy were deep-seated and genuine.

Somehow, she had reached his soul within that lonely place where he had withdrawn and slowly, she was pulling him back.

"I'm doing well under the circumstances Mikala, better now that we're speaking. Thank you so much for understanding and caring, I greatly appreciate it."

Yet he still had to find a way to change the subject because he hadn't been doing that well at all for weeks.

"You know Mikala, I'm calling you for a huge favor. I'm out at Kennedy right now, just landed. Sorry I didn't mention that earlier."

"My original plan was to head straight to Frisco, that is until my mother called me in London; she called me a second time in fact to say that dad was doing badly. So, I stopped here as a precaution. If you don't mind, I could use your best read on him. If he's hanging in there, I may skip it and continue to the west coast. It's a critical time for me. I could return and hopefully attend some of the trial after that."

Thinking about everything that his words implied had Mikala's mind racing as she strained to comprehend the meaning behind his call. Why wasn't she amazed that he was so close, or that it felt as if it were her duty to comfort him and that she knew precisely how to do that?

Most important, she didn't know how on earth she was able to recite so much information about his fiancé? She couldn't remember Brett mentioning any of it to her; but he must have.

She wondered if all the unknowns were somehow connected to the internal changes she experienced over the past several months. After living with them and finally embracing the phenomenon she likened them to gentle rivulets of positive emotions. They arrived periodically; they seemed to wash over her spirit and push against her rational tendencies that in the past resulted in harsh self-criticism, pessimism, and depression. The rivulets left her at peace as well about her present state and her personal future despite the mountain of work and new challenges and the nagging reality that she was approaching her third year without anyone, any man, in her life.

She had no idea where they came from. But they were part of her now.

Realizing that Joshua was waiting for her to respond she focused on the present.

"I'd be more than happy to share what I've seen recently working with your father."

She had to pause after saying that because she was beginning to sense Joshua's presence so strongly through the phone. It sparked a range of emotions, the strongest being the urgent desire to see him and talk with him again in person. It was entirely different than the pleasant vibes that remained after their first meeting. Something more significant and far weightier was added onto that.

At the same time, she felt the growing need to physically touch him, to make a tactile connection.

She had to struggle to quell the intense feelings and respond to his questions.

Before she could do that, an active tingling, an irritating itch, began in both of her palms. She looked down; the surface of her palms as well as the skin on the bottom of her fingers was visibly moving, agitated.

"Could you hold on a second, Joshua, I'll be right back to the phone, thanks."

She put it down and pressed her fingertips and palms hard together, squeezing for minutes until they were numb and red and still. Then she opened a window to admit the ocean's chilly air before grabbing the phone.

"Sorry for the delay," she said.

"Okay, here's how I see things. The first few days of trial greatly affected him. In his eyes the rules-driven legal process seemed stacked against him. And with the scheduling delays it just dragged on. The reality that he was unable to personally influence the process increased his anxiety. It stripped his earlier optimism."

"That's probably when your mother first called you."

"I contrast that to the man I knew right after I came on board. There were pressures during that time for sure. But he was mostly positive and charged up; now that rarely happens anymore."

"Our financial health at all camps has been severely impacted by the growing legal expenses and the big crimp in donations. Thank God it's end-of-season around the country and our cash needs are substantially reduced. He may not have mentioned it to you but there was also a big dust up a while back in California around our proposed marina purchase, more on that in a second."

"But some good news; the prosecutors in the criminal trespass case withdrew the charges against the boys so that was a welcome win. We all celebrated. It really picked up his spirits, for a while."

"Now back to California. There was some good news in that home invasion matter; it turned out to be a hoax all along. The guy who broke into the family's home out there pretending to be a *Sail Shape* zealot was convicted. Brett was confident that he could repair most of the PR damage, but he has no idea where he'll get the money to do that."

She paused to catch her breath before giving him the bad news.

"But this land case has so much at stake that it's overshadowing all the positives. And don't forget, he is being sued individually for negligence, so his personal assets are at risk. The truth is I've seen your father go up hill emotionally and then back down where he remains right now. I also don't think he's taking his meds, but I can't be sure."

"What I'm sure about is that he's aged five years just in the time that I've known him. I believe it's the current land trial even though he's not a big complainer, which is a problem since he holds everything bottled up inside. You know Joshua, I hate to say this and it's really none of my business, but I also believe that his separation from your mother is driving everything else down."

Hearing the word *separation* drove home the reality that Joshua had tried to sugarcoat; his mother wasn't merely working out of state, she hadn't just taken a better position with a business in California for the time being, his parents were separated and heading for divorce, face it.

"But he's tough," Mikala said, wanting to end on a high note. " I think he'll pull through it somehow; I certainly hope so."

It was exactly what he didn't want to hear. His father was really struggling and if he remained in New York to help him he'd hand the helm to Willosby.

She reacted to his silence.

"Are you okay, is there anything I can do to help?"

"Thanks for asking. Truth is I'm having an internal crisis right now. If I remain here and wait until the end of the trial, I'll miss the chance to skipper in the finals. Alternatively, if the timing works out, I could possibly finish the competition and fly back here to be with dad before the verdict is rendered."

"But you know what," he said, "that's some very selfish thinking on my part; I mean if his health is at risk what the hell am I hesitating for?"

"That's very honest and very self-critical, Joshua. It is a difficult decision, there's nothing easy about it. It's made even harder for you after… losing her. Can I be equally candid about myself?"

"Sure."

"Well, for entirely selfish reasons, I would really like to see you while you're in the States. I know that might sound crude but believe me when I say that I'm not trying to make any kind of move, particularly at this difficult time."

She paused, wanting to stop there, but she felt compelled to tell him the rest.

"The truth is I really enjoyed the brief get together with you at the camp. I've been thinking about it off and on since that time you know. I was certainly aware of your status back then—compliments of Brett—so my thoughts were altogether realistic. But you know, anyway… somehow now it seems that I have this strong…that I really must…. I'm sorry Joshua, I'm just going on too much… forgive me."

"You know what," he said quickly.

"I haven't forgotten our meeting either. I greatly enjoyed it. Is there anything wrong with acknowledging that? I don't think so. Truth is that when we separated, I missed speaking to you and I guess part of the reason I called was to hear your voice and say *hi* again."

He decided to tell her everything.

"To be perfectly honest it was much more than that; I had this strange, intense need to call you the minute I landed; it just happened without warning. It was almost as f my phone made the call without me. Can't explain it and I even tried to rationalize it away. But in the end, it made perfect sense to do so and I'm glad that I did."

Mikala's heart jumped.

"Thanks for letting me know it wasn't just me. I've had a few strange and very intense experiences myself; I get it. Maybe our thoughts somehow crossed each other and were joined out there in that great cosmic void," she said hoping to lighten the mood.

"You know, perhaps they did, and that's not a bad thing."

He was genuinely happy about their talk so far. It suddenly occurred to him that he hadn't spoken socially to another woman in months. And he had deliberately avoided speaking to several who had reached out to touch base with him after the memorial service. He had no desire.

"But about your father," she said

"In almost every conversation I've had with him during the past few months he's mentioned your sailing in the Cup race. To say he was proud of you would be an understatement. You've worked for that chance, and he'd want you to go to San Francisco and race hard."

"I've worked for the chance, sure" he said.

"I also want to be here to support him. Believe me, it hasn't always been that way. You see, I've learned a lot more about who he is as a man in addition to what drives him. And we've been able to talk more openly about the friction between us; I certainly accept my part in it. The big surprise for me was him becoming introspective and honest about his own behavior and its impact."

Mikala was unsure about what that all meant, but it sounded an awful lot like the kind of reset that she needed with her mother; an infusion of fresh air and perspective in an increasingly dysfunctional parent-child relationship

"So where does that leave you, here or there," she said?"

Despite her neutral sounding question more than anything else she wanted him to remain in New York, close to her.

"I think I'm going to try to do both," he said while thinking about a workable plan.

"I'll leave early tomorrow morning for Frisco; when I arrive, it'll be time to race. I'll just have to win four straight races and get back here a.s.a.p. The trial should still be in session."

On the one hand she was ecstatic to hear that he would return. On the other she felt strangely calm about it because part of her seemed to already know his plan. There was one other effect—it quieted the still strong urge within her to see him and touch him.

"That's a lot of miles in a very few days and tons of racing. It's a very aggressive plan," she said.

"But I suppose," she said playfully while smiling into the phone, "I shouldn't expect anything different having worked with your father."

"Touché, guilty as charged," he said.

"When I get back here Mikala, I also want to find a time for us to meet for dinner; maybe I could come by the camp for you after a trial day. It's a bit of a drive from where you are, but we could find a spot in Montauk, there are several great places."

"That would be fun, I look forward to it. But until then I've got tons of work to get done before I put the locks on the gates. It's taking me longer to sort through everything because Brett's not here to walk me through the details."

"Mikala, thank you so much for your condolences earlier and for sharing your perspective on my father. That was way more than I expected or deserved," he said.

"When I have the date firmed up for my return flight, I'll send you a text. I'm hoping that will be very soon. Until then, take good care."

"Goodbye Joshua. Good luck, good sailing, and safe travels."

Without warning the force within her reared up with a vengeance as if protesting the reality that he was leaving her again. To resist Mikala gripped her hands tightly together and squeezed them between her legs. The effort barely prevented her from grabbing the phone and calling him back; she desperately wanted to know the name and location of the hotel where he would be tonight.

Finally regaining control, she walked unsteadily to the bathroom mirror.

Chapter Twenty-Three: Gathering

BEFORE TURNING BACK, SHE LOOKED UNDER THE WING at the vast expanse of Chicago as they floated serenely over the immense city.

"You know BG, the last time I made this flight to the east coast I was basically a fugitive from my convent. Are you kidnapping me," Sarah asked playfully?

BG shook her head and smiled back, she glanced around before squeezing Sarah's waiting hand.

For a while at least, probably a long while, they both understood that they would live like this, their passion and love for one another guarded and confined in public. Doubts about the long-term viability of that existence had already seeped in.

"So did the Reverend Mother ask a lot of questions after you requested the one-week leave, other than why of course?"

"No, not really. At first, I think she assumed that I was just burned out. I also believe that she was feeling a little guilty about her punishment of me. My six-day a week, twelve-hour a day purgatory was her idea. But you know I so wanted to tell her the truth or nearly all of it. I do love her, and she has been so good to me over the years—more than just a spiritual mother. So anyway, I told her that your family had an important case in the New York courts and that your father was under a huge amount of physical and mental strain. I also mentioned that we'd become very good friends. Then I asked for permission to travel with you as your spiritual support."

"Well, did she ask any follow-up questions about how close we really were? Do you think that she was at all suspicious?"

BG could hear her own paranoia in the question.

"I really don't know," Sarah said patiently.

"But she did ask about your family. I think she made the decision based solely on what I told her about your mother and father. I was surprised that's for sure. But you know what, my little white lie of omission about us doesn't sit that well with me. I can't just fill up my life, our life, with them forever."

She understood exactly what Sarah meant. They were both growing more anxious over the future.

Sarah squeezed her hand and blew a secret kiss.

BG eased back in her seat while and yawned. Even with the burden of stealth she was mostly happy now and she loved Sarah even more. But occasionally she wondered if she had exchanged one kind of internal prison for another kind set up against the prying eyes of the outside world.

She remembered the recent call from her mother and the heightened concern she expressed about how dad's health was deteriorating. She had asked her how that could possibly happen given some of the favorable developments. The response startled her when her mother claimed that he wasn't following his usual routine anymore; he was late out of bed every morning and he was snacking incessantly. And his exercise plan that his physician had carefully designed for him had been put back in the closet with the machine. What her mother had carefully avoided mentioning was that her relocation to California was very likely the root cause of his unhealthy lifestyle changes.

What she hadn't anticipated was the response she received after she told her mother that she would be returning home with Sarah. She'd expected by then that her mother's earlier support for her would have waned, with everything returning to its proper unmentionable place. But rather than receding it had grown stronger. So here they were, a tall black woman in a blue warmup and sneakers and a small white woman in a high bonnet and white habit.

Thinking more about her mother, she remembered her call two weeks ago when she spilled the beans that Keisha and Senator Broderick might be more than legal colleagues. Her mother's speculation was based on Keisha's constant chatter about him whenever his name came up; the multiple mentions of his name were exclusively from Keisha.

BG really didn't know that much about him other than how professional he'd been with her assault case. But knowing her sister, if she was thinking seriously about a relationship then he must really be okay.

Something squeezed her hand and startled her awake. Through half-open eyes she saw a threatening white shroud looming. She recoiled as her eyes opened wide. The apparition quickly dissolved; it was only Sarah.

After touchdown she turned on her cell phone and watched the messages load. The one from her mother nearly caused her to stand up in the aisle and scream.

Your father had a stroke in the courtroom this morning; he's in critical condition. We are at Bonaventure Memorial Hospital, Long Island City. Pray for him. Call me when you land.

For ninety minutes Sarah sat uncomfortably in a white plastic chair in the middle of the crowded ICU visitors' room. Her personal moments of reflection and prayer for BG's father were constantly interrupted as families and friends of the critically ill approached her for prayer.

Finally, she sent a text to BG that she was overwhelmed, that she was taking the train into Manhattan to see her mother, and they would meet up later. After that the sad faced emoticon popped up on her phone; the words *I love you be safe* appeared.

She was surprised; she hadn't expected a reply from the **no-cell-phone** ICU ward. She smiled knowing that BG would always respond to her, always be there for support no matter how difficult the challenge.

The dreary train ride to Penn Station took almost two hours, track problems being the only offered explanation. That was followed by another hour and ten-minute ride on two different subway lines before finally arriving at her mother's stop. After that she was forced to walk the remaining mile—broken bus.

When she dragged herself up to the fifth floor, she was dirty and exhausted.

"Sarah, you look thoroughly spent. Here, let me help you out of that uncomfortable habit. You can wear these workout clothes that I got on sale the other day, they should fit you just fine and I doubt if I'll have time to wear them anyway. And take this shower gel with you to the washroom. Just remember to bring it back when you're finished; otherwise, it'll disappear without a trace. I'll take this dirty habit to the Laundromat in the morning."

It occurred to Melinda that she sounded exactly like her own mother used to sound when she was a girl. Relax and take a breath she scolded herself.

"I can't believe how long it takes to get around this place," Sarah groaned. "And after hours underground you come out and you're still in the City. Honestly, I could have been back in California given the total time it took me to get here from the hospital."

"Your right, the metro area is immense. But at least those of us on tight budgets—most of the City by the way—don't have to worry about having a car along with the high associated expenses. It works for me."

When she returned from the washroom Sarah decided to say what was on her mind for the entire trip.

"Mother, how did your testimony go at the trial? You promised that you would figure out a way to make things right."

"Yes, and I think I did okay. The one commitment that I made to myself was no more lies. So, I tried as best I could to navigate through it all without doing that again."

She looked at Sarah and laughed.

"When they asked me on the witness stand about the facts in the affidavit, I told the truth. I said that I couldn't really be certain at all about what I said twenty-seven years ago or what was said to me because it was ancient history. Your father's lawyer almost had an epileptic fit trying to get me to change that. But in the end, he sat down, thoroughly exasperated."

"And what about father, was he angry," Sarah said.

"Well, he was at first, but I think he realized that he had no right to be. He knows that you love BG, and he knows that his lawsuit would destroy her family and a huge part of you. If he had known about that at the beginning, I really think he would have decided against bringing the lawsuit, at least I hope he would have."

"So," Melinda said in a quiet voice spoken to herself," we'll just have to see how the judge rules."

***

Mikala was parked in the airport's cell phone lot waiting for Joshua's flight to arrive. With car off and doors locked she finally had her quiet time to decompress from the traffic Armageddon that she survived to get there.

But she remained anxious and concerned despite the calm because she didn't want to give him the impression when he arrived that she was casually available. In her mind that was only one notch better than being loose and desperate.

Nor was she there to offer him something that she wasn't yet ready to give, her heart. That truth forced her to ask the question that had haunted her since she broke-off her engagement, what did she want in a man and if she ever found that could she commit herself through thick and thin? Her present ambivalence convinced her that she had no clue about the answers.

Yet here you are anyway she derided herself, readily available to meet your newfound friend the minute he arrives. She was conflicted about the whole idea and began to waiver. Finally, she decided that it was better to send him a text that she'd been hung up in traffic and couldn't make it.

Would he believe her? It didn't matter.

She grabbed her cell phone. Before she could hit speed dial her fingers cramped severely on both hands, forcing her to drop the device and curl her hands into tight fisted balls. She couldn't open her hands

The timing and severity of the phenomenon rattled her. Even more so now because it was part of a long string of inexplicable occurrences, all of which indicated that she was no longer in complete control of herself.

Waiting for her hands to uncramp she slowly calmed down, her confidence gradually returned. It helped her gain a different perspective as she considered everything.

It was only natural for her to pick him up at the airport after Brett's stroke she believed. After all, his mother was still at the hospital, and it was merely a ninety-minute drive in from the camp for her. And she had wanted to visit Brett herself at the hospital anyway.

She also remembered that it was Joshua who had called her to say he was returning right away. He could've easily arranged a car service for himself. So, she wasn't being forward by offering him a ride. She was just helping. That's all this really was.

That's baloney, she had to admit it.

She'd seen Brett two days ago during visiting hours. And her route to the airport was a well-known traffic nightmare but she had happily volunteered anyway. Who was she trying to fool? She'd made herself available now for only one reason and she had to accept the reality that there was no force on earth, including her own free will, that could prevent her from seeing him and touching him.

Her mind drifted briefly away from her embattled personal space. She wondered how he'd made out in the races. Had he won four? I guess the results are on-line she remembered.

Thank God she was able to sit with Brett before his stroke and go through the upcoming tranche of pending bills and facility issues. What surprised her at the time more than anything was his acceptance of her recommendations and his confidence that she would make the right decisions on her own.

Brett's visible loss of energy and hope as she sat across from him was the most disturbing part. She remembered thinking that it was likely due to the unspoken truth that even with all her accounting magic, without a complete win in the land case camp gates around the country would remain closed next summer, locking out campers and staff alike. That reality may have pushed his heart too far.

Speaking of being locked out, she thought about her recent big blow up with her mother. Had she finally locked that woman out of her life? Was she completely on her own at last without the maternal chains? It certainly felt that way.

It all started when Mikala figured out from her mother's reluctant admissions that she had gone behind Mikala's back to check up on her with Brett. Zena finally confessed that she and Brett discussed whether Joshua had been in touch with Mikala by phone. Mikala couldn't figure out how her mother had figured out that there was the potential for more than a casual friendship between them. She had barely figured that out for herself. And Mikala had deliberately been very guarded whenever she talked with her mother about *Sail Shape* matters, never mentioning Joshua.

But her mother confronted her over it, accusing her of trying to hide her relationship with Joshua. Mikala's denials only served to stoke Zena's temper. She ridiculed the idea that Joshua Howard would have any genuine interest in her and accused her of being naive in thinking that he would be attracted to someone who had fallen so far down within her profession.

Choose someone else, Zena commanded. Make it someone more within your capabilities and at your level. Don't be an embarrassment to me yet again, she screamed into the phone.

It was the raw condescension in her mother's voice that pushed Mikala over the edge, making her finally fight back, finally fight for herself.

I looked through your hidden picture album with Brett Howard years ago you know, so precious. Given that missed opportunity, you've got some nerve being haughty with me. Just because you weren't good enough to win and keep Brett's love don't assume that I'm not good and capable enough to have his son love me. And you know what else, I don't need you meddling in my life anymore like you did with Mickey years ago and with my fiancé, both behind my back. Leave me alone, damn it!

Mikala had never experienced the foul fulsome rage of her mother's voice. When she decided to end the call in the middle of

Zena's profane tirade, she could have sworn that a puff of smoke arose from her cell phone after she hit the disconnect button.

It wasn't long before she started worrying again about Joshua. She really needed to know what it would take for him to recover and fully heal and how she could help him do that.

At least she'd been able to draw him out of his shell when they spoke, or maybe he just liked the sound of her voice and let her talk a blue streak. But no, that couldn't be it. They really had a deeper connection between them, one that was hard to explain given the minimal time they shared together. I was good.

The other strange thing was that she increasingly felt as if she personally knew his fiancé, Mirra. It was as if some firm bond had been established. That sensation of an unbreakable link had become tangible, and she could no longer ignore it.

In fact, there were times when she knew exactly how Mirra would feel about a given situation. It was unsettling but the unanticipated result was that she was able to communicate with Joshua in a much more meaningful way.

Could there really be a cosmic or spiritual linkage between them she wondered? Might Joshau be a kind of medium that allowed that connection to come to life? Was it something else, something through Mirra; was she the talisman in all this?

Nonsense, that's impossible her rational mind objected, but with far less conviction than it had weeks ago.

Suddenly she shivered, reacting to what felt like a small tactile pressure on her shoulders.

Was that a touch, she asked out loud?

Of course not. It's just chilly out here; she answered her own question.

She turned on the car and heater.

Once again, her doubts ascended.

Mirra must have been so remarkable to do what she did in Africa. What amazing strength and caring. Whenever he speaks about her his voice conveys his strong respect and love, even when he barely says more than a few words. Will her almost heroic image in his eyes prevent him from appreciating someone else's attributes, she fretted?

How long will it take him to recover she asked herself more urgently?

And if he finally heals, can he ever love me so deeply?

***

After watching Keisha for the past several hours—at times secretly—he knew that the meeting with her father would be a highly charged affair. It would also be the latest of several wrenching events that they both had been involved in together.

The range of litigation threatening *Sail Shape* was its own cauldron of emotions—full of dramatic moments, too close to predictably call, and emotionally draining. The most important of the cases resided in the hands of an inscrutable judge, a Brahmin from the old order. Occasionally he treated them fairly, but he had also ruled against them in haphazard fashion.

The most traumatic was Brett's collapse in open court, which had shaken them badly. Visiting him later at the ICU when he was unconscious and intubated had been even more emotionally draining.

Now Keisha's ancient family circumstances promised more turbulence. J's stake in it was brought into sharp relief by the feelings that he'd developed for her. She meant so much to him now after the many hours they spent together in the legal trenches. He finally admitted to himself that he cared deeply for her, and he would have to tell her that soon.

It had to be more than his imagination he told himself optimistically; she seemed to care about him as well.

During the flight from Albany, he watched her regress as the meeting with her father approached. Gradually she had become someone different from the fearless lawyer that he'd come to know well. From her questions and comments about what might transpire when she met her father to her frequent withdrawals, she seemed closer in time to that young girl that she was long ago when he walked out of her life; closer in distance to that youngster who had steeled herself to be brave in the face of that and whatever else followed.

The meeting would take place at an extended care facility for veterans. Her father's military service had been short, but he was honorably discharged and now leaned heavily on the GI health benefit.

At one point J had tried to convince her that he probably shouldn't be in the room with them and that he could wait in the lobby. After another attempt at that he stopped. Belatedly he understood that while he wasn't exactly a crutch his silent presence might be important and maybe he was a small part of her fortitude.

Minutes after they entered her father's faintly lit room the full glare of sunlight flooded through the corner windows. J wondered whether it was an omen. Her father lay prone and still under the top sheet and seemed to be awake as his head turned slightly toward them.

A metal table with a glass of water was close by the bed along with a single black chair; an extra one was brought in later.

Surprisingly there were no monitoring machines, IV's, or tubes, which J took as a bad sign. He wondered who had determined that it was too late for extraordinary measures, and why.

A stout nurse easily raised him up in bed and braced his back with several thick pillows. As the sunlight washed over, it revealed a sallow jaundiced face and stringy neck set between frail collarbones.

Keisha sat down; he could see her trying mightily to appear cool and collected before she spoke.

The initial chatting lasted for the first twenty minutes where they assumed pantomime roles much like ethereal shadow boxers, circling and jabbing at the other. The banter between them was polite enough, however, with neither one attempting to land a heavy blow.

Despite the surface correctness, J sensed that the sparring was going to end sooner rather than later as they inched closer to the reason they'd been estranged for thirty years.

So much like a mute spectator J sat in his chair and watched the gloves come slowly off. It soon evolved into the most extraordinary exchange he'd ever witnessed.

"Keisha, you do look good girl, I can tell you've been successful, no thanks to me that's for sure," he said hoarsely.

"Thank you, I'm doing okay," she said courteously.

"Daddy, this is Mr. Broderick. He's an attorney working on several cases with me up in Albany. He's from California."

The old man acknowledged him with a slight nod; after that J felt himself being checked over by the shrewd eyes of a long-time hustler. But the haggard face revealed nothing.

"Pleased to meet you Mr. Broderick. You probably have heard that I'm her trifling father, the one that abandoned her and kicked her to the curb."

J didn't quite know how to respond to that, so he settled on a pleased to meet you reply.

But the old man wasn't finished yet.

"Mr. Broderick, I can see that you have more concern for my daughter than working on some legal stuff. I'm unlikely to be around much longer but I do hope you can provide her some happiness in her life. That's something that I was unwilling to do."

Keisha broke in at that point.

"Daddy," she said scolding quietly, "let's not get started with Mr. Broderick quite so soon."

After that their conversation drifted to animated exchanges about everything irrelevant to the visit, including weather and sports.

Keisha finally realized that she had to put her cards on the table, or she had to be satisfied with wasting her trip.

She stood and moved closer to the bed, holding her tightly clasped hands in front of her. Her face was composed and resolute when she spoke.

"Daddy, I came here for a particular reason today. And that was to tell you that I forgive you. I forgive you unconditionally. I forgive you because I realized that you weren't in control back then, your vices were in control. I've lived long enough now to know how strong those can be. I've seen it in many trials and proceedings that I've been part of. I've gained some wisdom and spilled a lot of bitterness."

"But even still, the things that happened hurt me deeply, I will never be able to forget them."

She paused for a moment and closed her eyes before continuing.

"Despite everything I'm glad I came. I'm glad that you've been sober for quite a while now. And it's good to finally see you again."

The old man looked at his daughter while she spoke. He appeared relieved that the talk had turned real. When she finished, he closed his eyes, his chest heaved two or three times before settling down.

That's when J saw the first tears in his eyes. But the old man quickly grabbed a fistful of top sheet and wiped them off. Keisha reached into her purse and gave him several tissues. He thanked her and inhaled deeply as he steadied himself.

"Keisha," he said after clearing his throat again.

"I'm happy to see you girl. It's been so long and every day that it's been I count as a day of failure on my own part. Yet I dream about you often, not always pleasant things because of the guilt. I've also been workin on that forgiveness thing that you mentioned, trying to forgive my bull-headed and drug dependent self. It ain't easy and frankly I don't think I'll have enough time to get there to tell you the truth. Faith ain't never been my strong suit you know; that was your mother's department."

He paused and coughed.

"Yeah, you got it mostly right. I was out of control for a long time, but I also didn't care to be helped. I was arrogant about refusing help. I willingly let my demons control me. The only thing that mattered was what felt good to me at the time. And you took the brunt of that abuse, you and your sister and your mother before she passed. So yes, now that I've been sober,"

He had paused and choked up without completing the thought.

"And you know what," he said,

"It ain't no excuse worth telling."

He wiped his face again. His eyes were red; he tried to blink them dry.

J watched her face carefully, so many emotions.

Her father kept going.

"Now that I've been clean, my heart aches for what I didn't provide for you, what I failed to enjoy with you. There's no fool like an old fool…ain't that the truth," he said as he coughed up a thick brown mucus on the top sheet.

"I'm just happy for your aunt Lailani and that she was there. She's always been a solid woman; your mother loved her sister so much. And that Brett, damn near a superman. He did right by you, took you as his own. And I was ignorant enough once to hate them both for that."

Watching her J finally saw the business-like facade dissolve. Maybe she'd expected to come into the room, deliver her forgiveness speech, and walk out unaffected. If so, she was wrong.

The first puncture in the armor occurred when she reached for his hands after he started to tear up. Then, as he began to cry, she'd leaned over the hospital bed and hugged him for a long time. They rocked back and forth together, saying nothing. She finally sat down on the bed where they cried quietly in their own space.

That was when J felt his own emotions well up. He stood and walked over to the window, raising it for fresh air as he pulled himself together.

Keisha regained her composure. She asked her father if he remembered the song, the one he would sometimes sing to her when she was a little girl, just before bedtime.

"I sure do remember that song, it was *sleep my little angel. Right?*"

"Yes, that was it. You know that song stayed with me for many years after we were separated. It allowed me to summon up your voice if I closed my eyes and listened to the words in my mind. For some reason it made me feel that we weren't permanently separated from each other. As I grew older, I believed that one day we would meet again; not like this but somehow."

It seemed to J that the old man had finally run out of words; what more could he say? But when he finished drinking from a glass of water, he started up again.

"Before the Lupus took your mother, you was barely eight then, she and I talked for almost an entire night about what she wanted for your future and how I had to be the major one to deliver that for you, without her. She loved you so much, you know."

"Of course, it didn't take me long after she died to flaunt the dreams that she had. But guess what, your mother was smart back then, way smarter than me. On her dying bed she looked me in the eye and said that I wouldn't be able to destroy her dreams no matter how stupid I was bound to become. She said that she'd cooked you too well in her belly, prayed on you too long, and that you were tough and would shake off whatever life threw. Damn it, she was right. You didn't let a fool like me lay a glove on you."

That started more tears and hugging.

Keisha stood and held both of his hands.

She asked him to allow her to pray; he agreed.

That was when J recognized for the first time that she had a powerful prayer life. With her eyes closed she called boldly upon the Holy Spirit to give her father peace and comfort and to bind up his mental and physical wounds as he prepared for his journey. J felt its strong presence.

Seeing her there he finally understood the strength by which she had overcome her mother's death, a father's cruel abandonment, and a frightening assault as a young girl. It was a fortitude passed from mother to daughter in prayer, one nurtured by a loving aunt and true father.

He watched them say goodbye.

They separated as former adversaries, foes that had acquired a true understanding of the person on the other side. Had they discovered friendship, love, devotion, and perhaps renewal? The words seemed inadequate and trite to him. Perhaps the heavy seasoning of regret and loss rendered them meaningless after so long a time. But whatever the proper description, J believed that a father and daughter discovered something permanent and uplifting in that bright room.

Walking slowly away from the rehab center he placed his arm around her waist and drew her closer. She melded into him. Without speaking they both understood that this was the last time they would see her father alive.

In that moment he realized that his priority, his entire future, was next to him, holding him. California politics would come second, if at all.

He asked himself whether the future would have been so clear if he'd never met her? Would he have stayed in the lawsuits or bailed out under the cover of his campaign?

And would he have returned home as he had now to that hopeful freedom that he knew as a teenager when passion and commitment was his choice over propriety and form?

Epilogue

JOSHUA WAS PLEASED FROM THE VERY START of the voyage because the main shipyard back in Papeete did an excellent job completing the detailed work order transmitted from London by his charter company. He'd been warned that the reputation in that Tahitian port was sometimes for slovenly work. But as he admired again the metal braced rigging and sliding safety chair erected next to the high skipper's seat, he was grateful that the workmanship was perfectly executed for their needs. His father had easily been able to take the helm of the seventy-foot catamaran during his shifts at the wheel even though he hadn't walked again after last year's stroke.

For the past two weeks they had weighed in together on the best sail plans and appropriate weather windows to make several open-ocean crossings between far flung islands and atolls over the miles deep Pacific. It was that daily ritual between them while huddled around the nav station that had fully healed their ancient feuds against one other. During those intense times of planning the rest of the family laughed and enjoyed life aboard.

For Brett these were the familiar waters of the southern Pacific's Society Island chain. He'd brought with him his note-covered charts from the old days, but not for navigational purposes he said, since they hadn't been updated in almost forty years. After reviewing them he'd mentioned that the staunch winds and deep waters could be tricky at the sixteenth latitude, sometimes much better, sometimes far worse than the local weather forecast. But he'd promised everyone that the rewards from the voyage would be breathtaking. So far, all agreed.

Now they were heading out to the final island, outlying Bora Bora. After a few days in the sun, they would all board different charter flights back to stateside destinations.

Throughout the trip and to Joshua's surprise his father continually deferred to him to make all the tough skipper's decisions. And at the end of most crossings, he would ask him to pilot them through dicey inlets and approaches and get them safely at dock or at anchor. The old tensions and conflicts that Joshua used to experience whenever they were on board the same boat was a thing of the past, replaced by mutual respect.

Even though he'd long been a world-class skipper in his own right, he couldn't help but feel a sense of pride and satisfaction from his father's confidence.

Halfway into the cruise he finally relaxed, comfortable in his role as captain for the family.

After finishing a detailed boat check, they cast off lines and cruised serenely through the crowded marina. At the sea channel Joshua unfurled the main and head sail and steered close to the wind. They would approach the farthest elevated land point on Tahaa within sixty minutes. Once past that sheltering promontory they would be fully exposed to the open sea and wind.

As planned, Jazz and baby girl started to roll Brett's wheelchair aft to the lift station well before they reached the promontory. Joshua could see the energy in his father's face and in the set of his jaw. He knew it meant that he was preparing his mind and body once more for the rigor of the helm.

As a last to-do before the hand-off, Joshua looked through binoculars out beyond the point and saw the wind driving large blue rollers. From the quick scan he estimated a minimum thirty-knot blow along with twelve to fifteen-foot seas. He glanced at his gauges and sure enough the wind was already clicking up past twenty knots.

The impending conditions confirmed his final decision to lease the big cat rather than the stately sloop favored by his father. His thinking at the time had been that if they ever encountered extremely rough weather, stability would be paramount for his father as well as for the amateurs on the boat. Those conditions were now imminent.

Torrents of seawater began to arc up from the water line as the cat stubbornly dug into and over the increasingly rough seas. The throaty roar of the wind and sea along with the incessant slamming of the twin bows enveloped them all.

Not quite the idyllic weather forecast that they'd received from the local station that morning, he noted. As he took in more of the conditions, he considered for a moment whether they should return to port. But with three experienced crewmembers, including his father, baby girl and Mikala, he deemed the passage to be a reasonable risk.

As he unstrapped and prepared to relinquish the helm it occurred to him that he couldn't think of anyone that he would willingly hand a boat to in these conditions, other than to his father.

Baby girl and Jazz hoisted Brett up between them and then over onto the lift chair. They cranked the mechanical winch until he was level with the helm seat. Once there, Joshua moved over and helped slide him behind the big wheel, securing the double harness rig around his upper thighs and chest.

As he climbed down, he noticed that his father had remembered one thing that he'd forgotten; he wore tinted safety goggles around his neck in preparation for the spray.

Joshua checked the rigging one last time along with the crew disposition on deck. He asked who wanted to ride outside for the passage over. Baby girl, Sarah, and Mikala chose the deck. Jazz, Keisha, and Lailani retreated to the dry shelter of the cabin.

He looked at Sarah who seemed slightly lost. As he watched her struggle to keep her balance, he wasn't sure that her slight frame was up for the strain of the big waves that they would soon encounter. He also noticed that her life vest seemed to wrap around her small body like a deflated truck tire inner tube. He was about to suggest that she head inside when he noticed that baby girl had wedged herself low into a crevice between the main stays, securely bracing her back. Then she reached over and pulled Sarah down into her lap before clipping on safety lines; problem solved.

Moments later Brett turned the wheel ten degrees northwest and the rough slog across open sea started in earnest.

As his father navigated the tricky wave action and stiff gusts, Joshua tucked down into the transom area with Mikala in his arms. Out of sight he kissed her on her cheek and hugged her close. Together, they watched the azure blue sky and enjoyed partial shelter from the stiff blow.

In time the monotony relaxed him, and he remembered his childhood days when he and his father had handled much smaller boats together at the Albany Clear Lake Club, where it all began. That and many subsequent opportunities had been a great privilege. The full extent of that privilege and the fact that he'd groused about it for many years made him shake his head.

Increasingly all around them crystal blue seawater sprang up wildly as they plowed forward over endless steep rollers and surfed down the side of others. The tenor strained pitch from the rigging seemed to draw the myriad sea birds closer as they kept pace above the high mast and Kevlar sails. Not to be outdone, usual aquatic companions—flying fish off the beam and dolphins racing to keep ahead of the bow—joined the parade.

The reverie of the sea and why they'd both fallen in love with it was all around. Mikala smiled up at him, as entranced as he was by it all.

Two hours out of port and well beyond the sight of land the weather suddenly shifted. To the relief of all the winds dropped to twenty knots and the height of the waves eased by a third. His father nodded back in his direction and reluctantly he uncurled himself from around Mikala. She looked sad losing his shelter.

The agreed upon signal between them meant that it was time to check the charts and correct course, both paper and GPS. Neither of them liked to stretch a voyage longer than necessary if not required by weather or race tactics.

When the course adjustments were laid in, he returned to his comfortable position with Mikala in his arms. Brett turned slightly and shouted down his first question since taking the helm.

"So, Joshua, did your engineering team ever finally solve for why the American boat in Frisco was faster than your own on the upwind legs?"

"They solved it after many months of computer analysis," he said shouting his answer over the wind.

"Too late to make a difference of course but at least we know why we consistently lost the edge—the Americans used steel in their hydrofoil and dagger board engines, versus the lighter aluminum and composite that we had calculated would give us an advantage. In those exceptionally rough conditions that we faced throughout the finals we were damn lucky to win two of the races with that weight deficit. "

"Lucky," Brett said, skeptically?

He caught Mikala's eye at the same time and winked.

"Was it only coincidence," Brett said, "that you won those first two and that Willosby lost the final four races after you left for the hospital?"

Joshua thought about that before responding, trying to keep his ego out of his answer.

"Willosby was a very good skipper; he had racing guts for sure. His conditions, though, were rougher that mine during each of his four races as that low-pressure system offshore refused to break up. But it's true, I've never lost four races in a row ever, so who really knows what might have happened if I'd been able to stay, maybe an all-in rubber match after a 3-3 tie."

It was the same conclusion that Joshua reached when he watched video of the races and before seeing the final engineering report.

Brett nodded his head and then he looked over quickly at baby girl and Sarah snuggled up together; he issued one of his classic digs.

"Hey Sarah, did you sign baby girl up to be your yacht safety pillow on this voyage?"

Sarah blushed and shook her head at him while baby girl nodded her head vigorously and hugged her closer.

Mikala unfolded herself from beneath Joshua's shelter, leaving him as the one missing the other's presence this time. She stretched and stood quietly next to the metal rigging lift, content.

Her position in that space symbolized to Joshua what she had become, his father's strong right hand. More than that, she was discharging significant duties on behalf of the national board. It was the future that his father had once assumed would belong to Joshua.

He also remembered that she had been the first one to deliver to Brett the good news in the hospital after the ruling in favor of *Sail Shape* finally came down. In addition to everything else she had recently been spending half her time in California because the Marin County camp was only a few weeks from opening day. That had made his getting together with her from far off London a real challenge; it was something that he knew he would have to change very soon.

Brett looked down and smiled at her.

It was soon clear to him as he watched his father's slumping shoulders that he was growing exhausted, so he hugged Mikala and whispered to her to bring out his mother. No way was he going to suggest to his dad that he take a breather despite their much-improved relationship. He watched his mother talk him down from the helm with the promise of a snack that she had inside.

The easing winds and settling seas brought everyone out on deck an hour later just as the iconic twin peaks of Bora Bora appeared in the distance. They cheered the majestic site.

From their current position bearing down on the island the only evidence of the deadly barrier reef that encircled it was the subtle change in the color of the waves and sea state far off the bows. Joshua stayed well away from the submerged danger as he circumnavigated for two and one-half more hours to the narrow cut leading into the lagoon.

Before arriving, they cranked Brett up to the helmsman's' seat once more.

With that done Joshua ducked below to his cabin and carefully removed a blue urn from his sea bag. He crossed alone to the leeward side of the deck after glancing at Mikala who caught his eye and blew a knowing kiss. Lowering down into the transom he unsealed the urn and leaned back against the safety line, bracing wide-legged. He held it high above his head as the ashes flew from the mouth. They playfully suspended aloft as if possessing internal power, perhaps her sprinter's power he imagined. After keeping pace with the cat for an impossibly long time, the ashes disappeared beneath the waves. He lingered and reminisced.

After cruising through the opening into the calm lagoon the difference in sea state surprised everyone except Brett. He powered slowly forward after Joshua dropped the sails, gliding silently across the flat, green blue surface.

Everyone admired the lush tropical scenery that guarded the approach into the inner harbor.

Brett rounded a densely forested outcropping and edged them stern to into a hidden cove well away from the several scattered boats that lay at anchor. He was pleased that his special place was vacant and that aside from the towering plants and the stout trees that they used to tie up it hadn't changed much since his last visit.

Joshua and Mikala prepped and set out the food from the fridge while Jazz opened wine and arranged settings and glasses. Lailani added a dash of smooth jazz to the party with several CD's. Baby Girl gave Sarah a quick lesson in the art of hosing salt off the twin hulls.

In short order they all gathered around the large mid deck table. Mast and deck lights were switched on as the sun dropped quickly at that time of year.

The tinkling of silverware against glass rang out. Brett was clearing his throat, awaiting everyone's attention.

"Let me propose a toast to two of the finest attorneys that I have ever known. You know they went three for three last year; winning when no one thought that was possible. But their greatest win was finding each other. We celebrate their recent engagement, and we toast to a successful conclusion to Jazz's campaign for governor."

Everyone applauded.

Jazz hugged Keisha and stepped forward.

"Thanks so much. We're happy to make this first annual family cruise. And yes, we're very grateful that we found each other," he said looking into Keisha's eyes.

"There were times during the litigation when things got edgy, and the tension was severe. But she kept me on track. Her trial experience and instincts made the real difference. But more importantly, I've found someone special, a life partner. I love her dearly. To my future wife."

"Don't let him bamboozle you with that smooth political way of speaking," Keisha said as she stood with her arm around his waist.

"He's an extremely good lawyer and I'm convinced he'll win the election and make a huge difference for California. And he'll make an even bigger difference as my husband. Without realizing it I had been waiting for him for a very long time."

The full-on hug that followed caused a small uproar on board.

Joshua rapped loudly on his own wine glass as the applause faded. He looked at Mikala.

"I want to toast to a wonderful woman. She's patient, she's wise, and she's beautiful. She waited for me and helped me heal. Somehow, she knew exactly what I was feeling and what I needed. At this special time among us all I want to publicly declare my love and devotion to her."

Everyone cheered; no one was surprised by the open secret.

Mikala could only look at him and smile; she had no words. He was her man now and he fully loved her for who she was. She finally understood without understanding how that he was a special gift, Mirra's gift to her.

Lailani stood and walked over between baby girl and Sarah, kissing each of them on the cheek.

"To my daughter," she looked at Brett, "to our daughter and her dear love Sarah, two future doctors that will shine a dual light to identify and treat the needs of so many."

She turned to Sarah.

"Sarah, once again welcome to our family, your family now."

As she spoke the words Lailani believed that she would still be living on the west coast even after they graduated. Her executive role consumed most of her time and her travel schedule

387

was beyond hectic. Yet, she still saw baby girl much more often now than she had in previous years.

But in her private life she was lonely.

Brett couldn't allow anyone else to have the last word, so he rolled his wheelchair closer to the table and rapped on his glass once again until everyone quieted down.

"I just want to say this, I have to admit I'm finally getting up there and I've slowed down more than a little bit."

"Yes," he grinned as he conceded the next part, "the dawn does break over Marblehead."

After the several incredulous reactions to his admission faded, he continued.

"I've got to tell you though; I'm looking out at all of you, and I have two thoughts about the future. First, each one of you has a world of possibilities and opportunities ahead, you'll make the right choices, I'm sure. Second, I'm just waiting for someone to start producing the grandkids; I promise you this, I will spoil them!"

The collective laughter reverberated across the flat waters of the pitch-black lagoon to the base of the great twin mountains and back again.

Lailani shared in the good feelings though in her spirit she wondered whether she and Brett would help rear those future grandchildren together or apart in separate houses. She glanced over at him after that thought. He had removed his napkin from his lap, and he was staring intently at her. Had he somehow heard her doubts, she wondered? She smiled back to put his mind at ease.

He looked at her because he had missed her so much. It was why being on the cruise for an extended time had been special. But in two days he knew that she'd fly back home with baby girl and Sarah. He badly wanted to go with her, but he realized how difficult that would be in his present condition, even if she were to agree to a visit.

Lailani watched him position his hands firmly on top of the table after rolling his chair in closer.

Brett saw her smile back at him a few moments ago. She was also happy to be there he imagined, maybe as happy as he was.

They'd managed to talk with each other several times away from the others during the voyage and it had been pleasant. He didn't press her; he made sure to give her space.

Ready, he pushed the heels of his hands hard into the tabletop, determined to test something. He tightly compressed his abdomen and leaned forward in his wheelchair. While doing so images from an endless number of rehab sessions flashed through his mind along with the one constant refrain he'd taken into every painful appointment—you can do this when you're ready.

He removed his lower legs from the metal footrests before placing his palms back into position and pushing down hard. At the same time, he pressed his toes into his boat shoes trying to drive them through the deck; he rocked forward. Nothing.

What in God's name was he trying to do Lailani worried as she watched him; was there some issue with the wheelchair brakes? And why was he jerking in the chair like that; was it a stroke?

Alarmed, she rose quickly, her nurse's instincts kicking in.

Suddenly he was standing and looking at her; but this time his features had softened. And he was moving, walking slowly in her direction.

She looked down at his hands; he held them out palms up. With his steady balance she realized that he wasn't reaching for support.

Then she remembered; it all came back. He would always hold his hands outstretched like that when they were children, whenever they would start to dance.

Brett's announcement in Bora Bora that he couldn't wait to spoil the grandchildren was prescient, although it took more than three years before they started to arrive. Lailani's concern that she might raise them separate and apart turned out to be unfounded.

A year after the cruise Brett retired from *Sail Shape* due to his stalled physical recovery that left him able to walk but with limited mobility. Free from his decade's long commitment to the camps and lonely, he decided to sell the Albany house. After a year of inching closer together, he and Lailani finally agreed to purchase another home together. She retired three years later as CEO of the Calibri firm having been elected to that role after Tony's earlier departure.

Over the years their California Bay-side house became the gathering place for children and spouses and grandchildren.

***

Mikala and Joshua were married two years after the cruise. Zena Melody Jensen hosted the wedding and reception at her canyon estate in Mailbu after inching her way back into her daughter's heart. The newlyweds started the next generation twelve months later with a baby boy and baby girl delivered within one minute of each other.

After the failure of an outside executive brought in to replace Brett, Mikala was elected CEO by the board. Under her leadership donor support reached new highs with each of the twelve camps become financially self-sustaining. Camp enrollment continues to set records.

Joshua had already relocated his trading desk from London to San Francisco before her big promotion, which radically reduced his travel and work schedule. He spent the better part of three more years fine-tuning the management structure at the expanded four-campus warehouse in southern England, eventually naming Louise Afford as CEO.

***

With BG's support Sarah followed her heart, resigning from the order in her second year of medical school. She successfully pieced together government and private scholarship money to continue her schooling, including ongoing support from Melinda and Stewart as well as a generous anonymous gift from the Reverend Mother.

After completing residency, the two young physicians faced several employment barriers. They were finally hired as ER doctors at a failing medical facility on the south side of Chicago where they rose through the hierarchy to leadership roles. They engineered a complete transformation, the facility becoming a highly sought-after post for doctors and nurses desiring to help the underserved.

The punishing urban pace eventually took its toll. They accepted a generous offer from overseas where they established a badly needed medical center in the Volta region of Ghana. They were married there and soon adopted two girls and a baby boy. They are exploring surrogacy as they contemplate a family that includes a fourth child.

They make an annual pilgrimage to California to spend time with the extended family.

***

Jazz was elected governor of California, winning by the two-percentage point margin that Chad Pendleton predicted. Once in office he worked with the legislature to pull back run-a-way spending and taxation in exchange for focus against key educational and infrastructure initiatives. He ran for a second term, winning by a landslide.

Keisha relocated from Albany to join him in Sacramento after she convinced Bill Harpin that the firm could profitably expand in California. In time the office grew to fifteen attorneys. One of her hires was Stephen Whalen, a young attorney that she knew when he was a law student at her Albany office.

Keisha and Jazz were married in a small private ceremony shortly after her move. As the mother of two now, she always mentions her other full-time job involving her kids whenever she stays late at the office.

Her boys are enrolled at the Marin *Sail Shape* camp and have shown promise as young helmsmen. They also enjoy spending much of the summer and at least one or two holidays each year at the California house with their cousins, grandma, and grandpa.

***

Wilma and Jemal completed PhD studies together at Oxford. They were married on the same afternoon as their graduation ceremony, fulfilling a secret pact made between them sophomore year. They refused to consider regular employment opportunities after graduation, instead taking a huge risk to start a software development venture that finally turned a profit after four tough years. Having recently completed a successful private placement they have a chance at real growth, doubling the number of programmers and expanding their highly rated software offerings.

In addition to executive duties running day-to-day operations, Wilma marked her eighth month of pregnancy and yet has no plan to step away as delivery looms.

Jemal founded two computer and math-based warehouses in Africa to follow up on the needs that emerged from his Kid Genius! network. Several dozen of his overseas graduates enroll each year in regional colleges within their own borders. A much smaller number transfer to the warehouses in London and continue their studies at area universities, including Oxford and Cambridge.

Of late Jemal's prolific output of innovative software has slowed. Increasingly he has become a distracted bundle of nerves as he waits the imminent arrival of his baby girl.

***

Shana and Theo dated off and on for many years. The distance and cultural divide between northern and southern California made it hard.

During that time Shana enrolled in night law school. She completed her J.D. and passed the California Bar during a tough five-year stretch. After that she was hired as an adjunct professor at Loyola Law School where she taught civil procedure, property, and constitutional law. Determined to have a greater social impact she recently decided to put out her own shingle and start a family law practice.

Theo's Berkeley paper eventually folded, and he worked for a couple of years as a freelance investigative journalist based in Sacramento. That experience made him an attractive hire for the Los Angeles Sun Tribune where he became deputy bureau chief for political affairs. The new role required that he relocate to Los Angeles where he started night school at U.C.L.A. to complete his B.A.

Theo's relocation allowed him to spend more time with Shana.

They were recently spotted at a Rodeo Drive jewelry store with the initials HW that Theo had walked into on a whim as they were exploring Beverly Hills shops together. Shana had been surprised when they were looking around the store and the salesperson referred to Theo by name, even though no introductions had occurred.

Before she could ruin his headline, he quickly removed a ring box from his pocket and knelt on one knee.

Acknowledgements

I AM VERY GRATEFUL TO SEVERAL PROGRAMS at the Miami Book Fair, where support for emerging writers motivated me to enlarge the history set forth in my first novel, *Onset*. *Precious Things* grew from early drafts to final manuscript over several years. Thank you to Allison Devereux who presented at the Book Fair and provided honest feedback on my intermediate draft.

Other valuable programs at the Miami Book Fair assisted my search for an agent. Many thanks to Liz Van Hoose for insightful agent search tips and for helping me craft the right query letter. Help with a winning pitch and productive agent search was received from Arielle Eckstut and David Henry Sterry. Much value was also contained in their comprehensive Essential Guide.

Very helpful assistance was received from workshops at Litquake in San Francisco, including tips from publishing panelist Andrea Avery, Christina Julian, Ho Lin, Shobha Roa as well as Vicki DeArmon, Anna Ghosh, Liz Parker and Gayle Wattwawa. Imagination expanding talks at Litquake by Aaron James and Jaimal Yogis were timely inspiration.

Heartfelt thanks to Candelaria Silva-Collins for excellent feedback on the earliest draft and for taking the time from her busy writing schedule to provide useful insights.

Valuable feedback from readers of my first novel, *Onset*, provided both motivation and insights as I completed this book. Many thanks to everyone and I hope you enjoy the evolution of the voyage represented by *Precious Things*.

A most grateful thank you to my wife, Portia, my most loyal fan and supporter, who believed in this work always and who took the time and patience from the earliest moments to help me shape the story into its final form.

www.ingramcontent.com/pod-product-compliance
Lightning Source LLC
Chambersburg PA
CBHW071148020726
47502CB00002B/320